STORM WARNING

UNOFFICIAL GRAPHIC NOVEL #3 FOR FORTNITERS

NATHAN MEYER
ILLUSTRATED BY ALAN BROWN

Sky Pony Press
New York

Sky Pony Press books may be purchased in bulk at special discounts for sales promotion,
corporate gifts, fund-raising, or educational purposes. Special editions can also be created
to specifications. For details, contact the Special Sales Department, Sky Pony Press, 307
West 36th Street, 11th Floor, New York, NY 10018 or info@skyhorsepublishing.com.

Sky Pony® is a registered trademark of Skyhorse Publishing, Inc.®, a Delaware corporation.

Visit our website at www.skyponypress.com.

10 9 8 7 6 5 4 3 2 1

Library of Congress Cataloging-in-Publication Data is available on file.

Cover design by Brian Peterson
Cover illustration by Alan Brown

Paperback ISBN: 978-1-5107-5716-5
E-book ISBN: 978-1-5107-5720-2

Printed in the United States of America

STORM WARNING

UNOFFICIAL GRAPHIC NOVEL #3
FOR FORTNITERS

CHAPTER 1: SYSTEM FAILURE

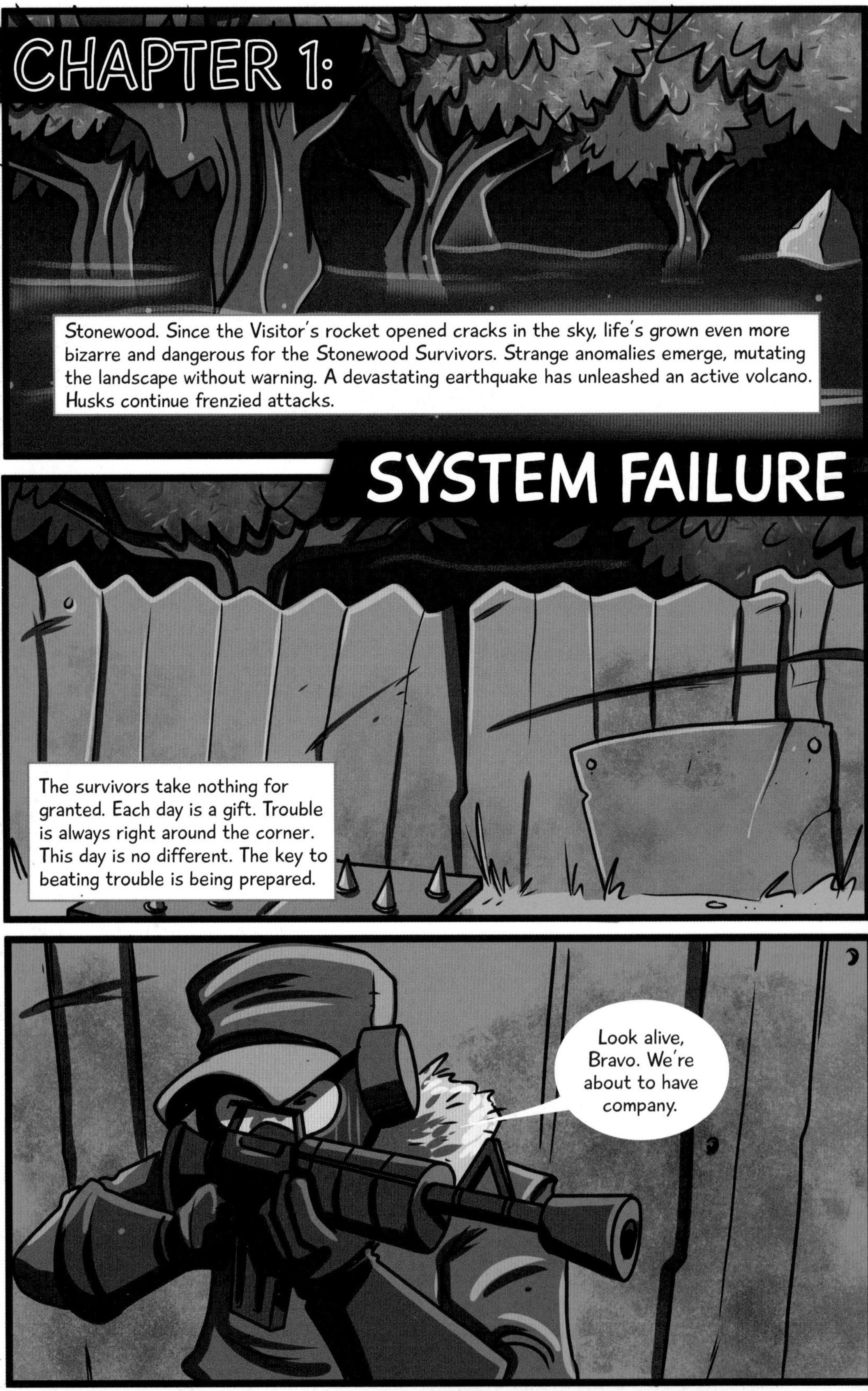
Stonewood. Since the Visitor's rocket opened cracks in the sky, life's grown even more bizarre and dangerous for the Stonewood Survivors. Strange anomalies emerge, mutating the landscape without warning. A devastating earthquake has unleashed an active volcano. Husks continue frenzied attacks.
The survivors take nothing for granted. Each day is a gift. Trouble is always right around the corner. This day is no different. The key to beating trouble is being prepared.
Look alive, Bravo. We're about to have company.

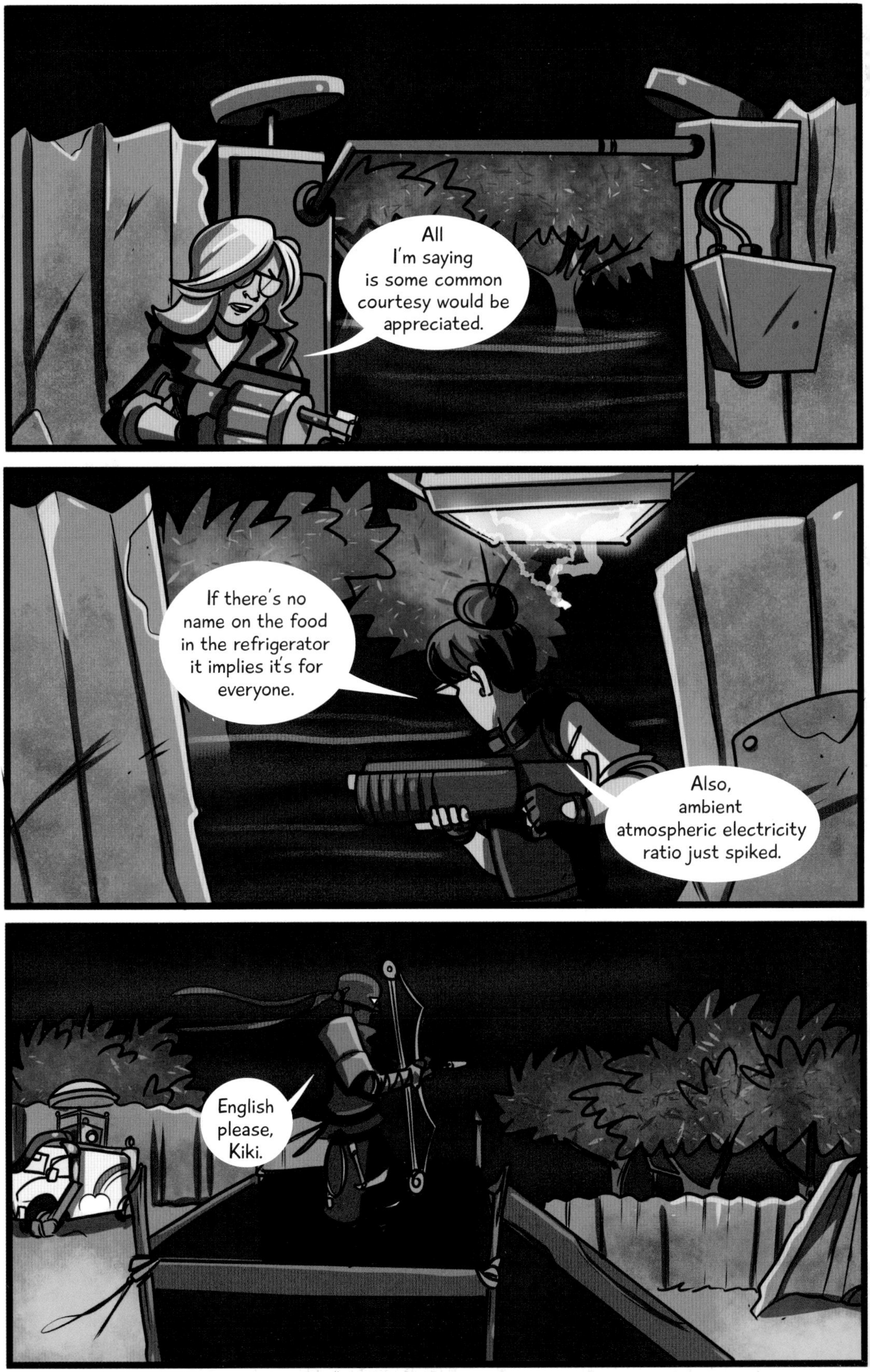
All I'm saying is some common courtesy would be appreciated.
If there's no name on the food in the refrigerator it implies it's for everyone.
Also, ambient atmospheric electricity ratio just spiked.
English please, Kiki.

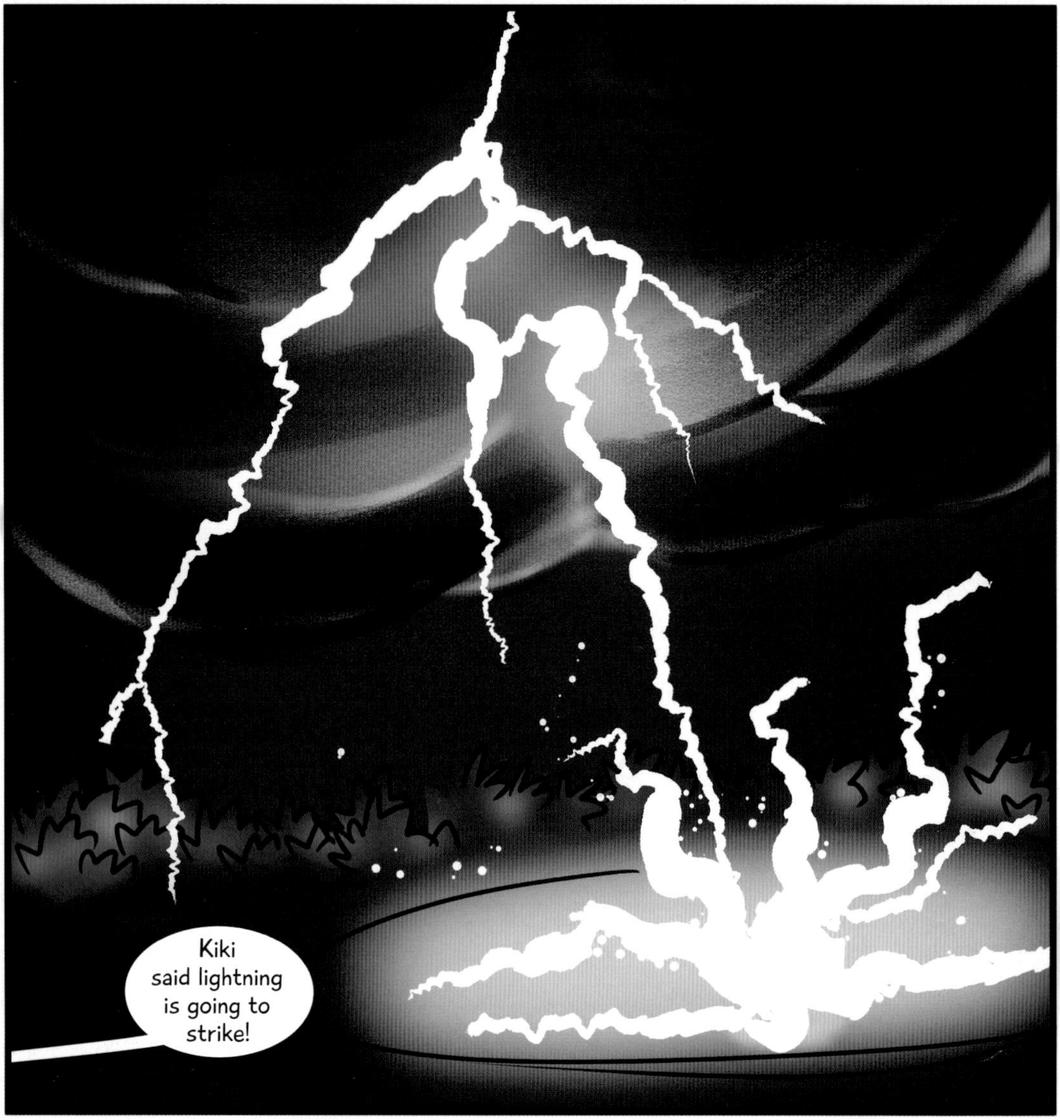
Kiki said lightning is going to strike!

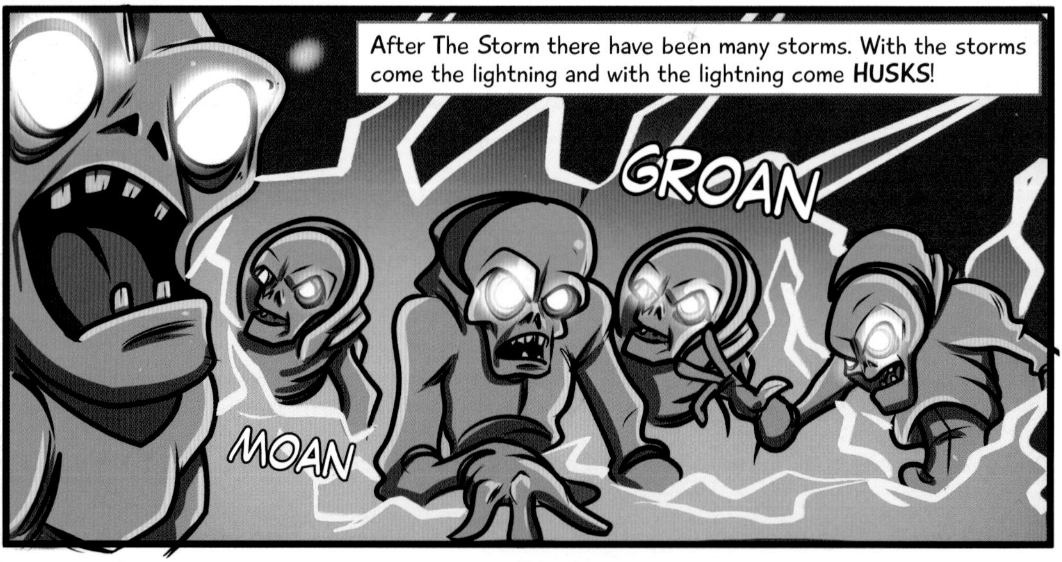
After The Storm there have been many storms. With the storms come the lightning and with the lightning come HUSKS!
GROAN
MOAN

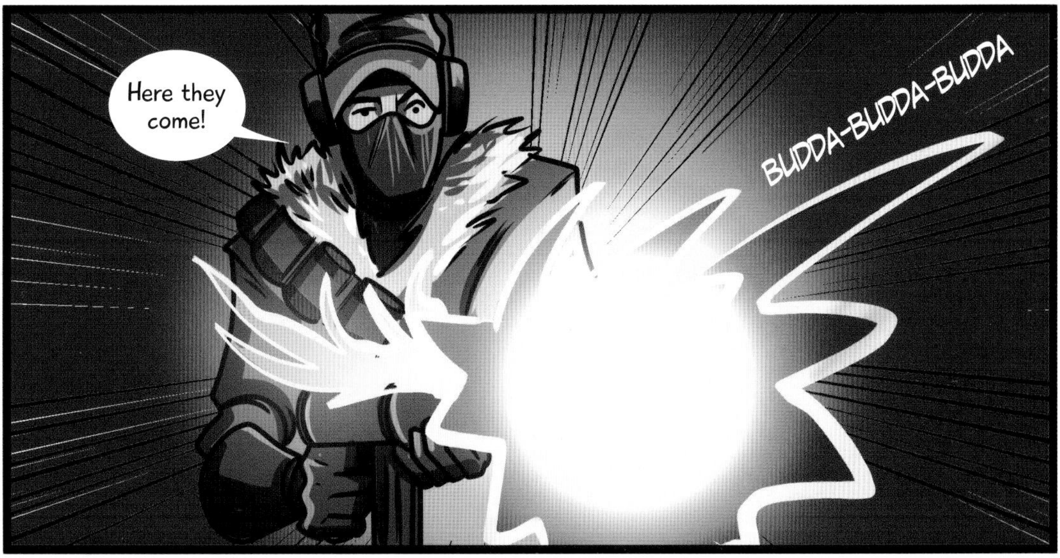
Here they come!
BUDDA-BUDDA-BUDDA

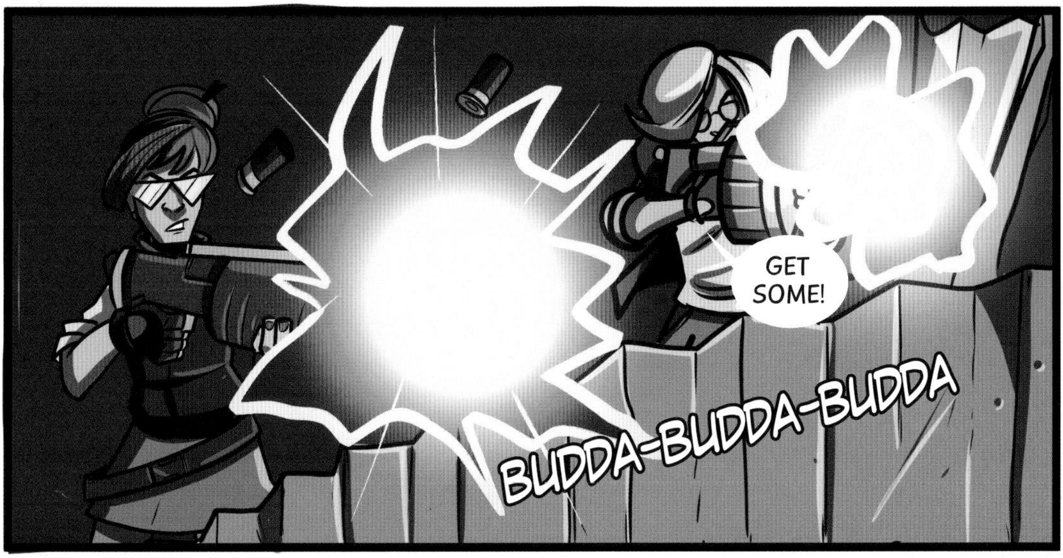
GET SOME!
BUDDA-BUDDA-BUDDA

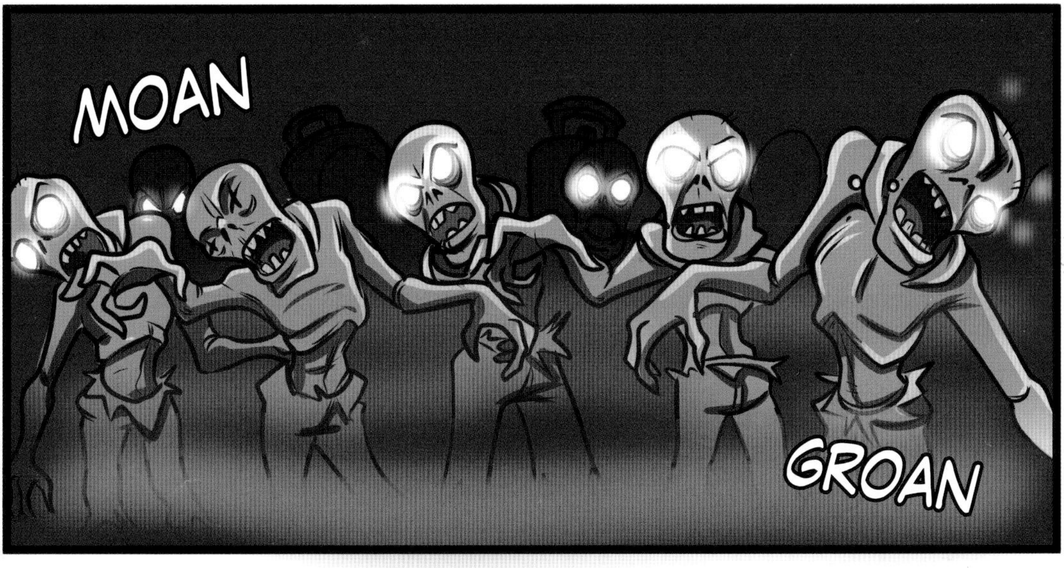
MOAN
GROAN

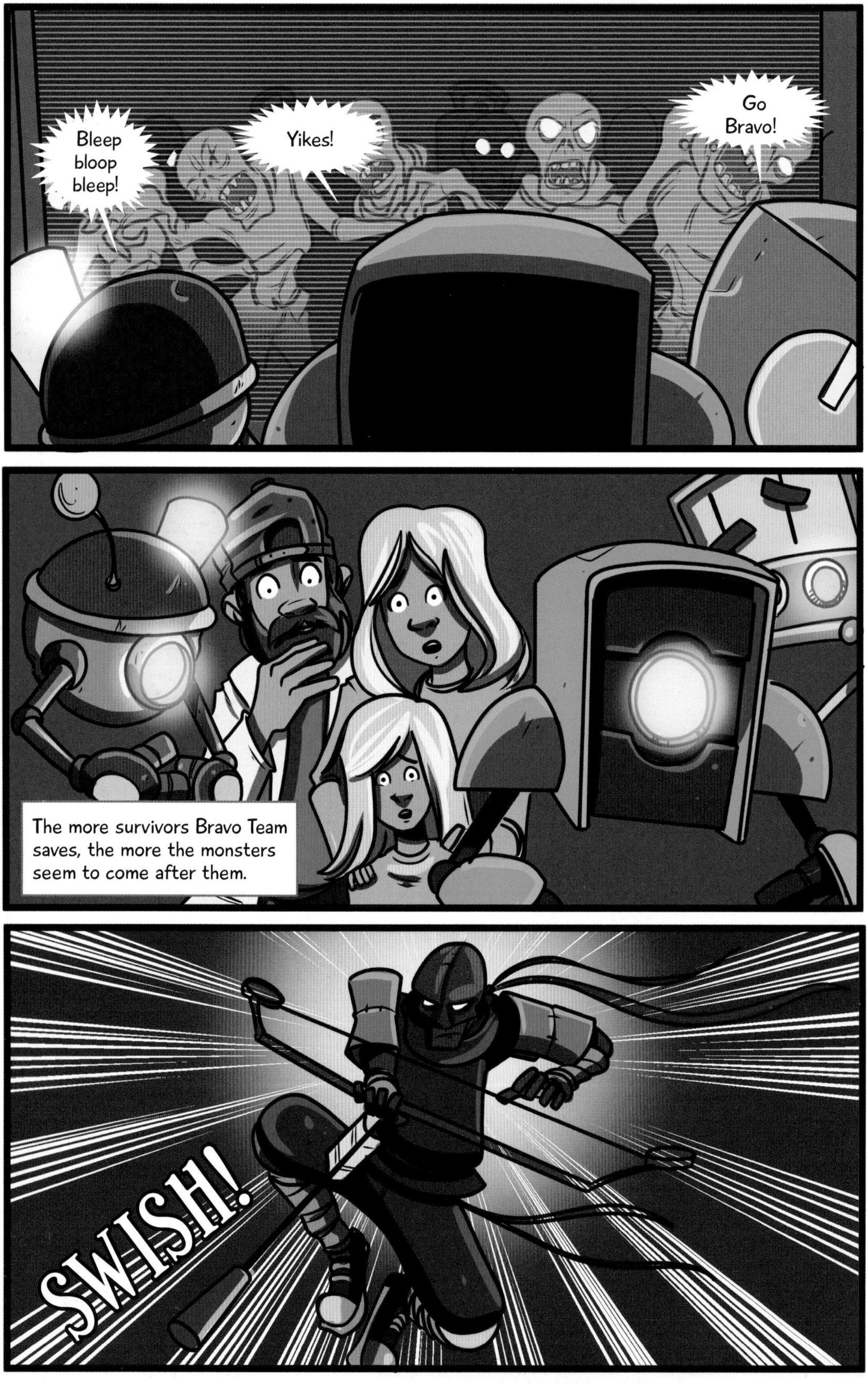
Bleep bloop bleep!
Yikes!
Go Bravo!
The more survivors Bravo Team saves, the more the monsters seem to come after them.
SWISH!

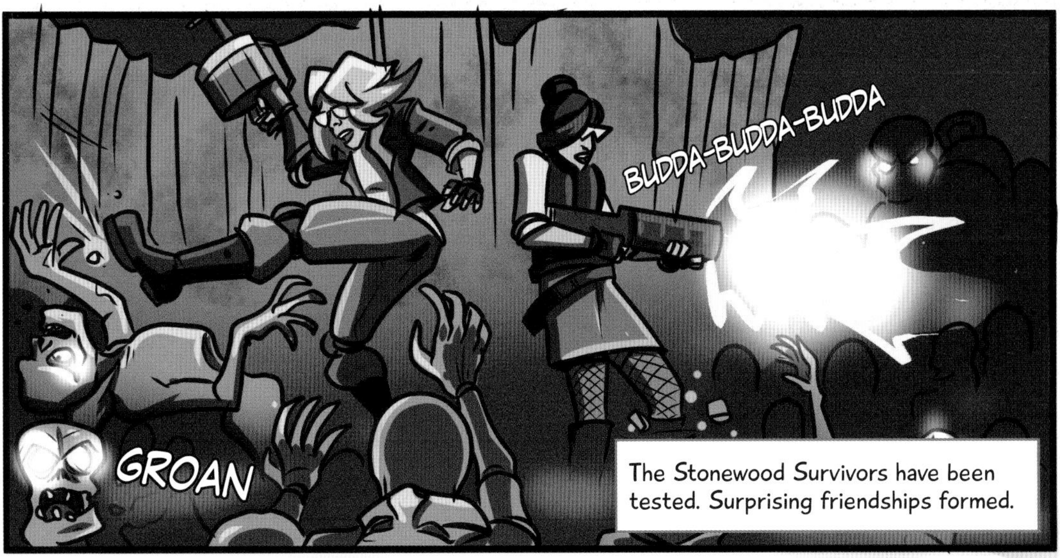
BUDDA-BUDDA-BUDDA
GROAN
The Stonewood Survivors have been tested. Surprising friendships formed.

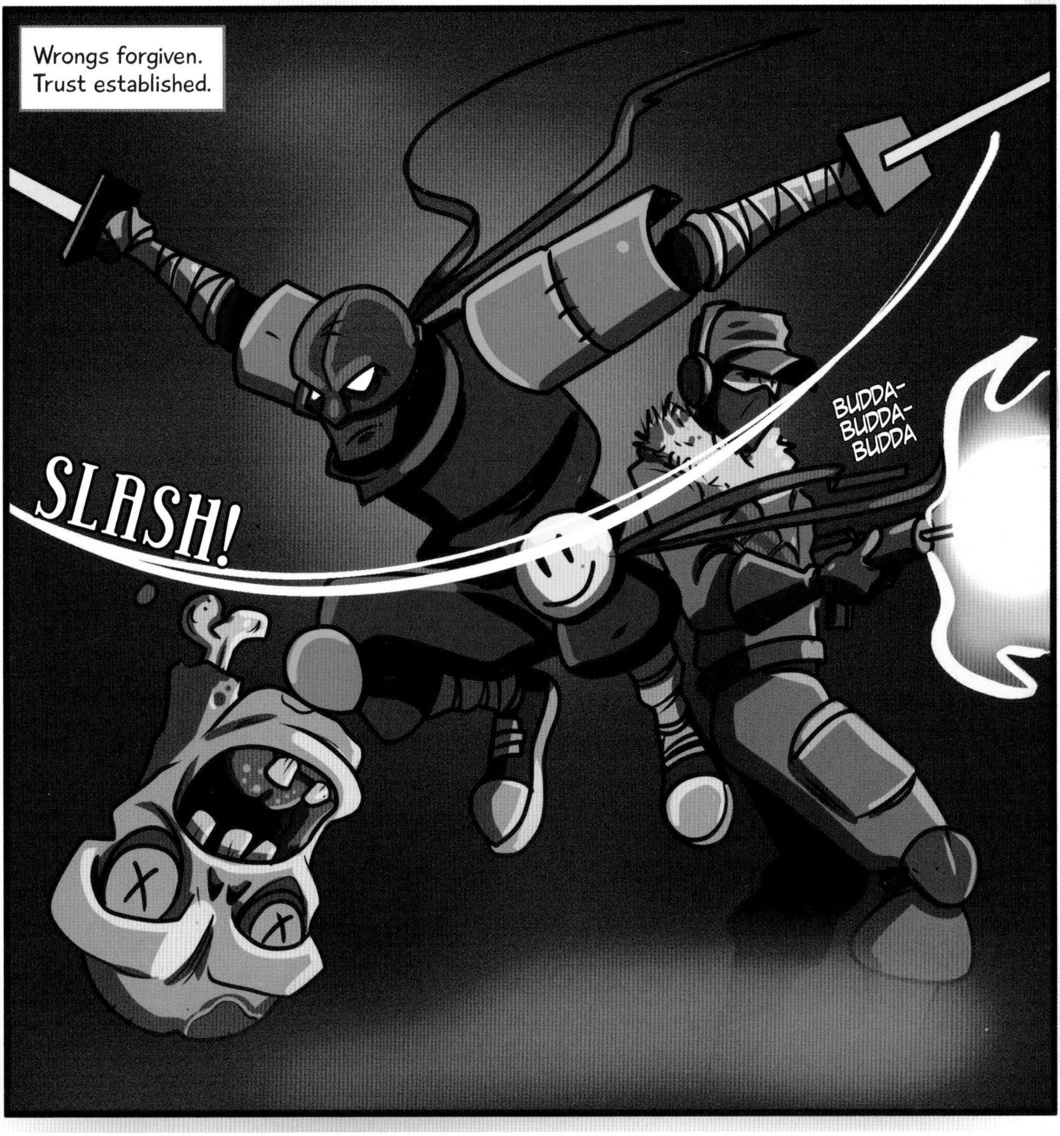
Wrongs forgiven. Trust established.
SLASH!
BUDDA-BUDDA-BUDDA

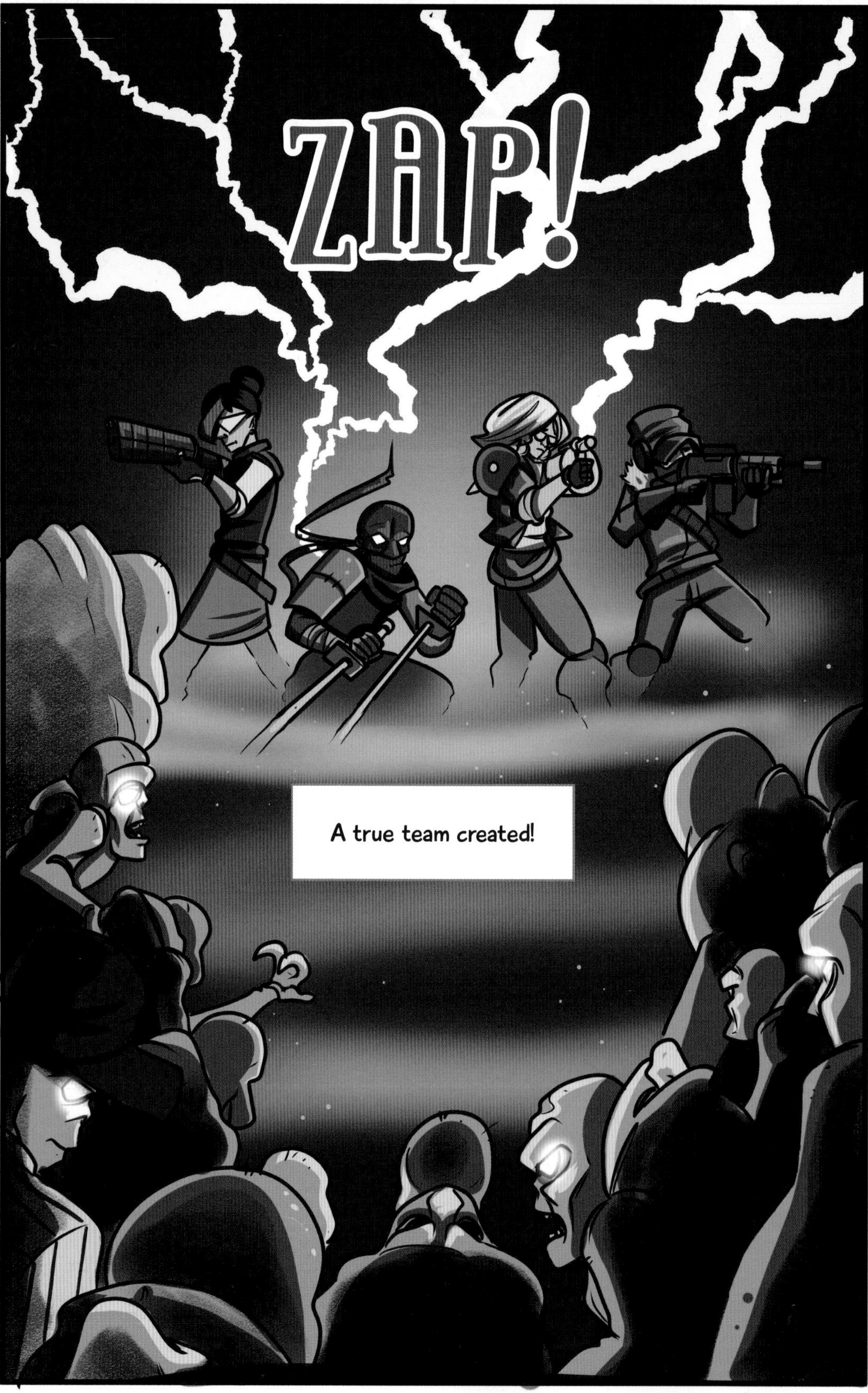
ZAP!
A true team created!

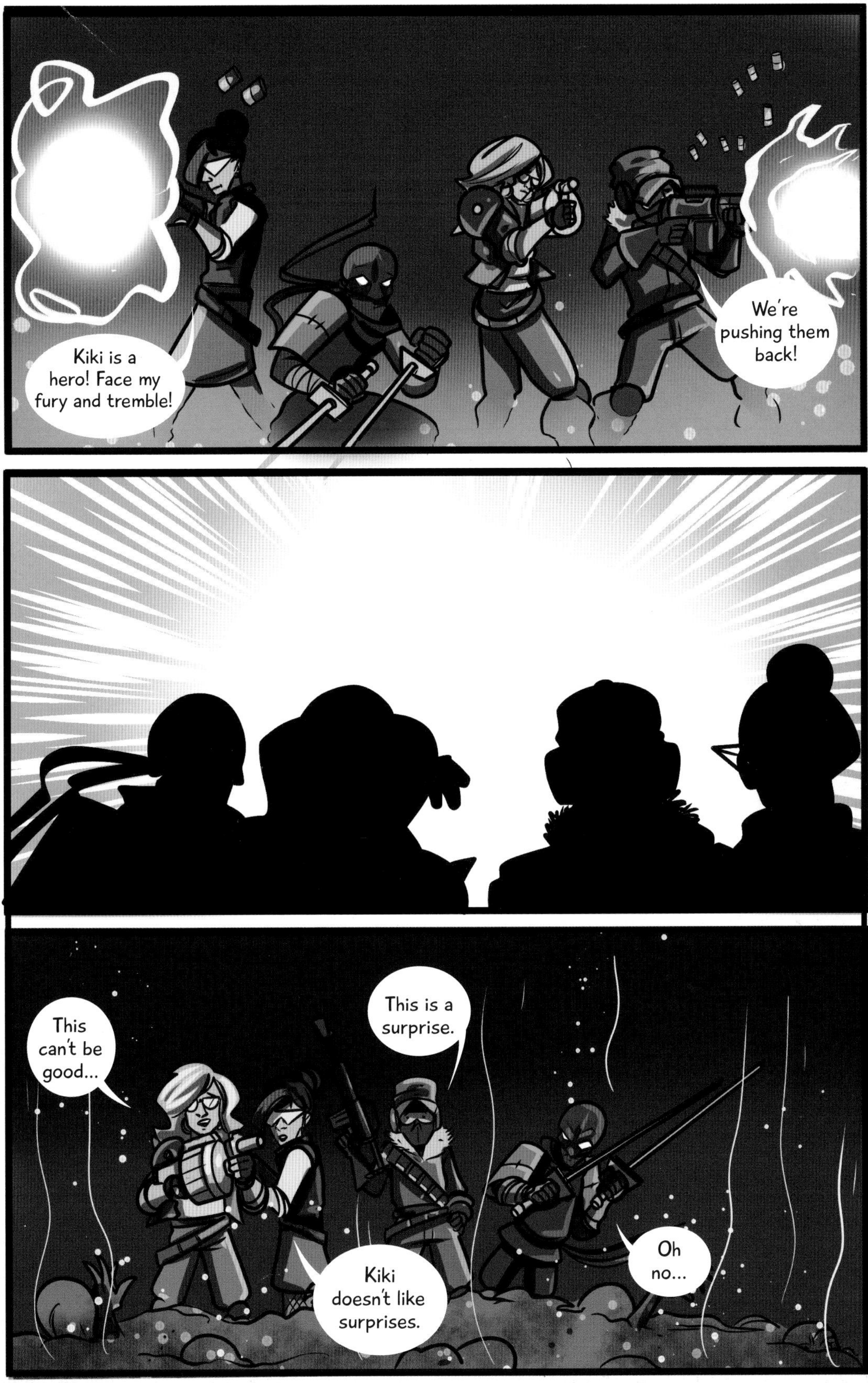
Kiki is a hero! Face my fury and tremble!
We're pushing them back!
This can't be good...
This is a surprise.
Kiki doesn't like surprises.
Oh no...

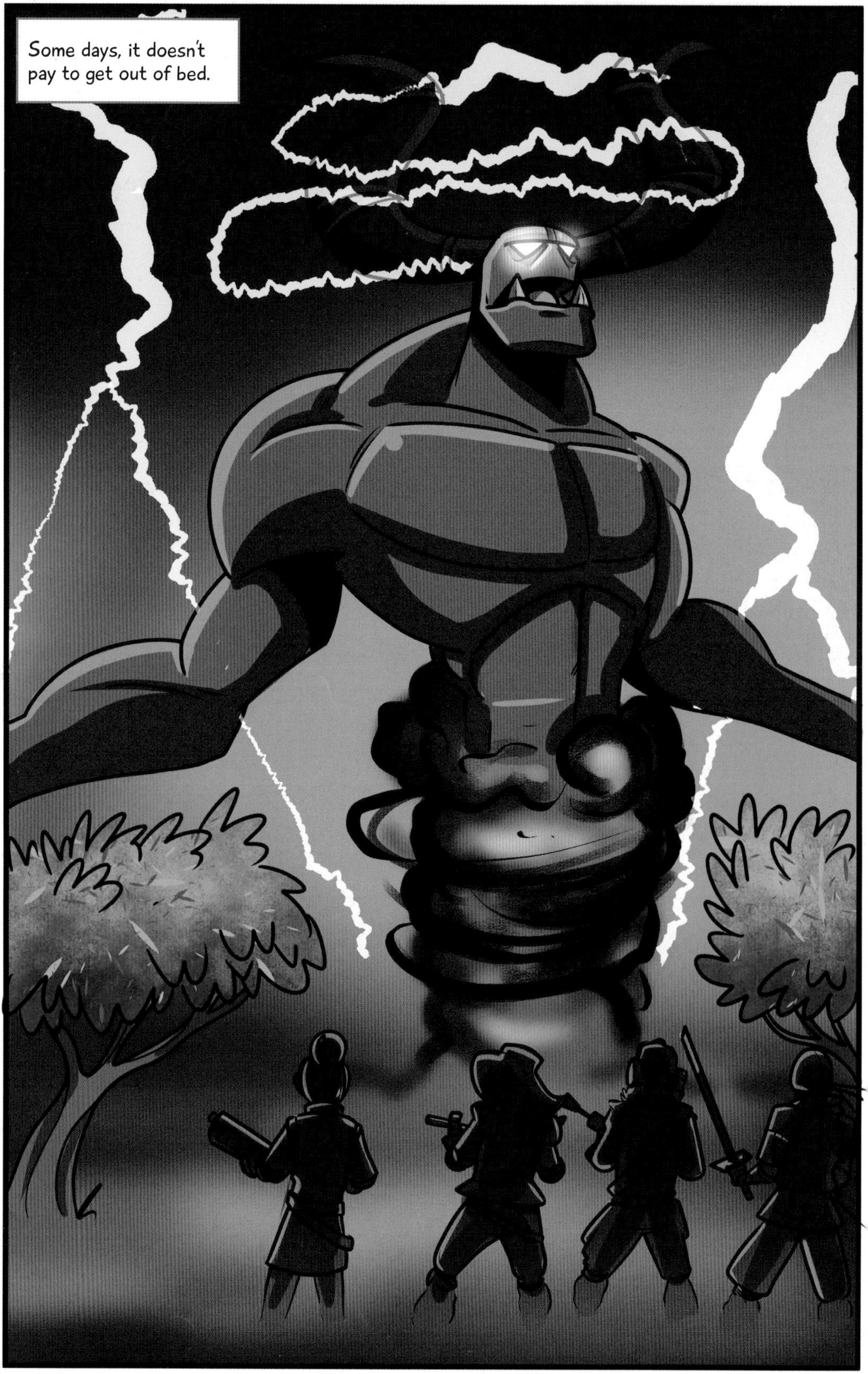
Some days, it doesn't pay to get out of bed.

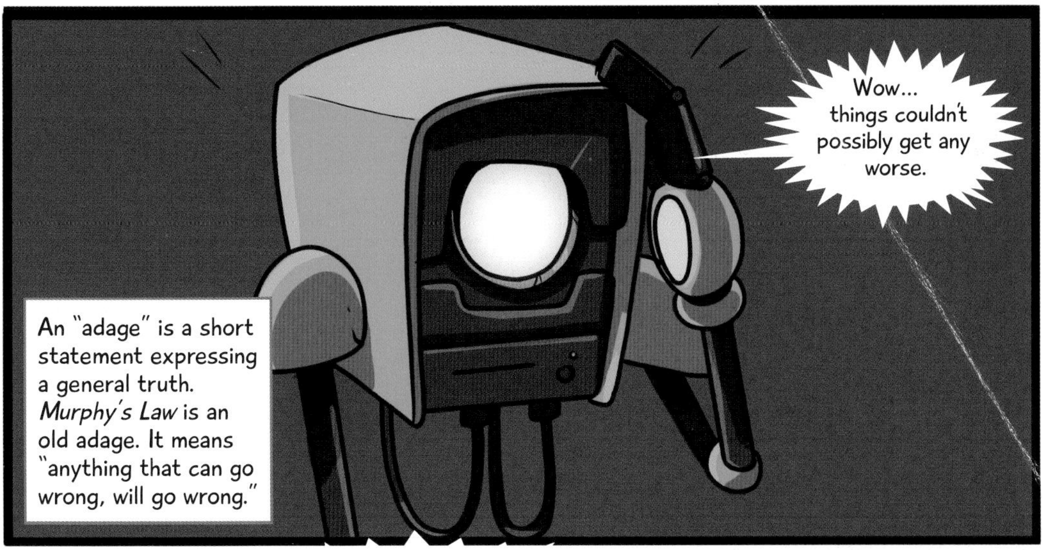
Wow... things couldn't possibly get any worse.
An "adage" is a short statement expressing a general truth. *Murphy's Law* is an old adage. It means "anything that can go wrong, will go wrong."

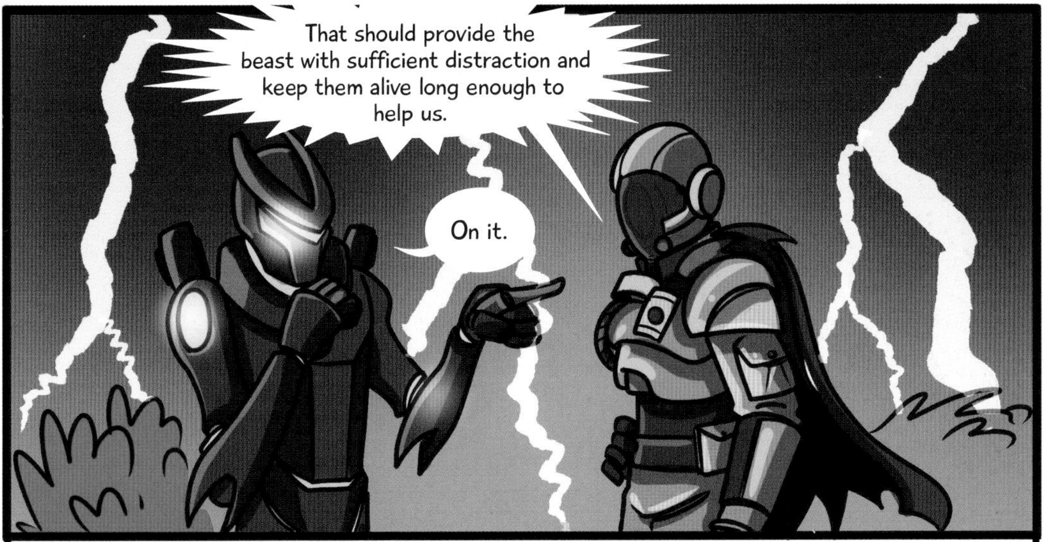
That should provide the beast with sufficient distraction and keep them alive long enough to help us.
On it.

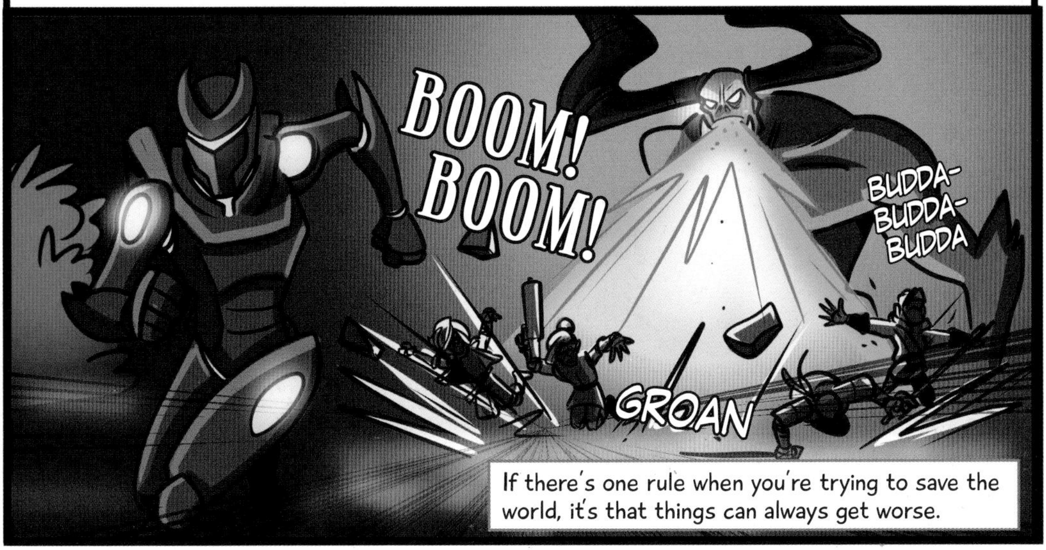
BOOM! BOOM!
BUDDA-BUDDA-BUDDA
GROAN
If there's one rule when you're trying to save the world, it's that things can always get worse.

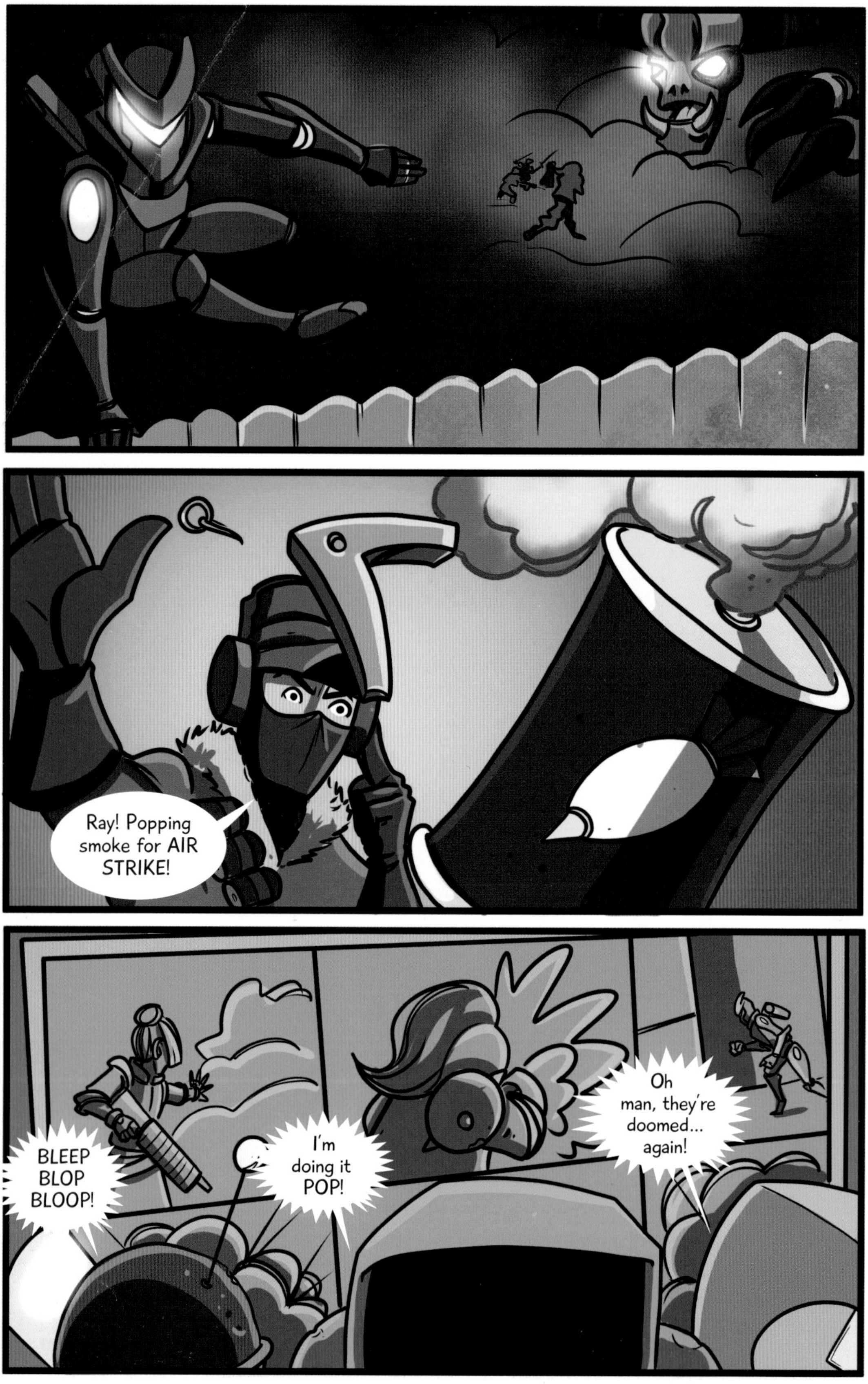
Ray! Popping smoke for AIR STRIKE!
BLEEP BLOP BLOOP!
I'm doing it POP!
Oh man, they're doomed... again!

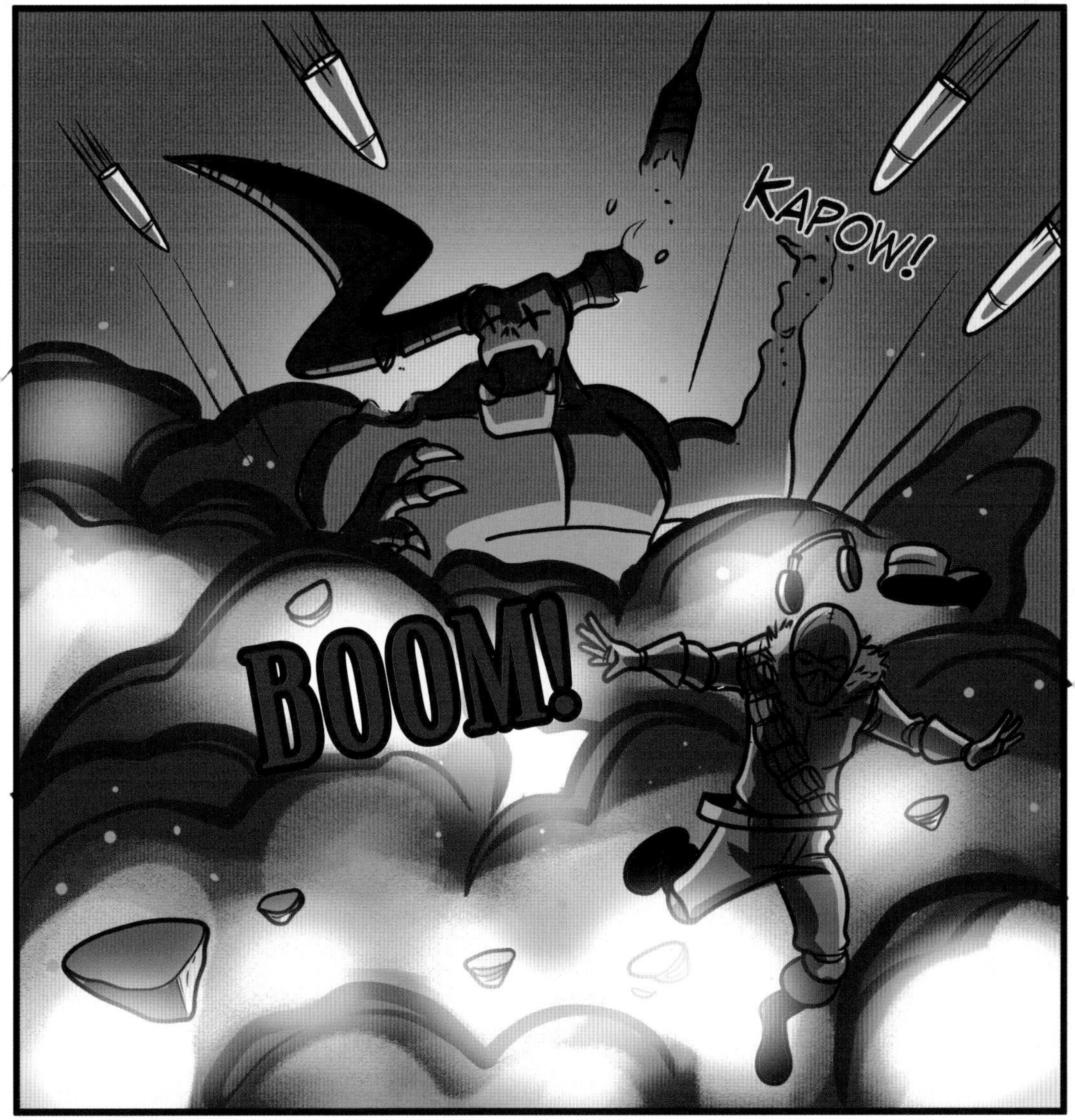
KAPOW!
BOOM!

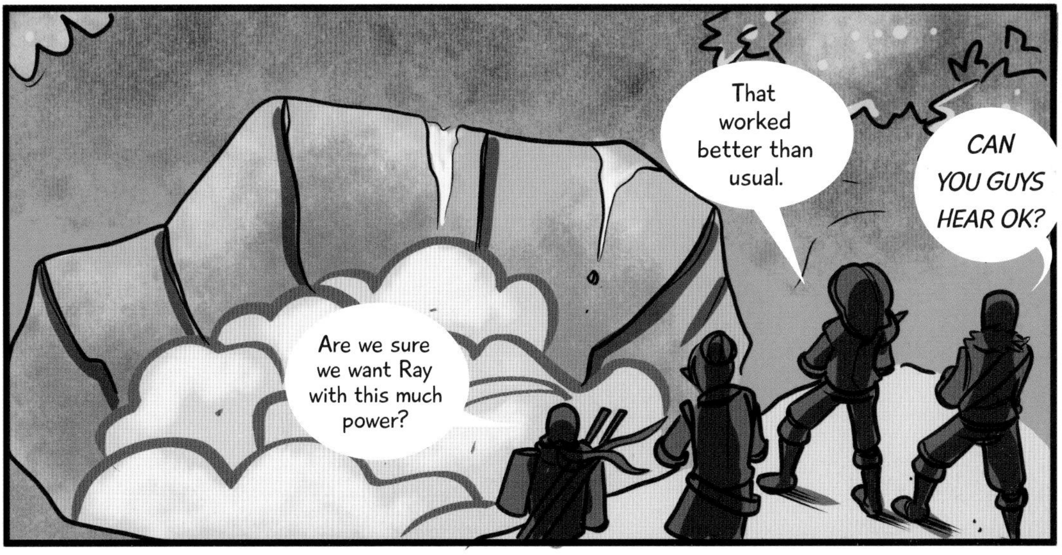
That worked better than usual.
CAN YOU GUYS HEAR OK?
Are we sure we want Ray with this much power?

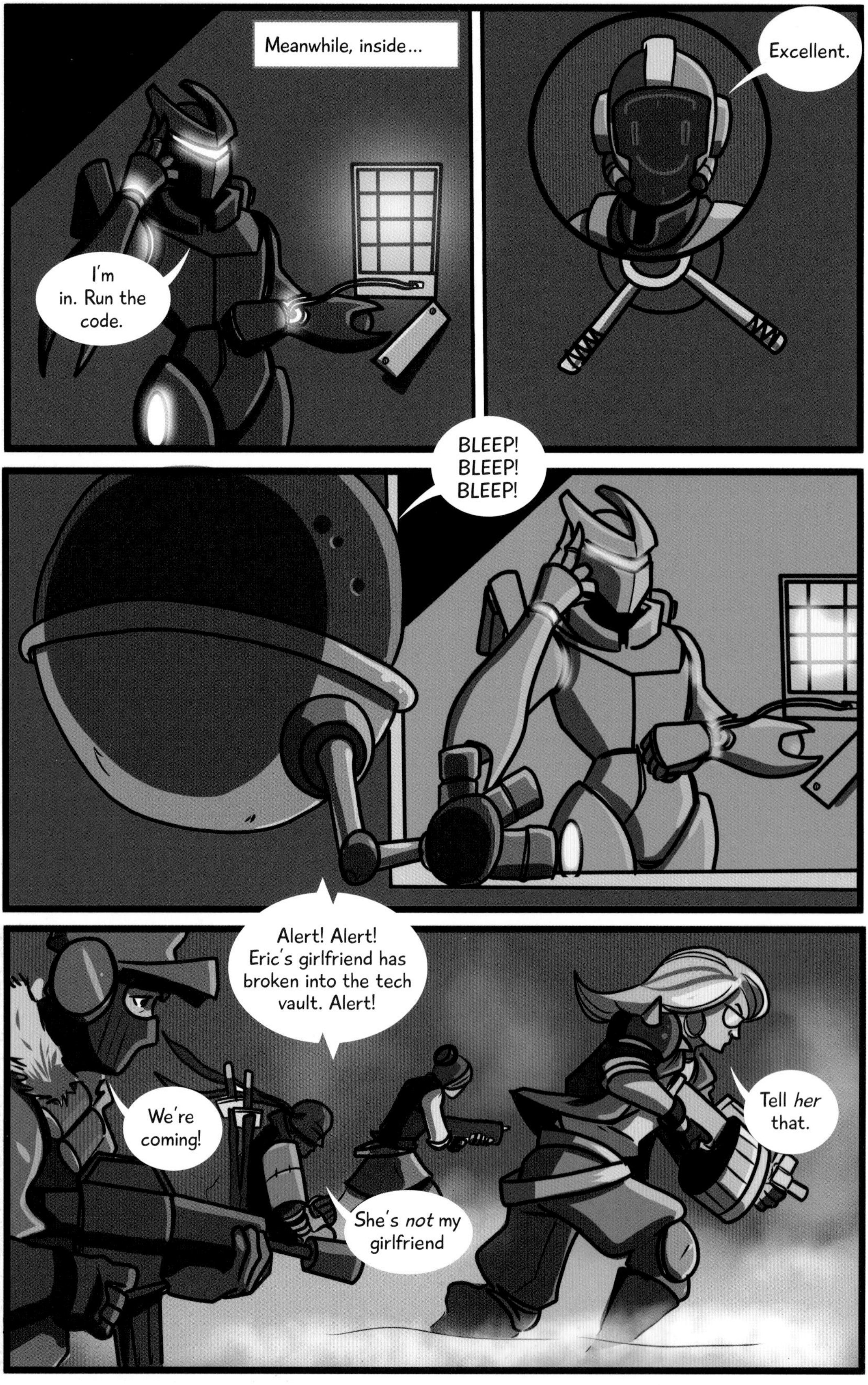
Meanwhile, inside...
I'm in. Run the code.
Excellent.
BLEEP! BLEEP! BLEEP!
Alert! Alert! Eric's girlfriend has broken into the tech vault. Alert!
We're coming!
Tell *her* that.
She's *not* my girlfriend

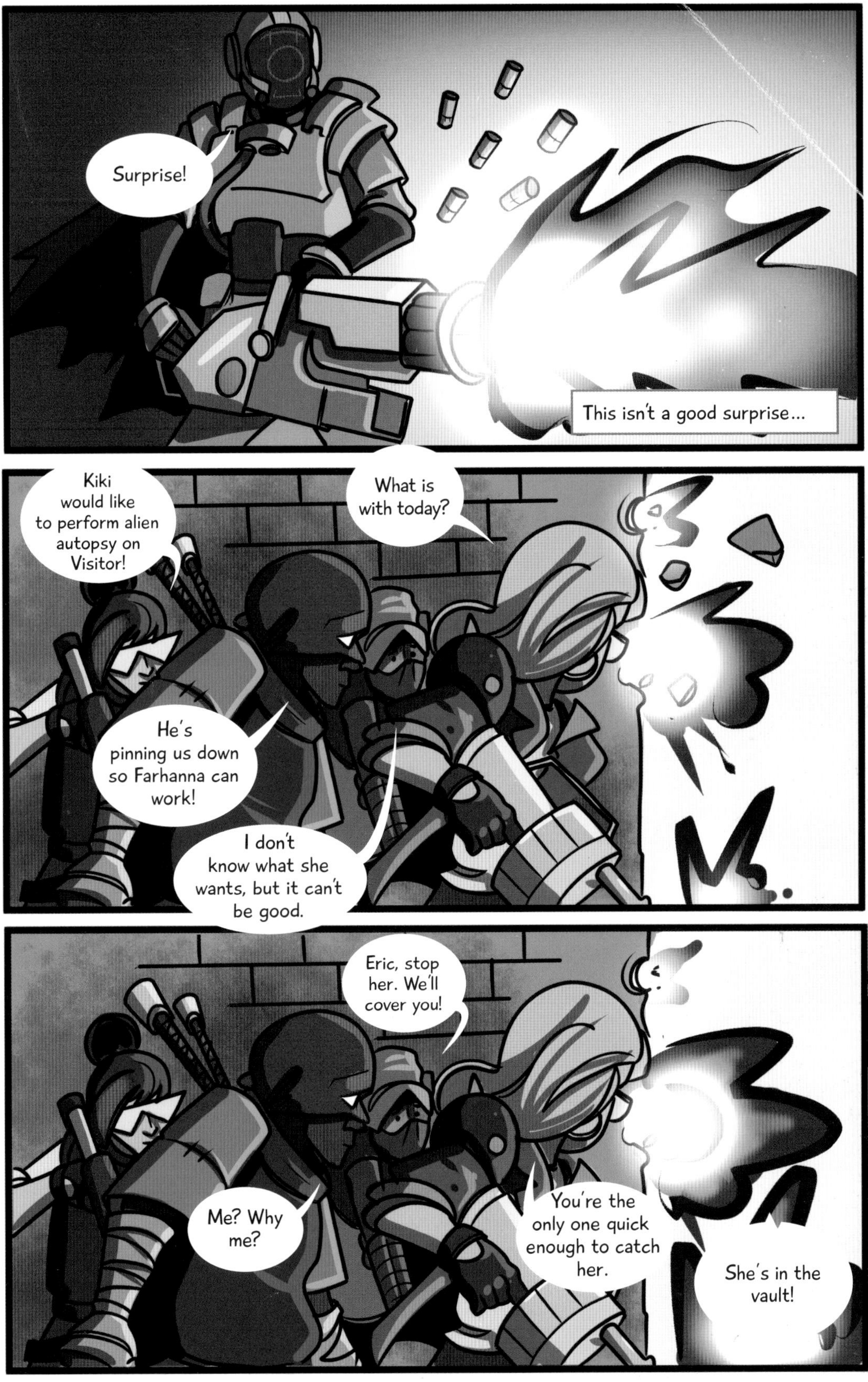
Surprise!
This isn't a good surprise...
Kiki would like to perform alien autopsy on Visitor!
What is with today?
He's pinning us down so Farhanna can work!
I don't know what she wants, but it can't be good.
Eric, stop her. We'll cover you!
Me? Why me?
You're the only one quick enough to catch her.
She's in the vault!

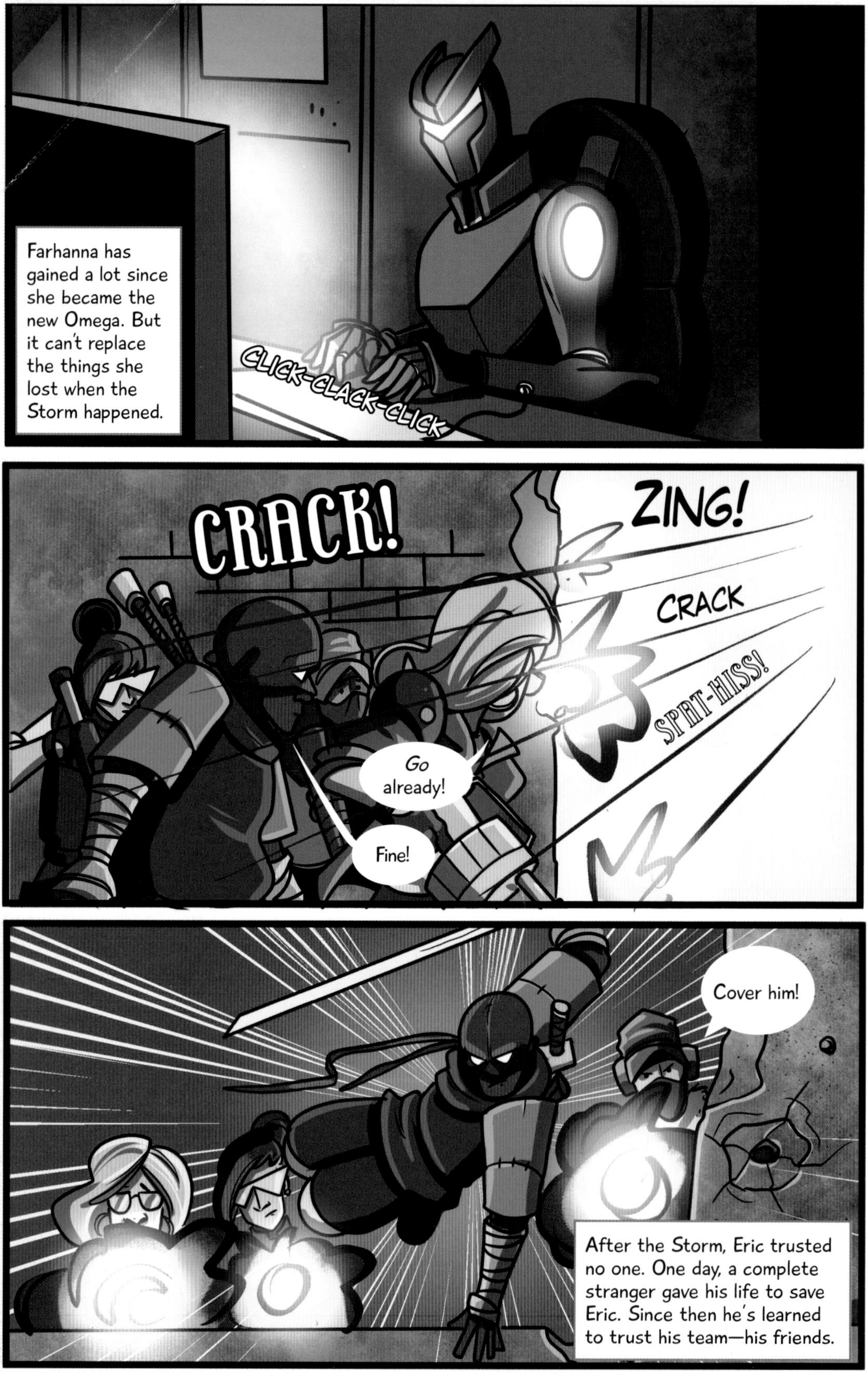
Farhanna has gained a lot since she became the new Omega. But it can't replace the things she lost when the Storm happened.
CLICK-CLACK-CLICK
CRACK!
ZING!
CRACK
SPAT-HISS!
Go already!
Fine!
Cover him!
After the Storm, Eric trusted no one. One day, a complete stranger gave his life to save Eric. Since then he's learned to trust his team—his friends.

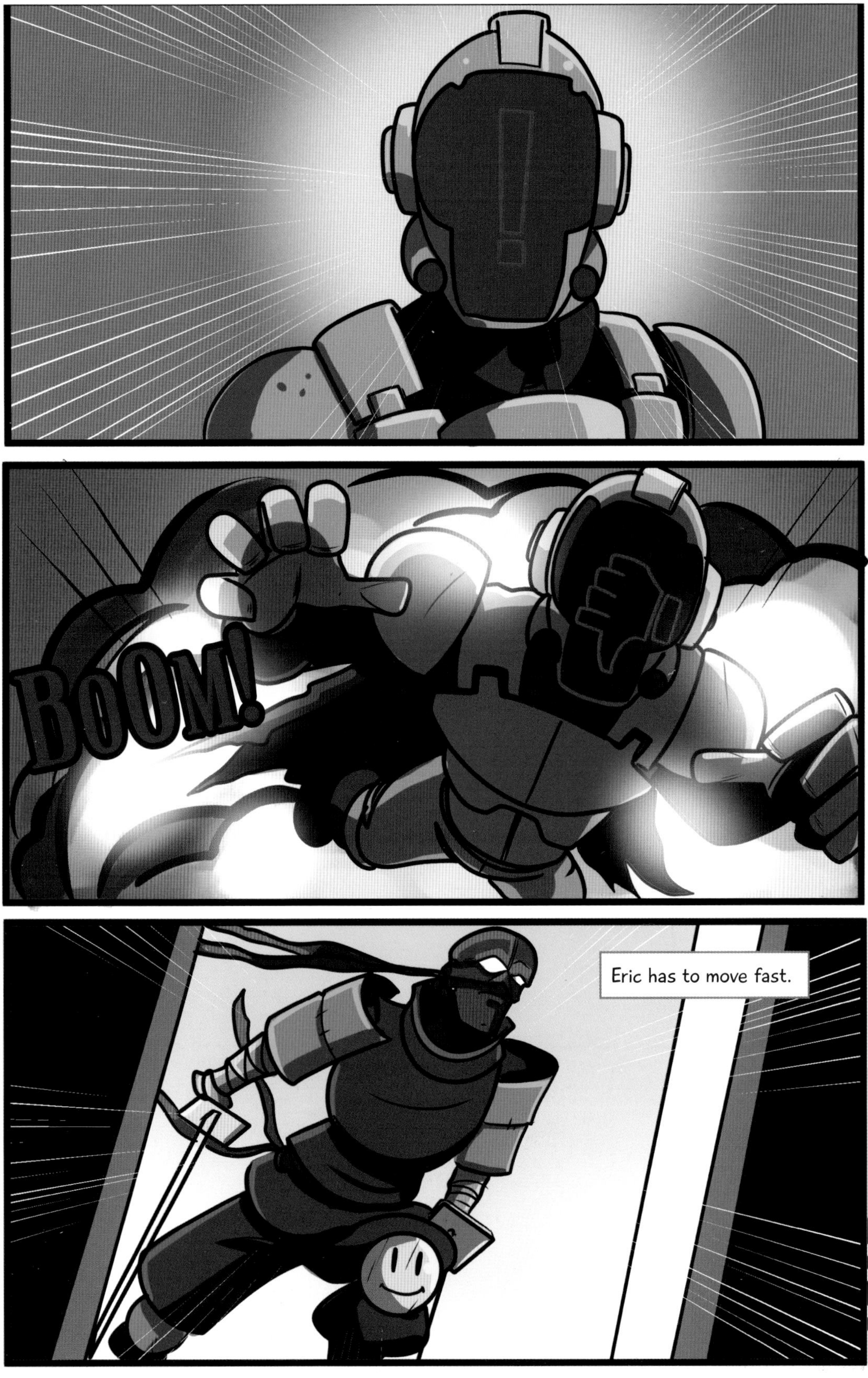
BOOM!
Eric has to move fast.

There's no room for error.

He's got to bring his A game...

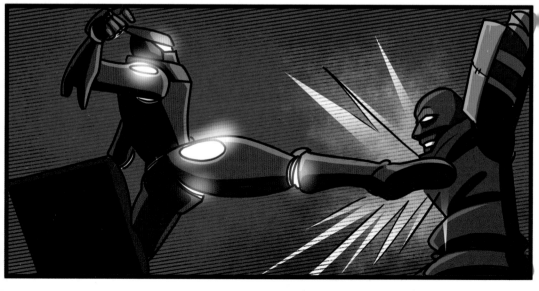

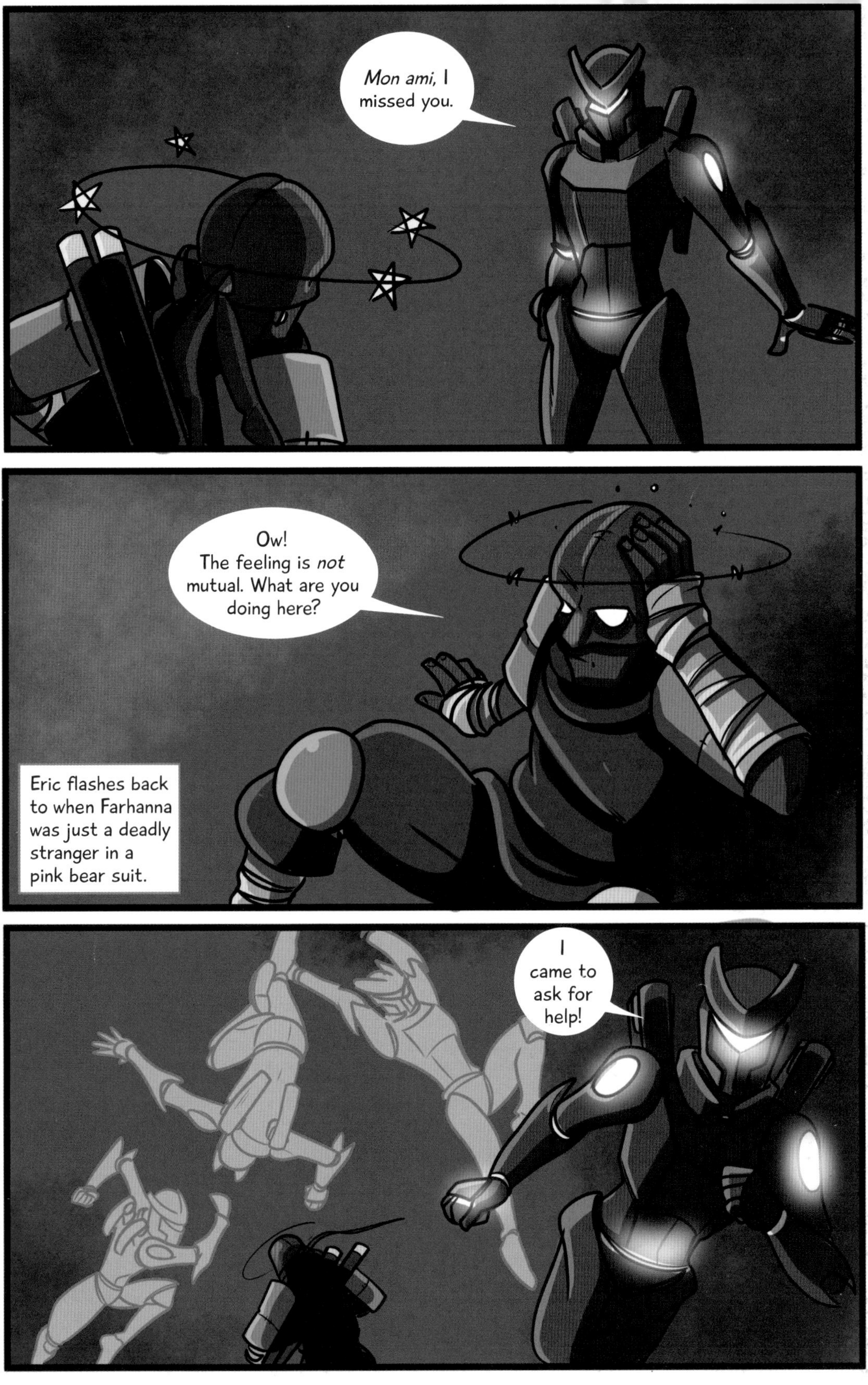
Mon ami, I missed you.
Ow! The feeling is *not* mutual. What are you doing here?
Eric flashes back to when Farhanna was just a deadly stranger in a pink bear suit.
I came to ask for help!

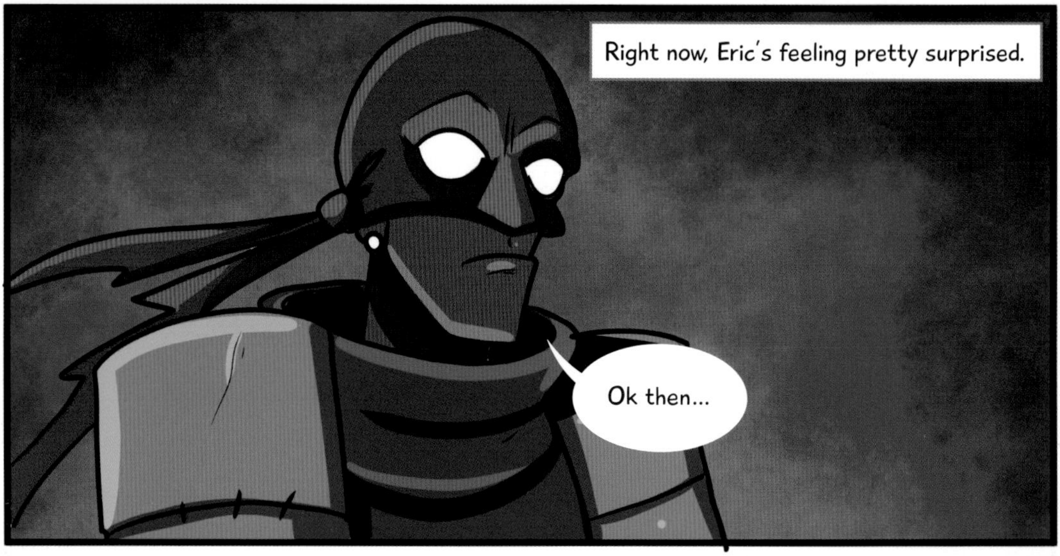
Right now, Eric's feeling pretty surprised.
Ok then...

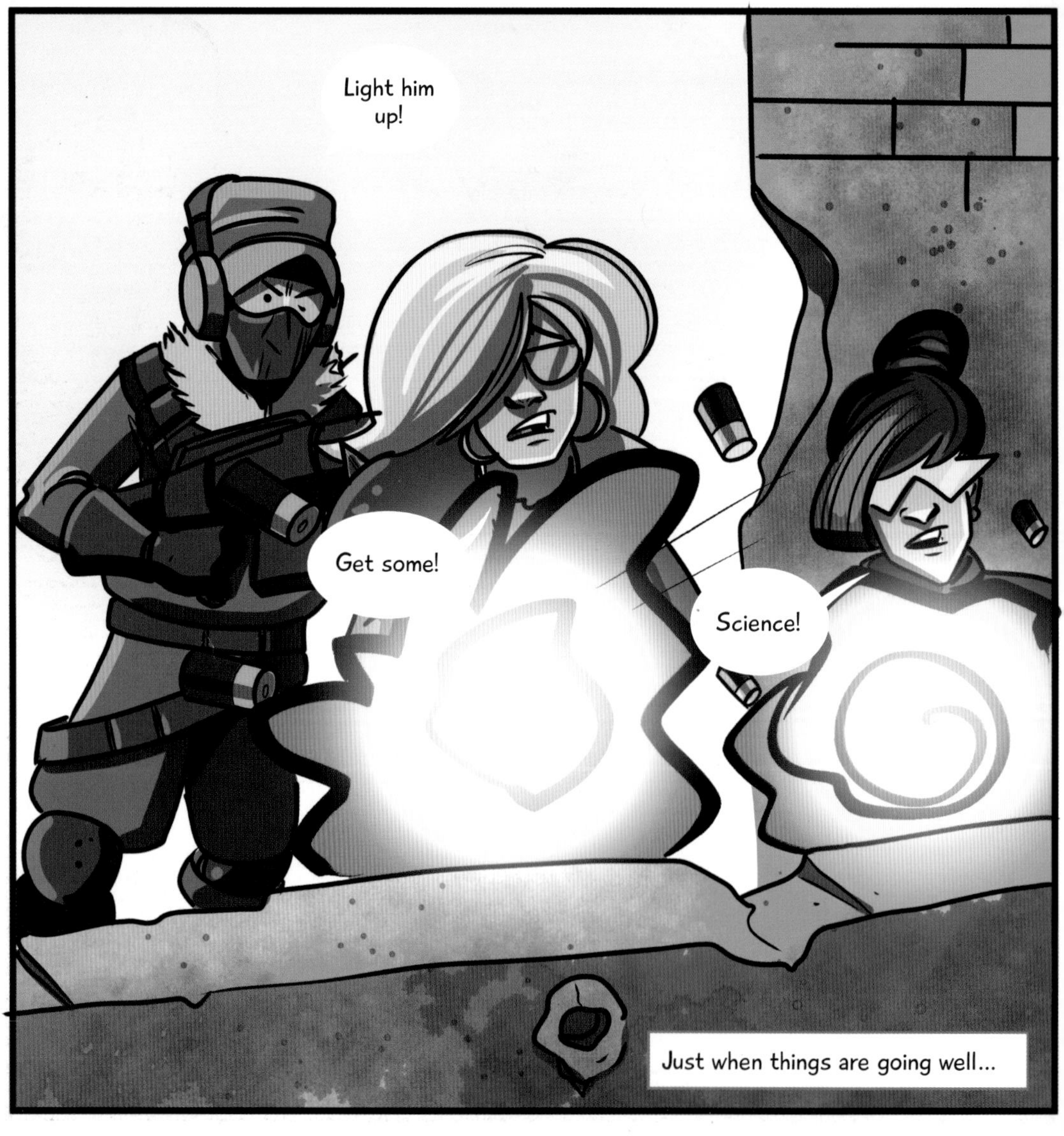
Light him up!
Get some!
Science!
Just when things are going well...

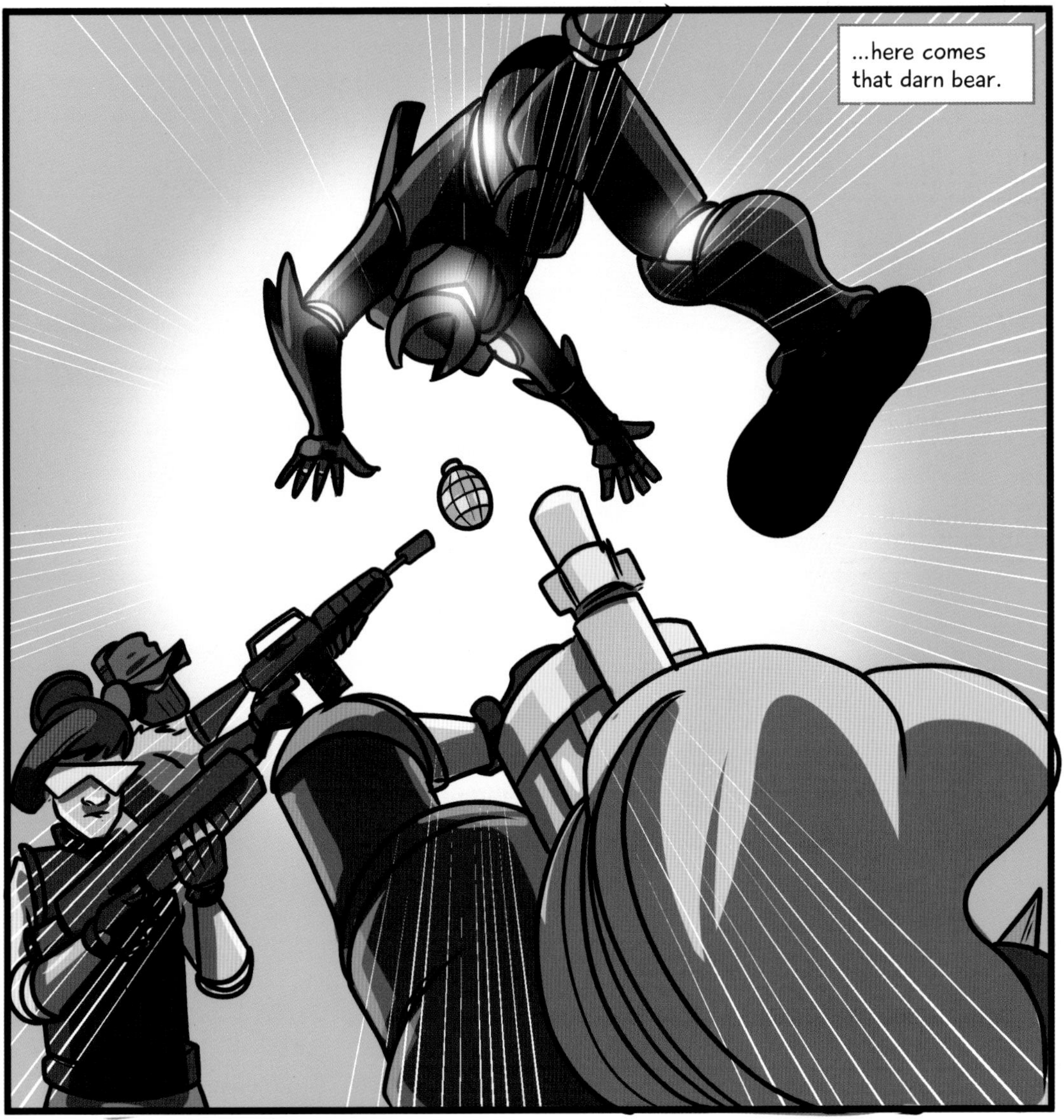
...here comes
that darn bear.

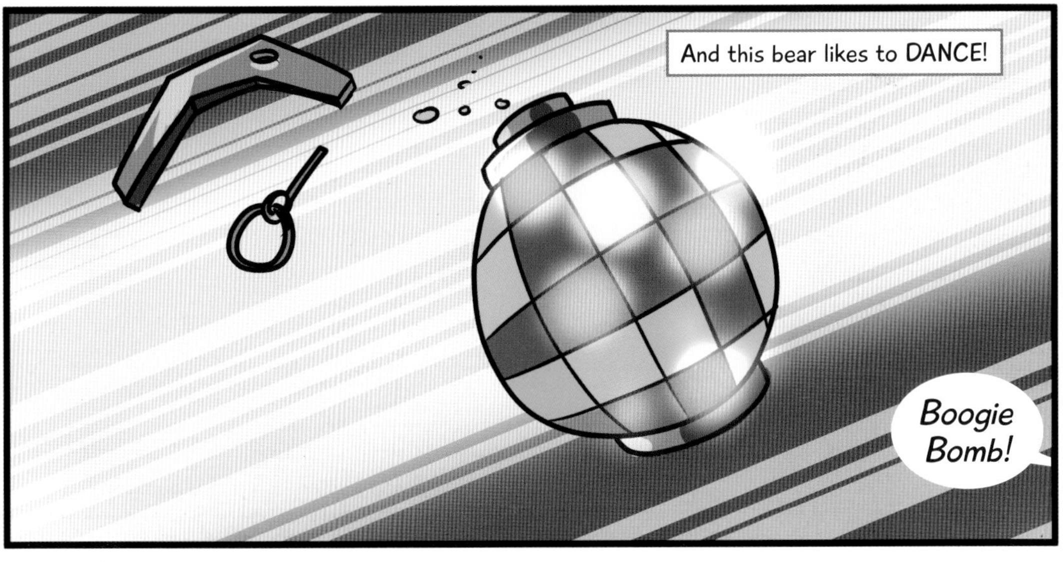
And this bear likes to DANCE!
Boogie Bomb!

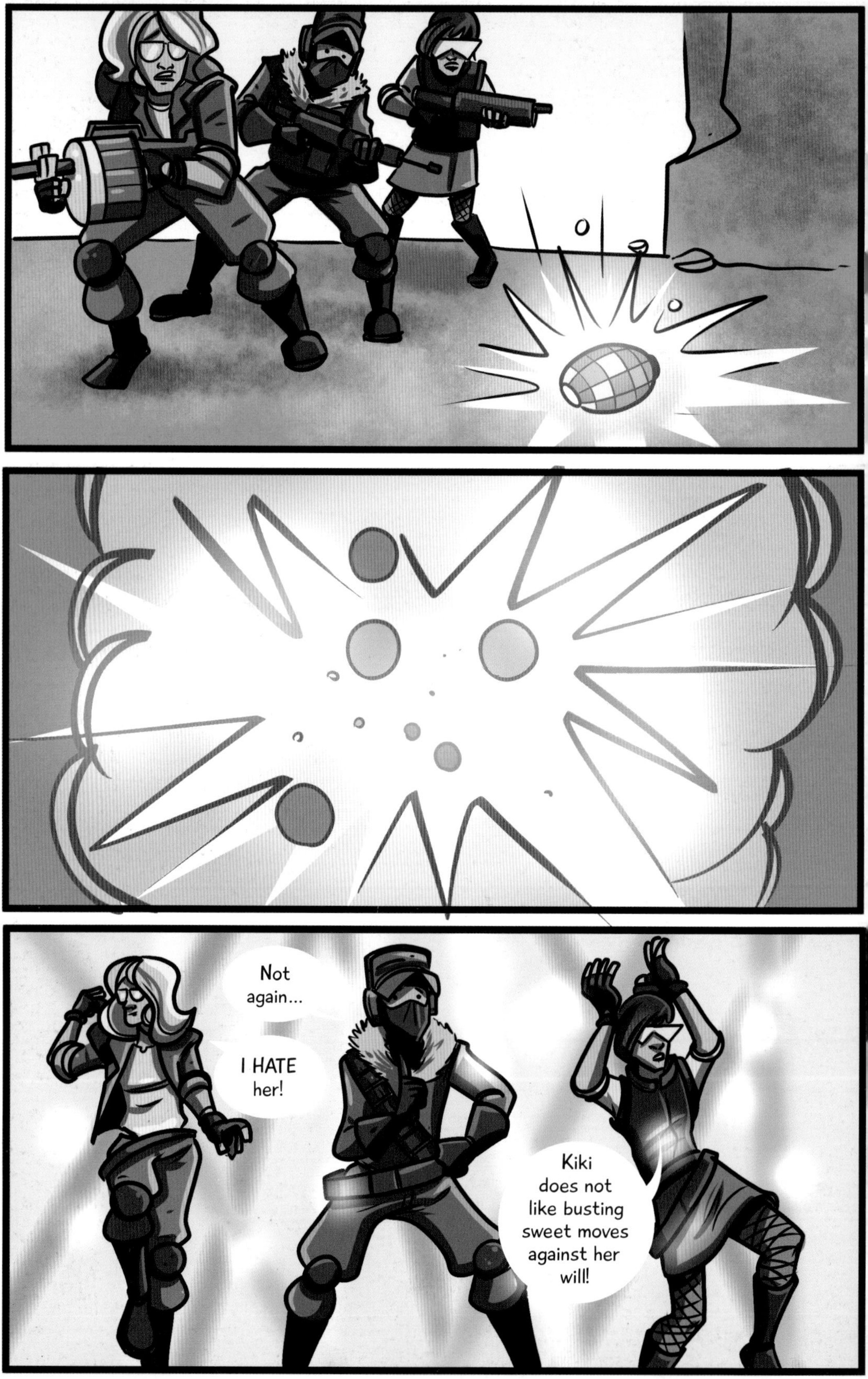
Not again...
I HATE her!
Kiki does not like busting sweet moves against her will!

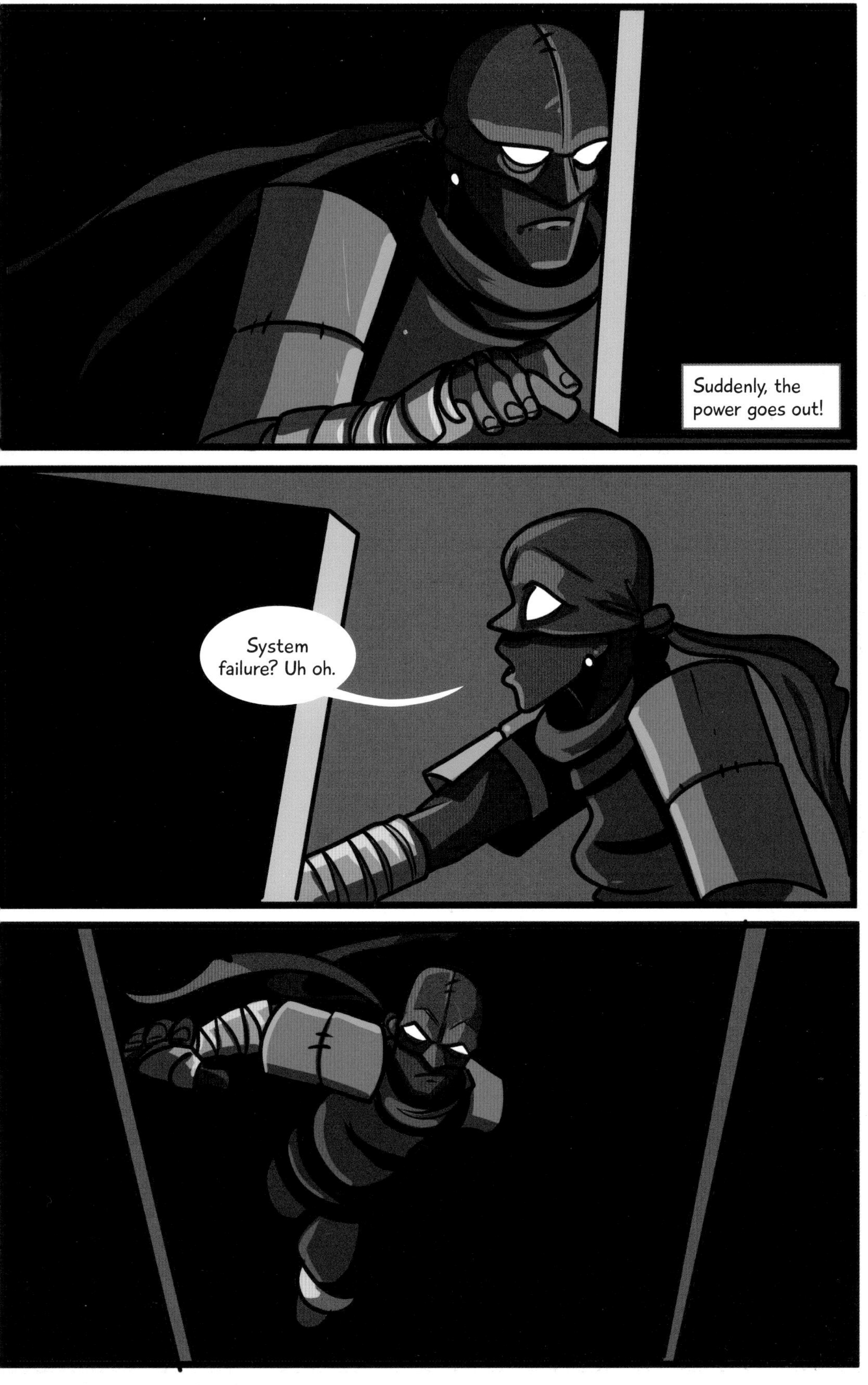
Suddenly, the power goes out!
System failure? Uh oh.

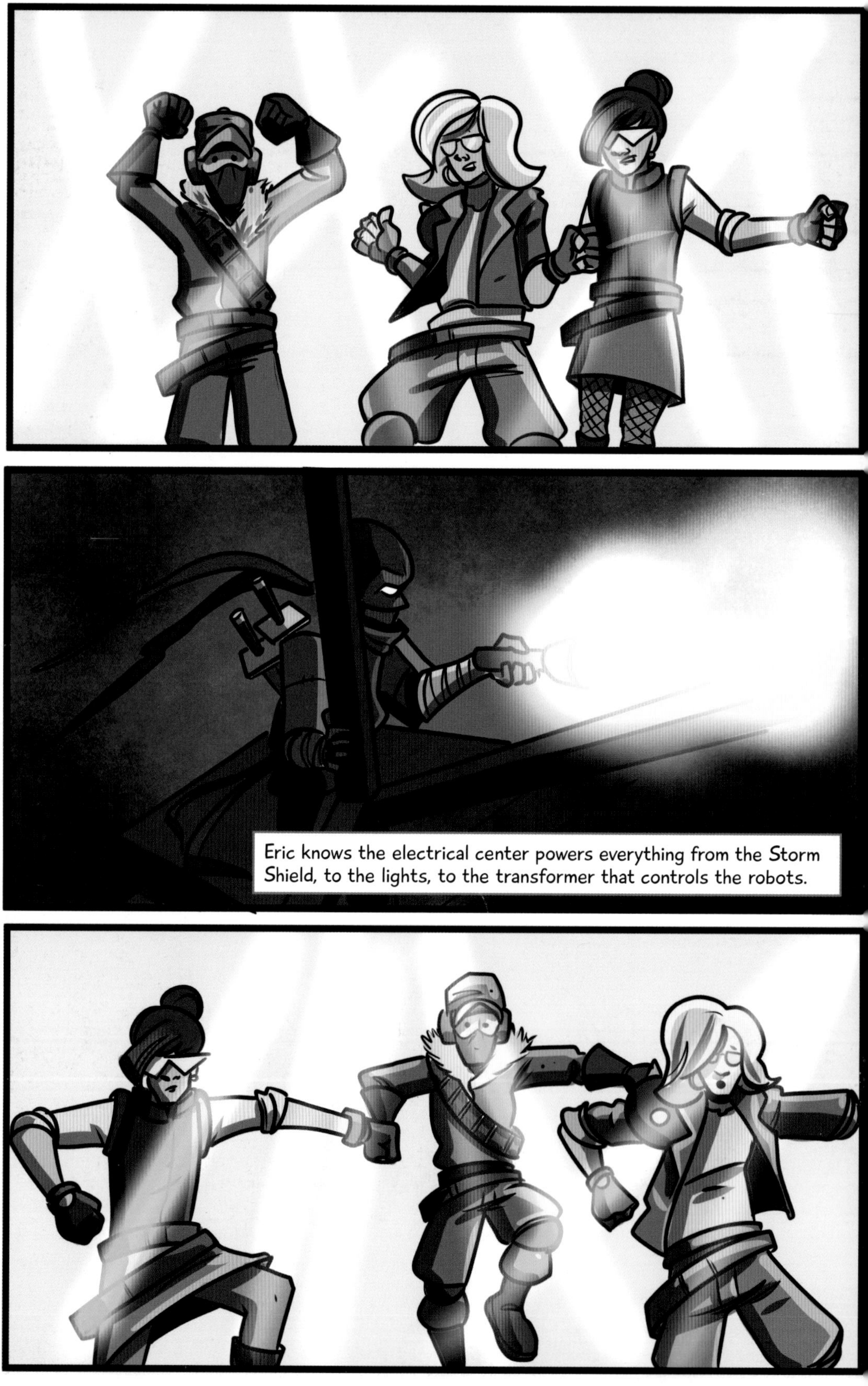
Eric knows the electrical center powers everything from the Storm Shield, to the lights, to the transformer that controls the robots.

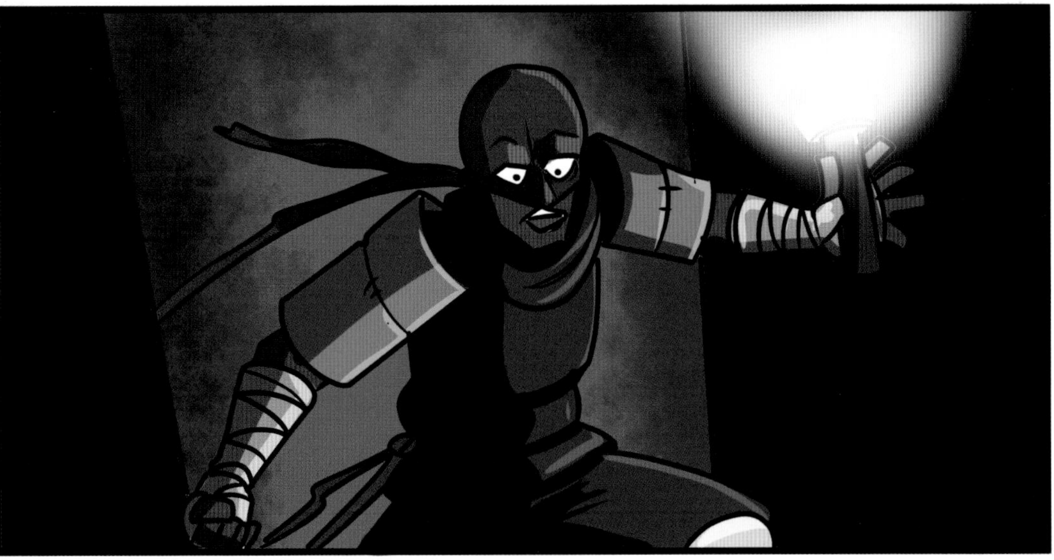

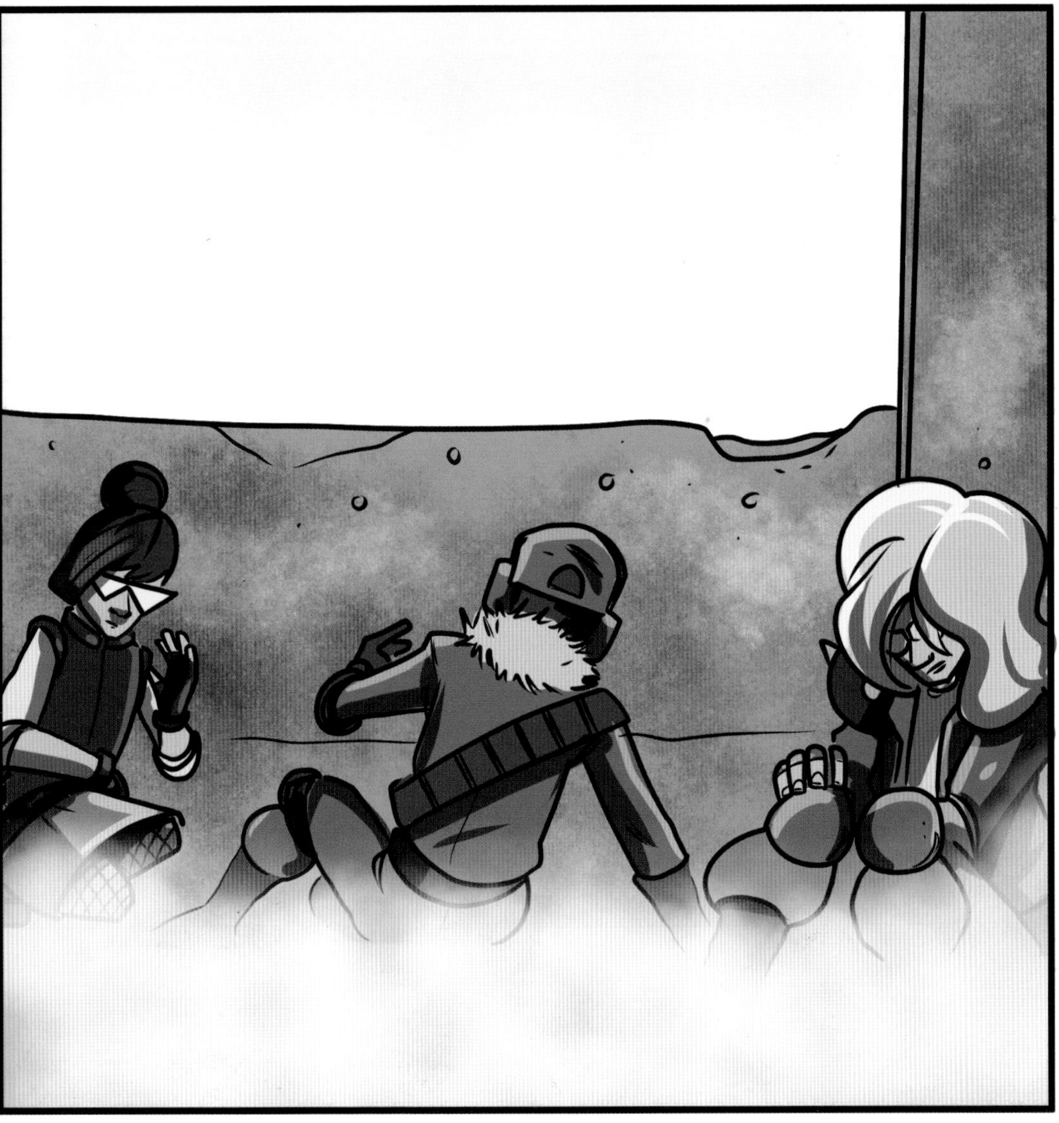

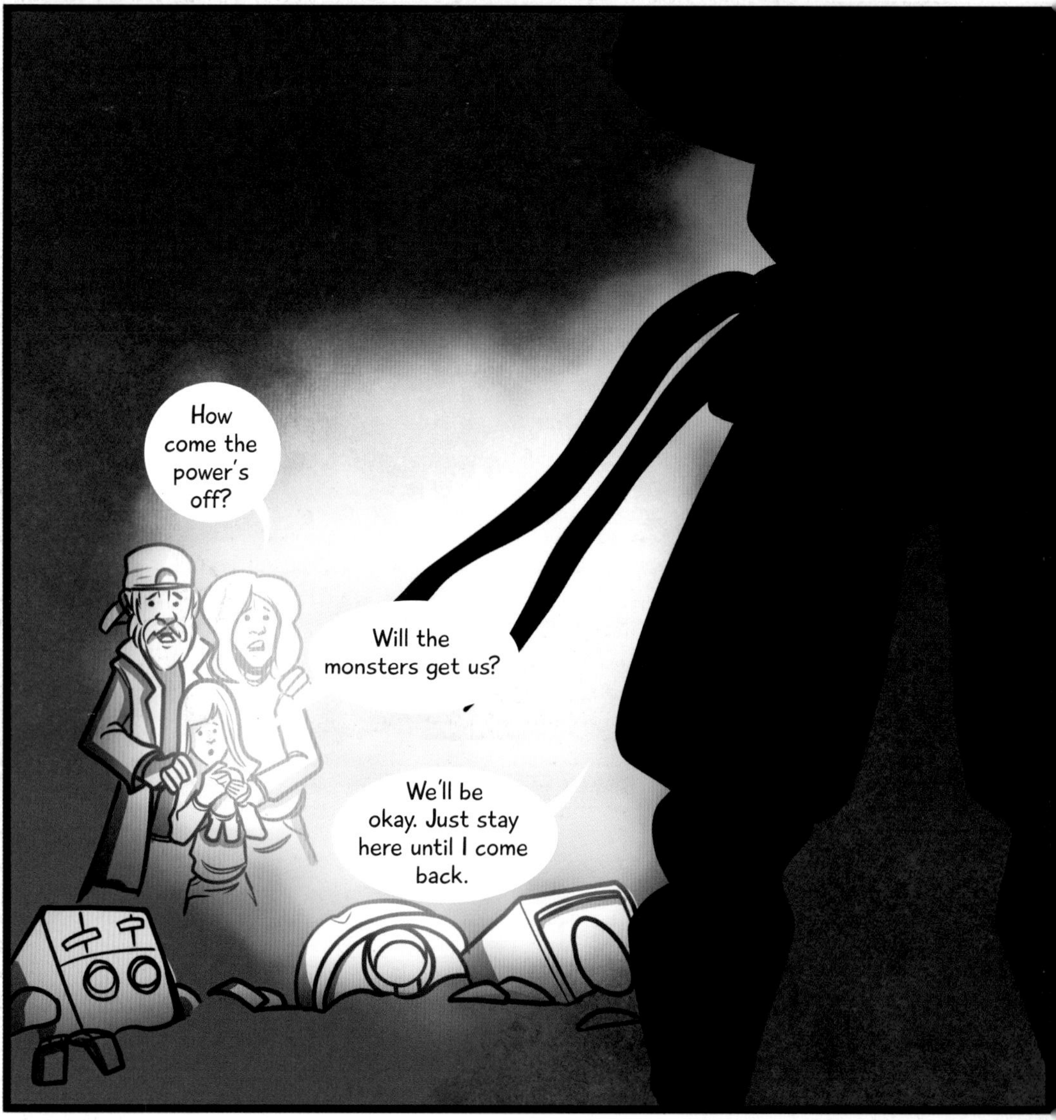
How come the power's off?
Will the monsters get us?
We'll be okay. Just stay here until I come back.

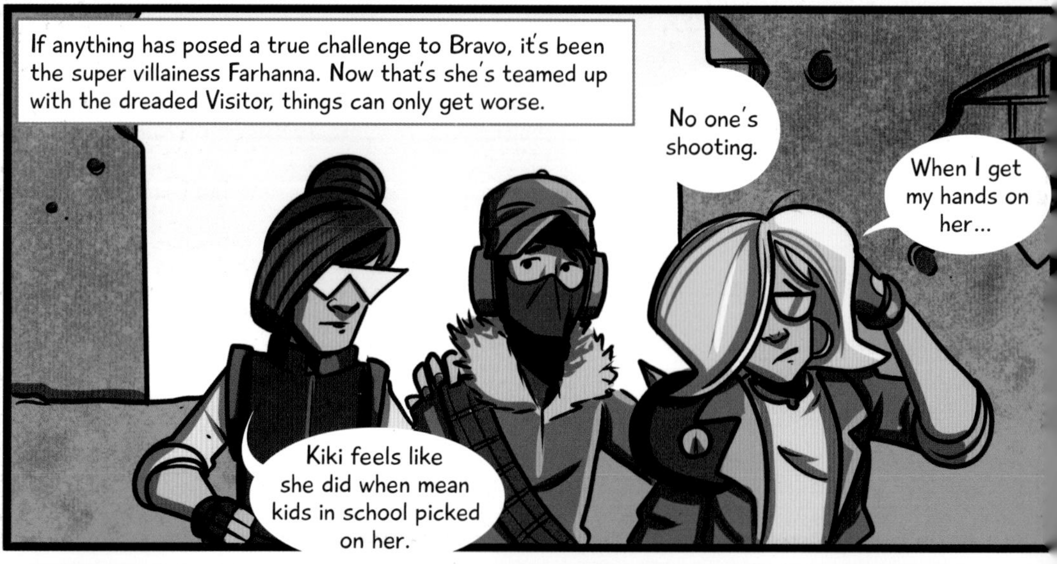
If anything has posed a true challenge to Bravo, it's been the super villainess Farhanna. Now that's she's teamed up with the dreaded Visitor, things can only get worse.
No one's shooting.
When I get my hands on her...
Kiki feels like she did when mean kids in school picked on her.

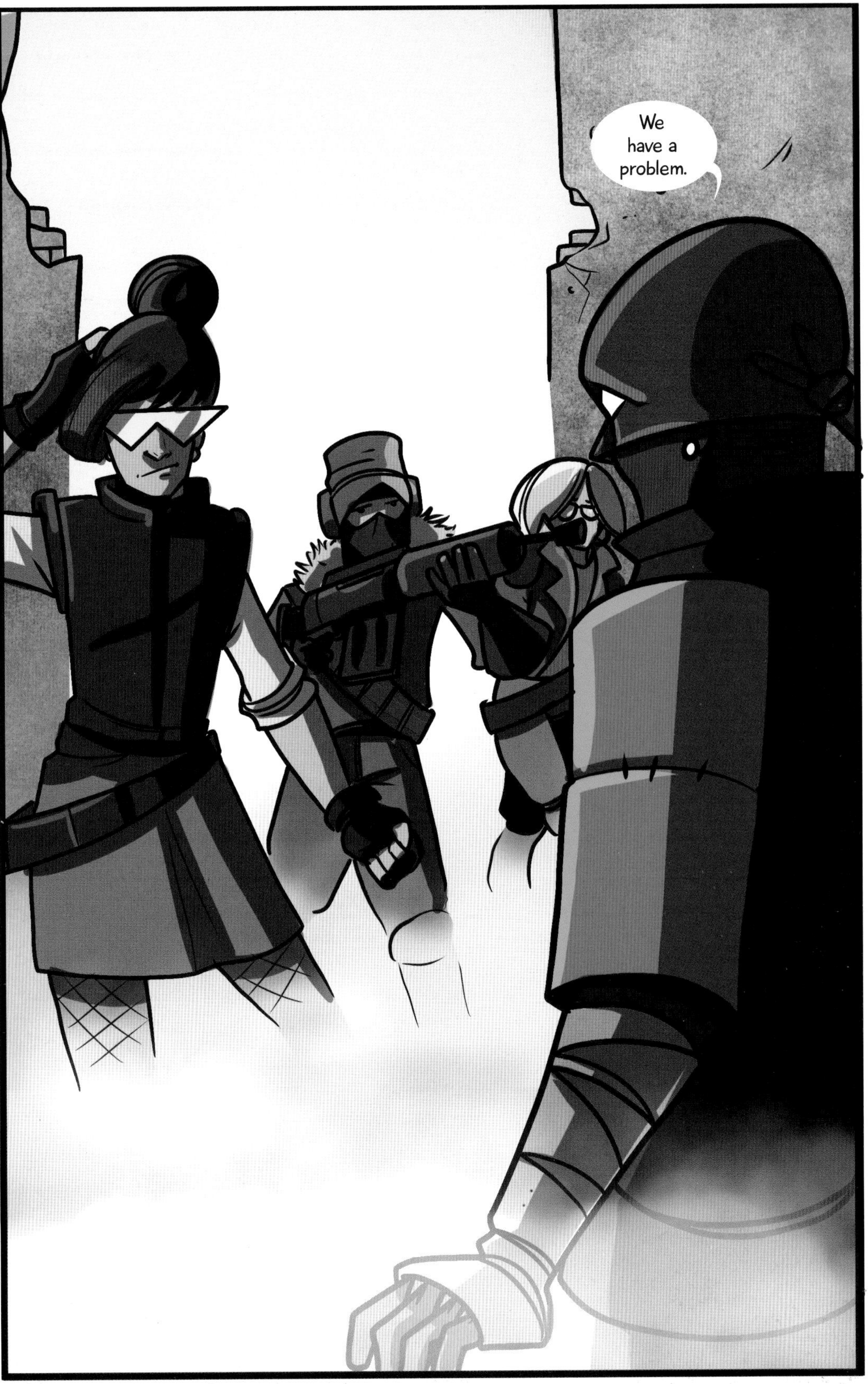
We have a problem.

CHAPTER 2: CODE RED!

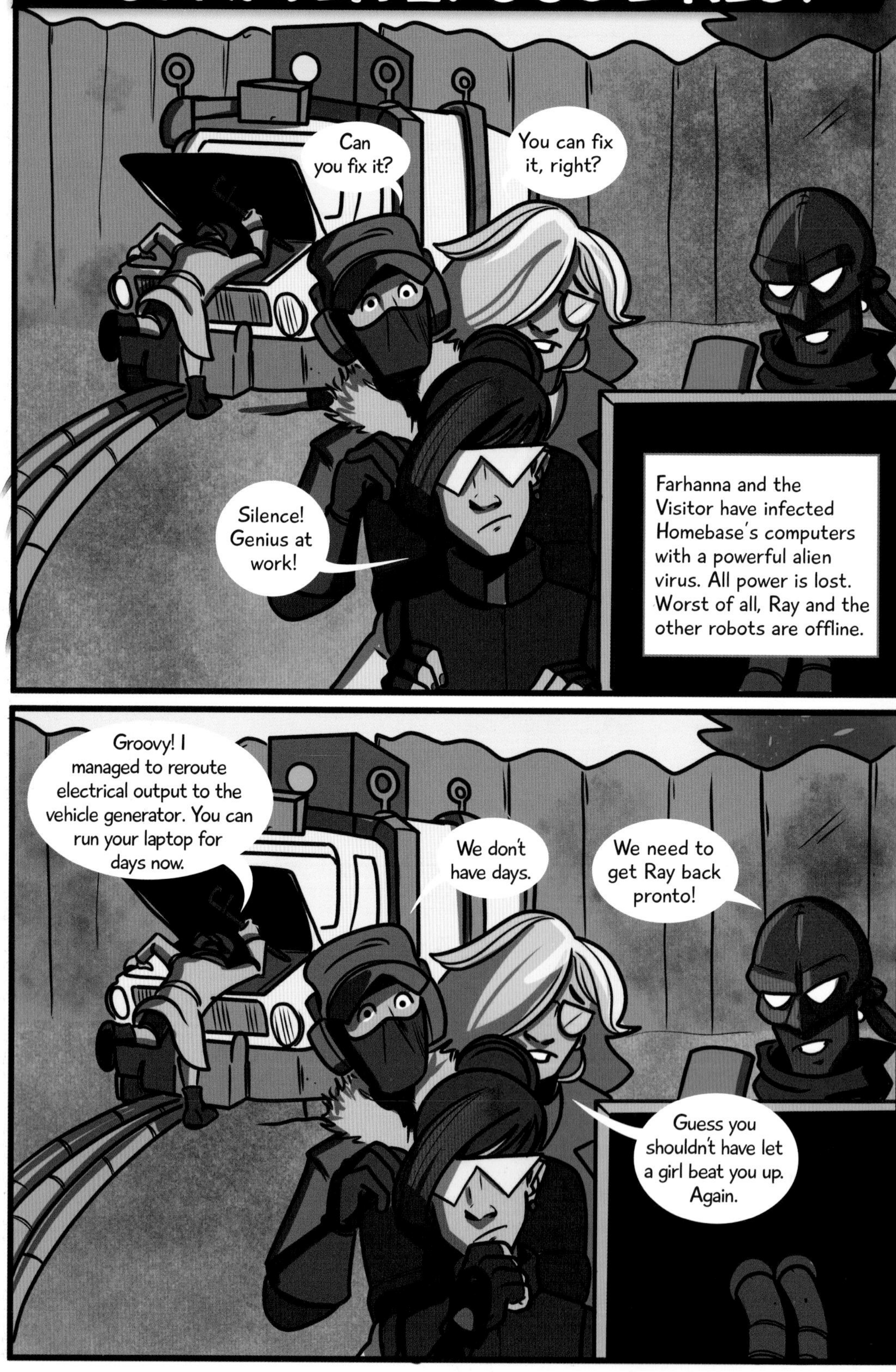
Can you fix it?
You can fix it, right?
Silence! Genius at work!
Farhanna and the Visitor have infected Homebase's computers with a powerful alien virus. All power is lost. Worst of all, Ray and the other robots are offline.
Groovy! I managed to reroute electrical output to the vehicle generator. You can run your laptop for days now.
We don't have days.
We need to get Ray back pronto!
Guess you shouldn't have let a girl beat you up. Again.

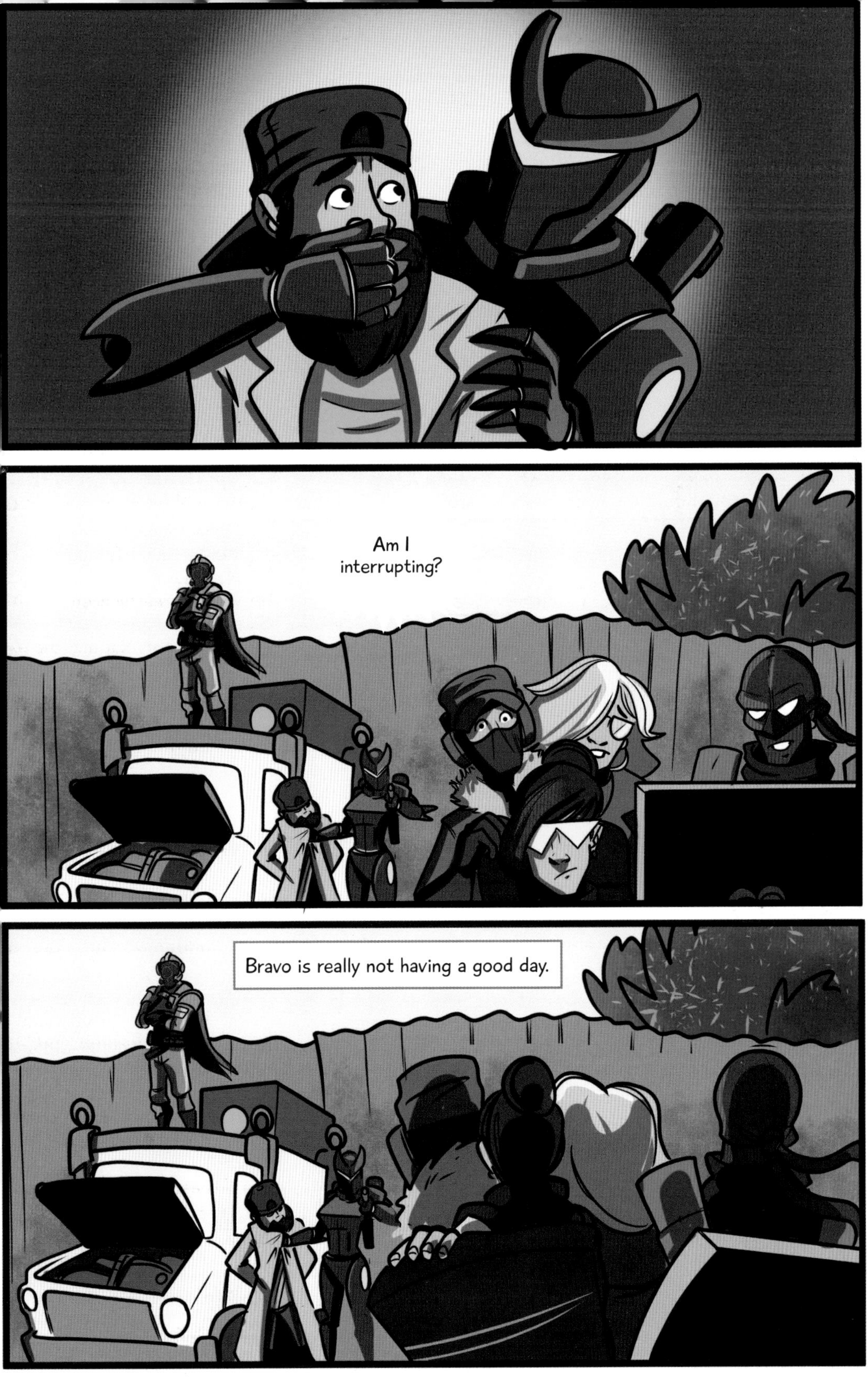
Am I interrupting?
Bravo is really not having a good day.

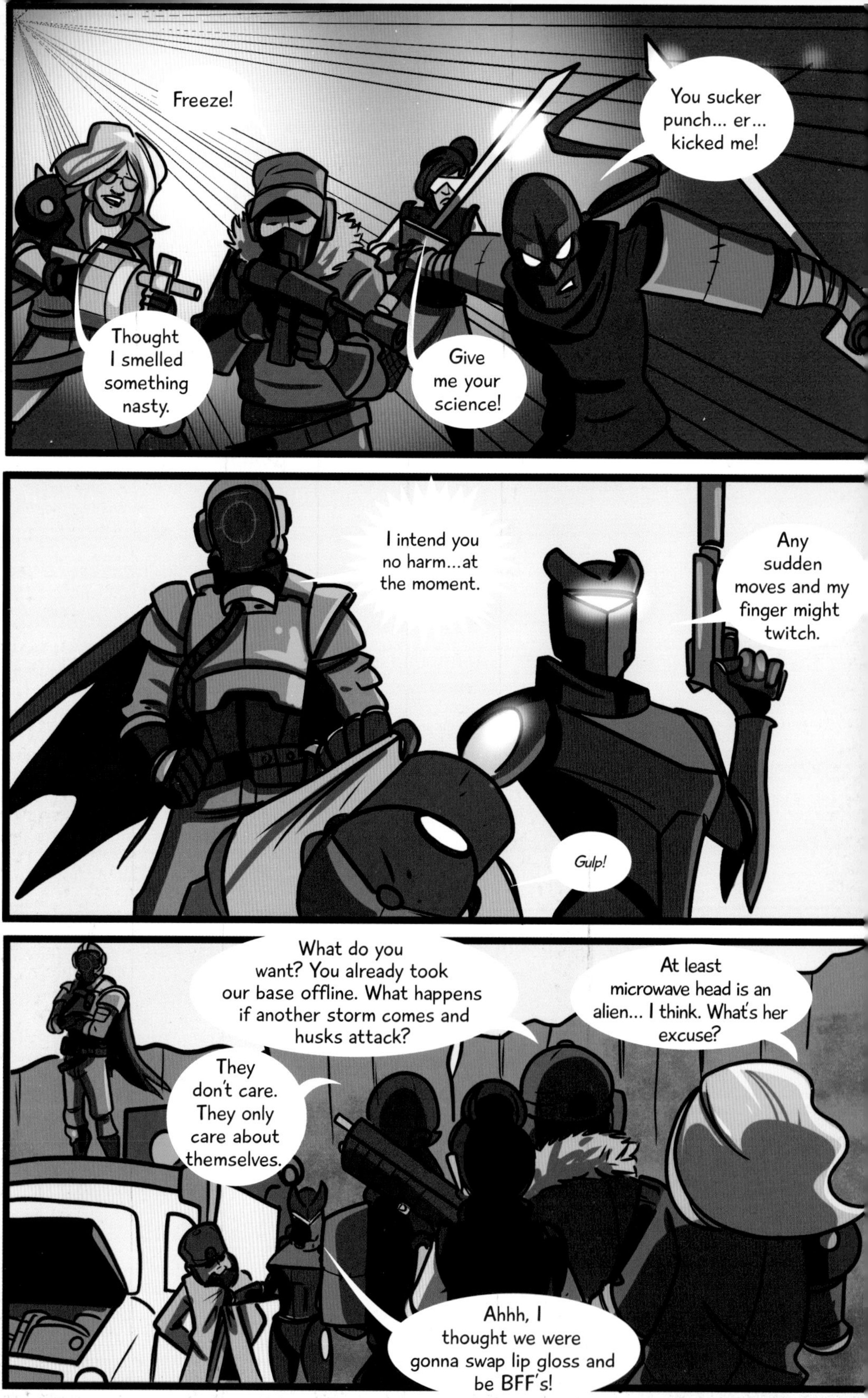

Freeze!
You sucker punch... er... kicked me!
Thought I smelled something nasty.
Give me your science!
I intend you no harm...at the moment.
Any sudden moves and my finger might twitch.
Gulp!
What do you want? You already took our base offline. What happens if another storm comes and husks attack?
At least microwave head is an alien... I think. What's her excuse?
They don't care. They only care about themselves.
Ahhh, I thought we were gonna swap lip gloss and be BFF's!

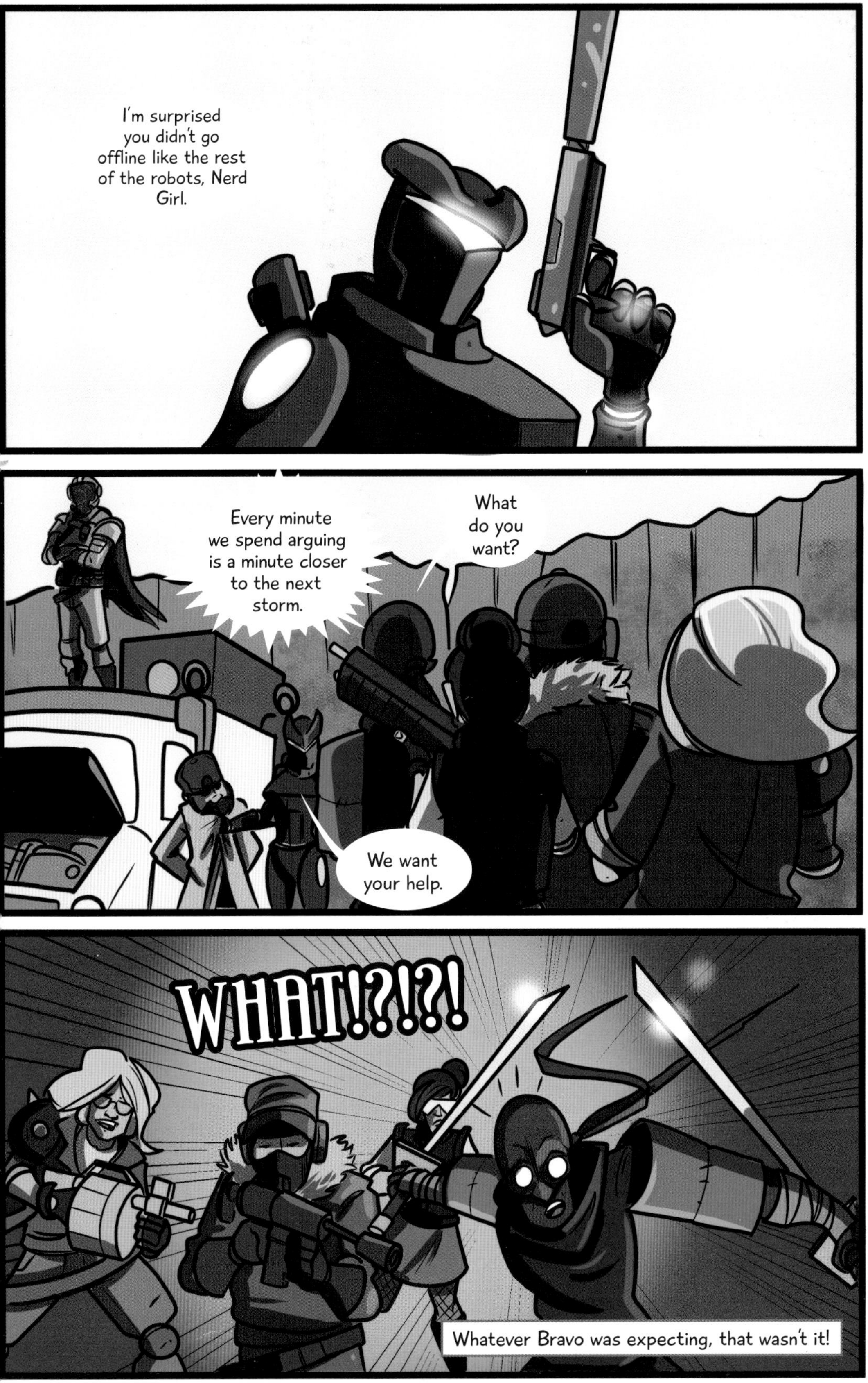
I'm surprised you didn't go offline like the rest of the robots, Nerd Girl.
Every minute we spend arguing is a minute closer to the next storm.
What do you want?
We want your help.
WHAT!?!?!
Whatever Bravo was expecting, that wasn't it!

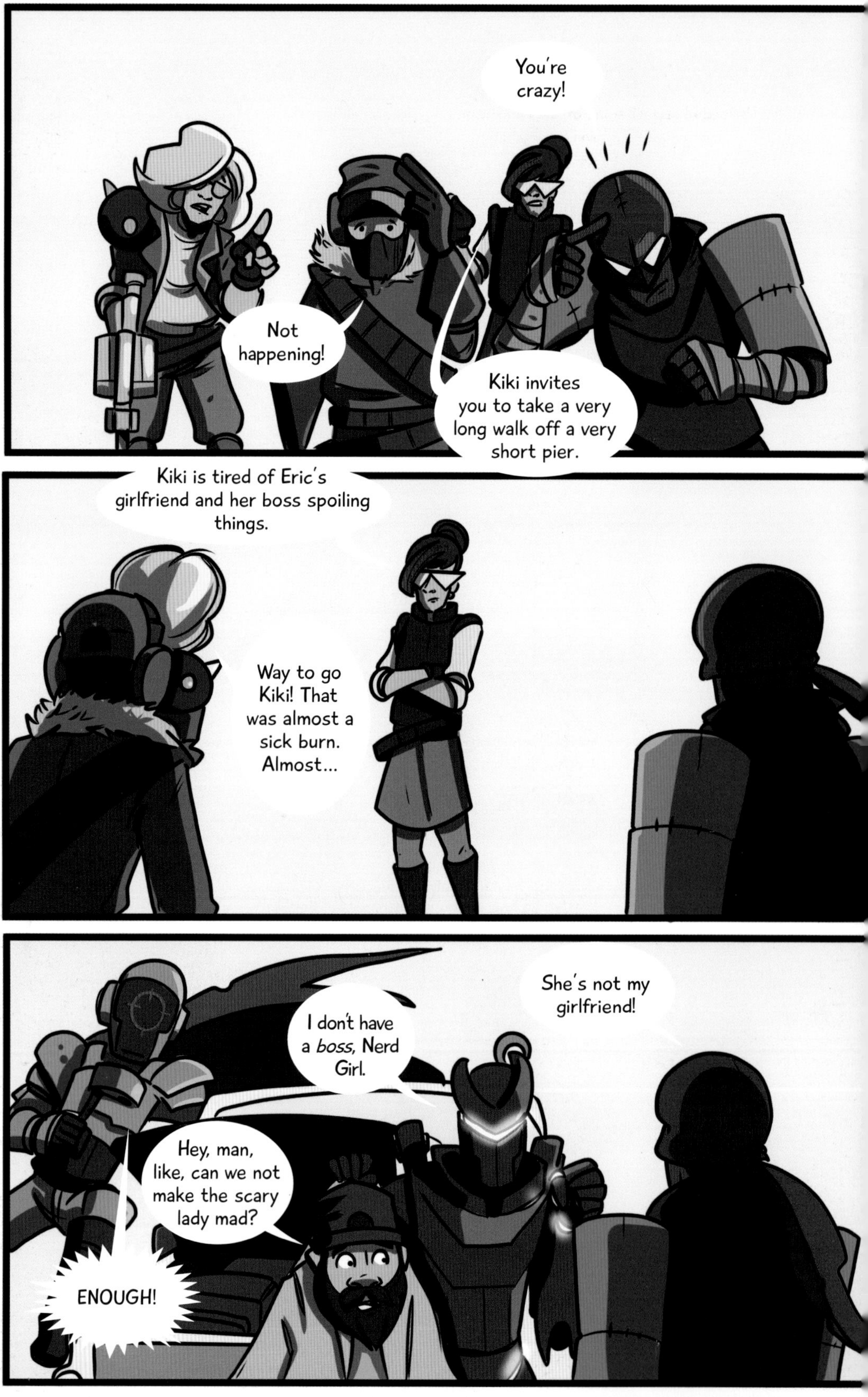
You're crazy!
Not happening!
Kiki invites you to take a very long walk off a very short pier.
Kiki is tired of Eric's girlfriend and her boss spoiling things.
Way to go Kiki! That was almost a sick burn. Almost...
She's not my girlfriend!
I don't have a *boss*, Nerd Girl.
Hey, man, like, can we not make the scary lady mad?
ENOUGH!

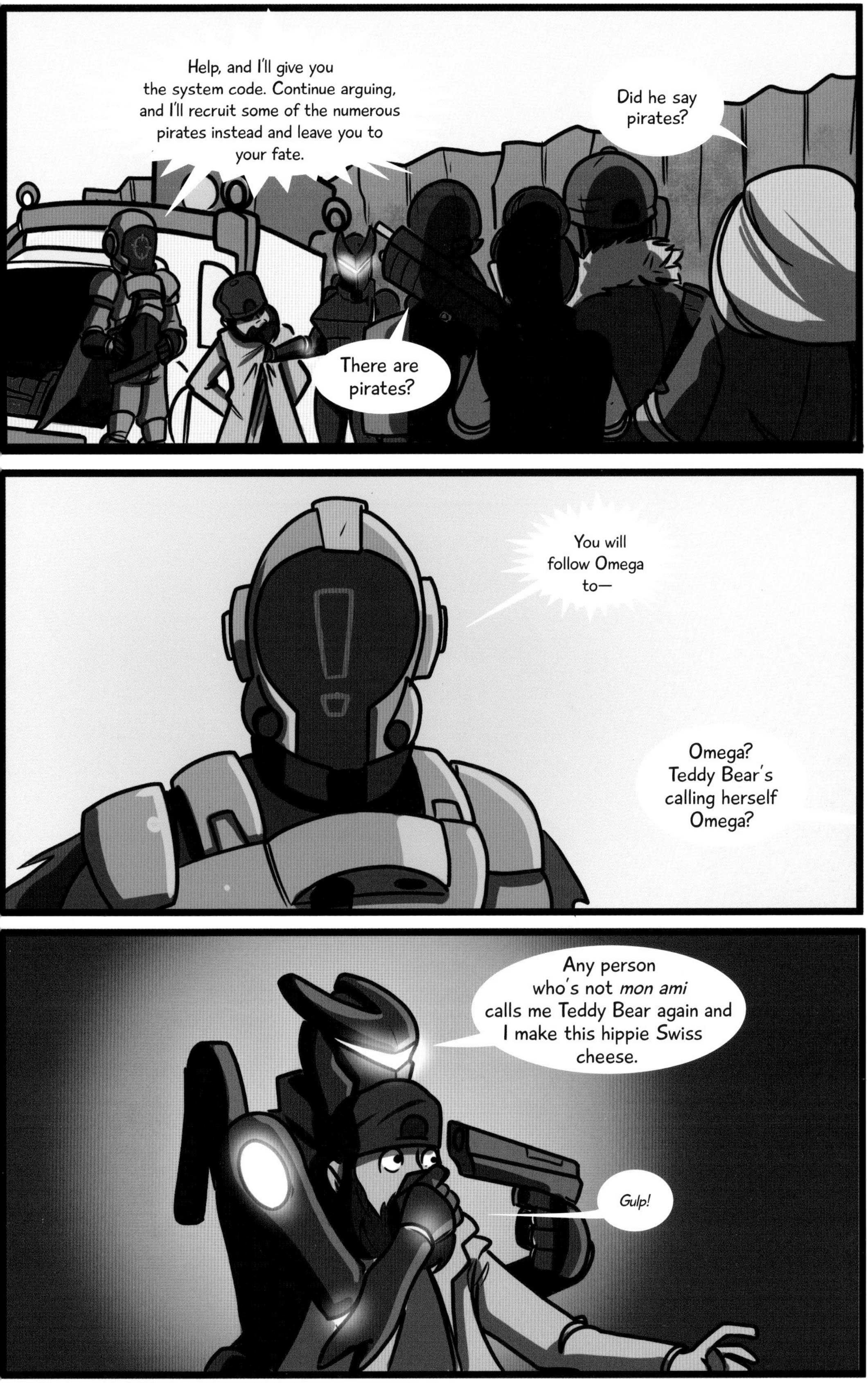
Help, and I'll give you the system code. Continue arguing, and I'll recruit some of the numerous pirates instead and leave you to your fate.
Did he say pirates?
There are pirates?
You will follow Omega to—
Omega? Teddy Bear's calling herself Omega?
Any person who's not *mon ami* calls me Teddy Bear again and I make this hippie Swiss cheese.
Gulp!

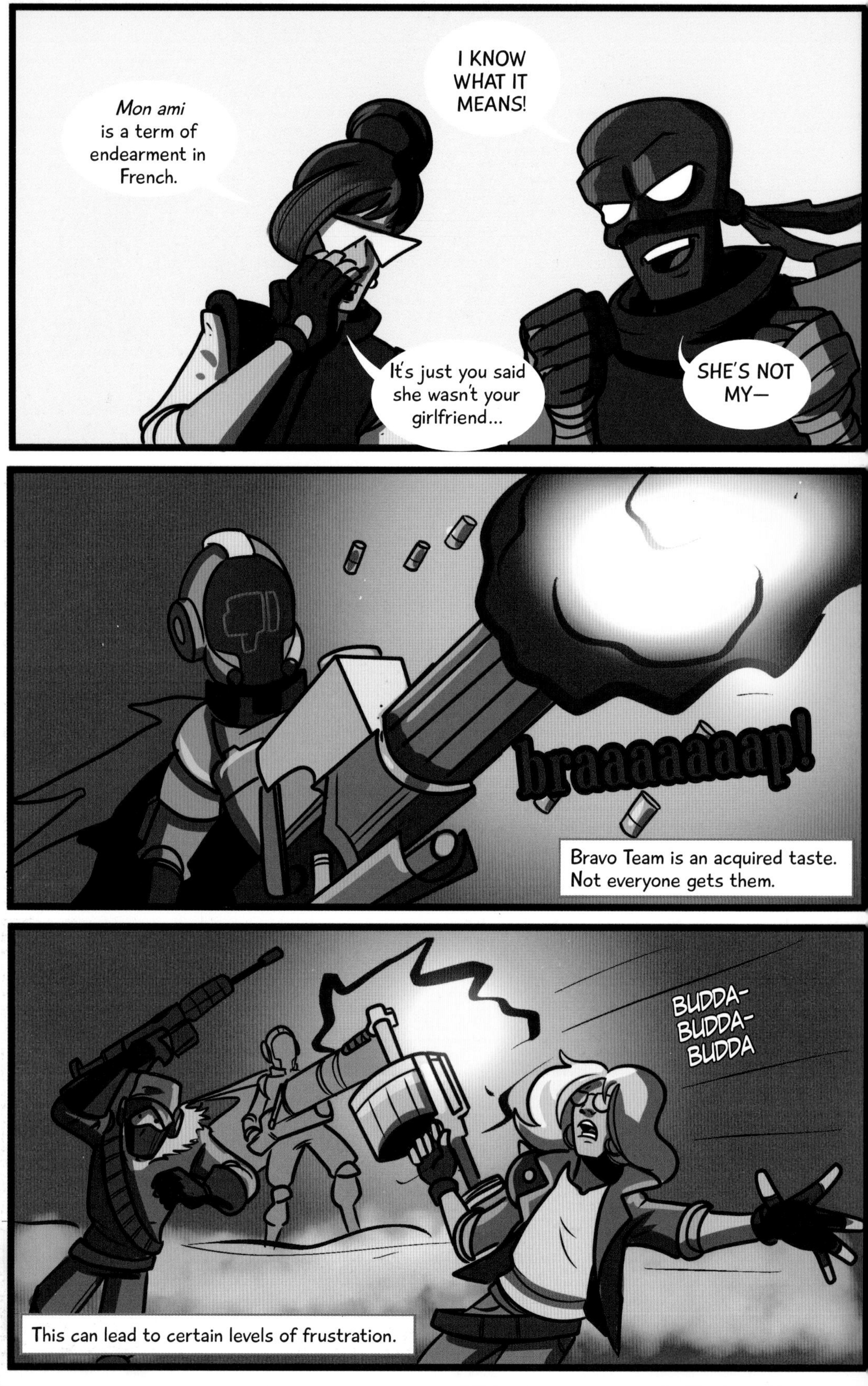
Mon ami is a term of endearment in French.
I KNOW WHAT IT MEANS!
It's just you said she wasn't your girlfriend...
SHE'S NOT MY—
braaaaaaap!
Bravo Team is an acquired taste. Not everyone gets them.
BUDDA-BUDDA-BUDDA
This can lead to certain levels of frustration.

I SAID, ENOUGH!!!

I do not have the time or patience for this. But Omega assures me you four are the ones for the job.

I will provide you with codes to reboot your system once you have completed the task I require of you.

But continue this incessant, childish bickering, and there will be consequences!

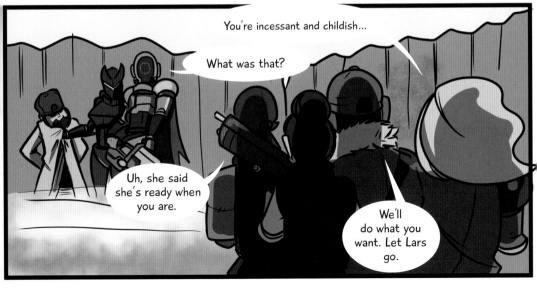

You're incessant and childish...

What was that?

Uh, she said she's ready when you are.

We'll do what you want. Let Lars go.

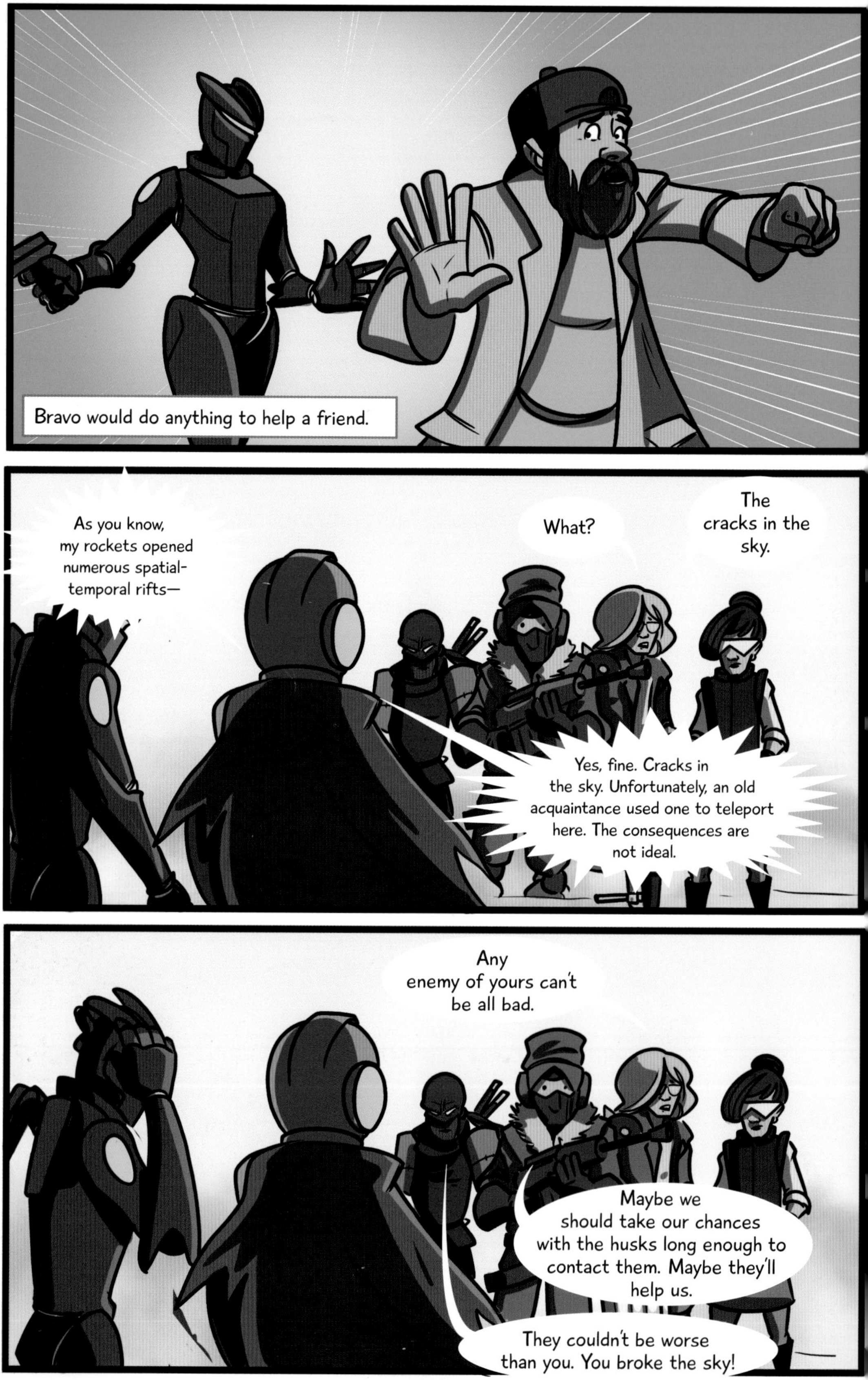

Bravo would do anything to help a friend.
As you know, my rockets opened numerous spatial-temporal rifts—
What?
The cracks in the sky.
Yes, fine. Cracks in the sky. Unfortunately, an old acquaintance used one to teleport here. The consequences are not ideal.
Any enemy of yours can't be all bad.
Maybe we should take our chances with the husks long enough to contact them. Maybe they'll help us.
They couldn't be worse than you. You broke the sky!

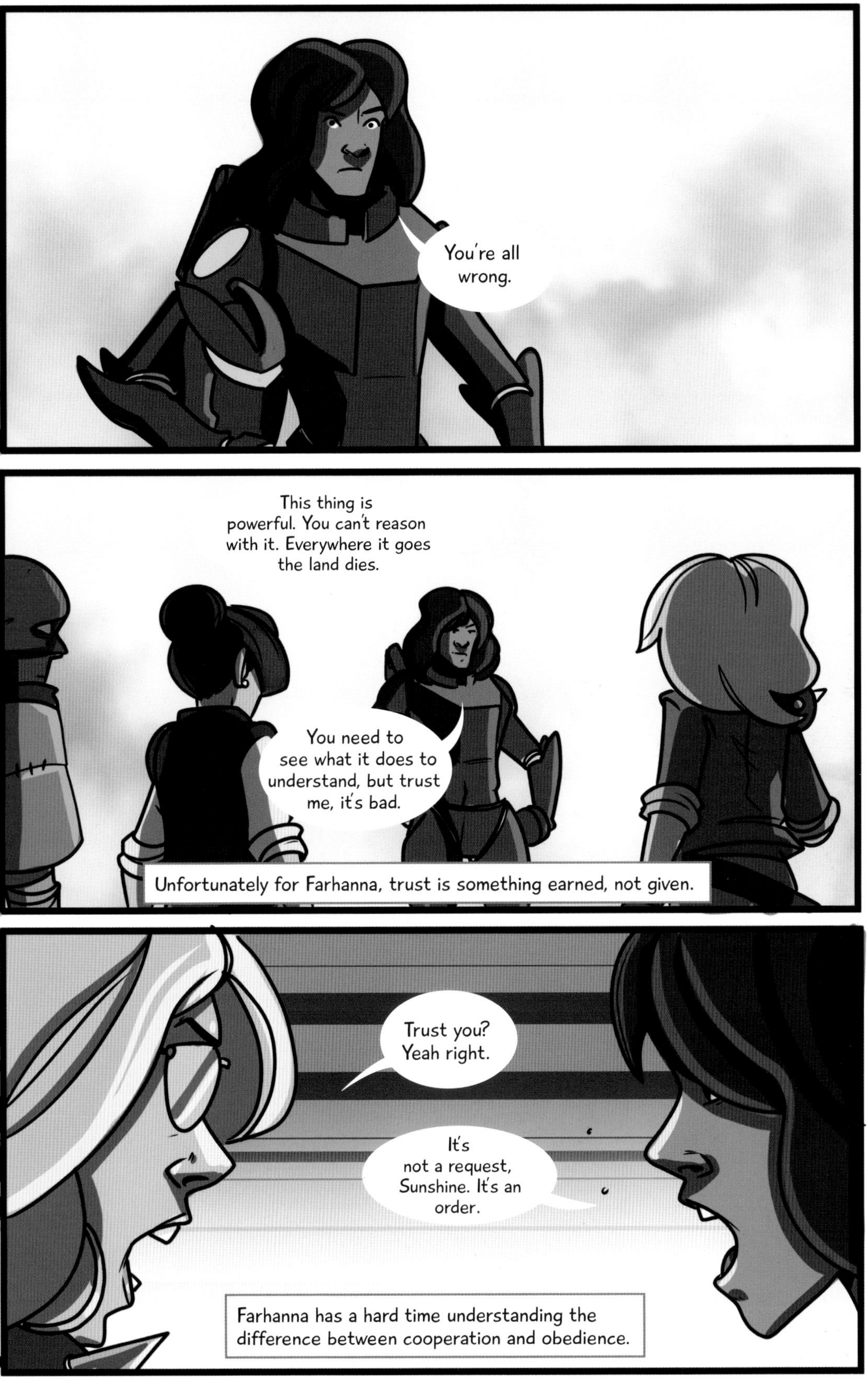
You're all wrong.
This thing is powerful. You can't reason with it. Everywhere it goes the land dies.
You need to see what it does to understand, but trust me, it's bad.
Unfortunately for Farhanna, trust is something earned, not given.
Trust you? Yeah right.
It's not a request, Sunshine. It's an order.
Farhanna has a hard time understanding the difference between cooperation and obedience.

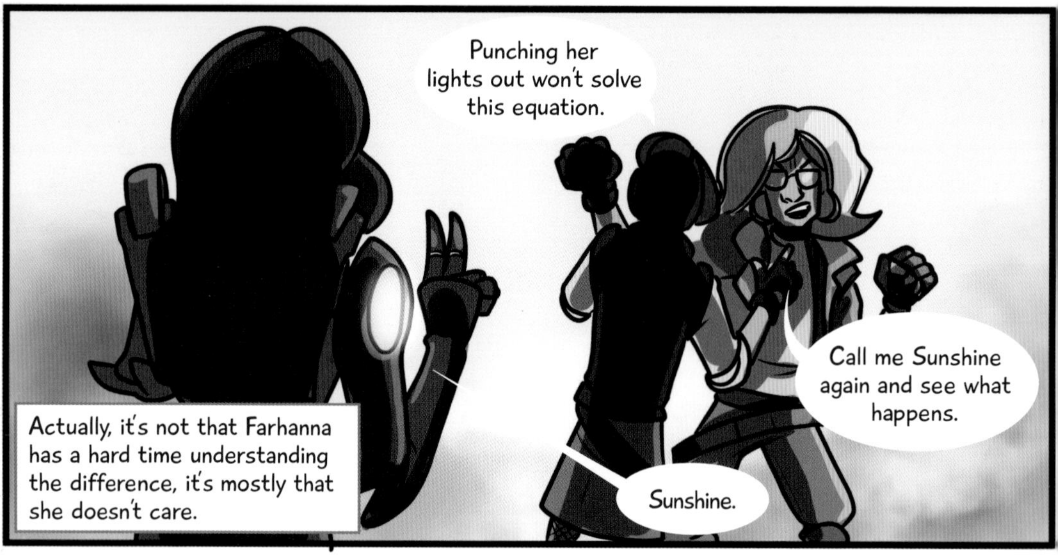
Actually, it's not that Farhanna has a hard time understanding the difference, it's mostly that she doesn't care.
Punching her lights out won't solve this equation.
Call me Sunshine again and see what happens.
Sunshine.

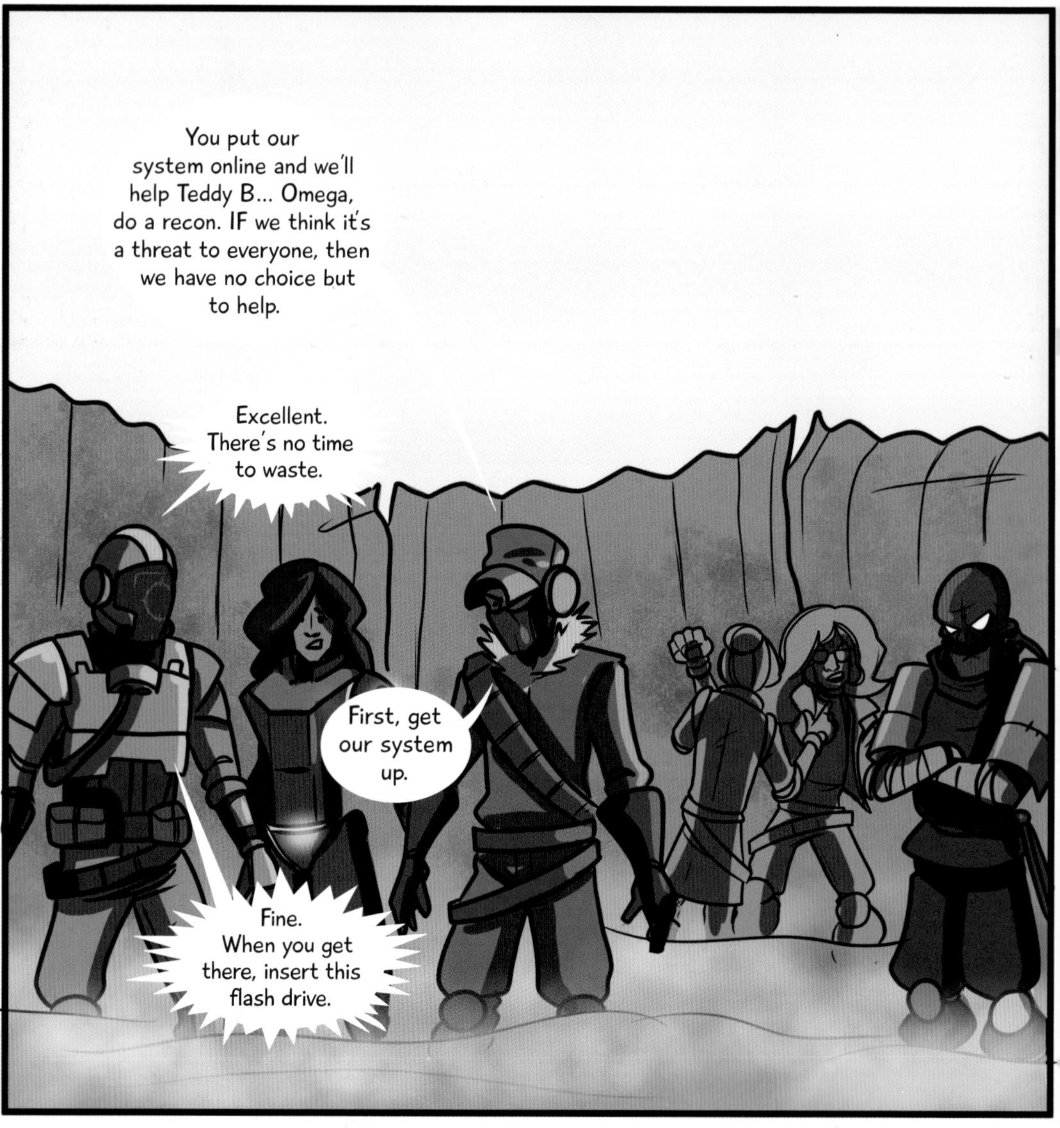
You put our system online and we'll help Teddy B... Omega, do a recon. IF we think it's a threat to everyone, then we have no choice but to help.
Excellent. There's no time to waste.
First, get our system up.
Fine. When you get there, insert this flash drive.

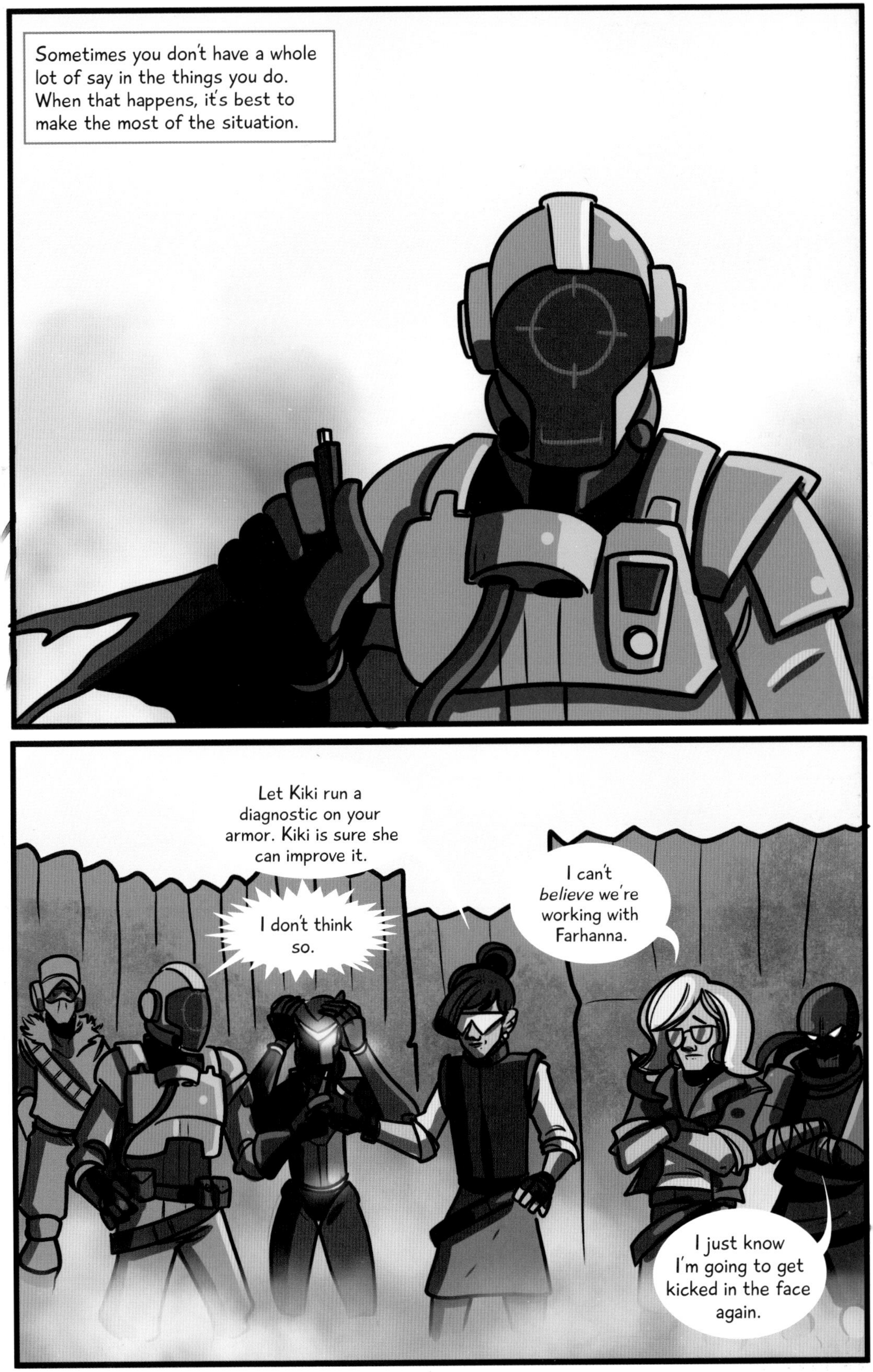
Sometimes you don't have a whole lot of say in the things you do. When that happens, it's best to make the most of the situation.
Let Kiki run a diagnostic on your armor. Kiki is sure she can improve it.
I don't think so.
I can't *believe* we're working with Farhanna.
I just know I'm going to get kicked in the face again.

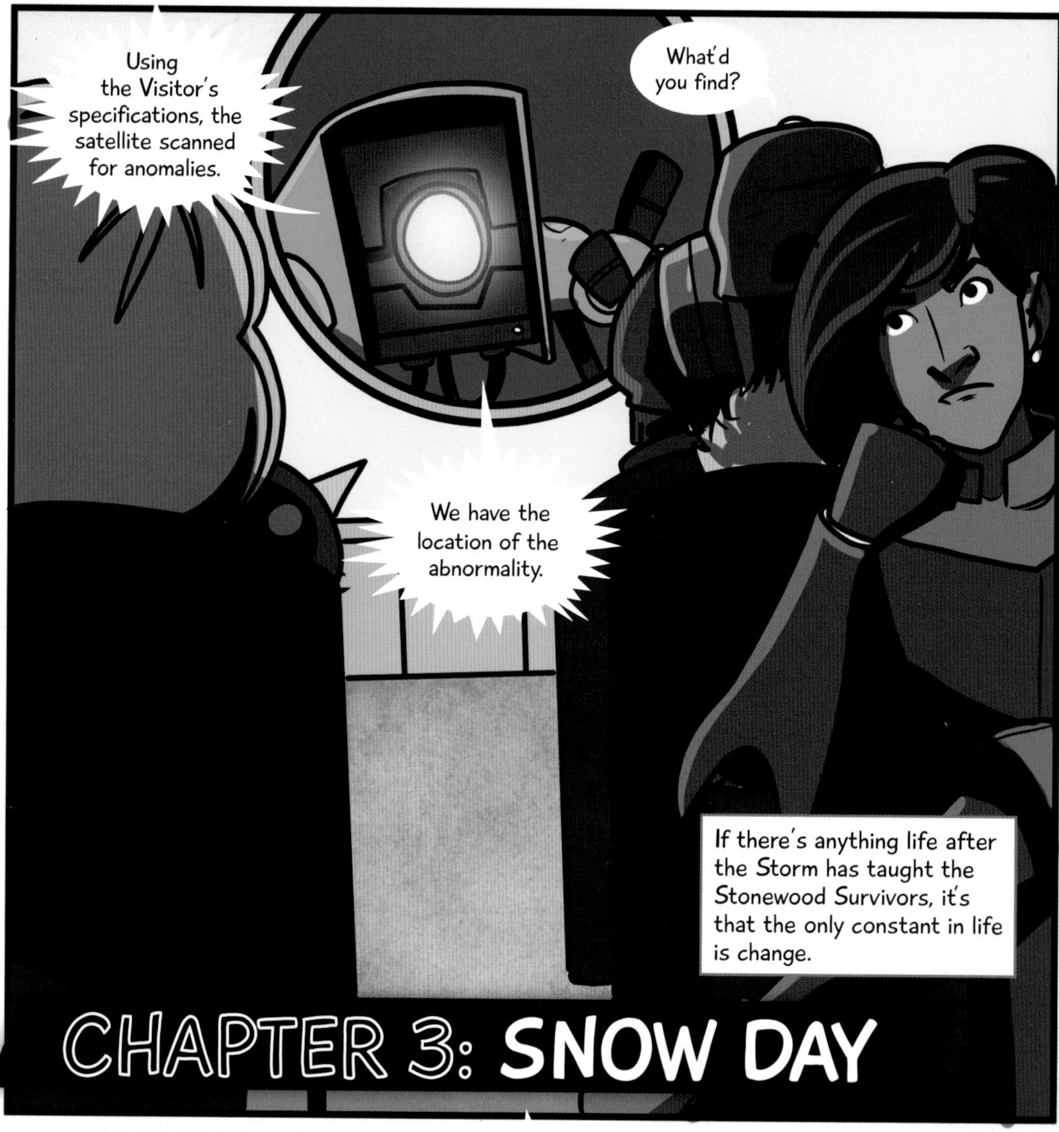
Using the Visitor's specifications, the satellite scanned for anomalies.
What'd you find?
We have the location of the abnormality.
If there's anything life after the Storm has taught the Stonewood Survivors, it's that the only constant in life is change.
CHAPTER 3: SNOW DAY

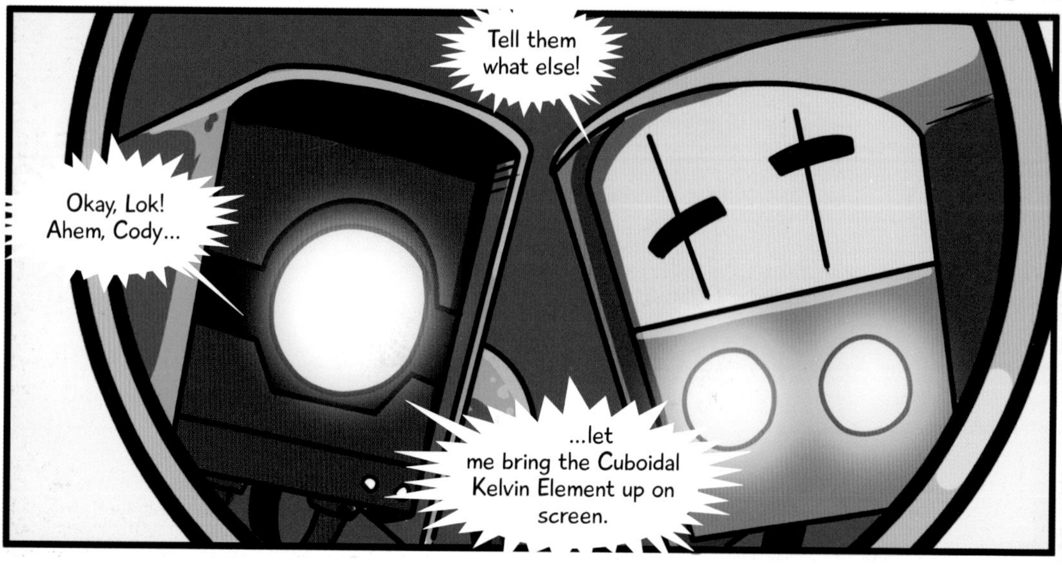
Tell them what else!
Okay, Lok! Ahem, Cody...
...let me bring the Cuboidal Kelvin Element up on screen.

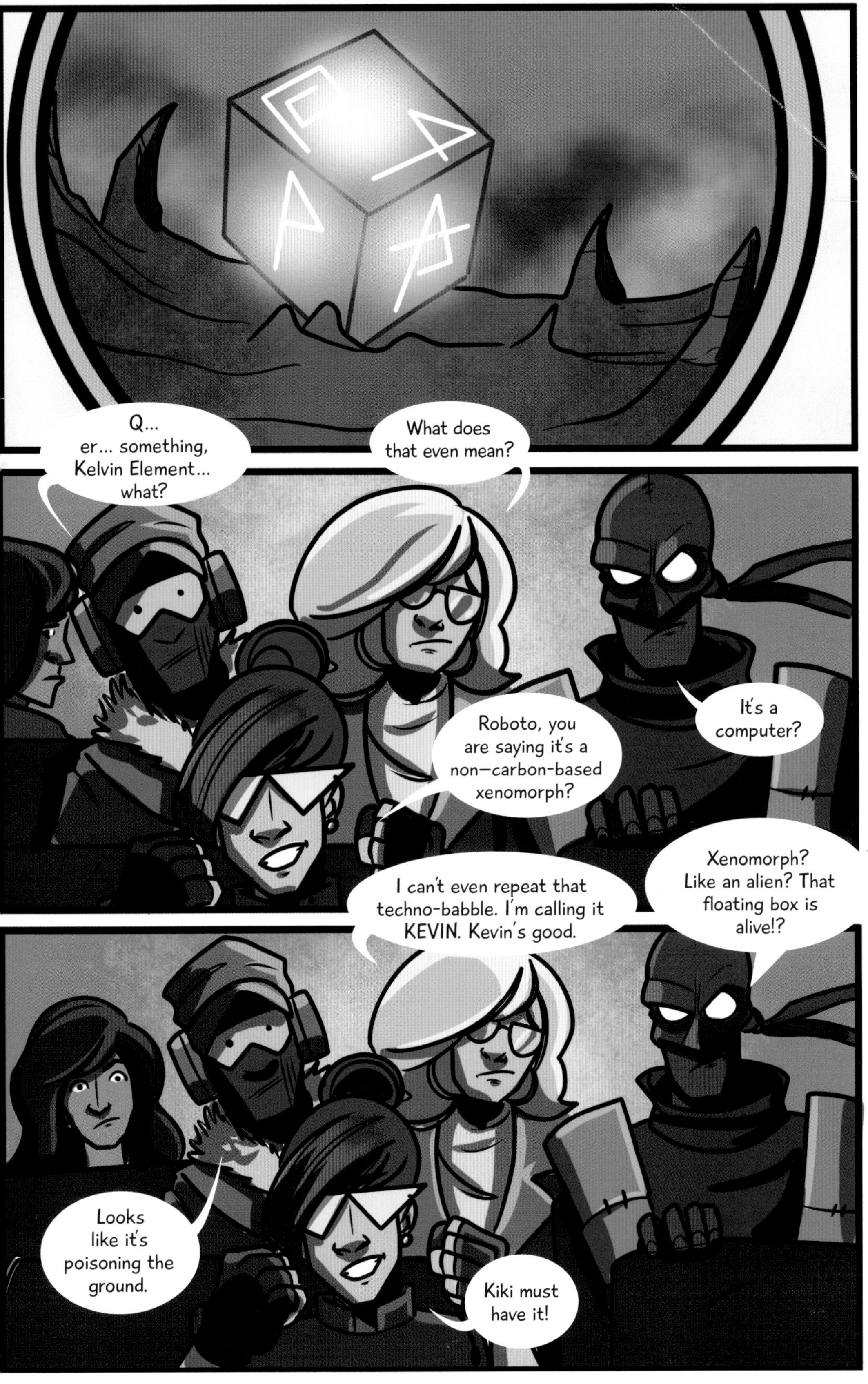
Q... er... something, Kelvin Element... what?
What does that even mean?
It's a computer?
Roboto, you are saying it's a non–carbon-based xenomorph?
Xenomorph? Like an alien? That floating box is alive!?
I can't even repeat that techno-babble. I'm calling it KEVIN. Kevin's good.
Looks like it's poisoning the ground.
Kiki must have it!

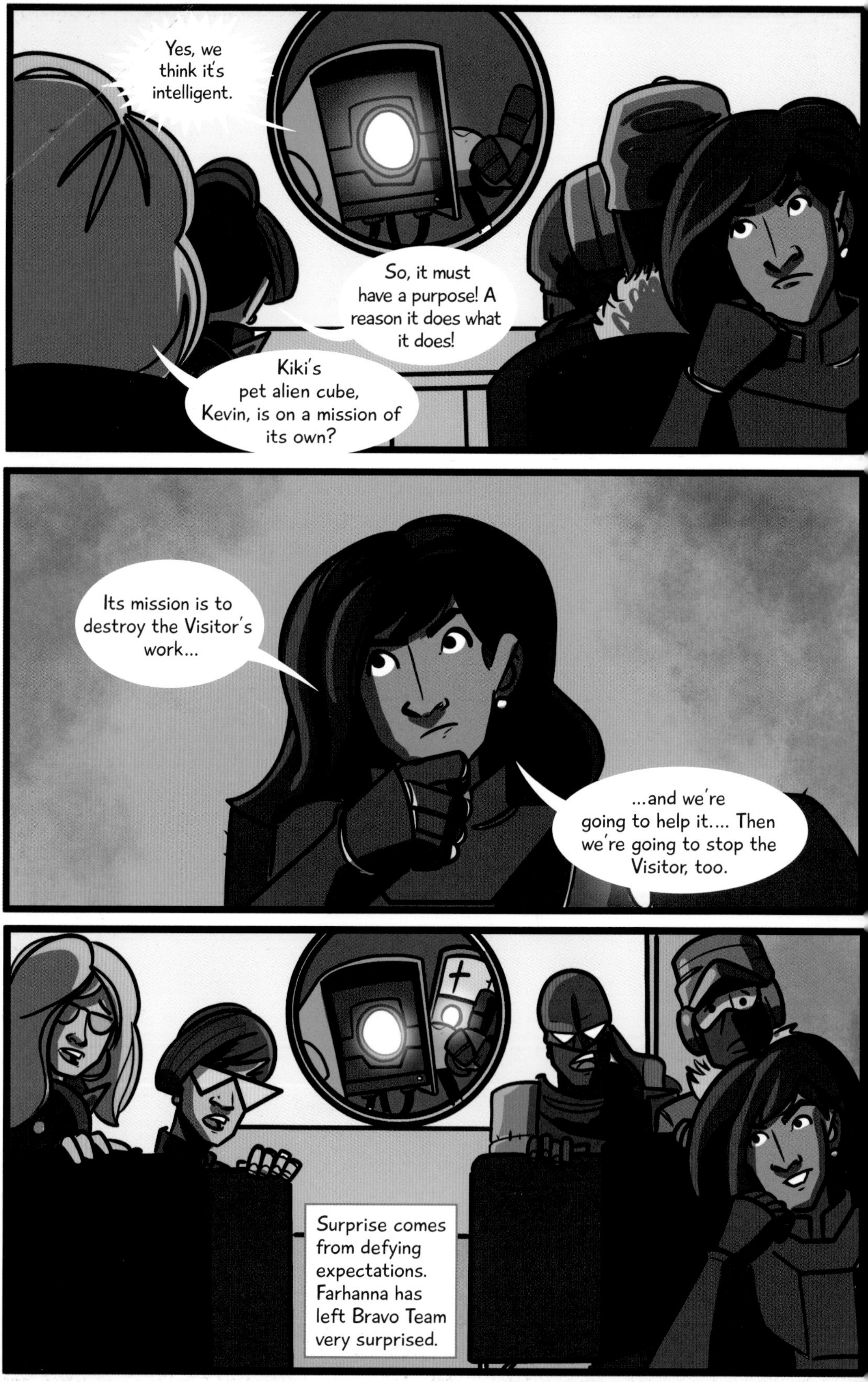
Yes, we think it's intelligent.
So, it must have a purpose! A reason it does what it does!
Kiki's pet alien cube, Kevin, is on a mission of its own?
Its mission is to destroy the Visitor's work...
...and we're going to help it.... Then we're going to stop the Visitor, too.
Surprise comes from defying expectations. Farhanna has left Bravo Team very surprised.

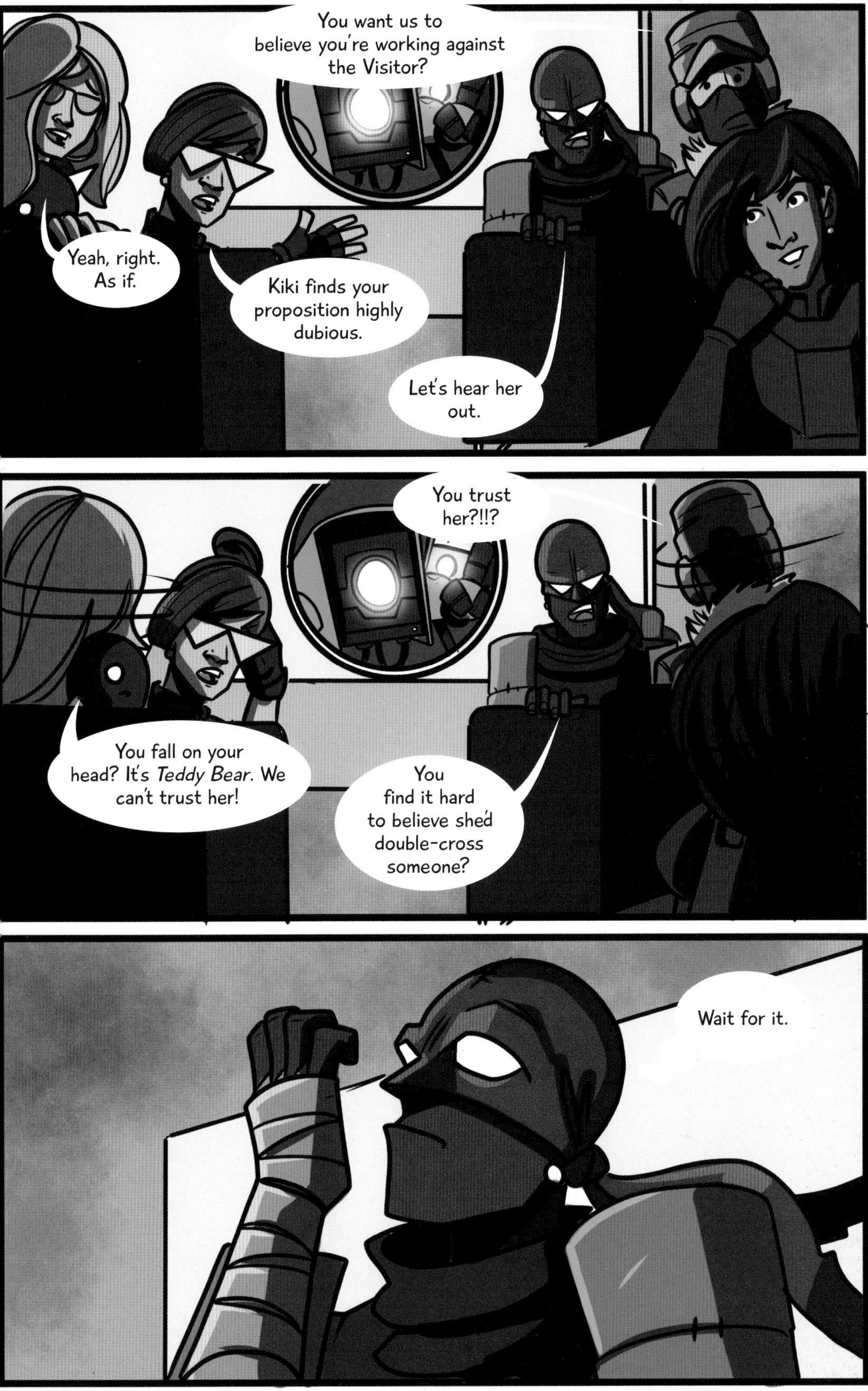
You want us to believe you're working against the Visitor?
Yeah, right. As if.
Kiki finds your proposition highly dubious.
Let's hear her out.
You trust her?!!?
You fall on your head? It's *Teddy Bear*. We can't trust her!
You find it hard to believe she'd double-cross someone?
Wait for it.

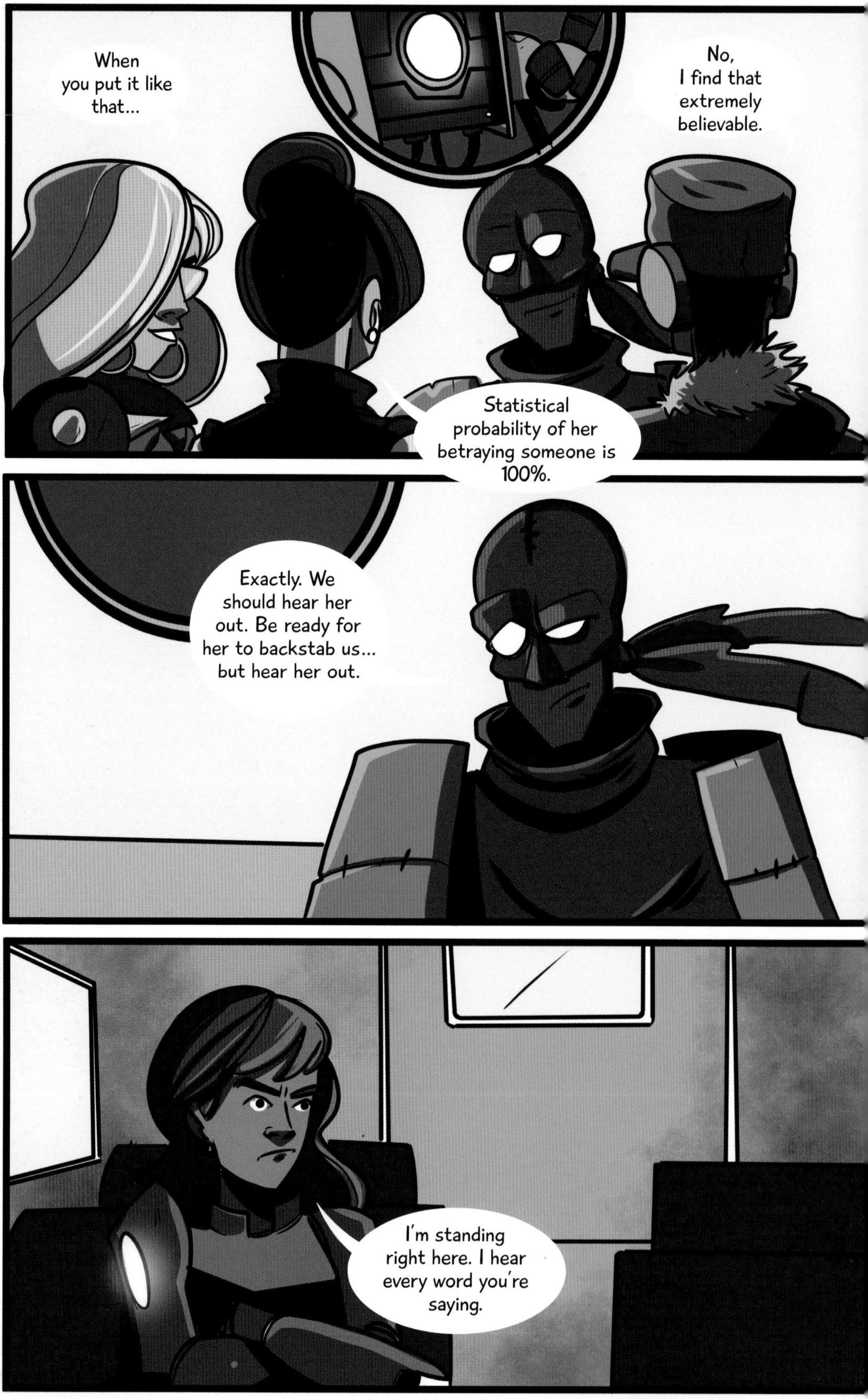
When you put it like that...
No, I find that extremely believable.
Statistical probability of her betraying someone is 100%.
Exactly. We should hear her out. Be ready for her to backstab us... but hear her out.
I'm standing right here. I hear every word you're saying.

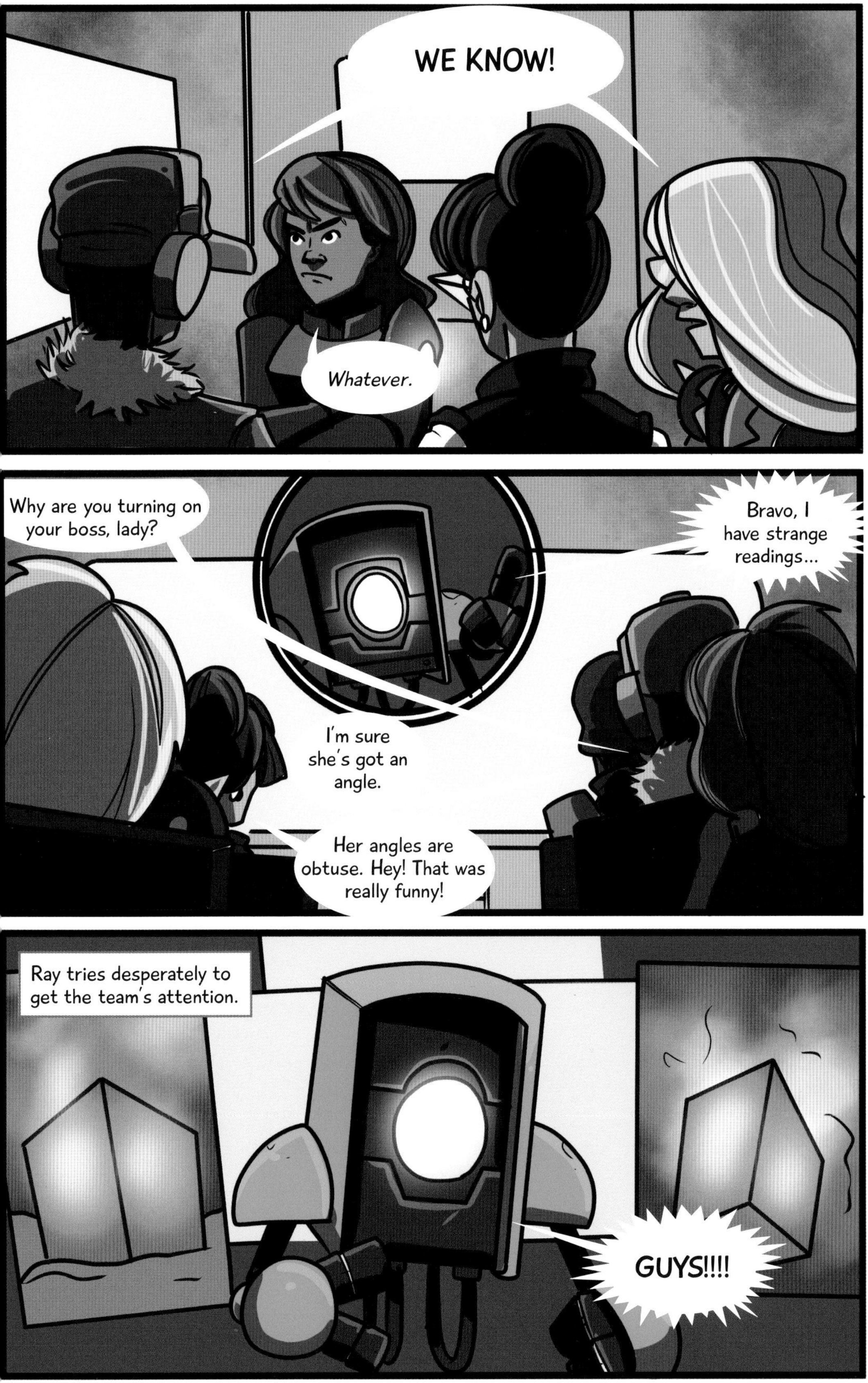
WE KNOW!
Whatever.
Why are you turning on your boss, lady?
Bravo, I have strange readings...
I'm sure she's got an angle.
Her angles are obtuse. Hey! That was really funny!
Ray tries desperately to get the team's attention.
GUYS!!!!

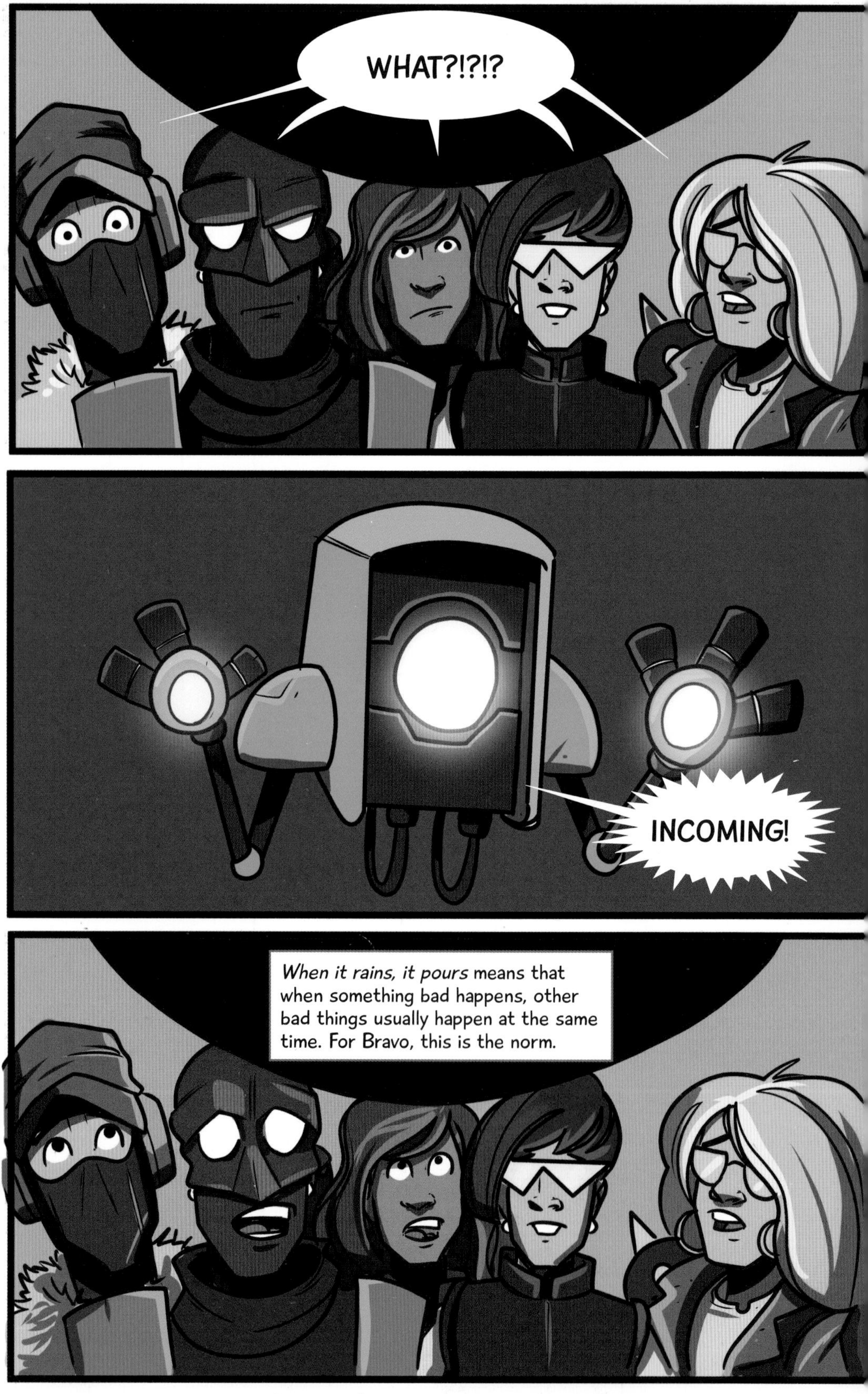
WHAT?!?!?
INCOMING!
When it rains, it pours means that when something bad happens, other bad things usually happen at the same time. For Bravo, this is the norm.

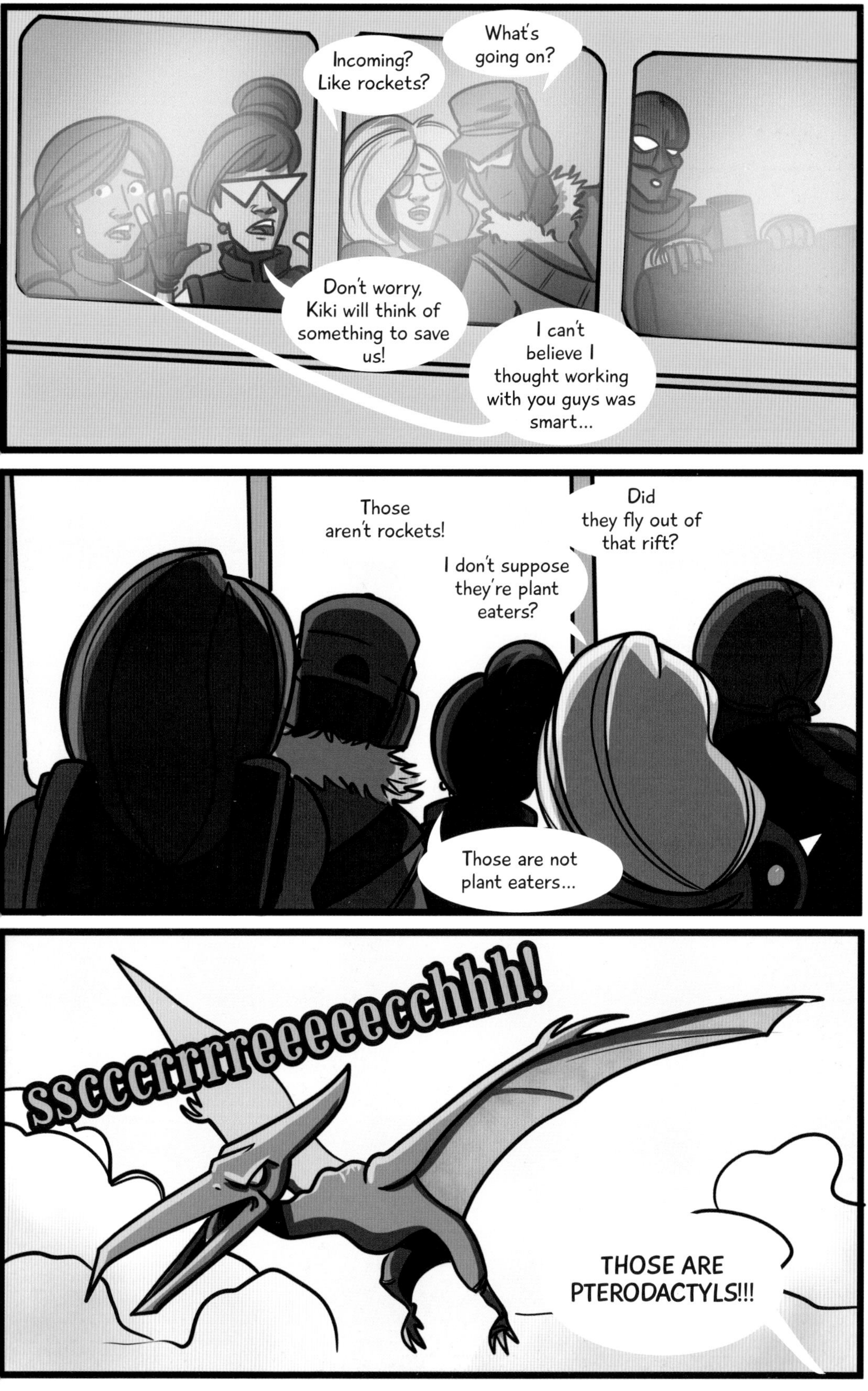
Incoming? Like rockets?
What's going on?
Don't worry, Kiki will think of something to save us!
I can't believe I thought working with you guys was smart...
Those aren't rockets!
Did they fly out of that rift?
I don't suppose they're plant eaters?
Those are not plant eaters...
sscccrrrrreeeeeecchhh!
THOSE ARE PTERODACTYLS!!!

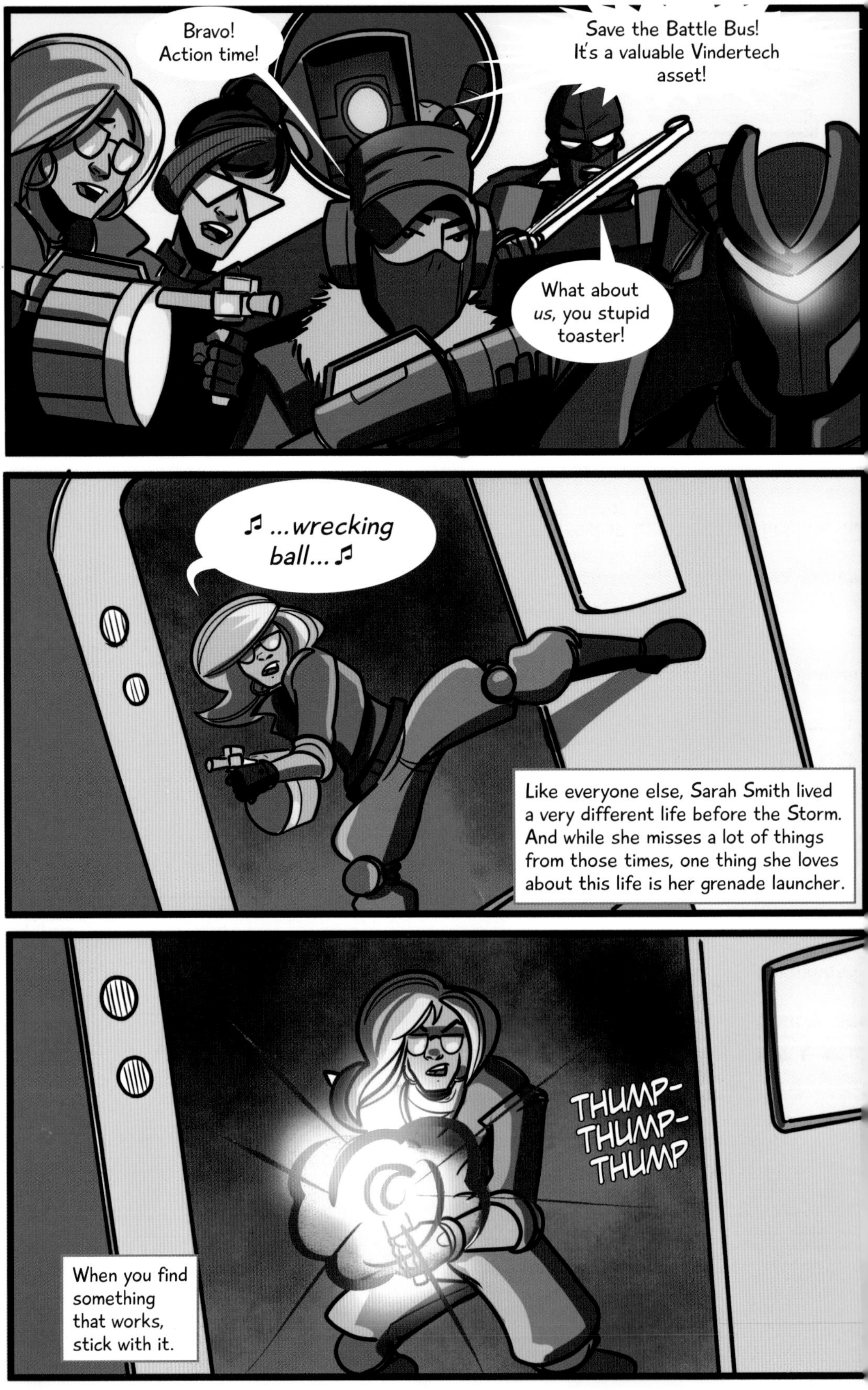
Bravo! Action time!
Save the Battle Bus! It's a valuable Vindertech asset!
What about *us*, you stupid toaster!
♫ ...wrecking ball... ♫
Like everyone else, Sarah Smith lived a very different life before the Storm. And while she misses a lot of things from those times, one thing she loves about this life is her grenade launcher.
THUMP-THUMP-THUMP
When you find something that works, stick with it.

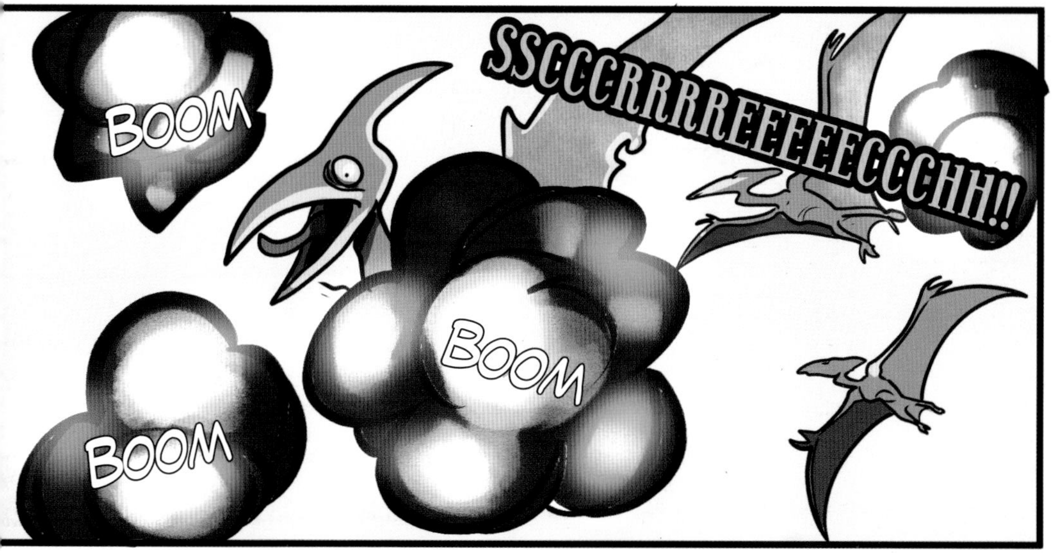
BOOM
SSCCCRRRRREEEEEECCCHH!!
BOOM
BOOM

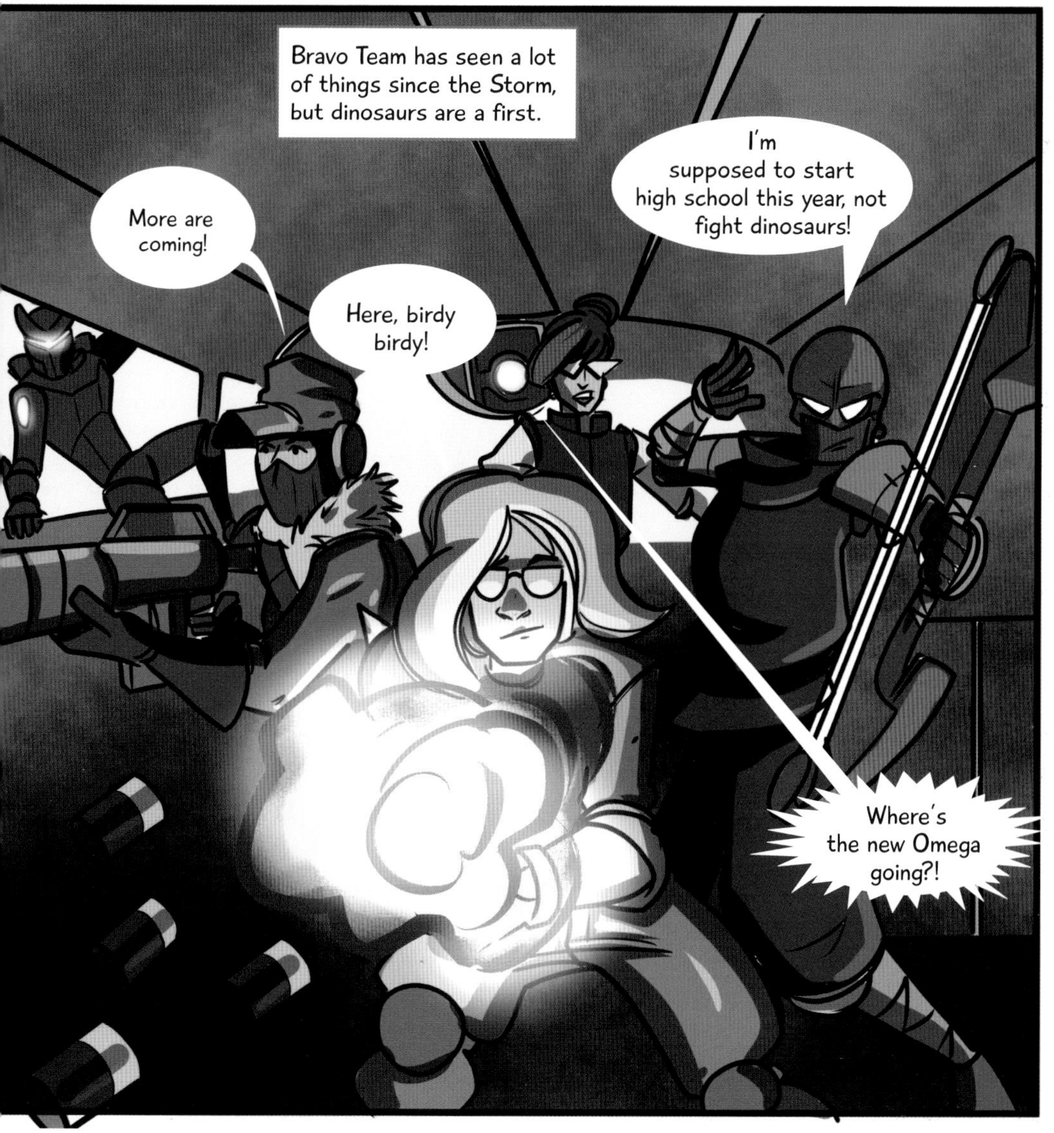
Bravo Team has seen a lot of things since the Storm, but dinosaurs are a first.
More are coming!
Here, birdy birdy!
I'm supposed to start high school this year, not fight dinosaurs!
Where's the new Omega going?!

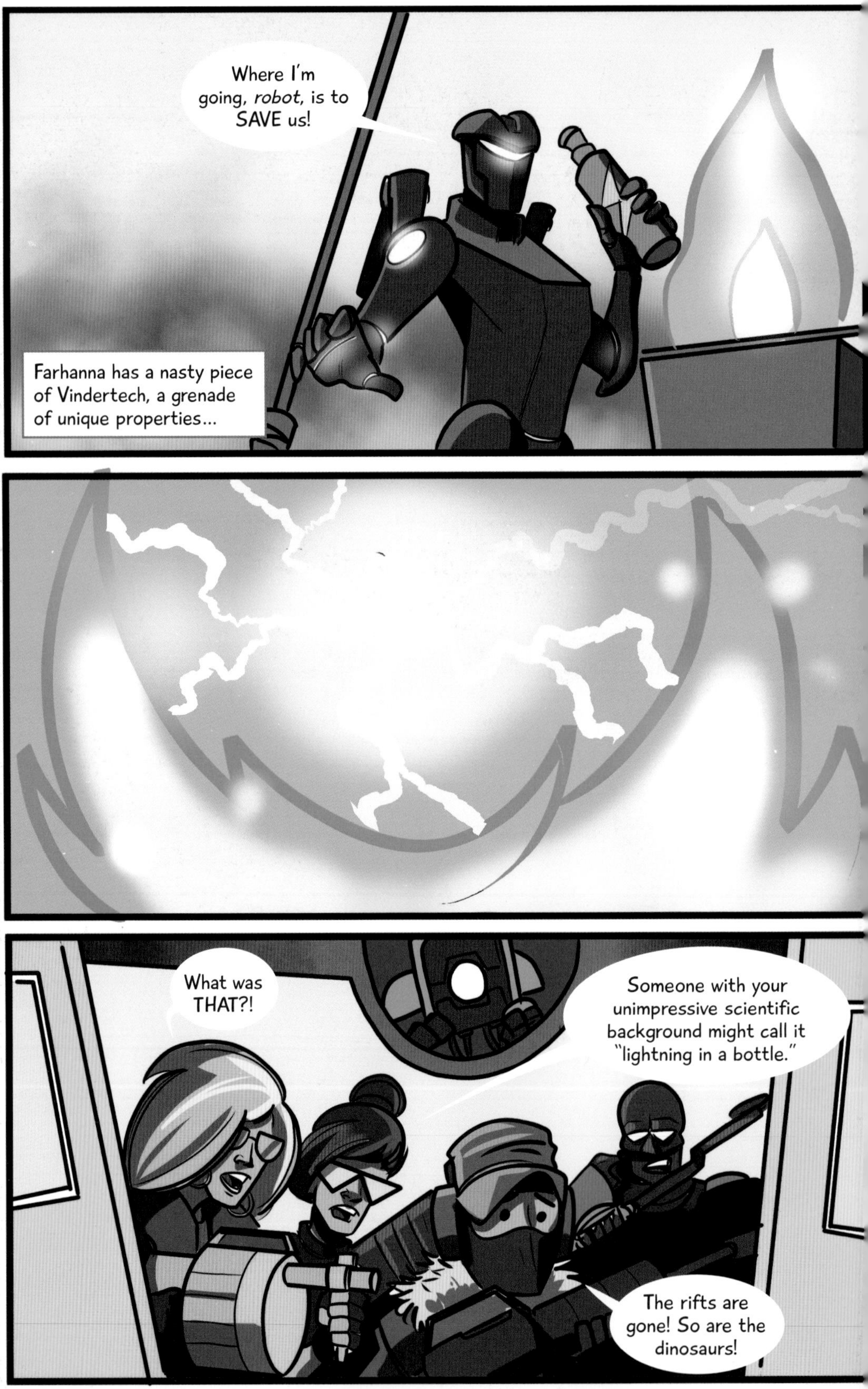
Where I'm going, *robot,* is to SAVE us!
Farhanna has a nasty piece of Vindertech, a grenade of unique properties...
What was THAT?!
Someone with your unimpressive scientific background might call it "lightning in a bottle."
The rifts are gone! So are the dinosaurs!

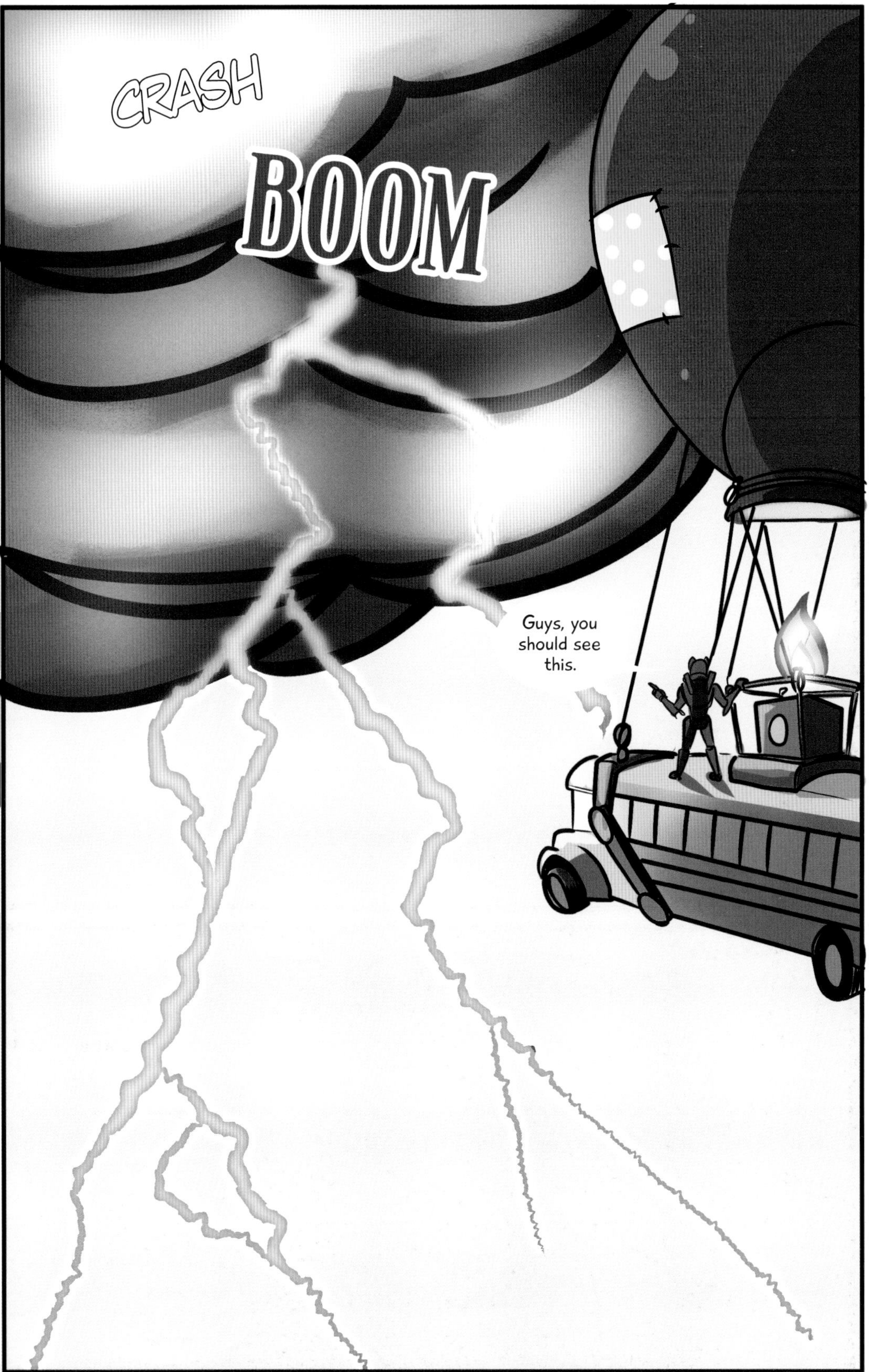
CRASH
BOOM
Guys, you should see this.

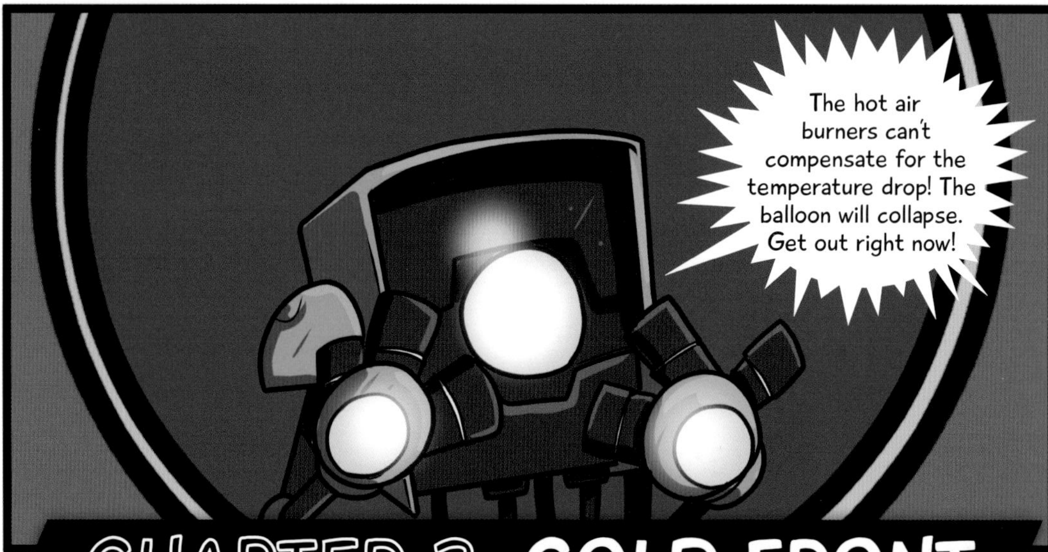
The hot air burners can't compensate for the temperature drop! The balloon will collapse. Get out right now!

CHAPTER 3: COLD FRONT

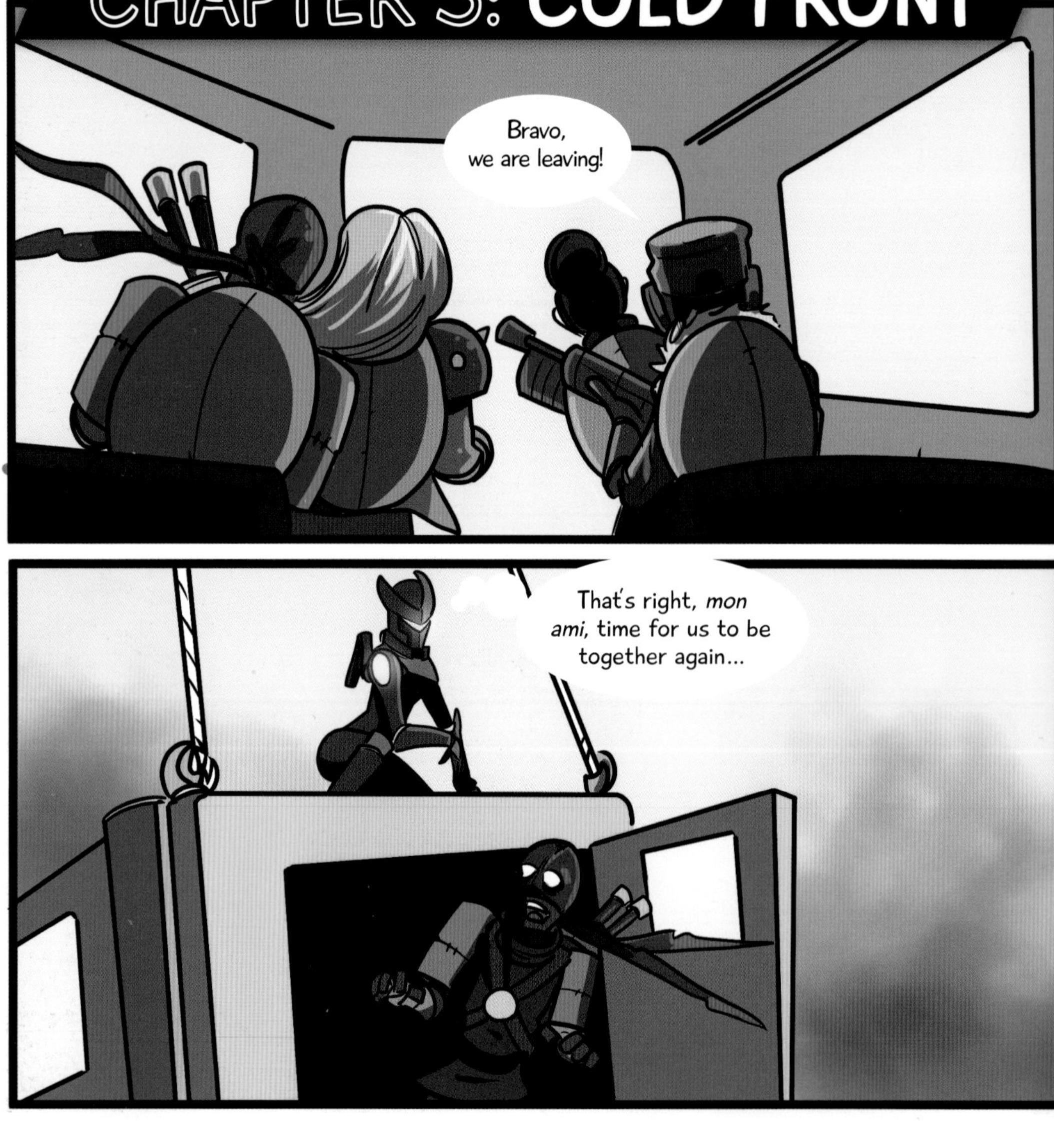
Bravo, we are leaving!
That's right, *mon ami*, time for us to be together again...

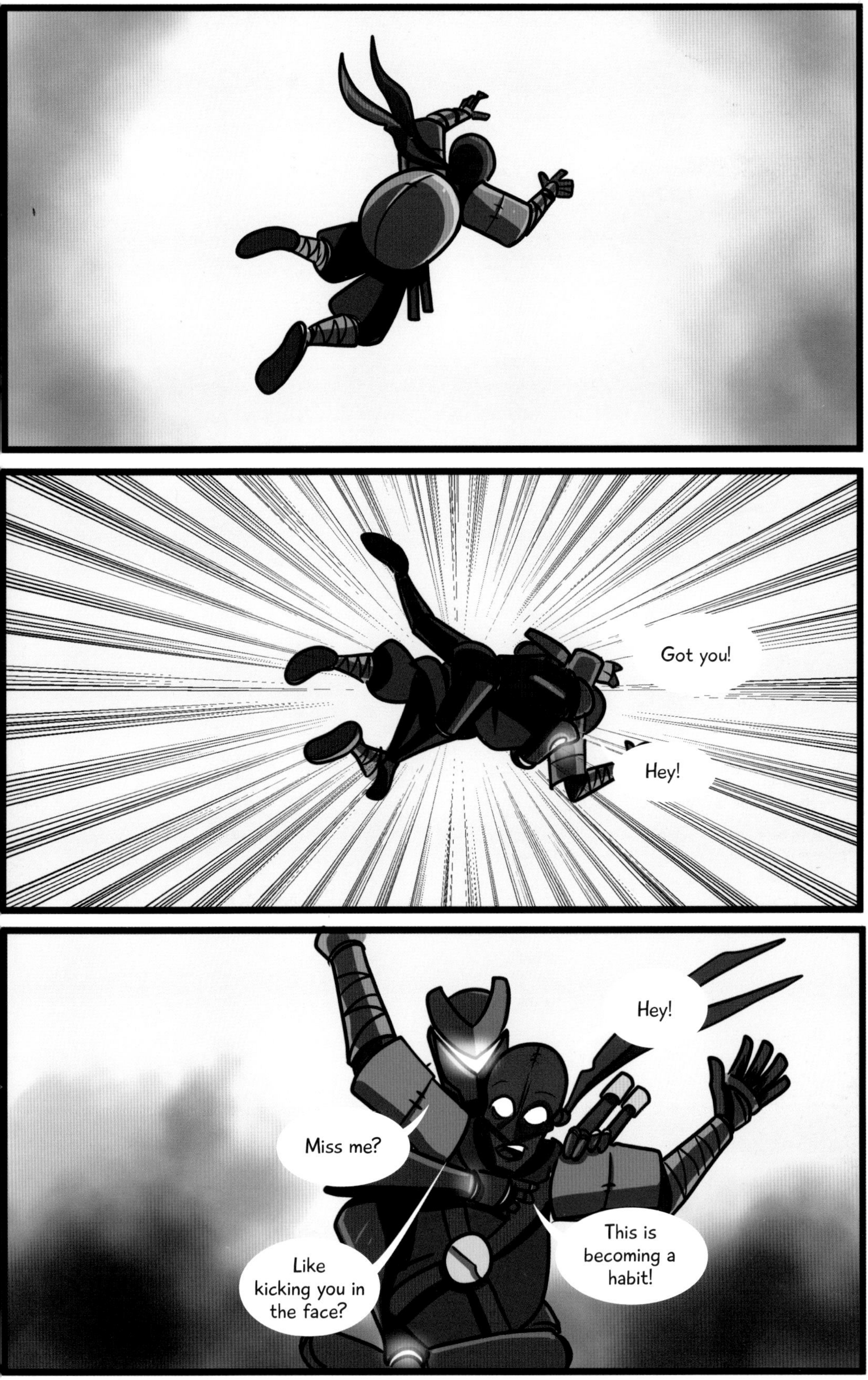
Got you!
Hey!
Hey!
Miss me?
Like kicking you in the face?
This is becoming a habit!

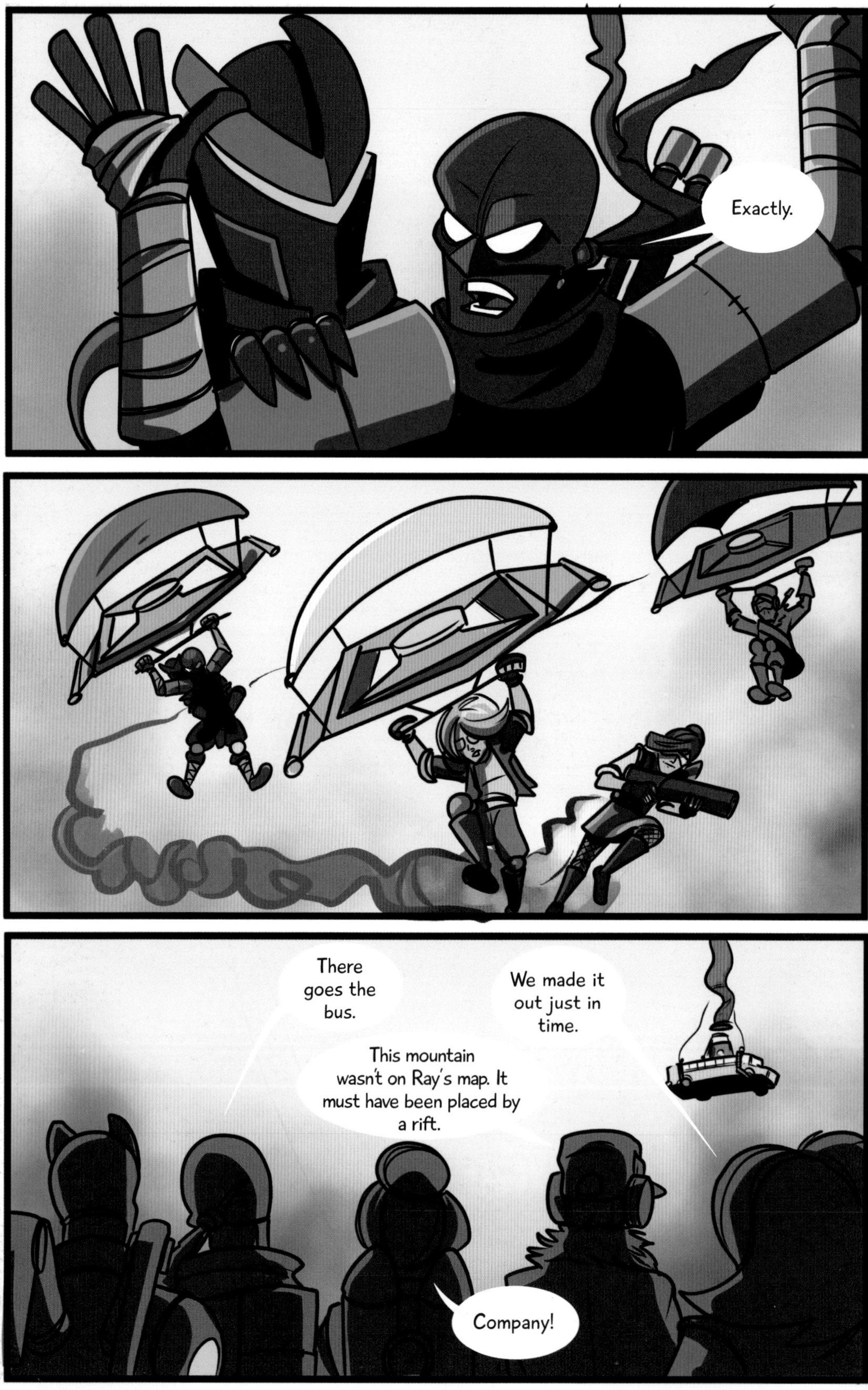
Exactly.
There goes the bus.
We made it out just in time.
This mountain wasn't on Ray's map. It must have been placed by a rift.
Company!

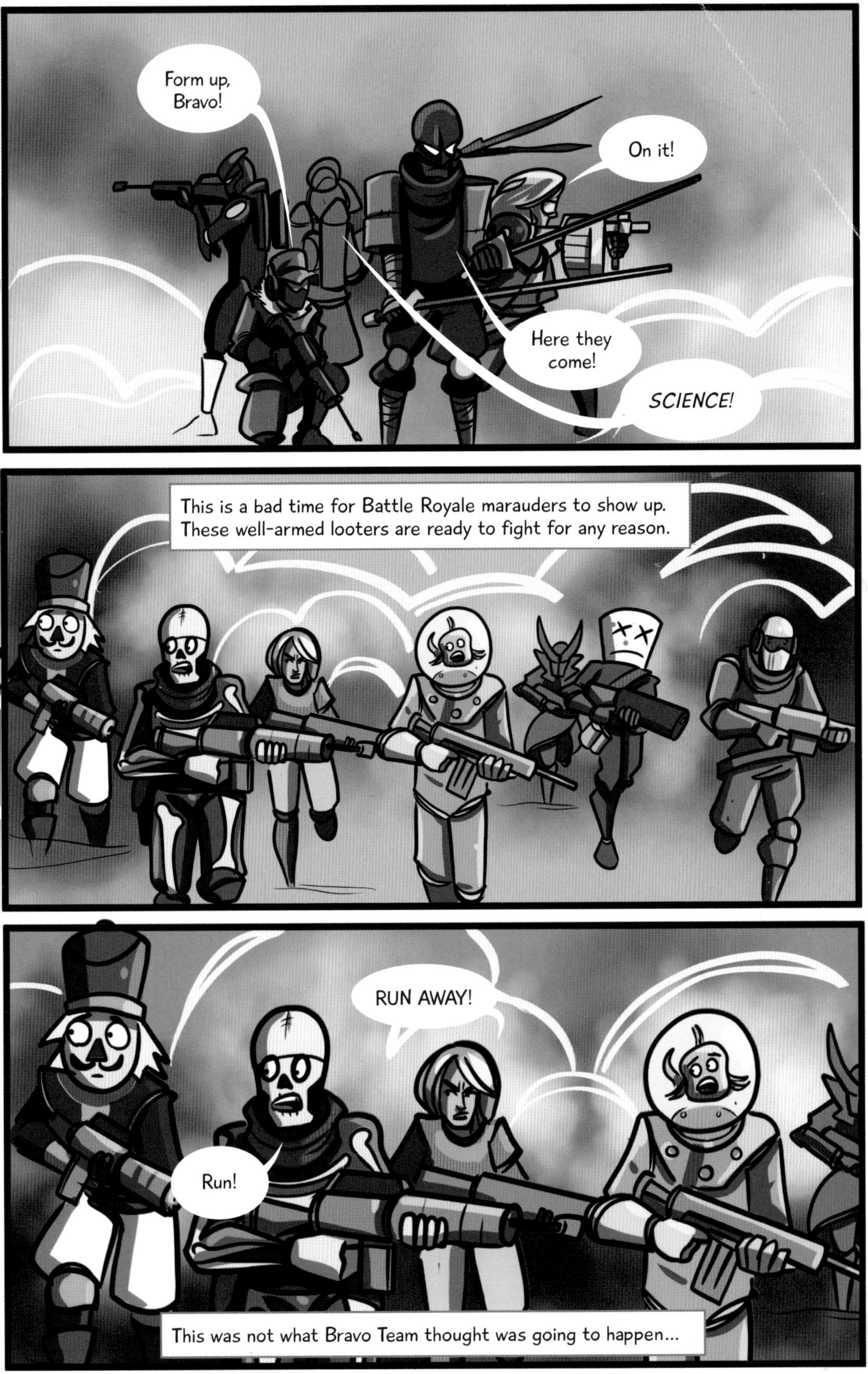
Form up, Bravo!
On it!
Here they come!
SCIENCE!
This is a bad time for Battle Royale marauders to show up. These well-armed looters are ready to fight for any reason.
RUN AWAY!
Run!
This was not what Bravo Team thought was going to happen...

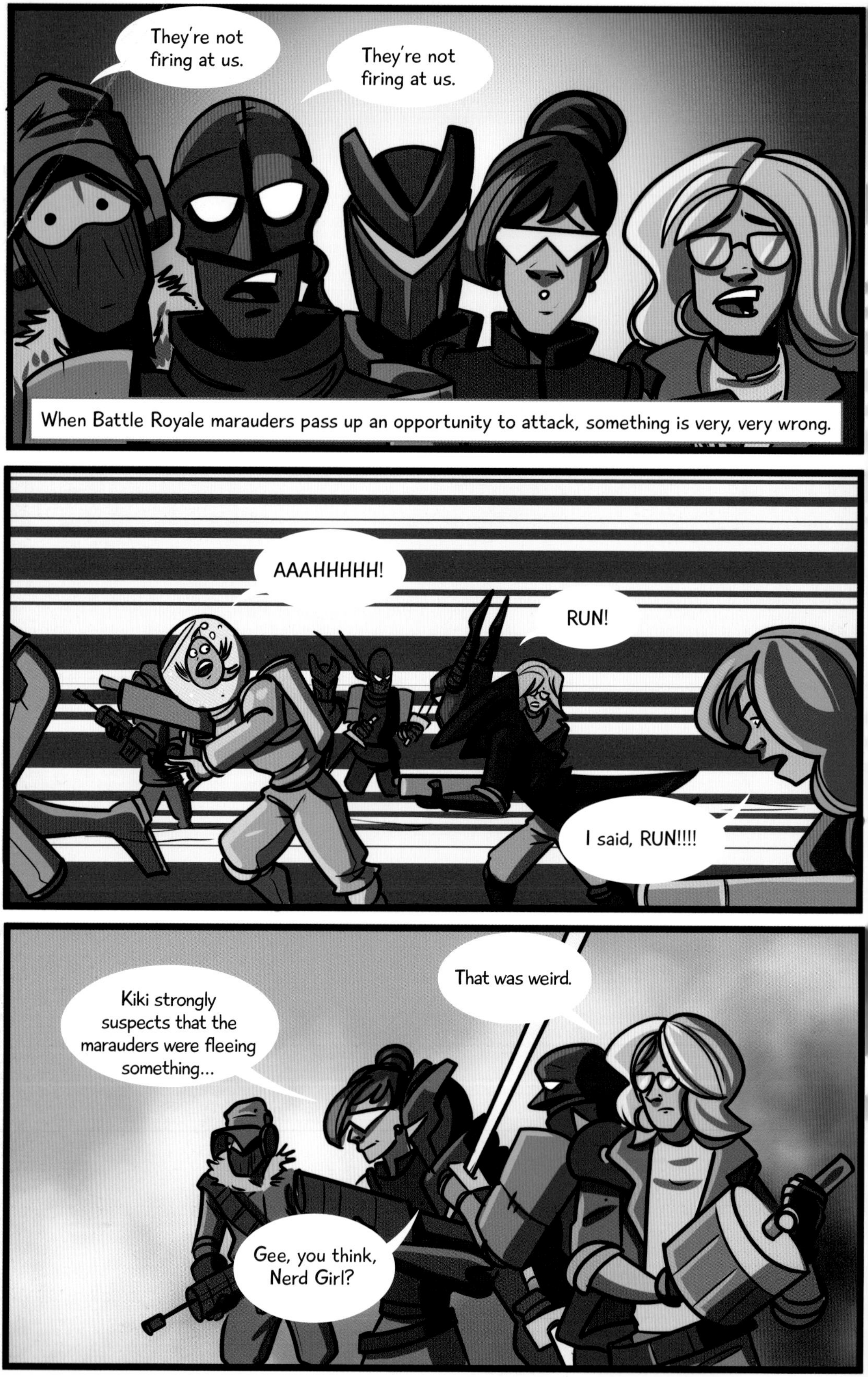
They're not firing at us.
They're not firing at us.
When Battle Royale marauders pass up an opportunity to attack, something is very, very wrong.
AAAHHHHH!
RUN!
I said, RUN!!!!
Kiki strongly suspects that the marauders were fleeing something...
That was weird.
Gee, you think, Nerd Girl?

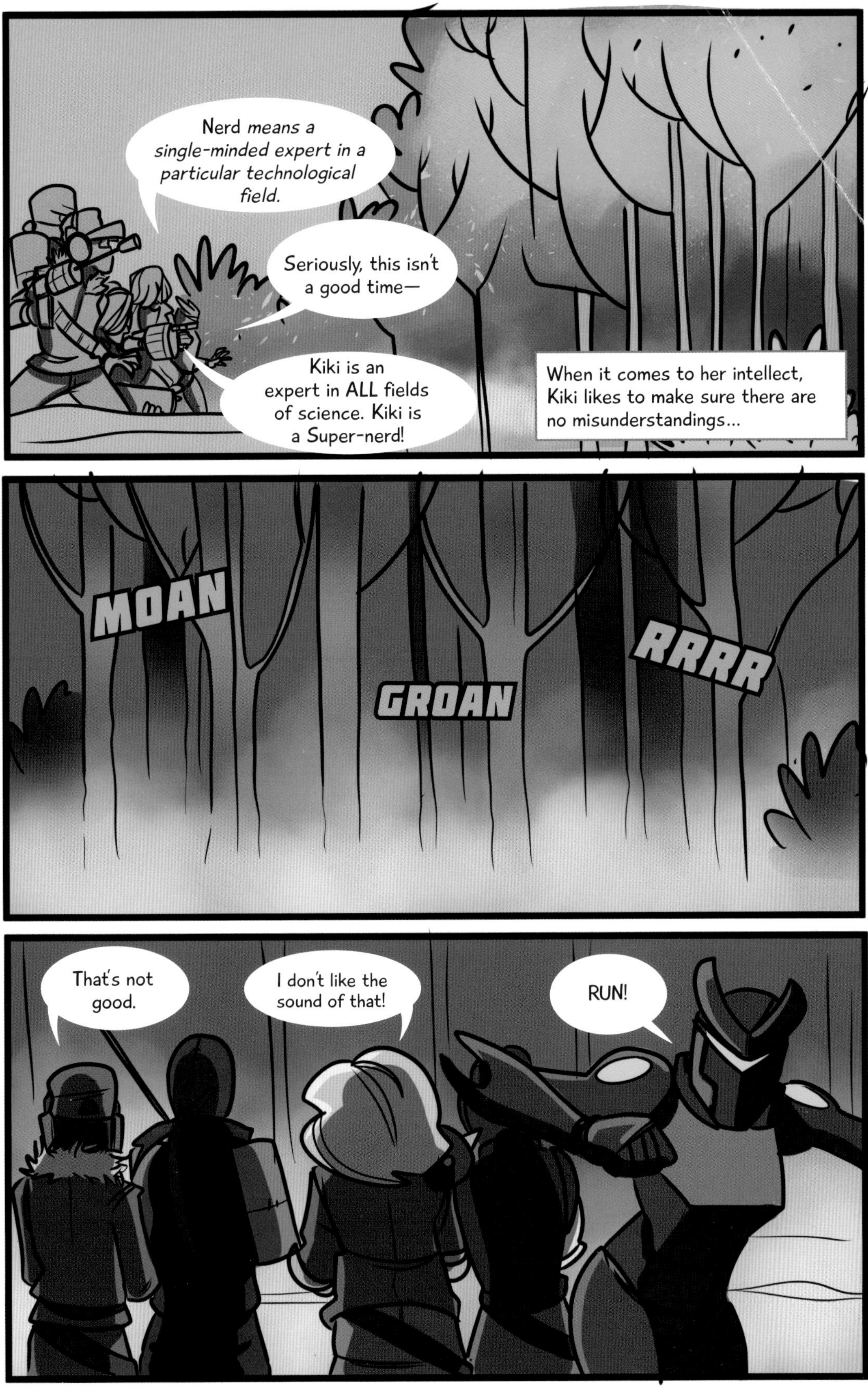
Nerd *means* a single-minded expert in a particular technological field.
Seriously, this isn't a good time—
Kiki is an expert in ALL fields of science. Kiki is a Super-nerd!
When it comes to her intellect, Kiki likes to make sure there are no misunderstandings...
MOAN
GROAN
RRRR
That's not good.
I don't like the sound of that!
RUN!

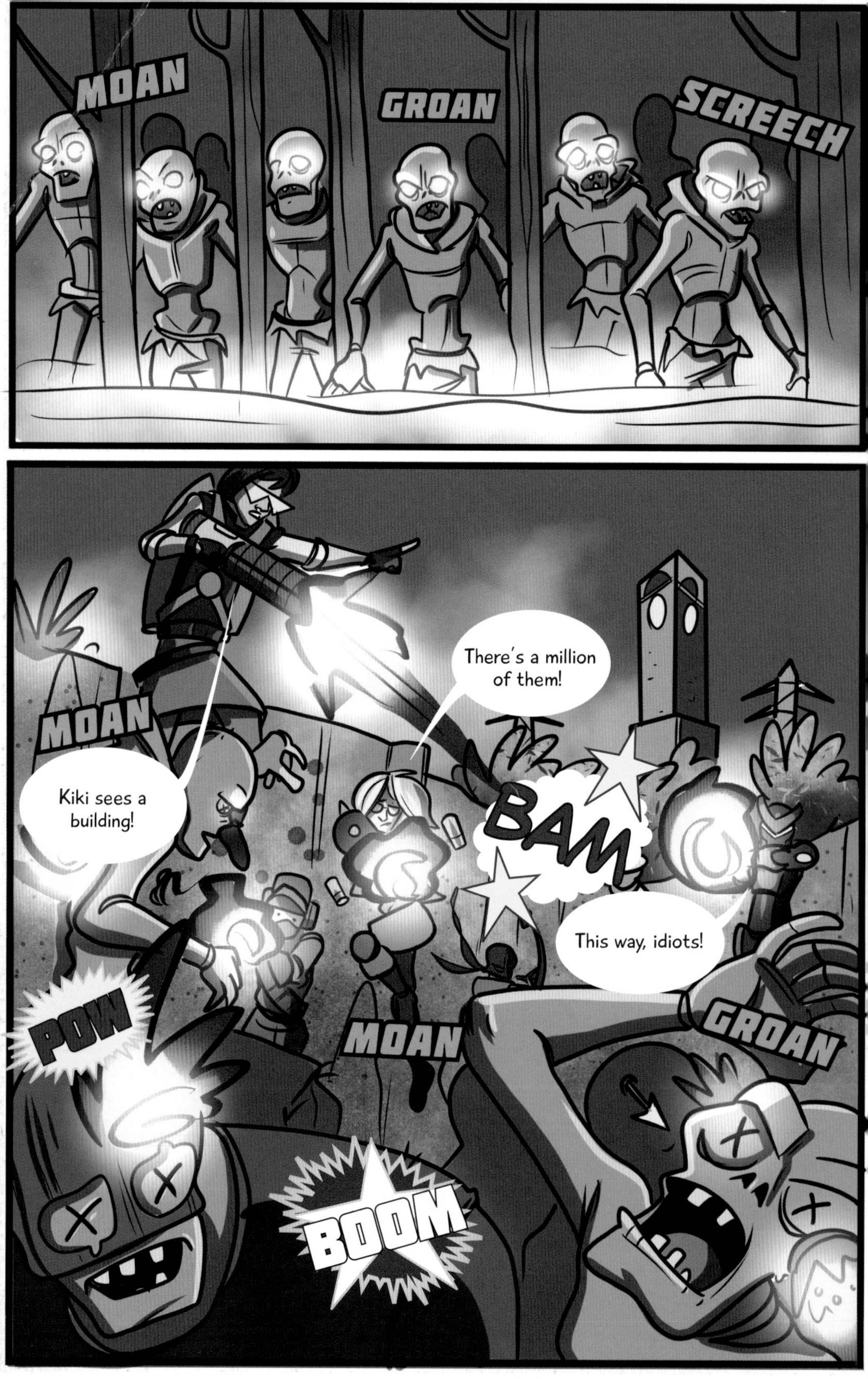
MOAN
GROAN
SCREECH
MOAN
There's a million of them!
Kiki sees a building!
BAM
This way, idiots!
POW
MOAN
GROAN
BOOM

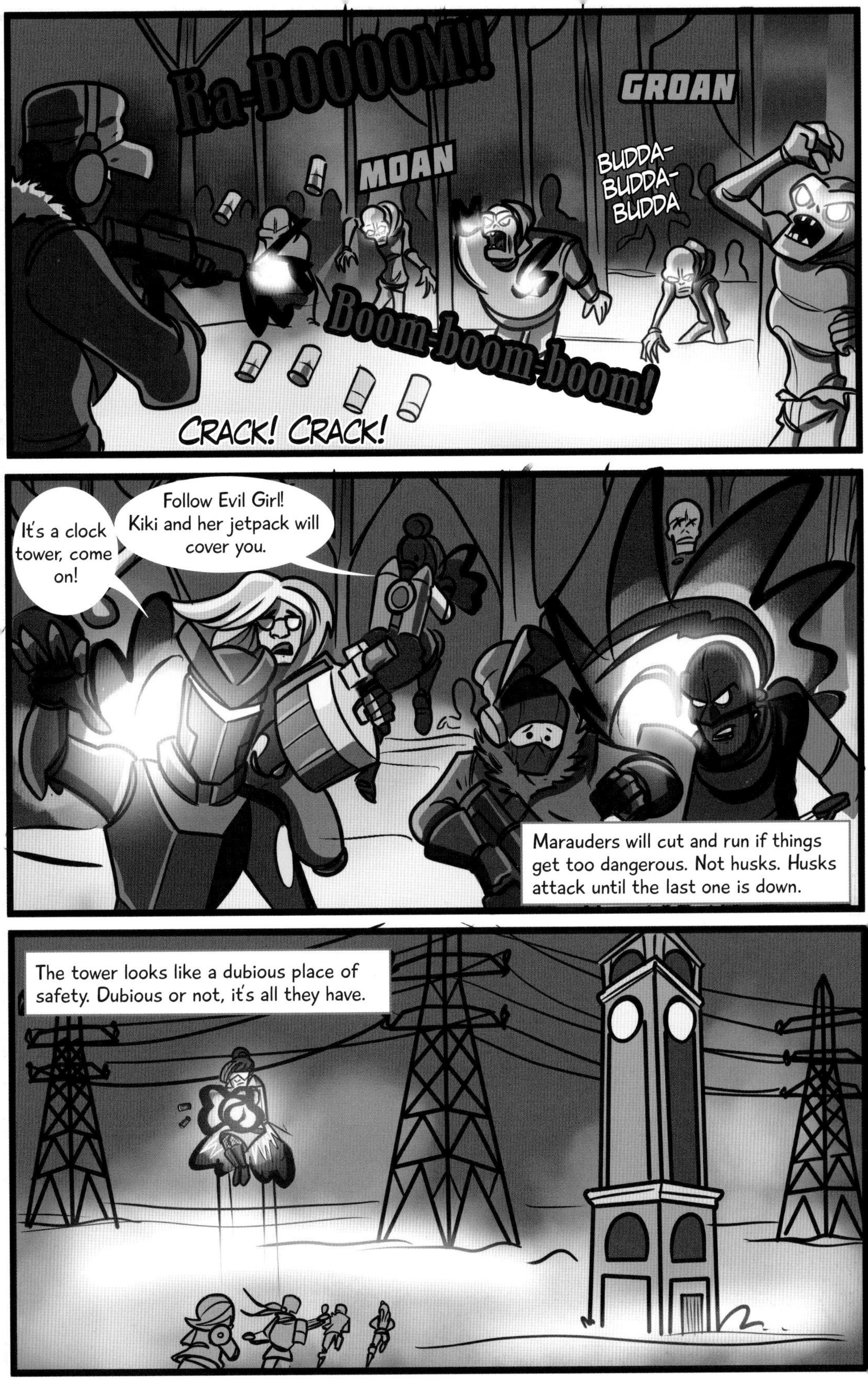
Ra-BOOOOM!!
GROAN
MOAN
BUDDA-BUDDA-BUDDA
Boom-boom-boom!
CRACK! CRACK!
It's a clock tower, come on!
Follow Evil Girl! Kiki and her jetpack will cover you.
Marauders will cut and run if things get too dangerous. Not husks. Husks attack until the last one is down.
The tower looks like a dubious place of safety. Dubious or not, it's all they have.

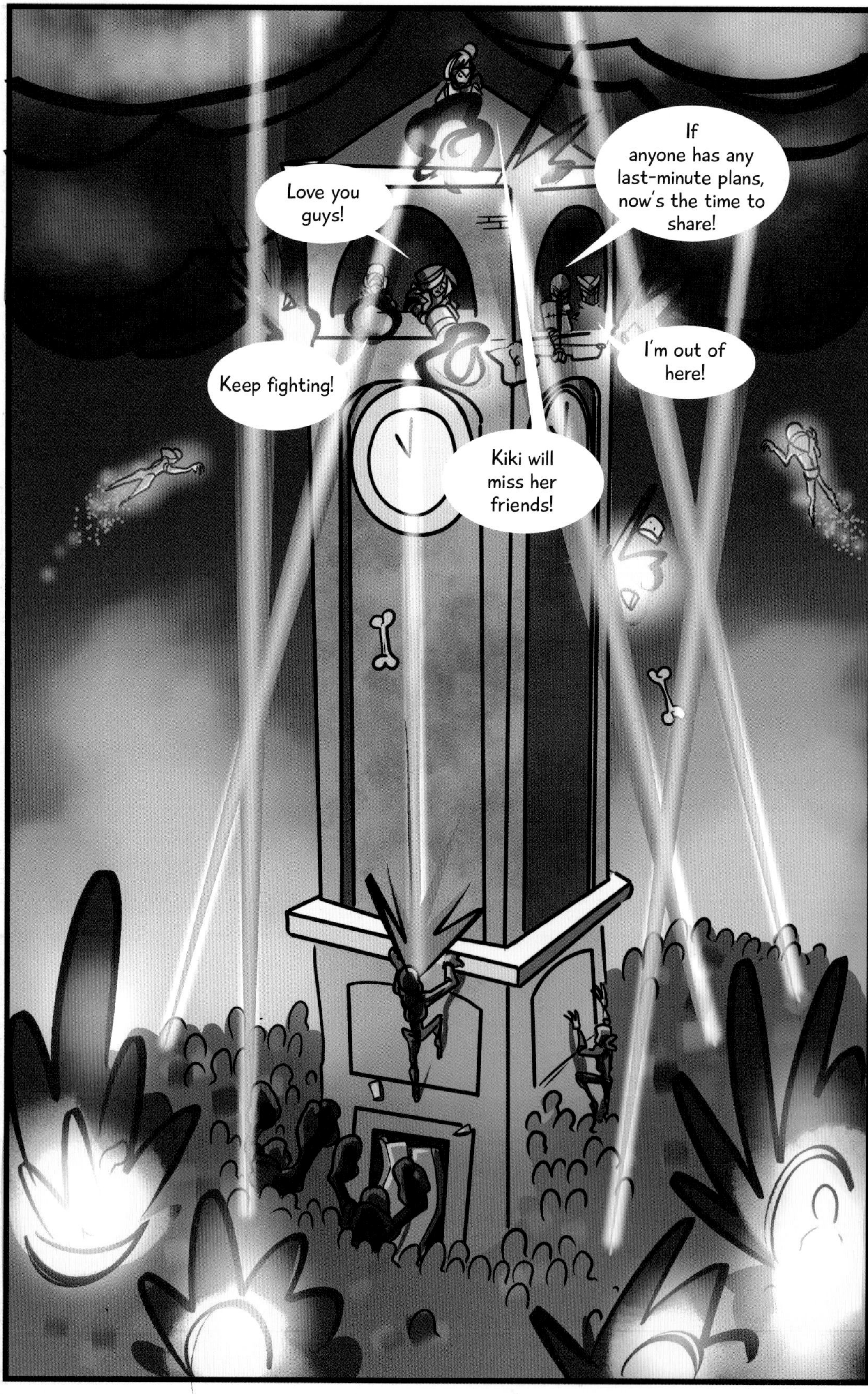
Love you guys!
If anyone has any last-minute plans, now's the time to share!
Keep fighting!
I'm out of here!
Kiki will miss her friends!

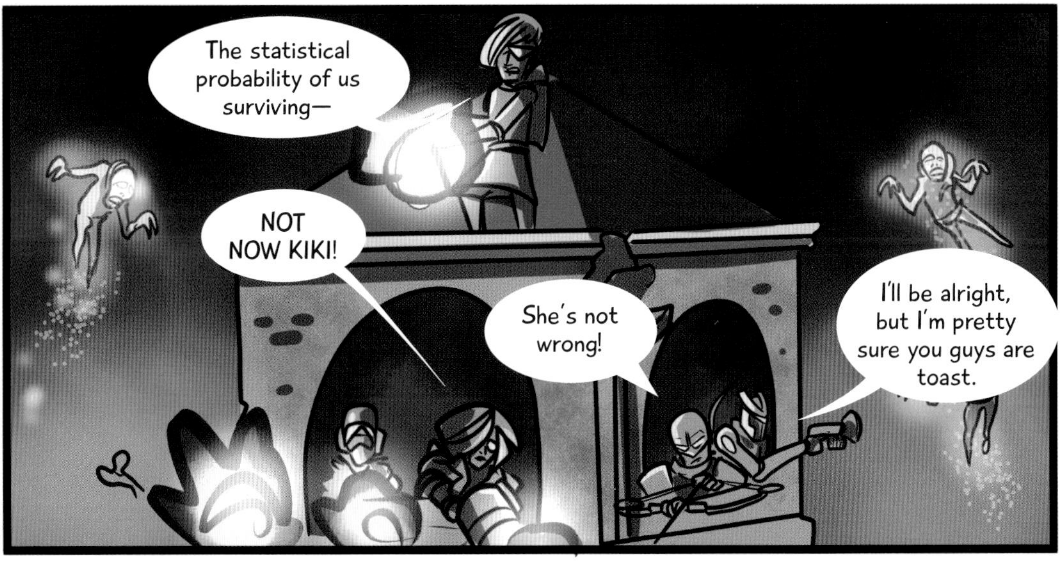
The statistical probability of us surviving—
NOT NOW KIKI!
She's not wrong!
I'll be alright, but I'm pretty sure you guys are toast.

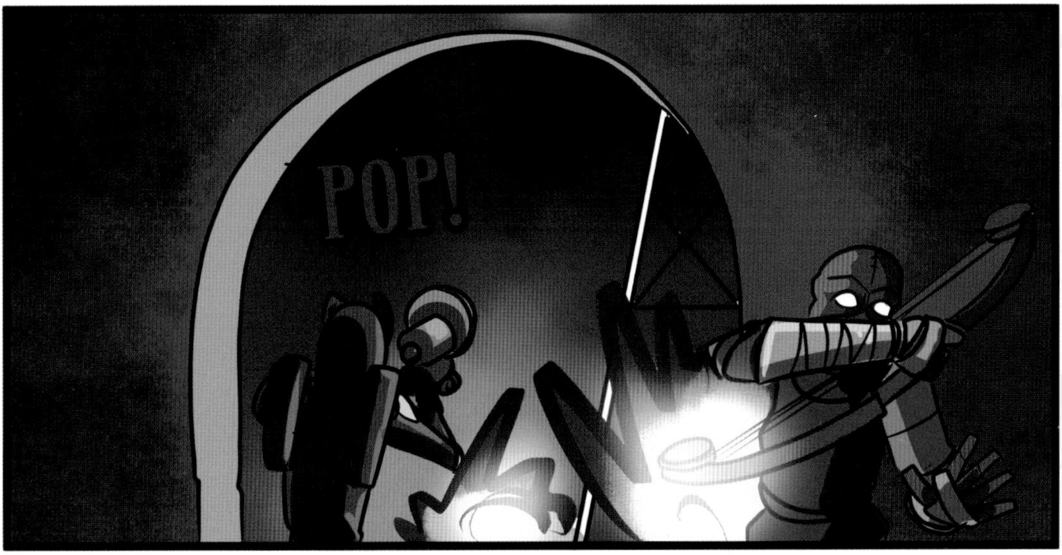
POP!

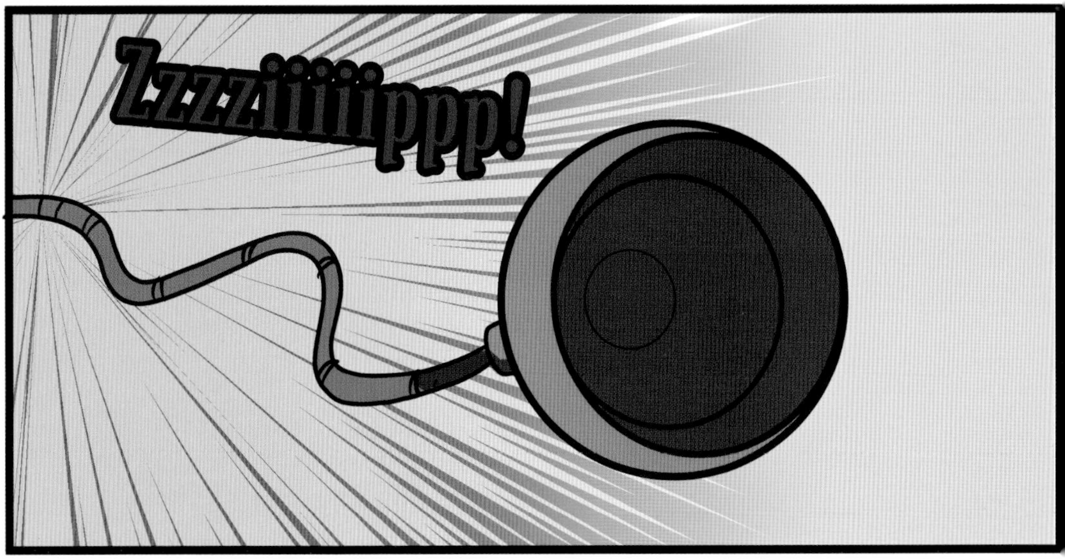
Zzzziiiiippp!

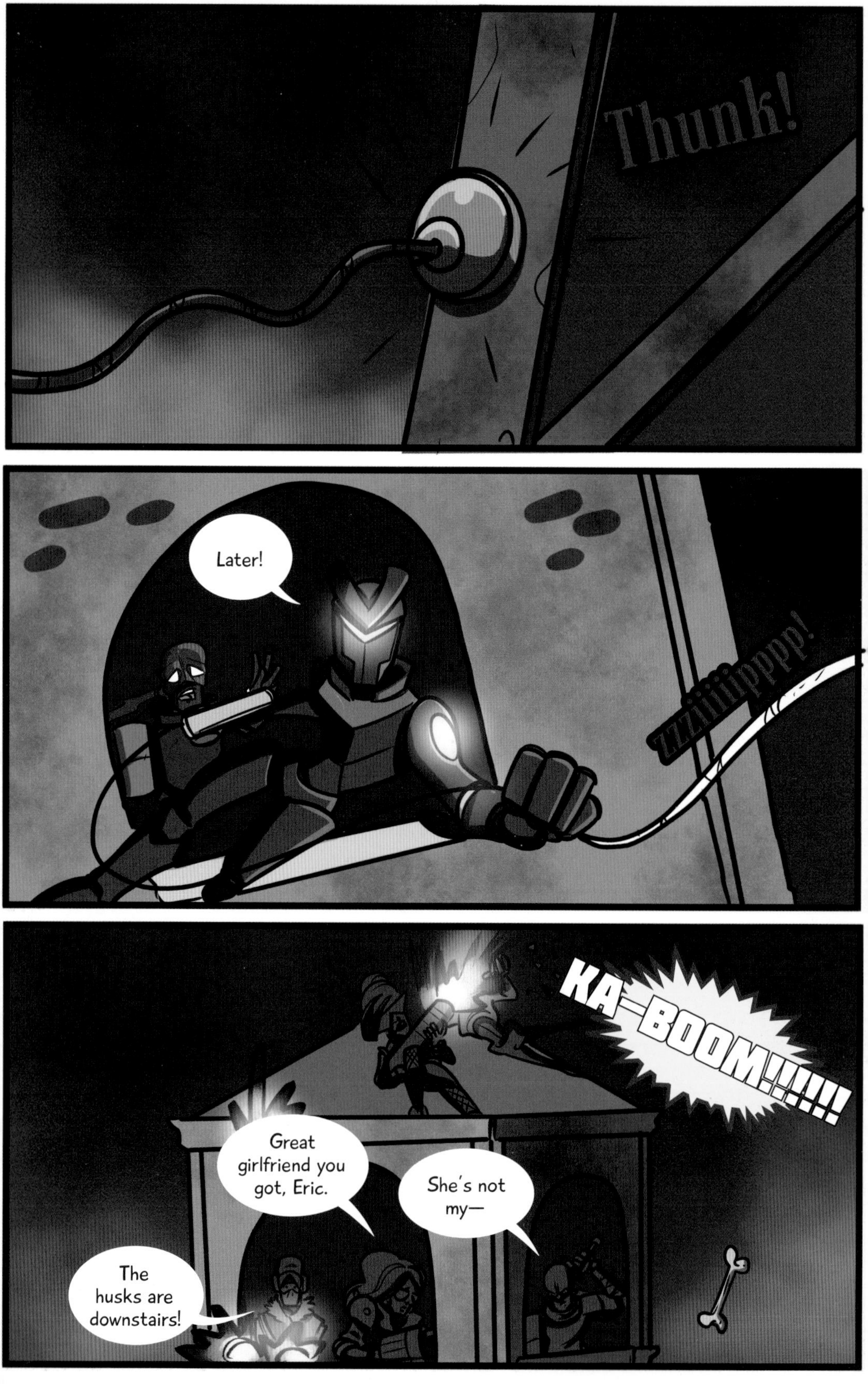
Thunk!
Later!
Zziiiiipppp!
KA-BOOM!!!!!!
Great girlfriend you got, Eric.
She's not my—
The husks are downstairs!

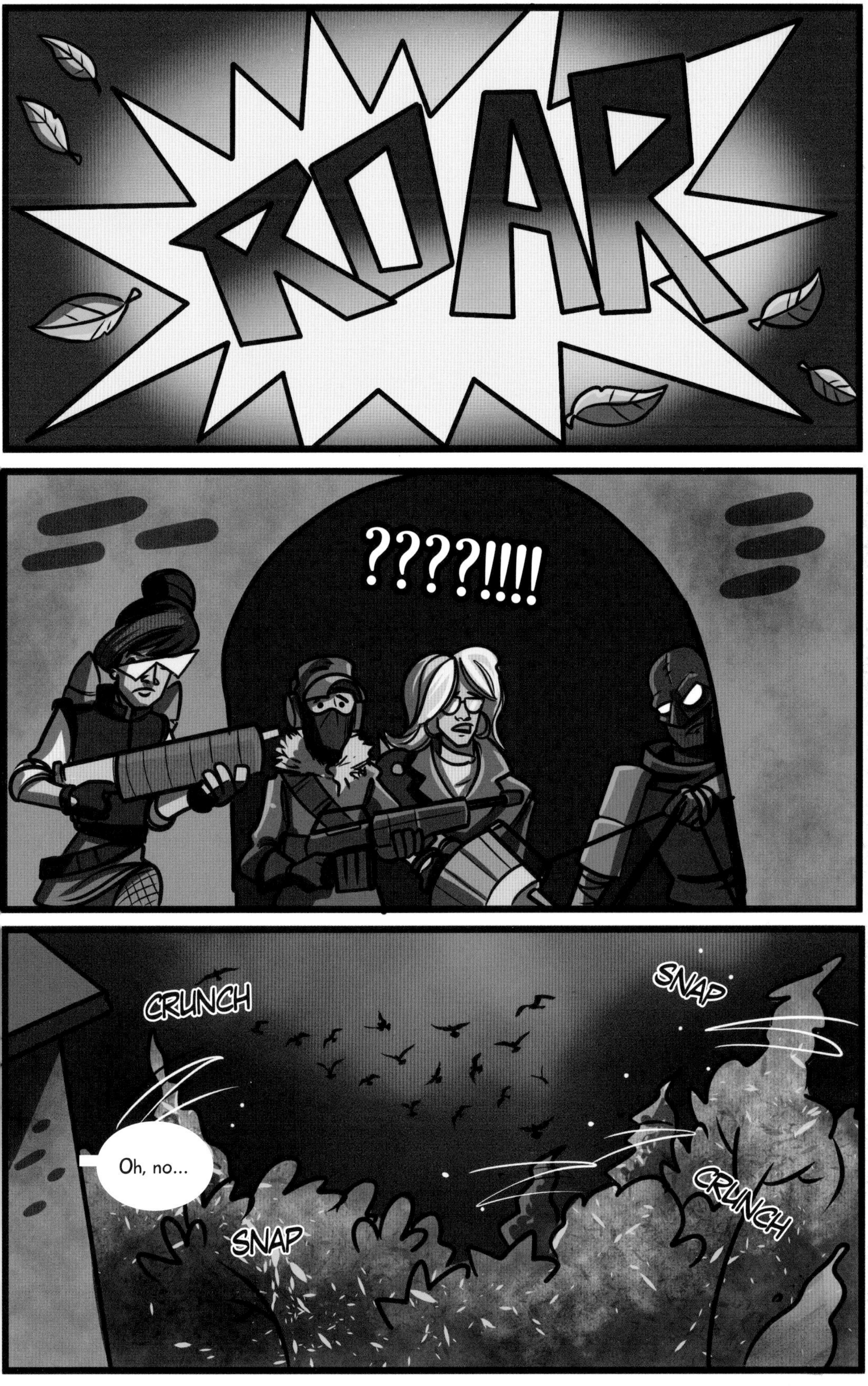
ROAR
????!!!!
CRUNCH
SNAP
Oh, no...
SNAP
CRUNCH

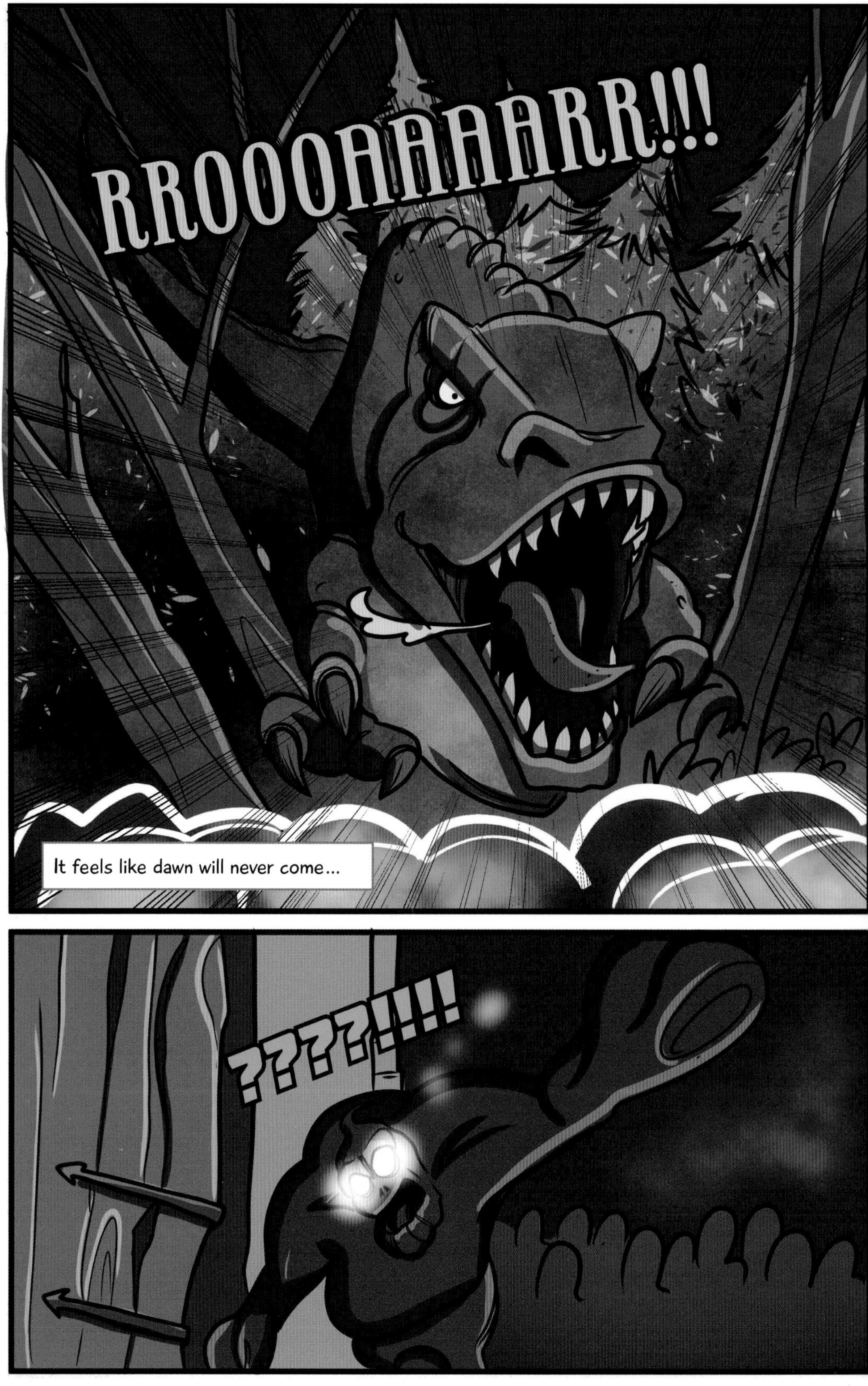
RROOOAAAAARR!!!
It feels like dawn will never come...
????!!!!

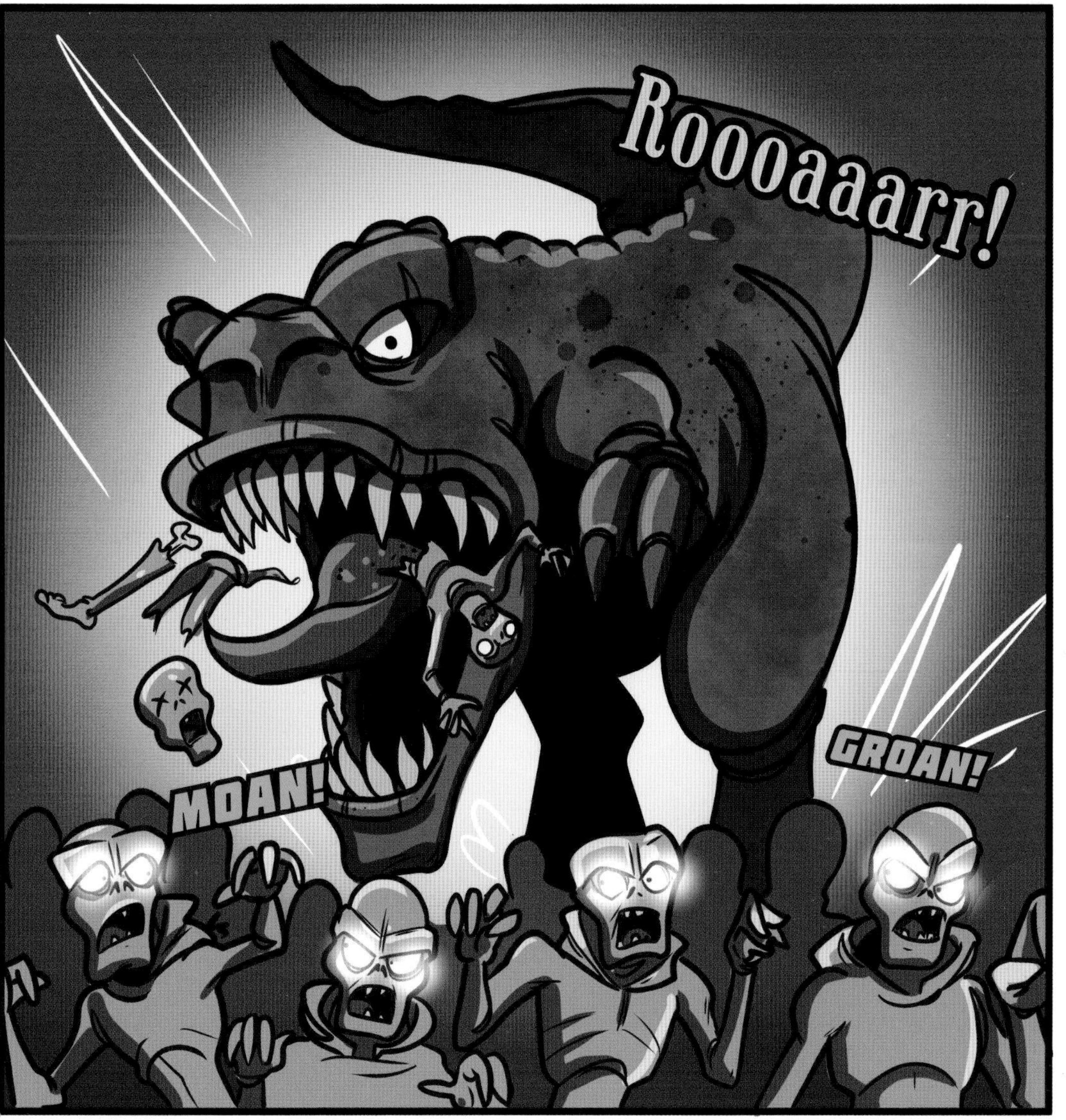
Roooaaaarr!
MOAN!
GROAN!

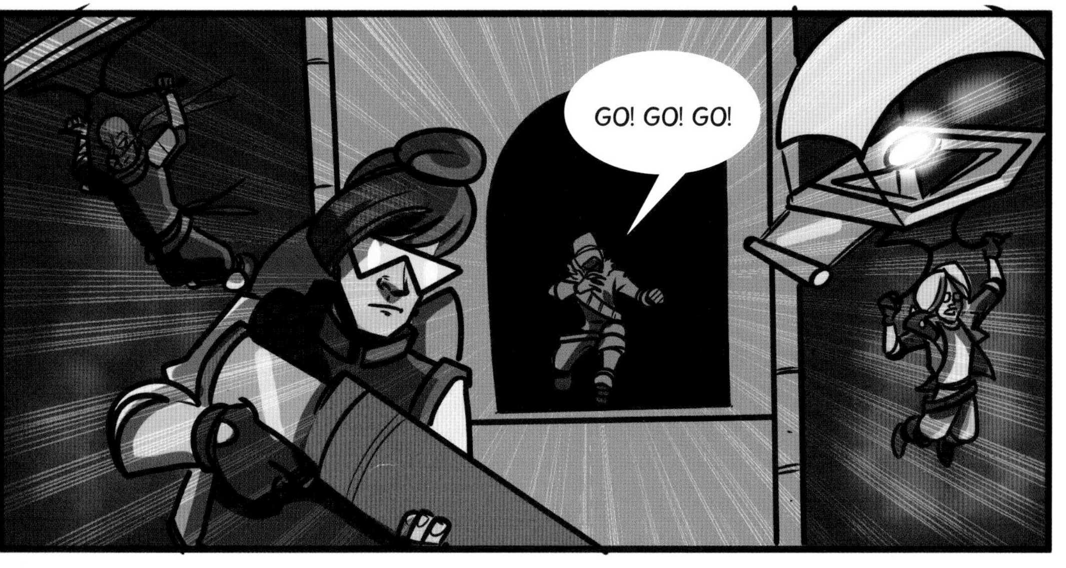
GO! GO! GO!

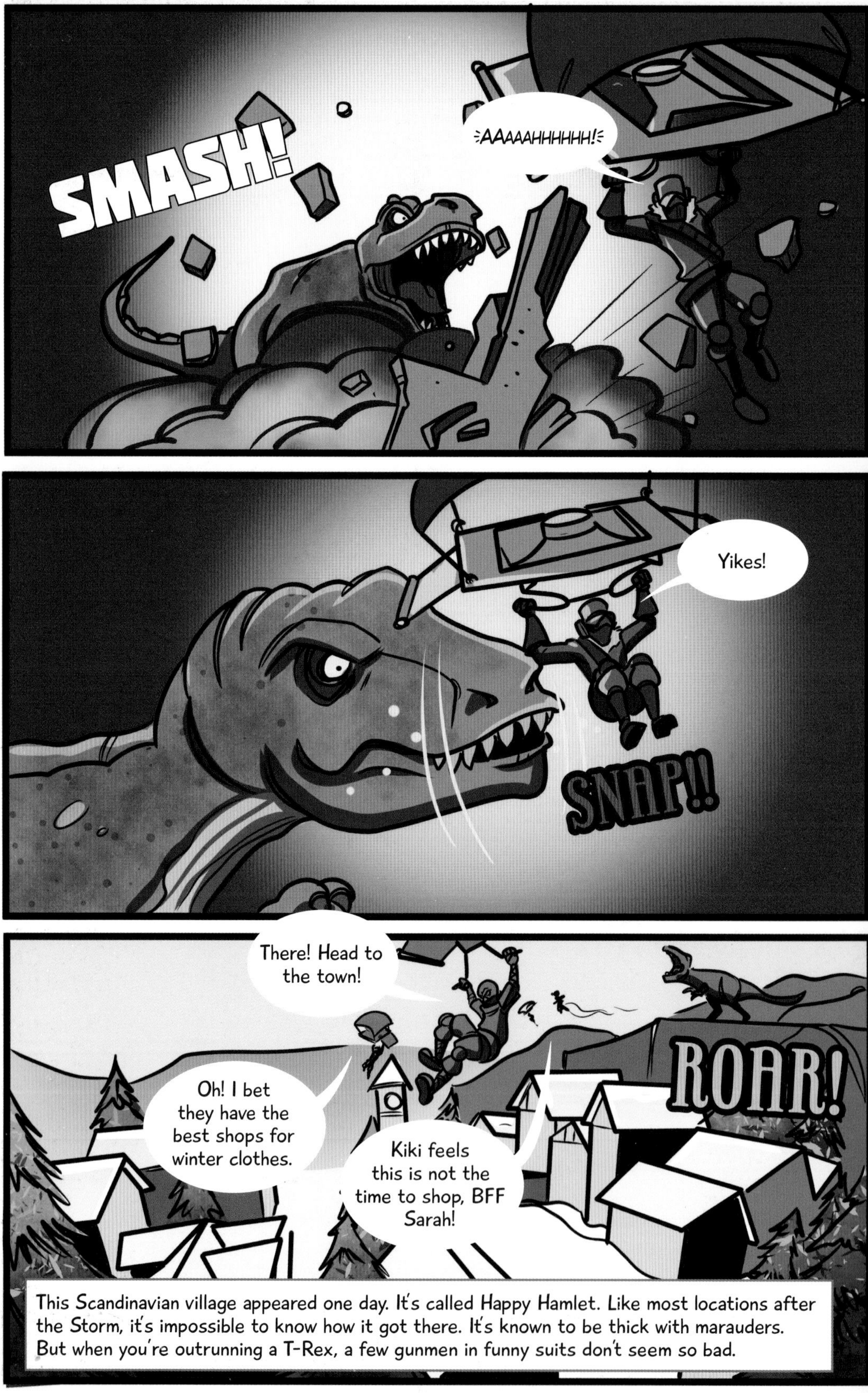
SMASH!
AAAAAHHHHHH!
Yikes!
SNAP!!
There! Head to the town!
Oh! I bet they have the best shops for winter clothes.
Kiki feels this is not the time to shop, BFF Sarah!
ROAR!
This Scandinavian village appeared one day. It's called Happy Hamlet. Like most locations after the Storm, it's impossible to know how it got there. It's known to be thick with marauders. But when you're outrunning a T-Rex, a few gunmen in funny suits don't seem so bad.

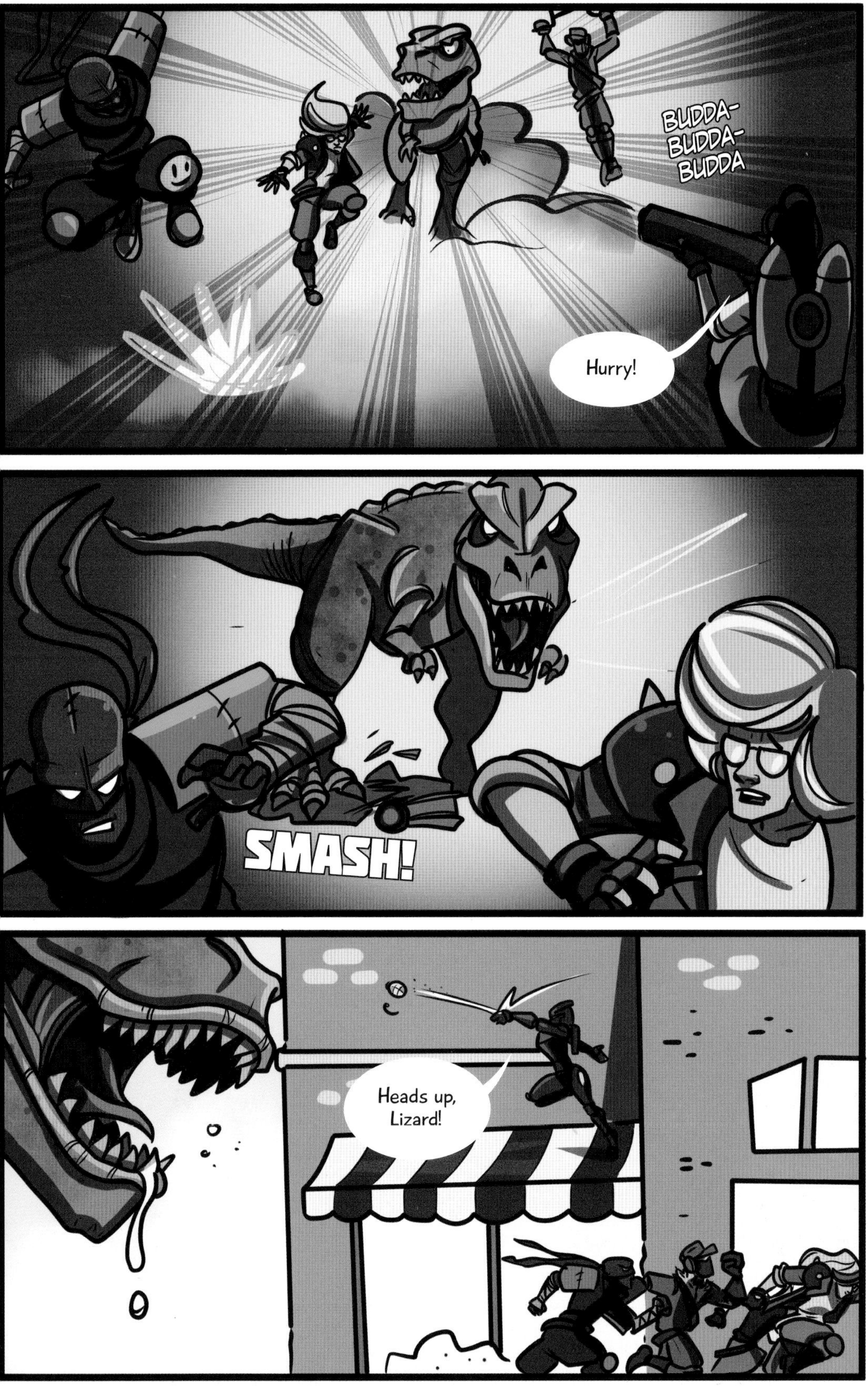
BUDDA-
BUDDA-
BUDDA
Hurry!
SMASH!
Heads up, Lizard!

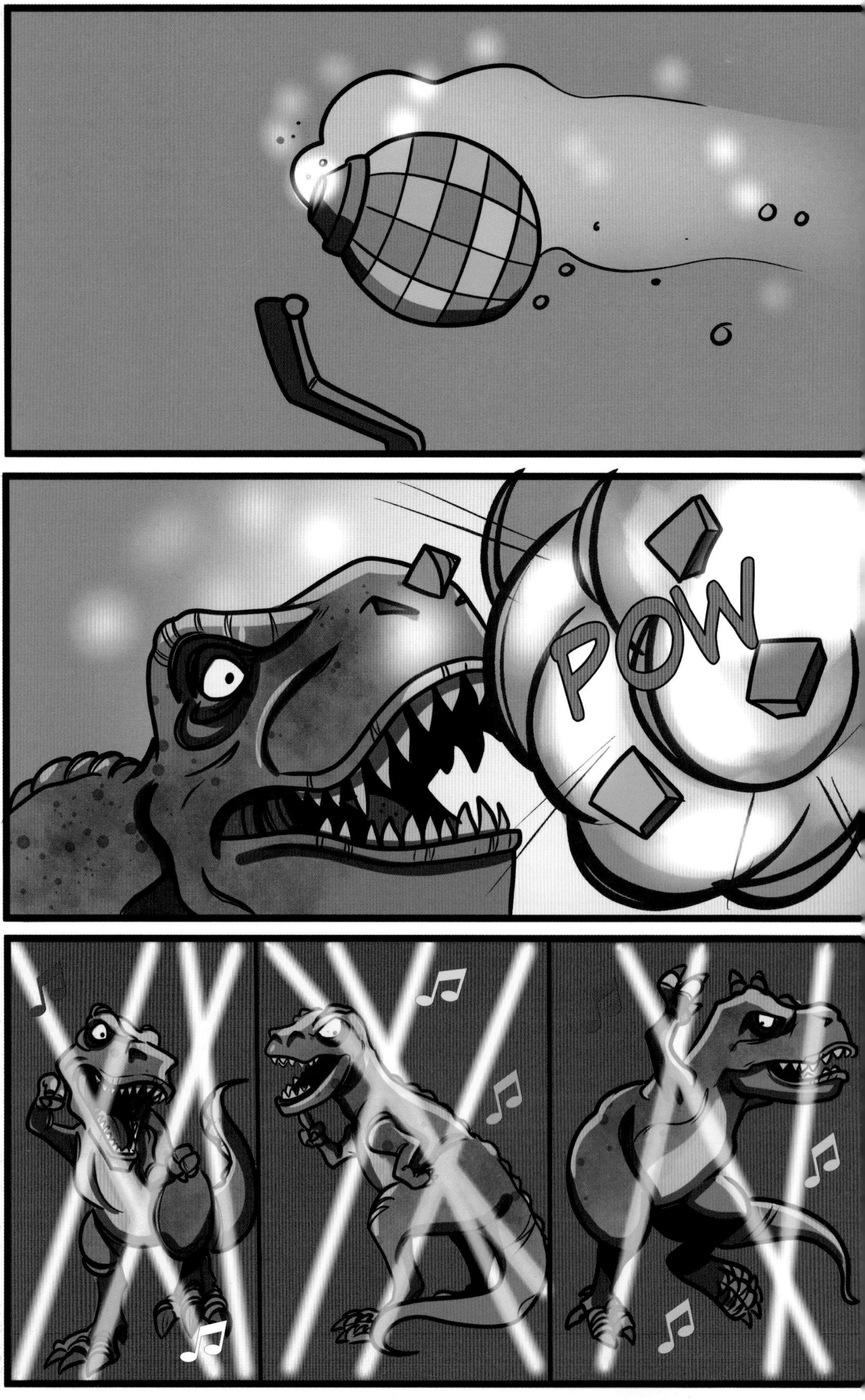
POW

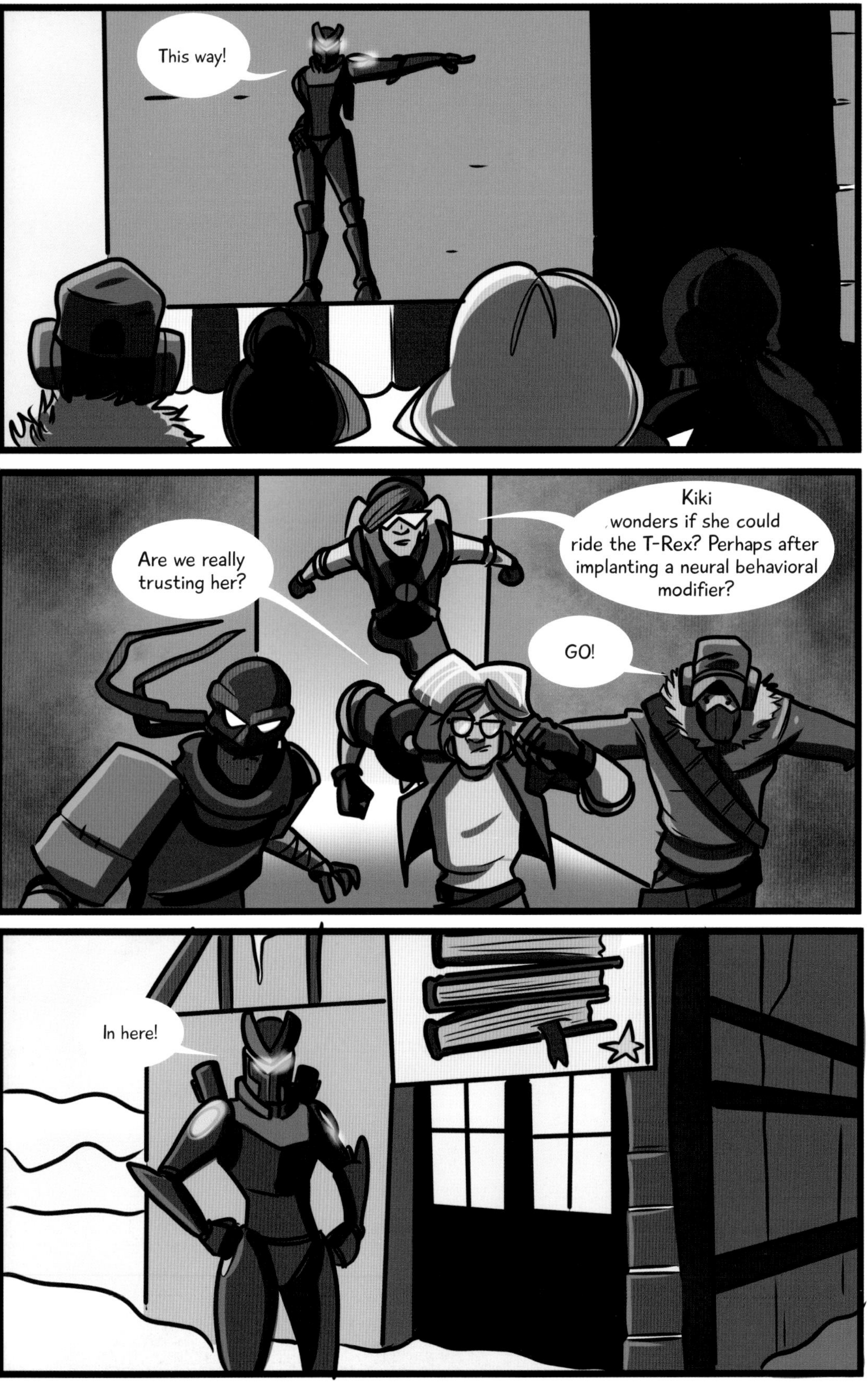
This way!
Are we really trusting her?
Kiki wonders if she could ride the T-Rex? Perhaps after implanting a neural behavioral modifier?
GO!
In here!

CHAPTER 5: DOWN THE RABBIT HOLE

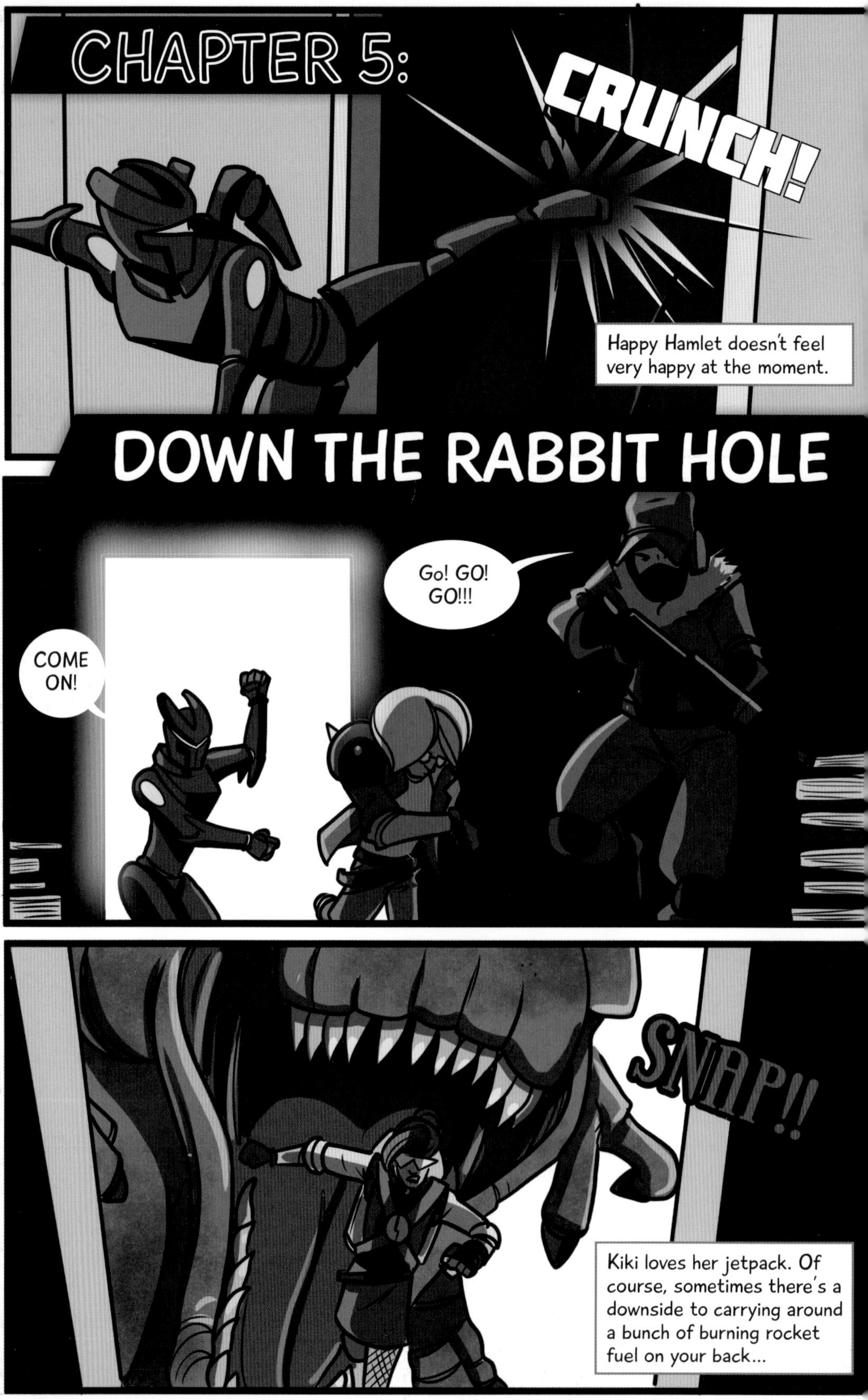
CRUNCH!
Happy Hamlet doesn't feel very happy at the moment.
Go! GO! GO!!!
COME ON!
SNAP!!
Kiki loves her jetpack. Of course, sometimes there's a downside to carrying around a bunch of burning rocket fuel on your back...

BANG!

I got you, Kiki!

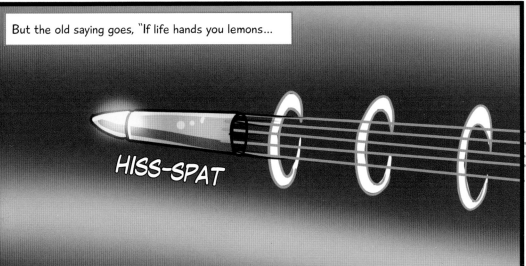

But the old saying goes, "If life hands you lemons...

HISS-SPAT

CRACK

WHOOSH

BOOM!

...make lemonade!

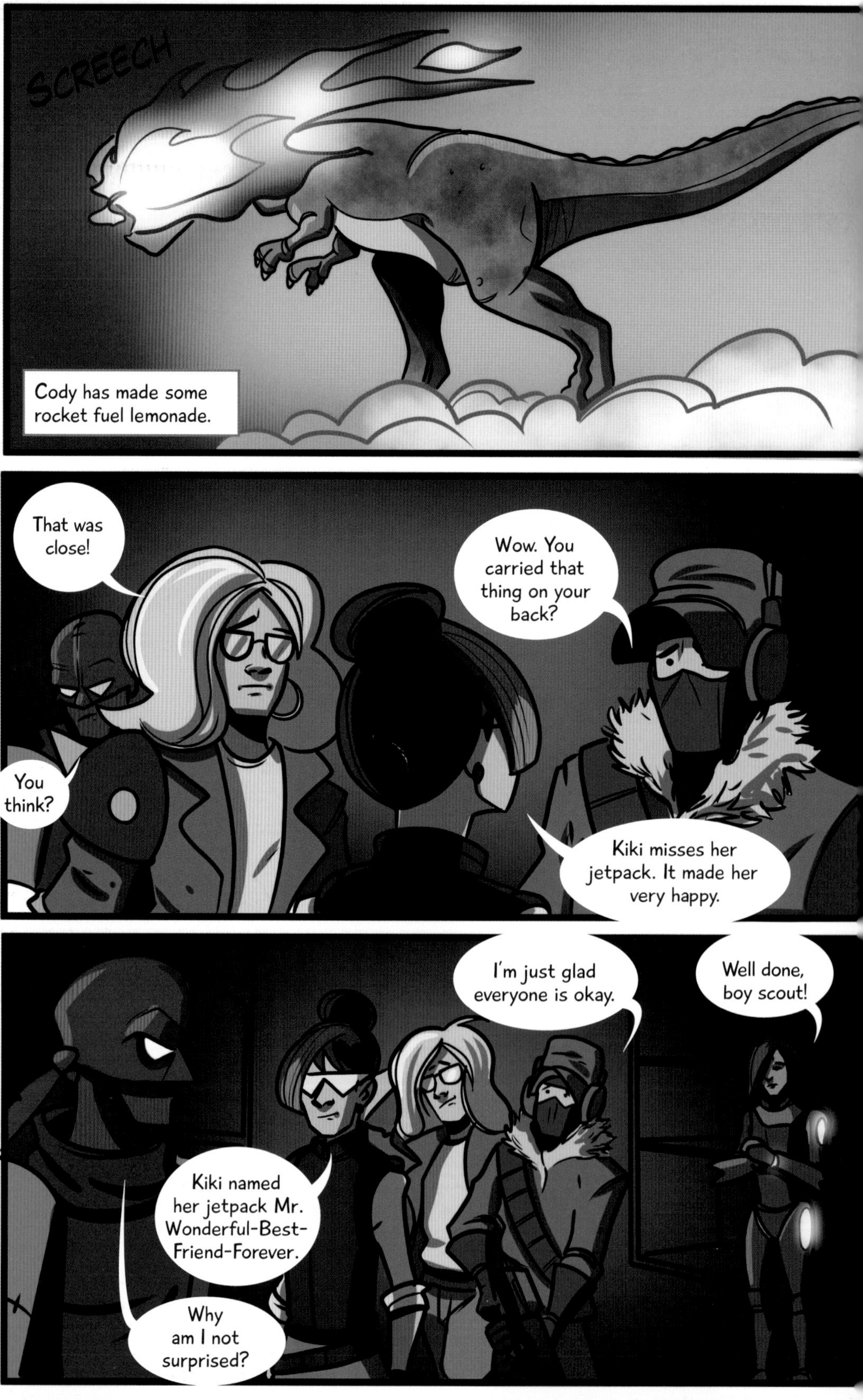
SCREECH
Cody has made some rocket fuel lemonade.
That was close!
You think?
Wow. You carried that thing on your back?
Kiki misses her jetpack. It made her very happy.
I'm just glad everyone is okay.
Well done, boy scout!
Kiki named her jetpack Mr. Wonderful-Best-Friend-Forever.
Why am I not surprised?

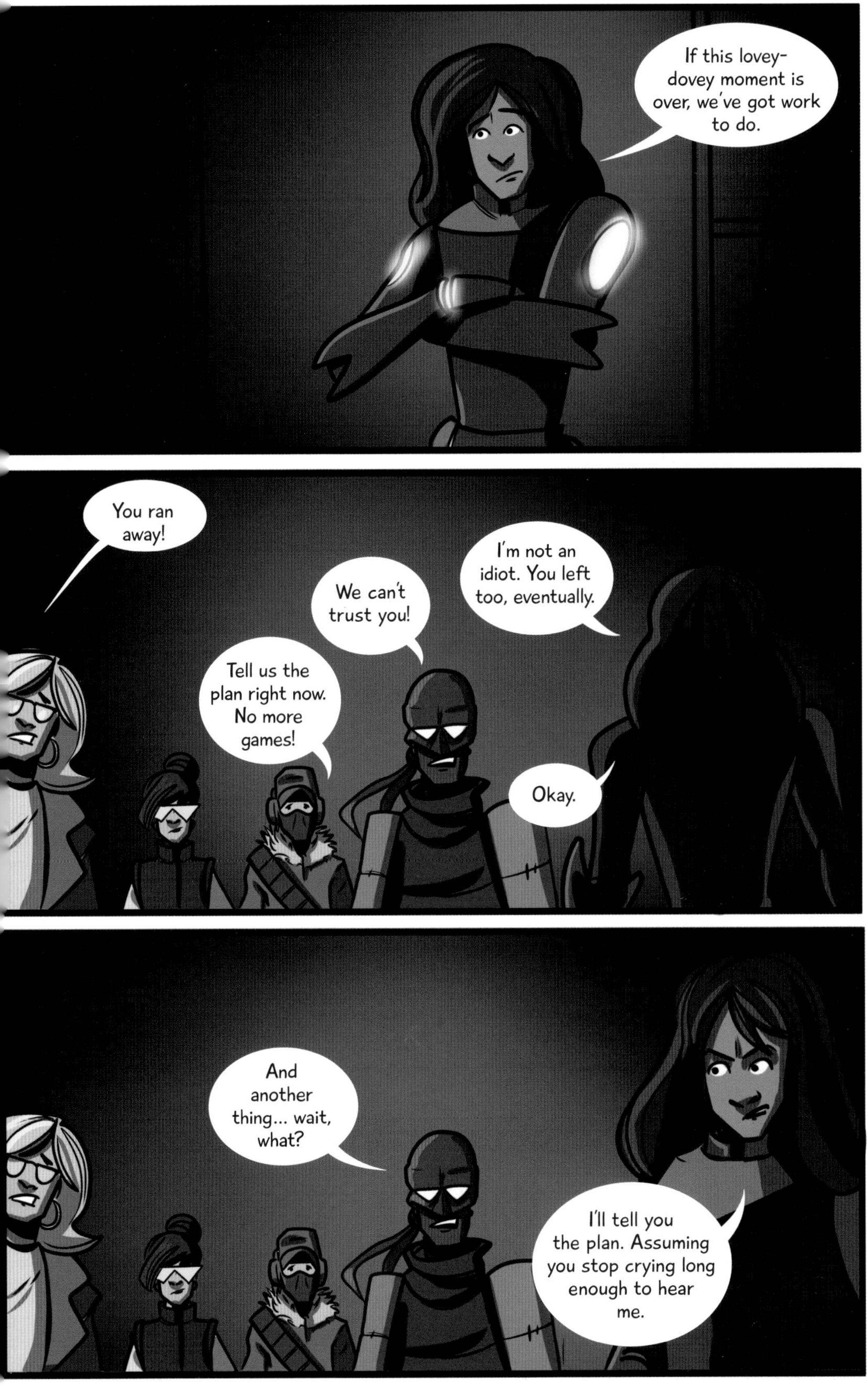
If this lovey-dovey moment is over, we've got work to do.
You ran away!
We can't trust you!
Tell us the plan right now. No more games!
I'm not an idiot. You left too, eventually.
Okay.
And another thing... wait, what?
I'll tell you the plan. Assuming you stop crying long enough to hear me.

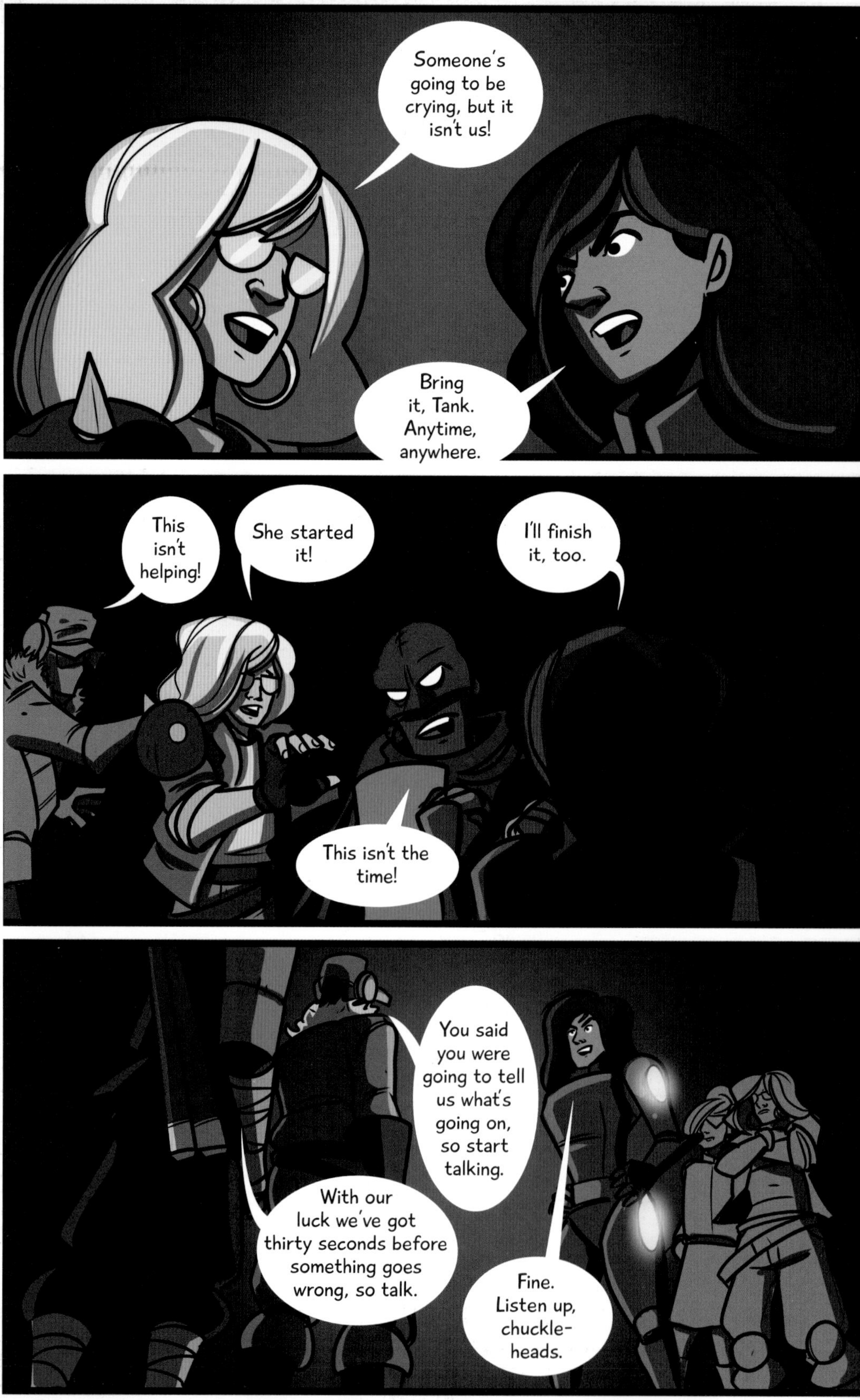
Someone's going to be crying, but it isn't us!
Bring it, Tank. Anytime, anywhere.
This isn't helping!
She started it!
I'll finish it, too.
This isn't the time!
You said you were going to tell us what's going on, so start talking.
With our luck we've got thirty seconds before something goes wrong, so talk.
Fine. Listen up, chuckle-heads.

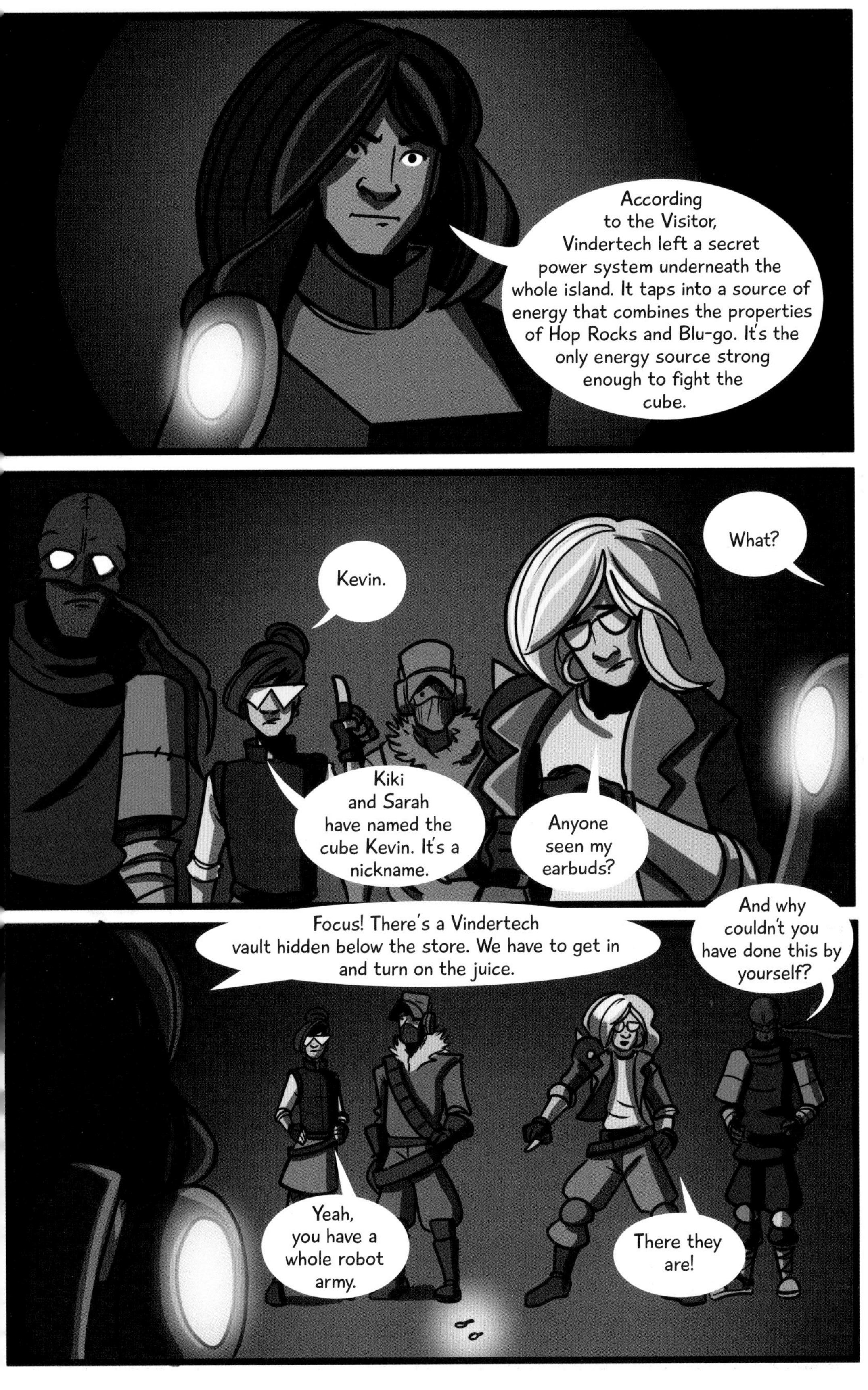
According to the Visitor, Vindertech left a secret power system underneath the whole island. It taps into a source of energy that combines the properties of Hop Rocks and Blu-go. It's the only energy source strong enough to fight the cube.
Kevin.
What?
Kiki and Sarah have named the cube Kevin. It's a nickname.
Anyone seen my earbuds?
Focus! There's a Vindertech vault hidden below the store. We have to get in and turn on the juice.
And why couldn't you have done this by yourself?
Yeah, you have a whole robot army.
There they are!

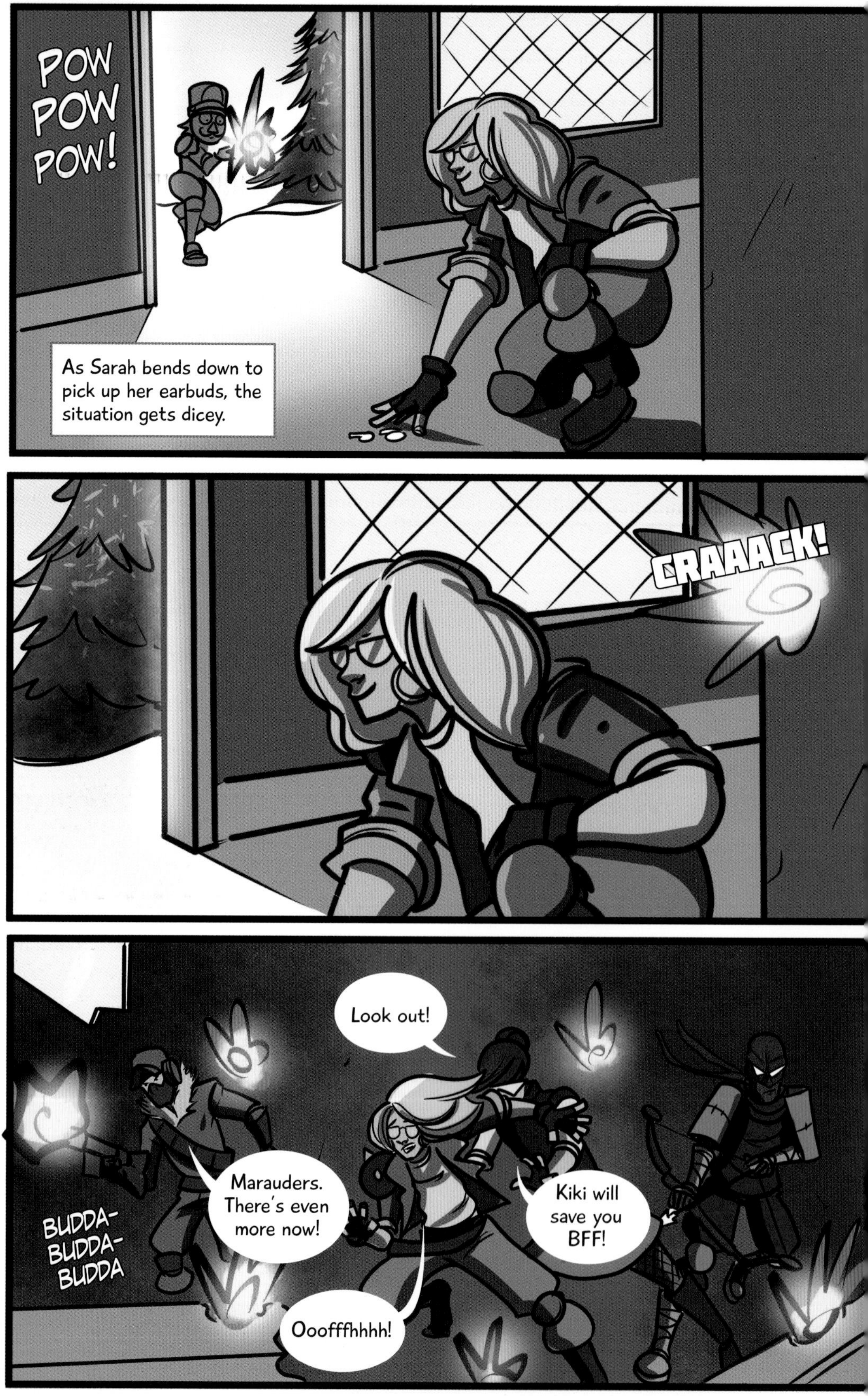
POW POW POW!
As Sarah bends down to pick up her earbuds, the situation gets dicey.
CRAAACK!
Look out!
Marauders. There's even more now!
Kiki will save you BFF!
Oooffhhhh!
BUDDA-BUDDA-BUDDA

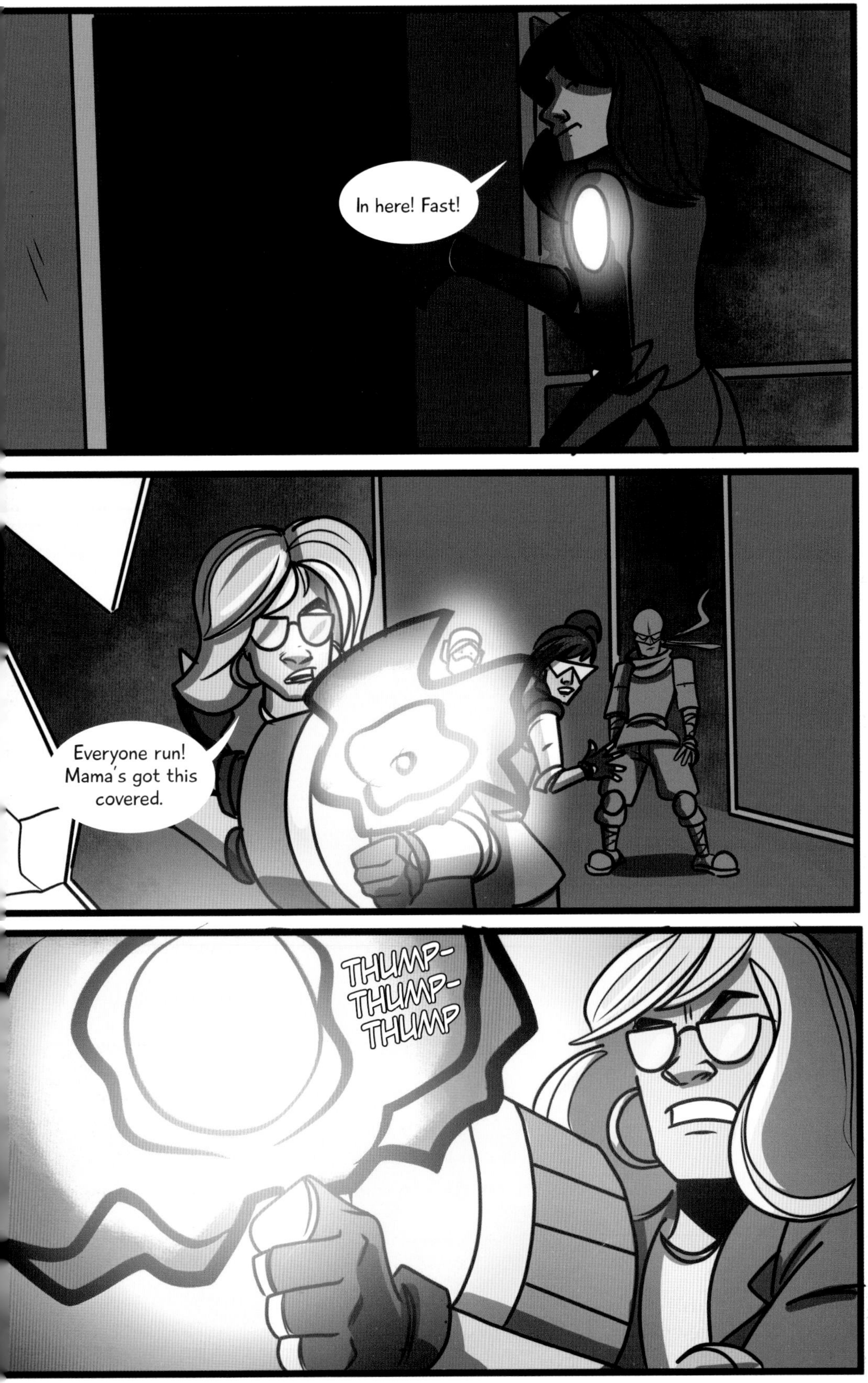
In here! Fast!
Everyone run! Mama's got this covered.
THUMP-THUMP-THUMP

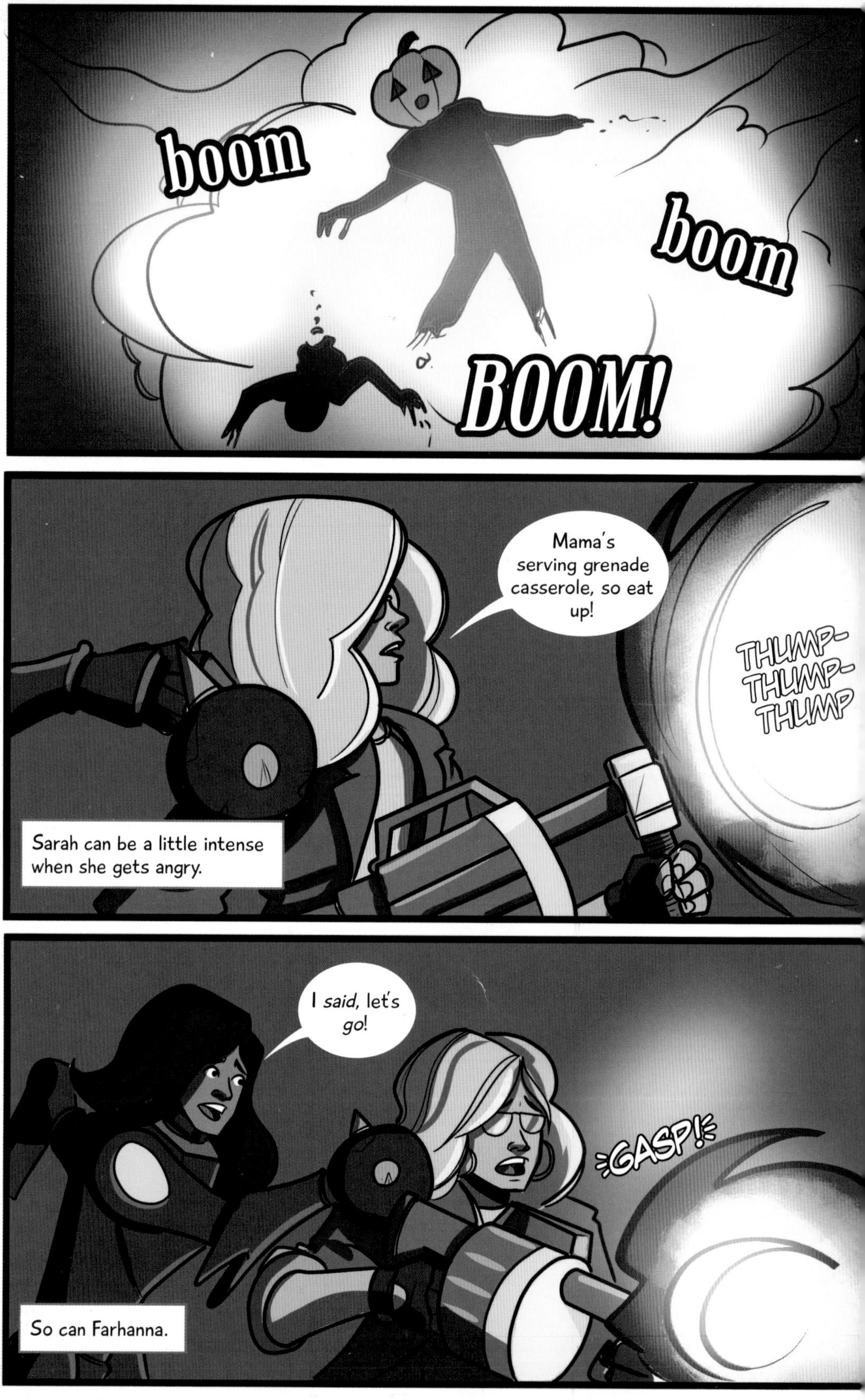
boom
boom
BOOM!
Mama's serving grenade casserole, so eat up!
THUMP-THUMP-THUMP
Sarah can be a little intense when she gets angry.
I said, let's go!
GASP!
So can Farhanna.

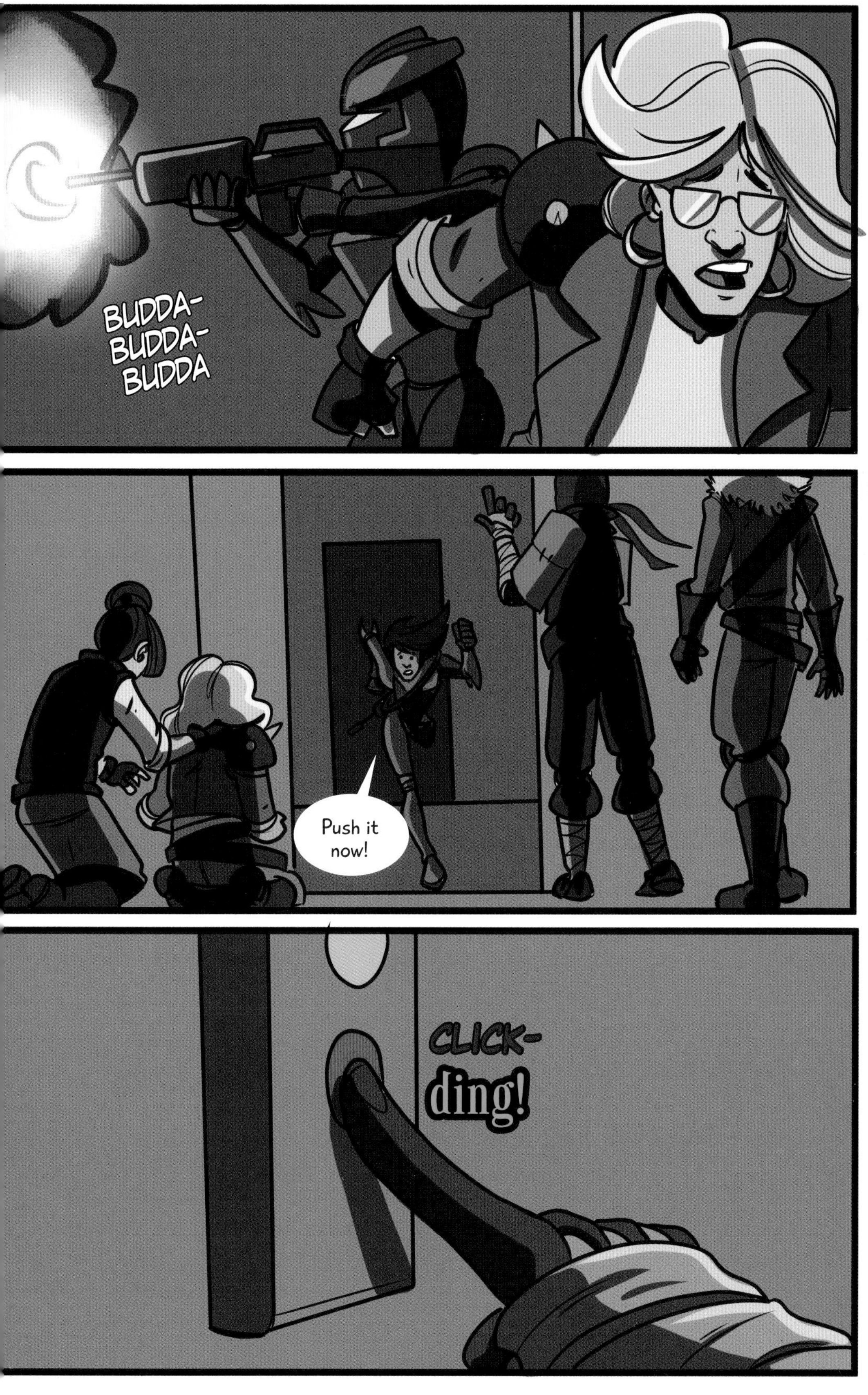
BUDDA-
BUDDA-
BUDDA
Push it now!
CLICK-
ding!

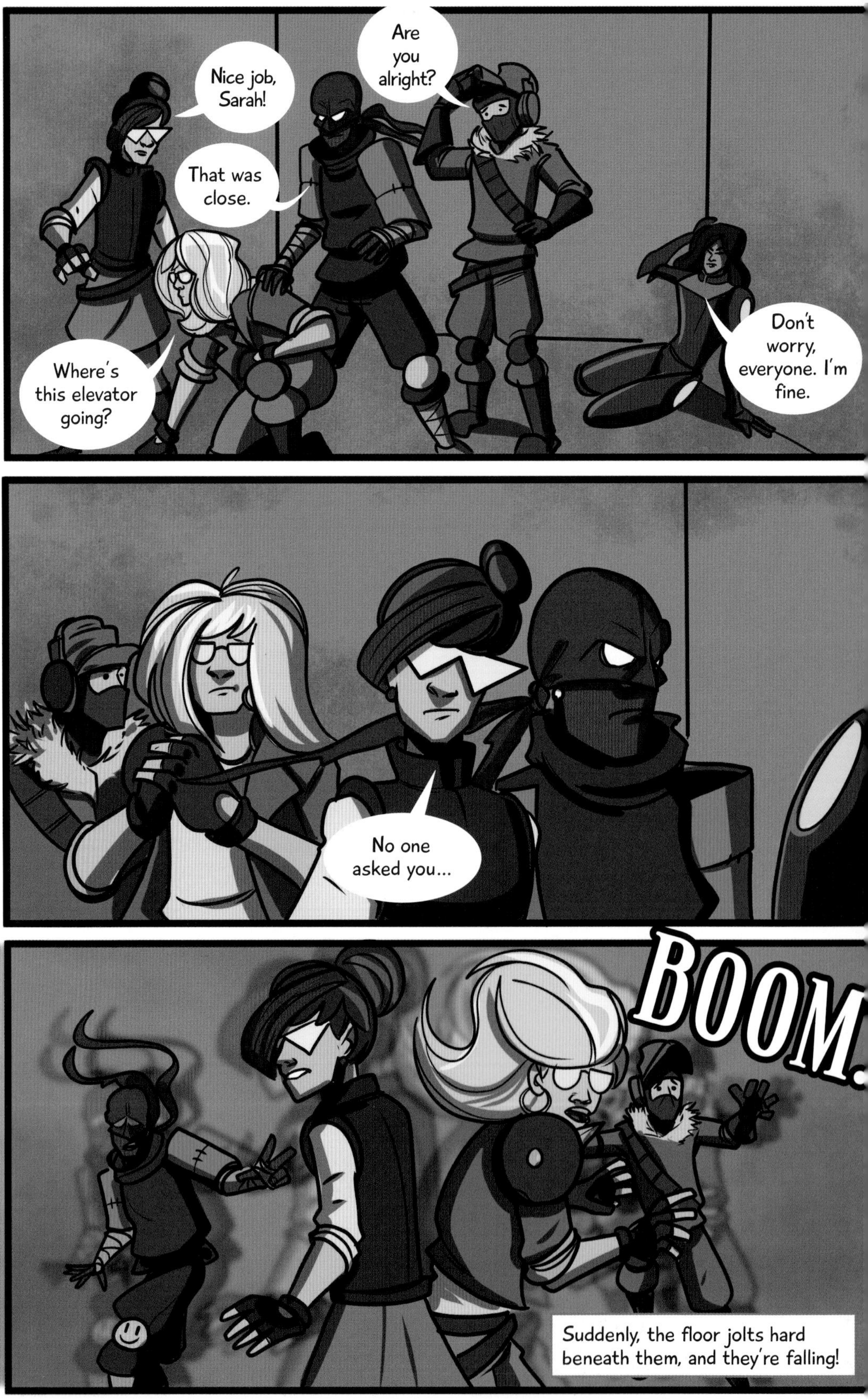
Nice job, Sarah!
Are you alright?
That was close.
Where's this elevator going?
Don't worry, everyone. I'm fine.
No one asked you...
BOOM.
Suddenly, the floor jolts hard beneath them, and they're falling!

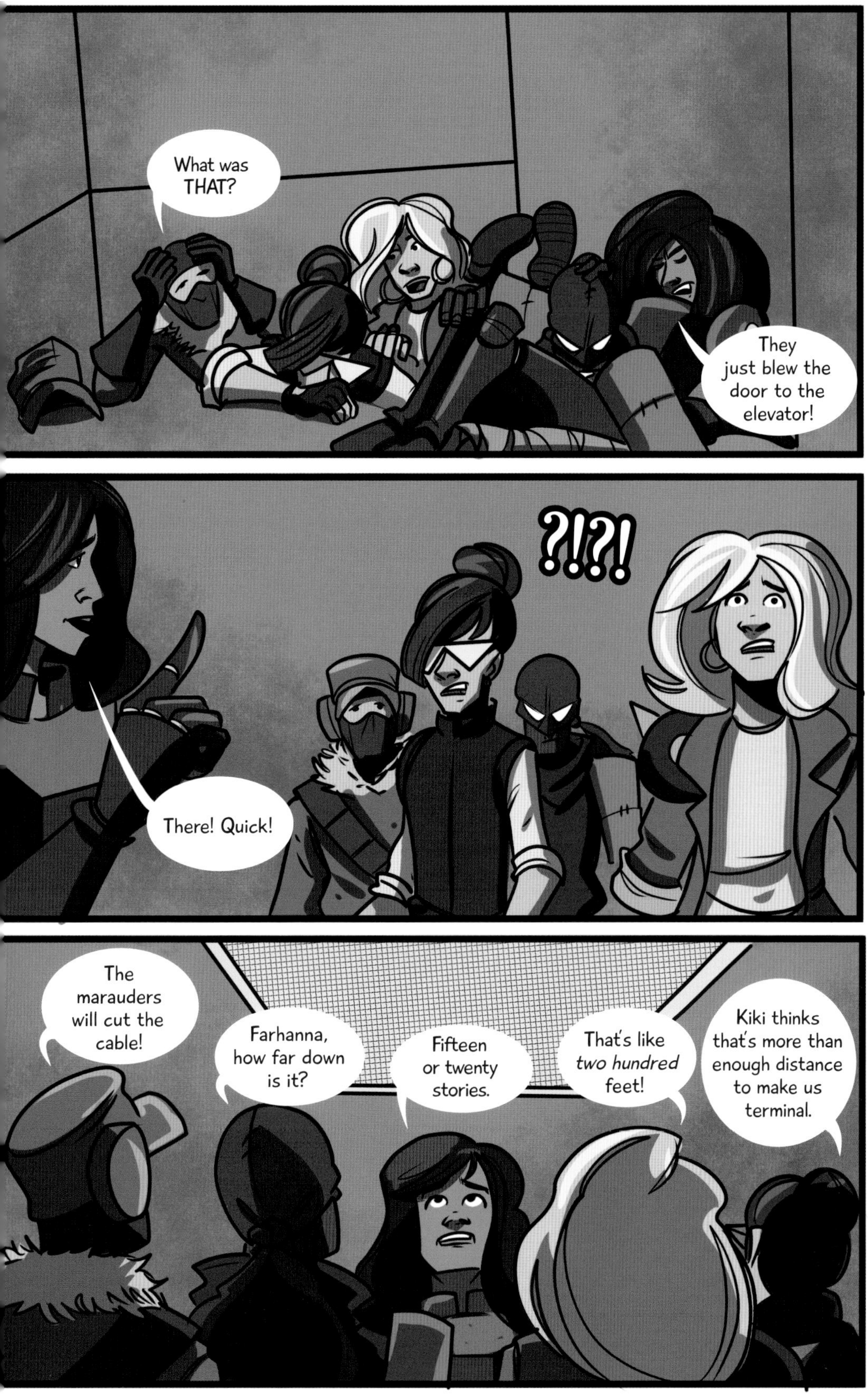
What was THAT?
They just blew the door to the elevator!
?!?!
There! Quick!
The marauders will cut the cable!
Farhanna, how far down is it?
Fifteen or twenty stories.
That's like *two hundred* feet!
Kiki thinks that's more than enough distance to make us terminal.

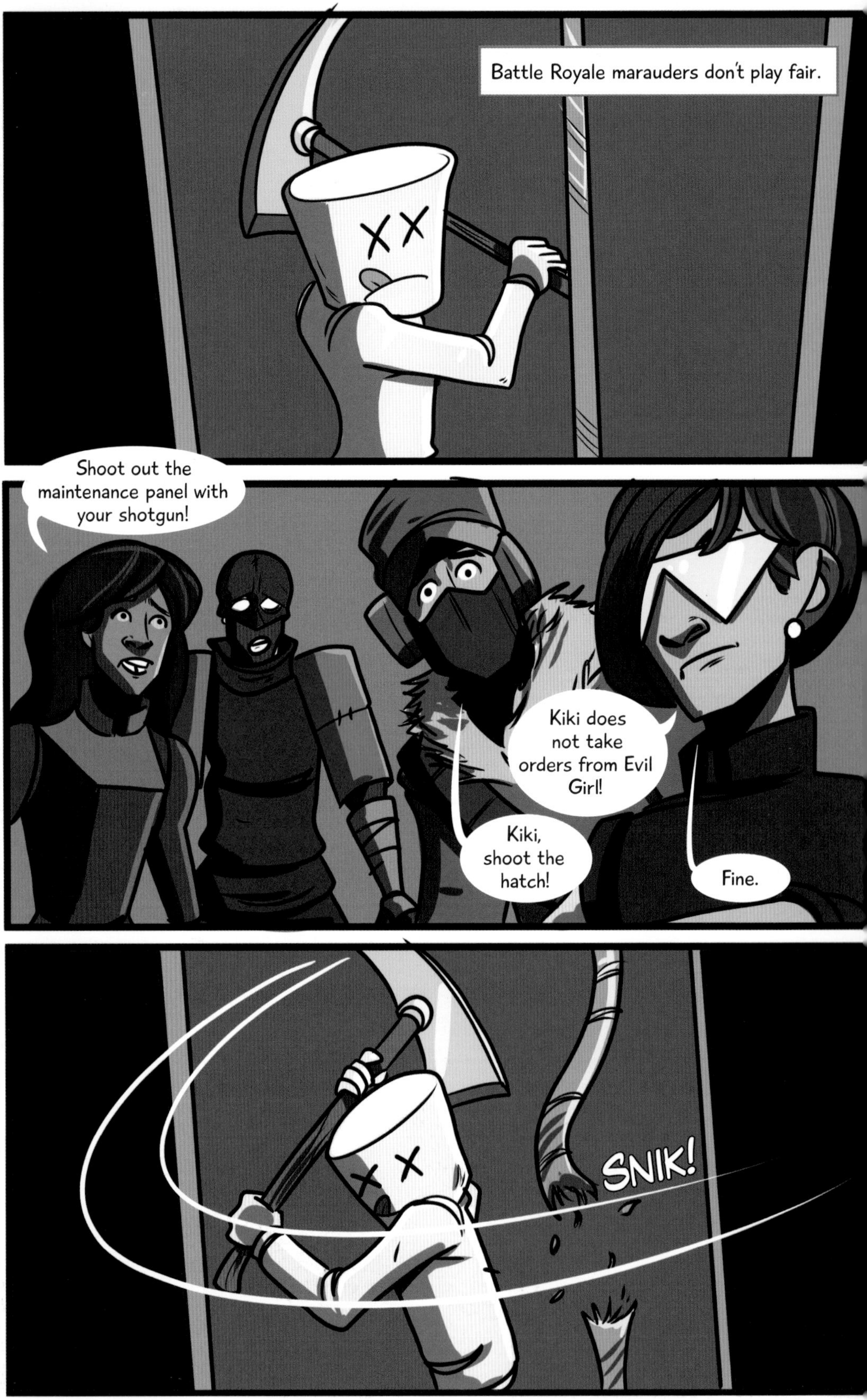
Battle Royale marauders don't play fair.
Shoot out the maintenance panel with your shotgun!
Kiki, shoot the hatch!
Kiki does not take orders from Evil Girl!
Fine.
SNIK!

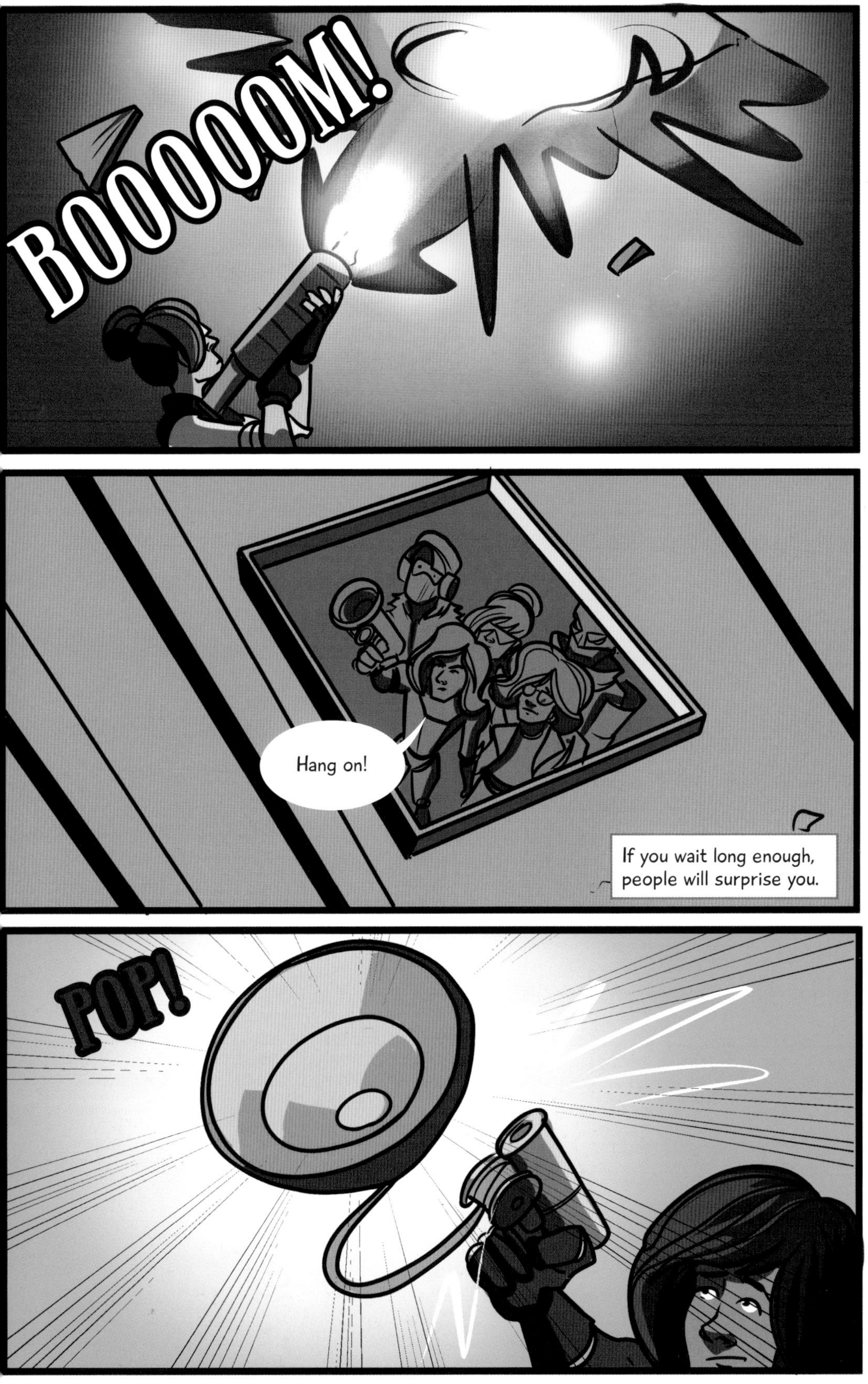
BOOOOOM!
Hang on!
If you wait long enough, people will surprise you.
POP!

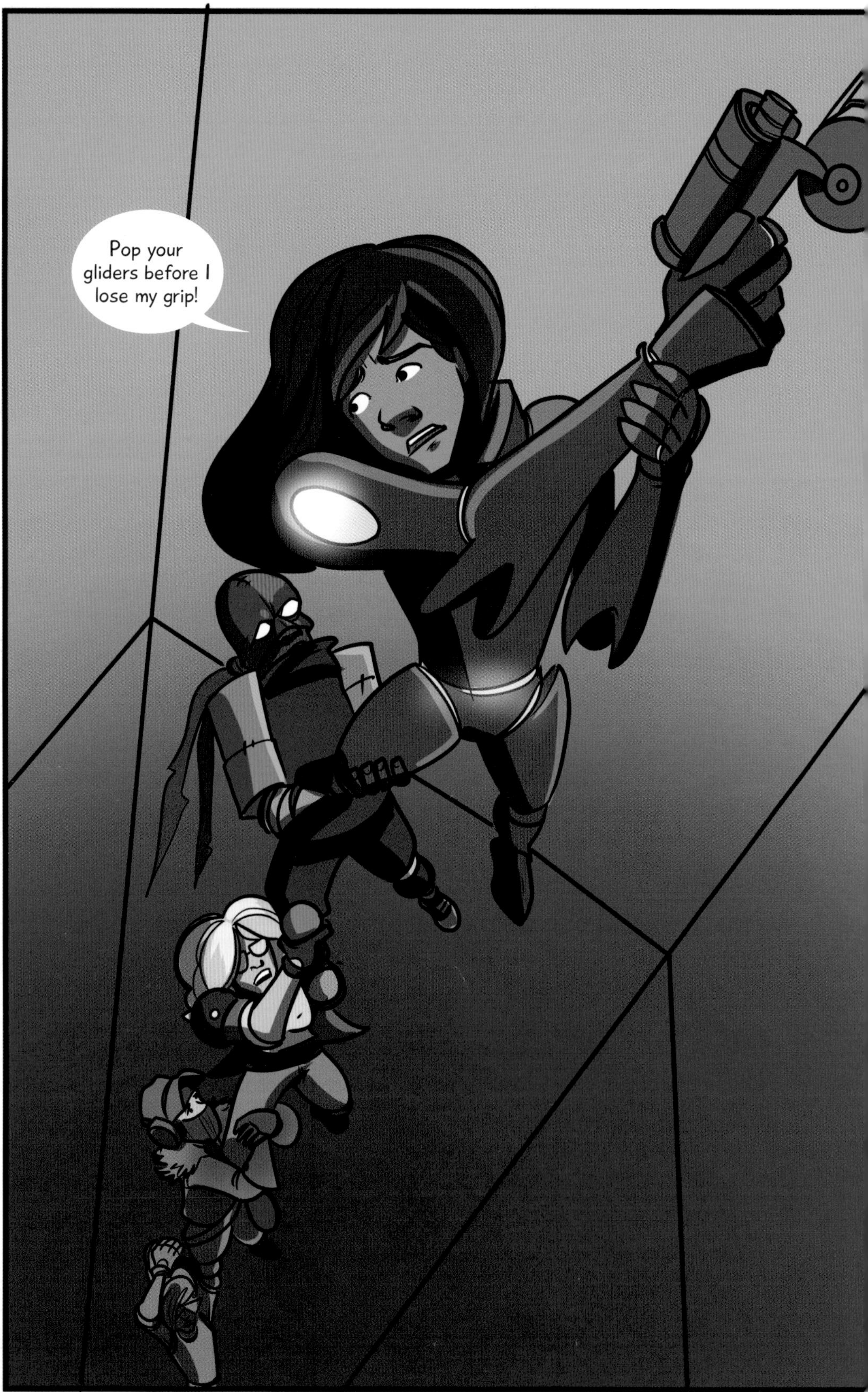
Pop your gliders before I lose my grip!

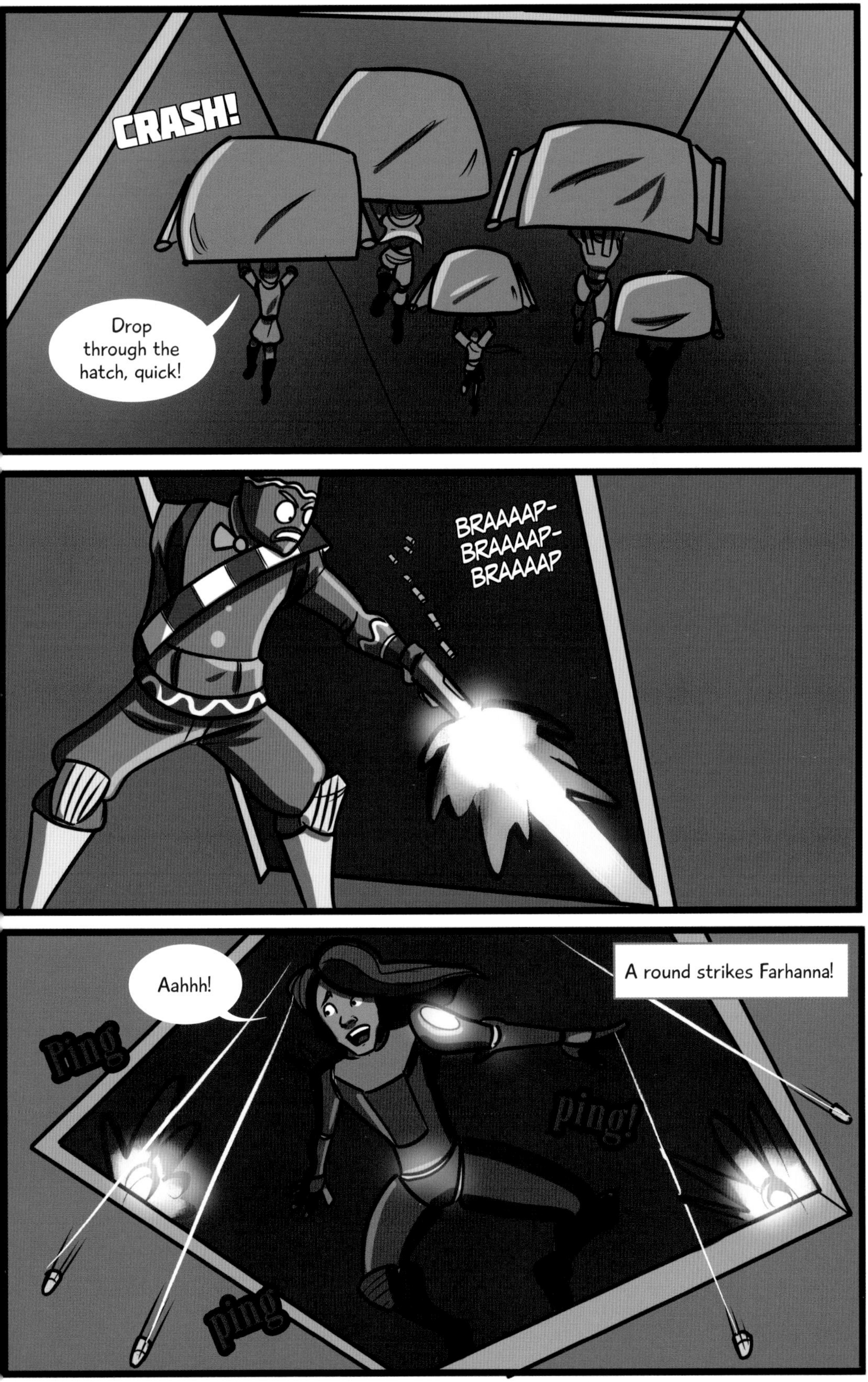
CRASH!
Drop through the hatch, quick!
BRAAAAP- BRAAAAP- BRAAAAP
A round strikes Farhanna!
Aahhh!
Ping
ping!
ping

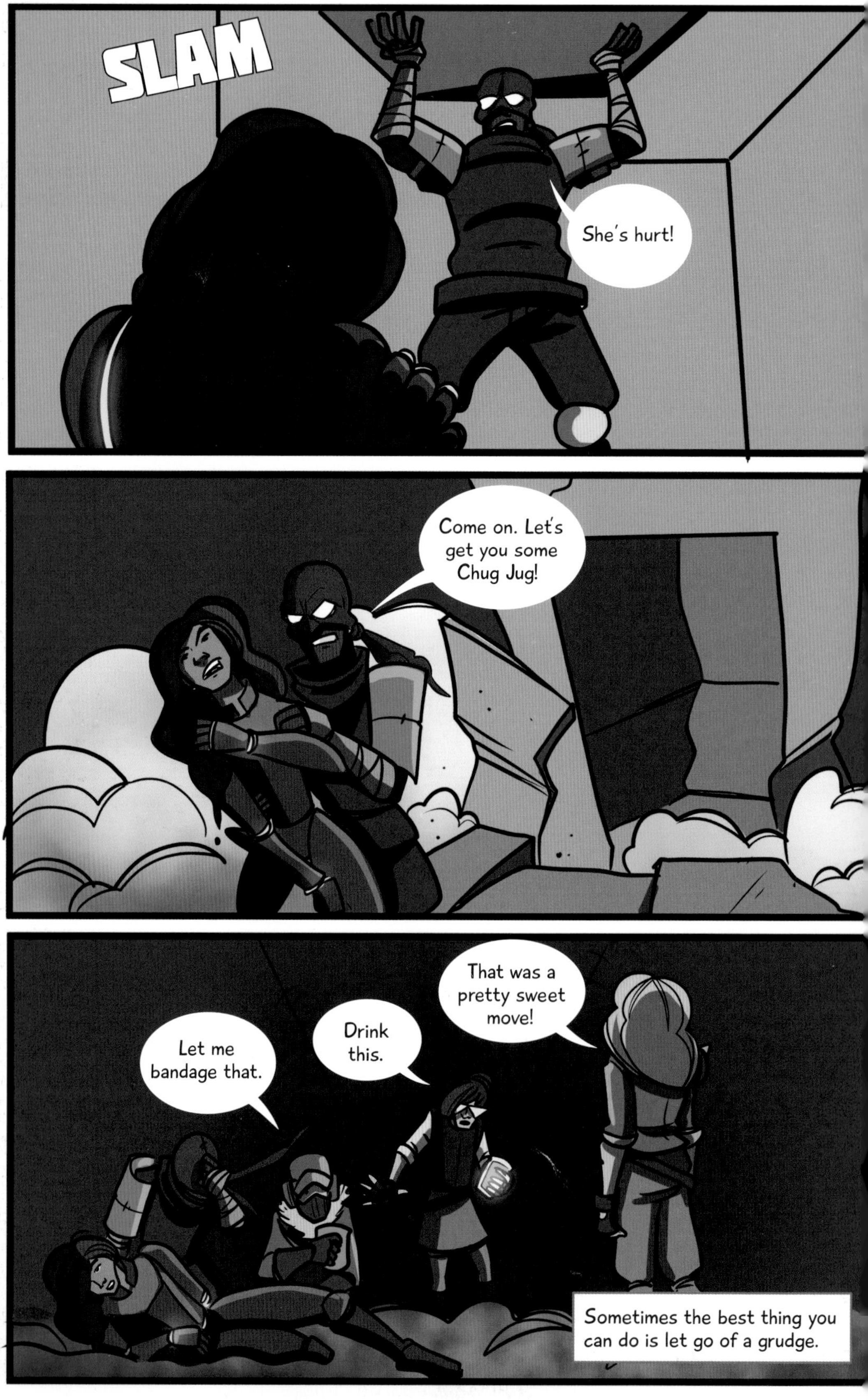
SLAM
She's hurt!
Come on. Let's get you some Chug Jug!
Let me bandage that.
Drink this.
That was a pretty sweet move!
Sometimes the best thing you can do is let go of a grudge.

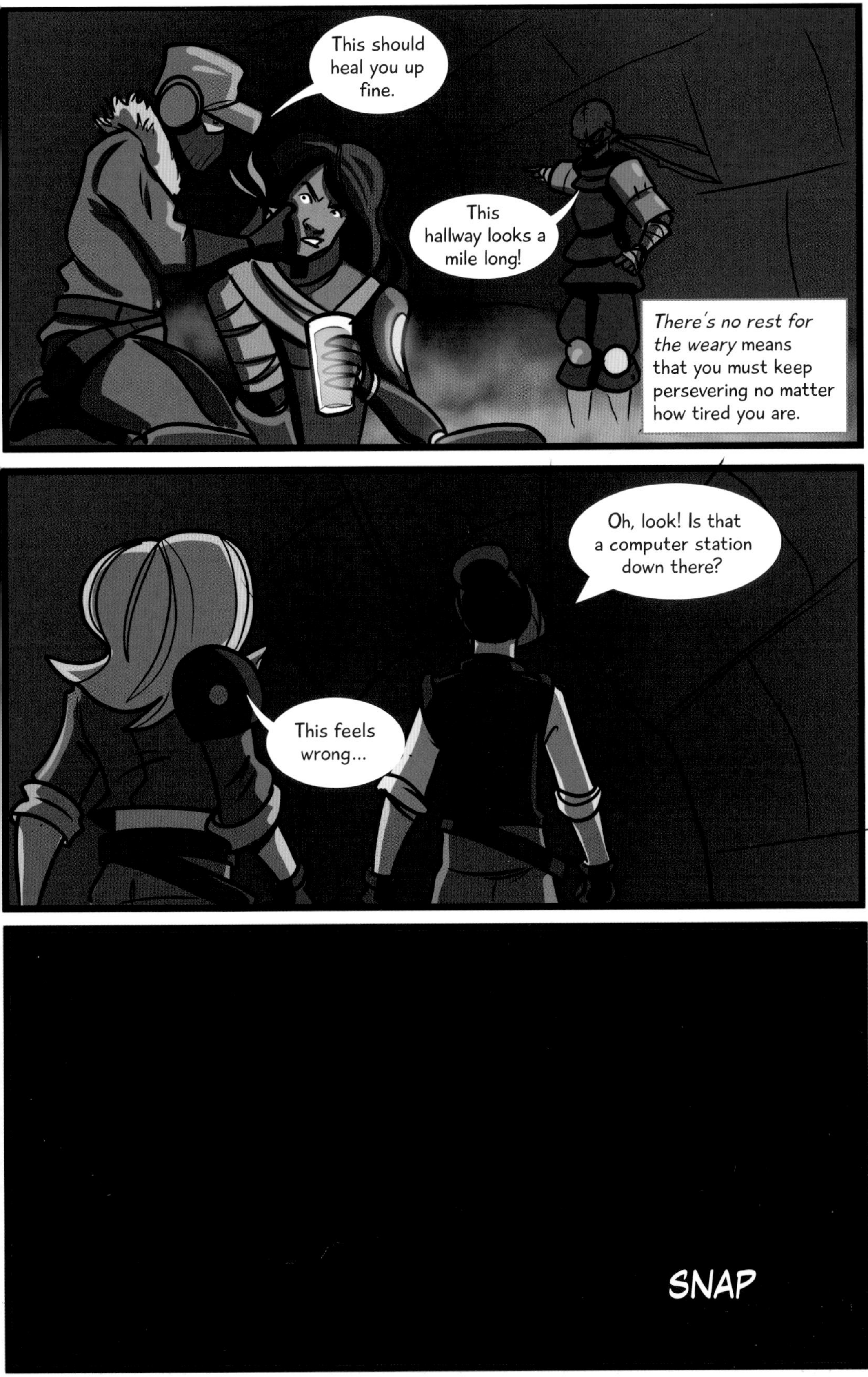
This should heal you up fine.
This hallway looks a mile long!
There's no rest for the weary means that you must keep persevering no matter how tired you are.
Oh, look! Is that a computer station down there?
This feels wrong...
SNAP

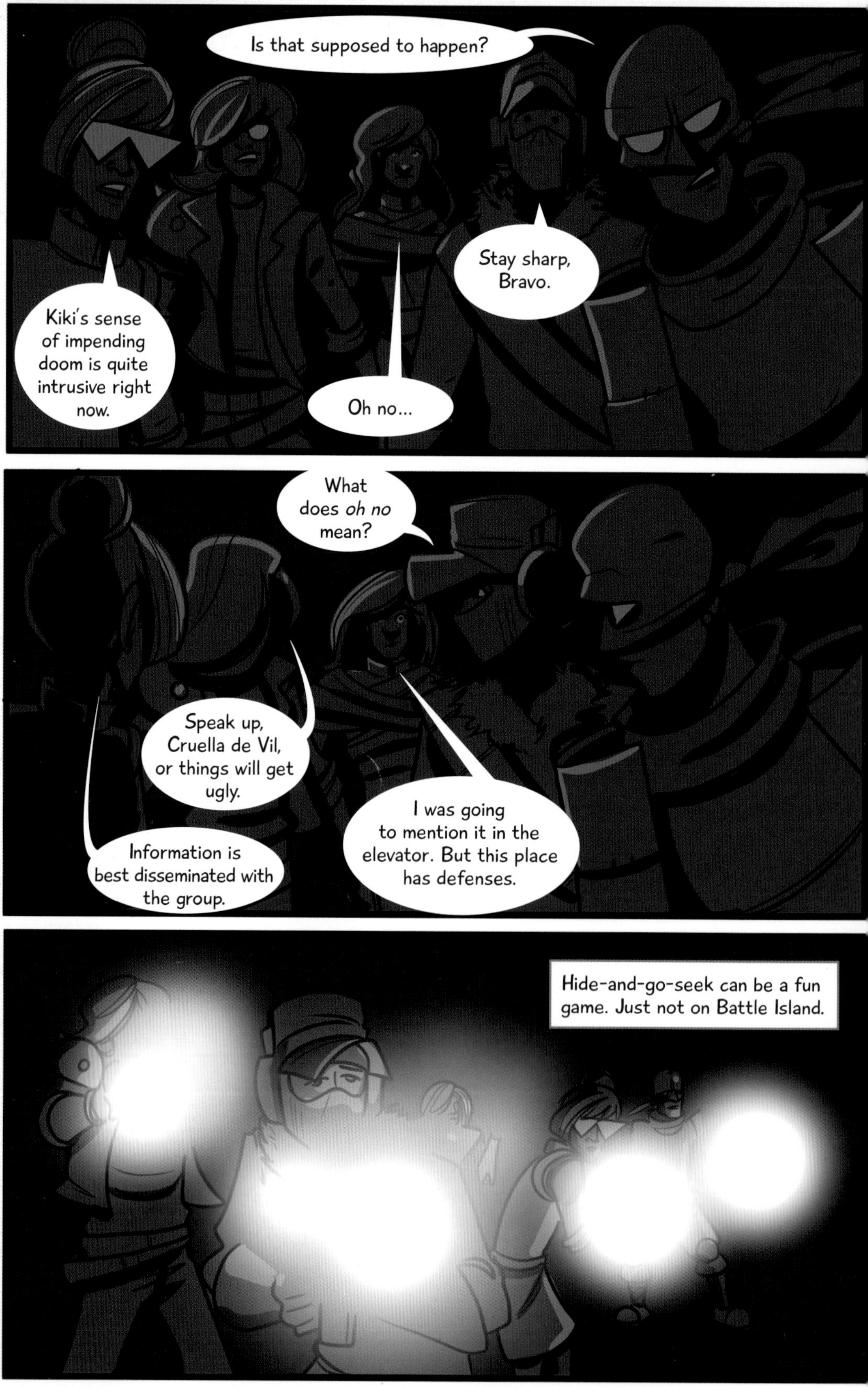
Is that supposed to happen?
Kiki's sense of impending doom is quite intrusive right now.
Oh no...
Stay sharp, Bravo.
What does *oh no* mean?
Speak up, Cruella de Vil, or things will get ugly.
Information is best disseminated with the group.
I was going to mention it in the elevator. But this place has defenses.
Hide-and-go-seek can be a fun game. Just not on Battle Island.

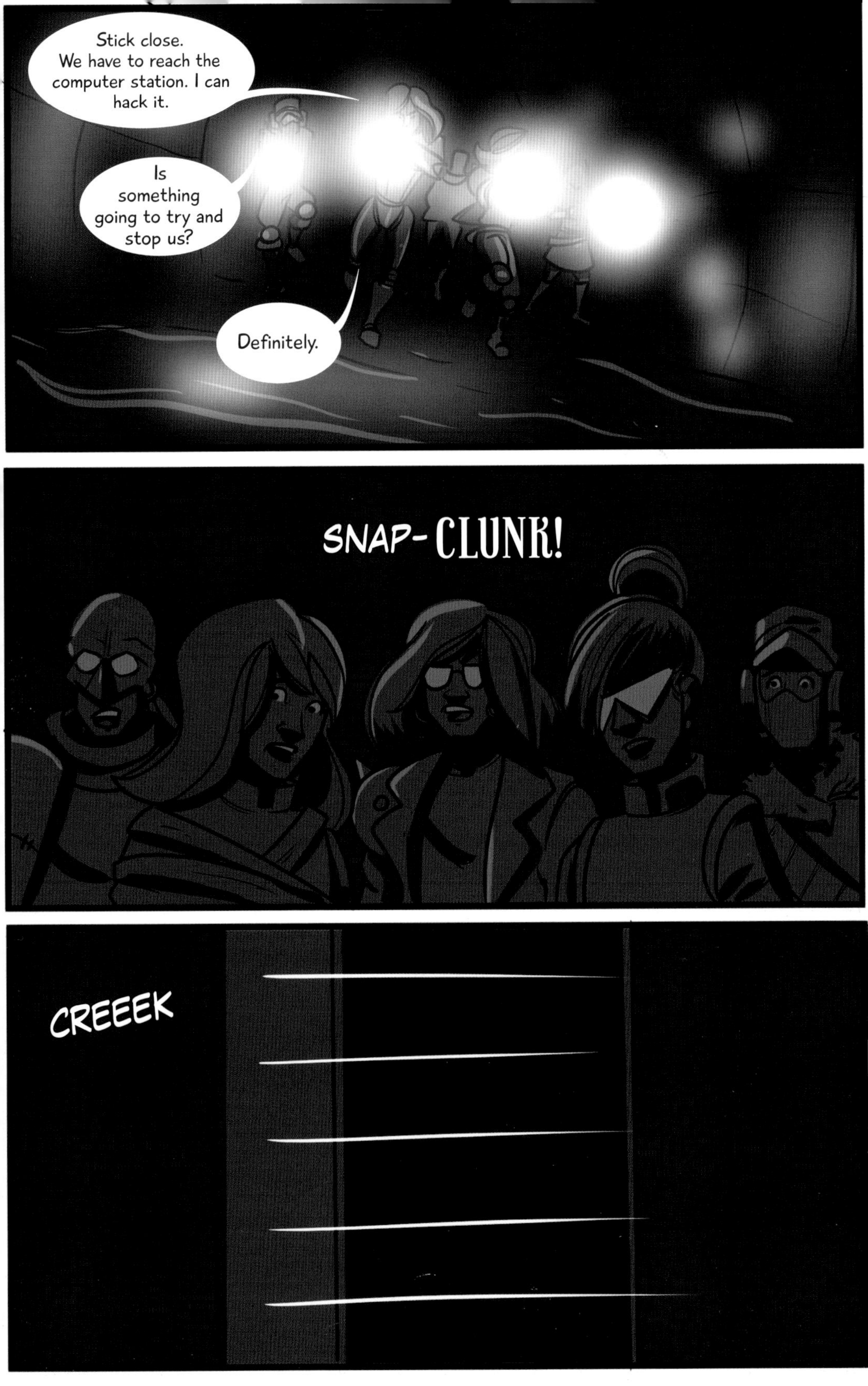
Stick close. We have to reach the computer station. I can hack it.
Is something going to try and stop us?
Definitely.
SNAP- CLUNK!
CREEEK

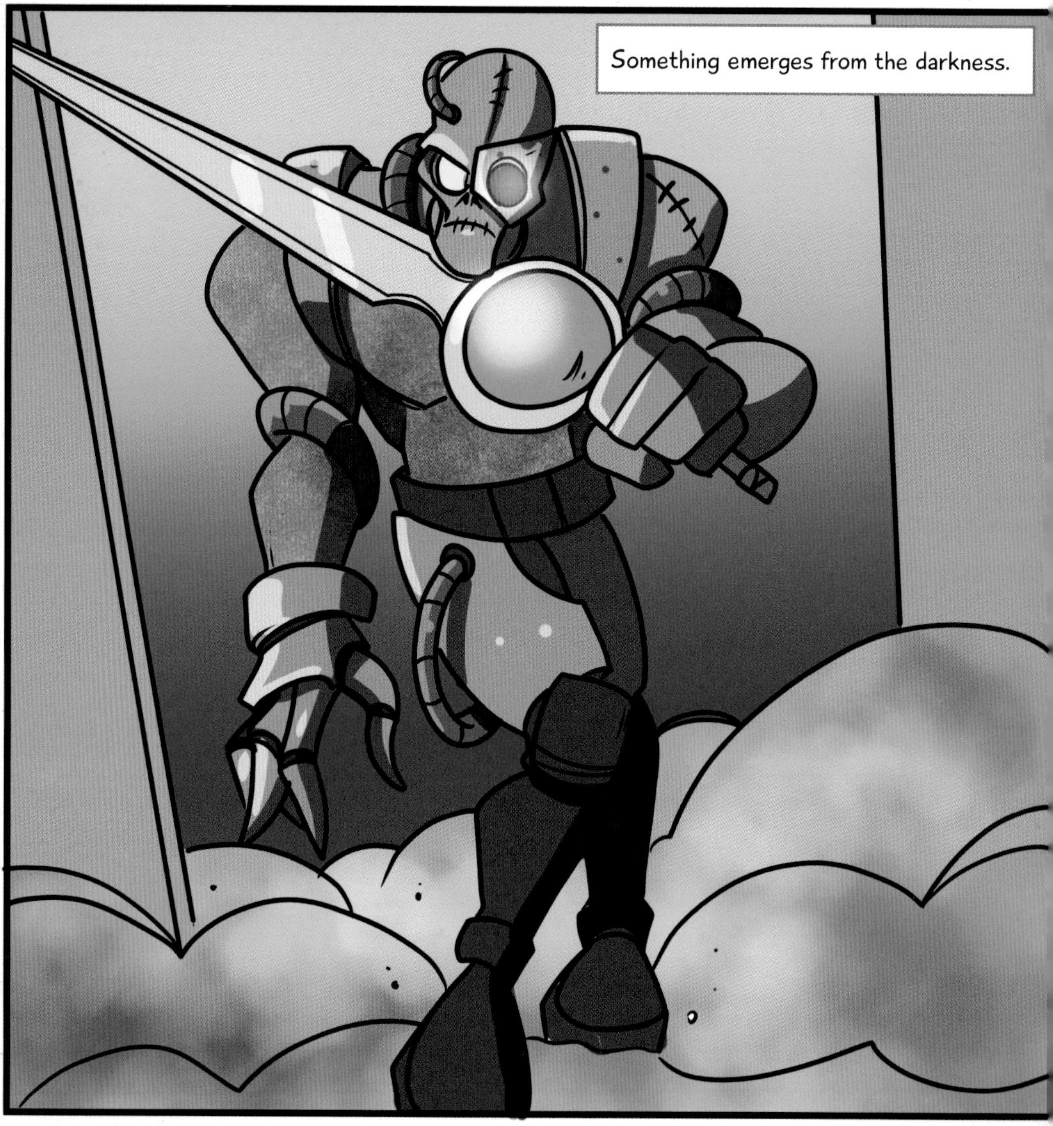
Something emerges from the darkness.

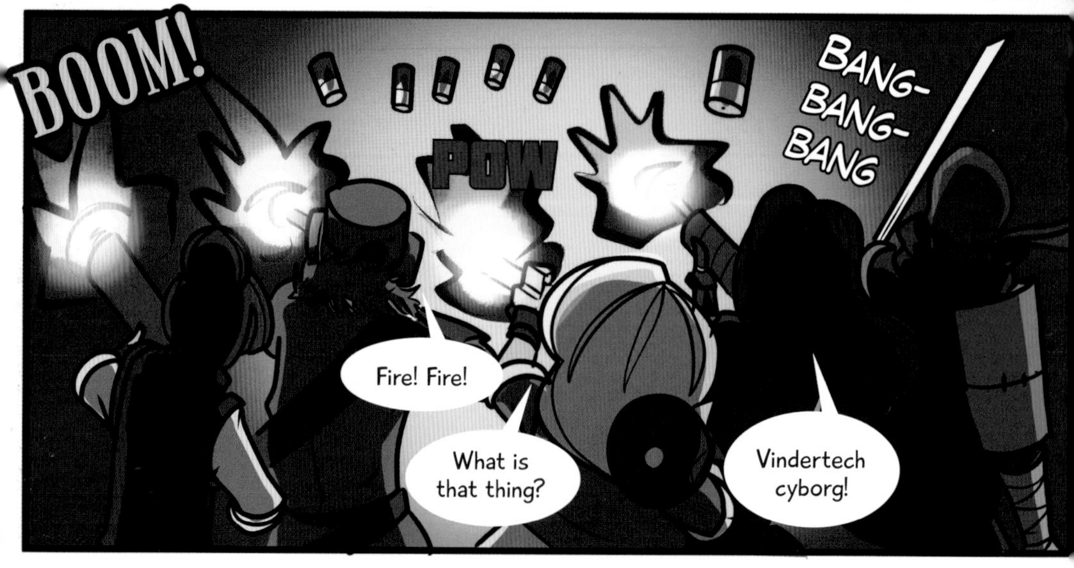
BOOM!
POW
BANG-
BANG-
BANG
Fire! Fire!
What is that thing?
Vindertech cyborg!

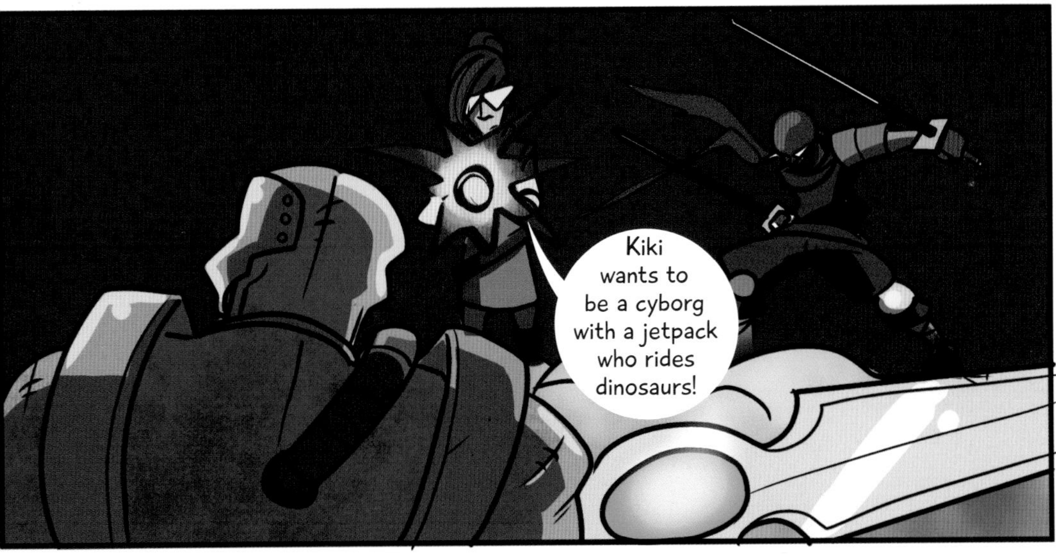
Kiki wants to be a cyborg with a jetpack who rides dinosaurs!

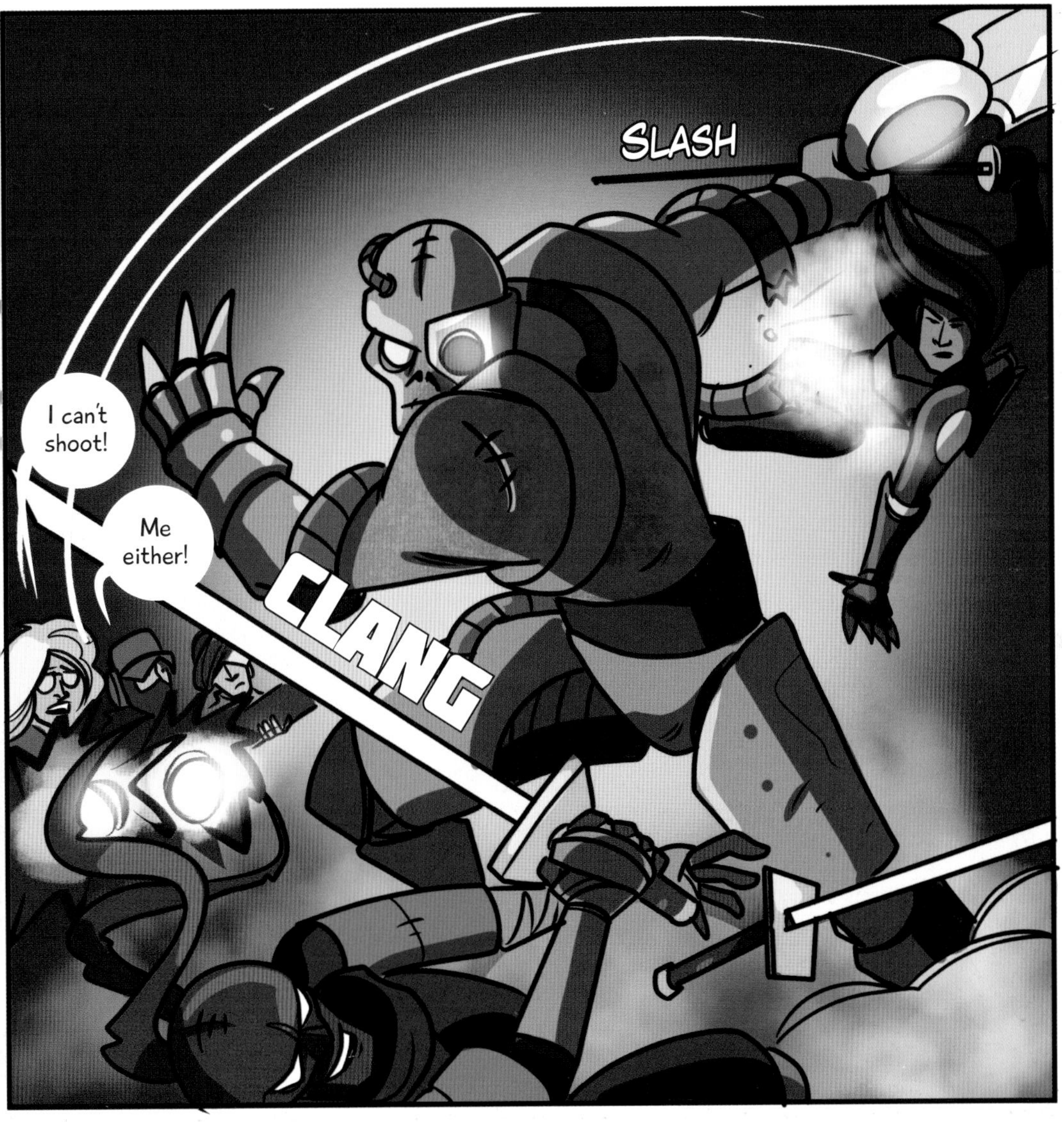
SLASH
I can't shoot!
Me either!
CLANG

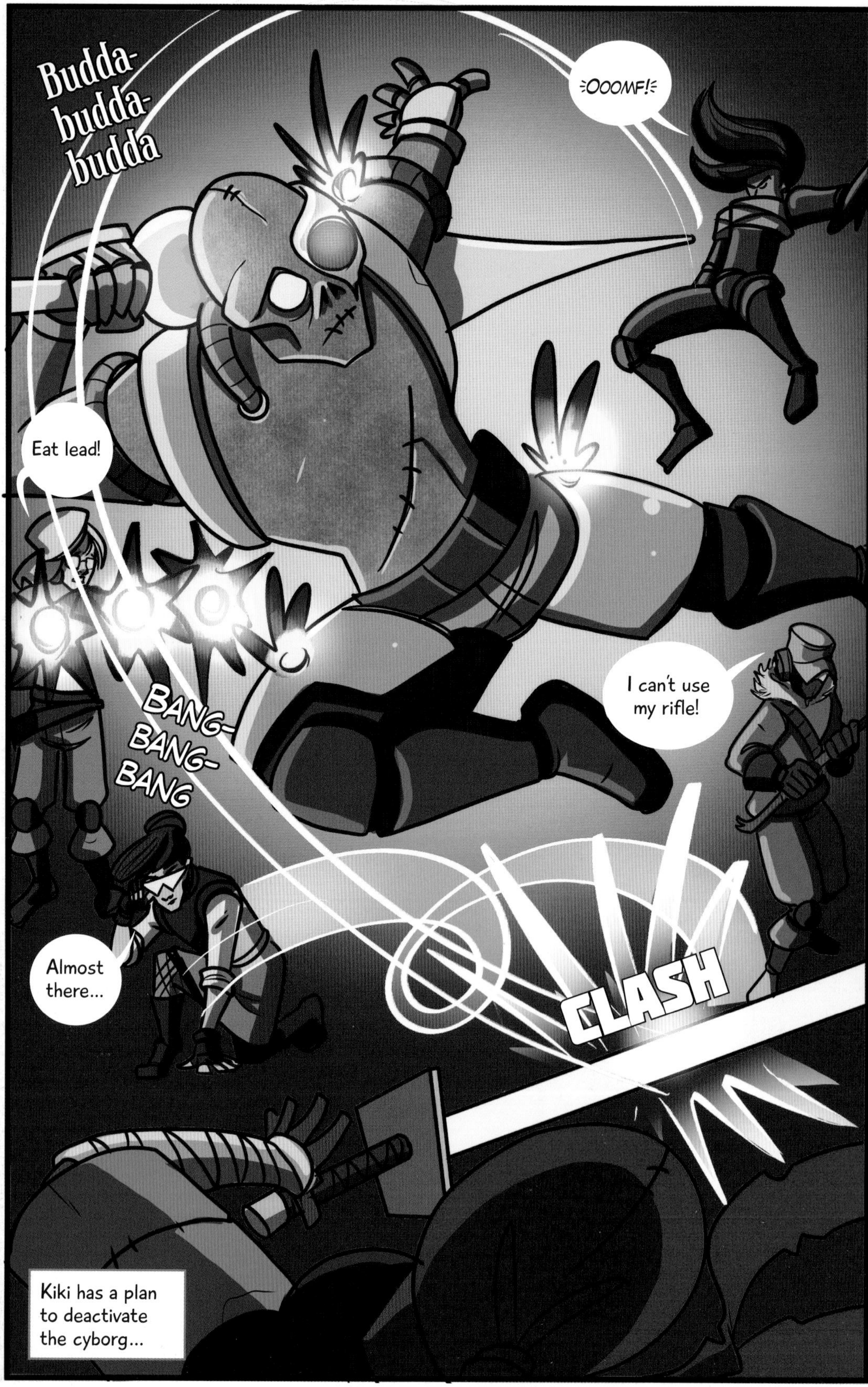
Budda-budda-budda
OOOMF!
Eat lead!
BANG-BANG-BANG
I can't use my rifle!
Almost there...
CLASH
Kiki has a plan to deactivate the cyborg...

For everyone's sake, it had better work.

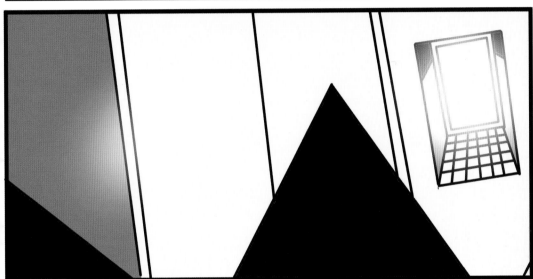

I II III V VIII
XIII XXI
XXXIV LV

One, Two, Three, Five, Eight, Thirteen, Twenty-One, Thirty-Four, Fifty-Five...

Come on Kiki, all of life is mathematics! You know this!

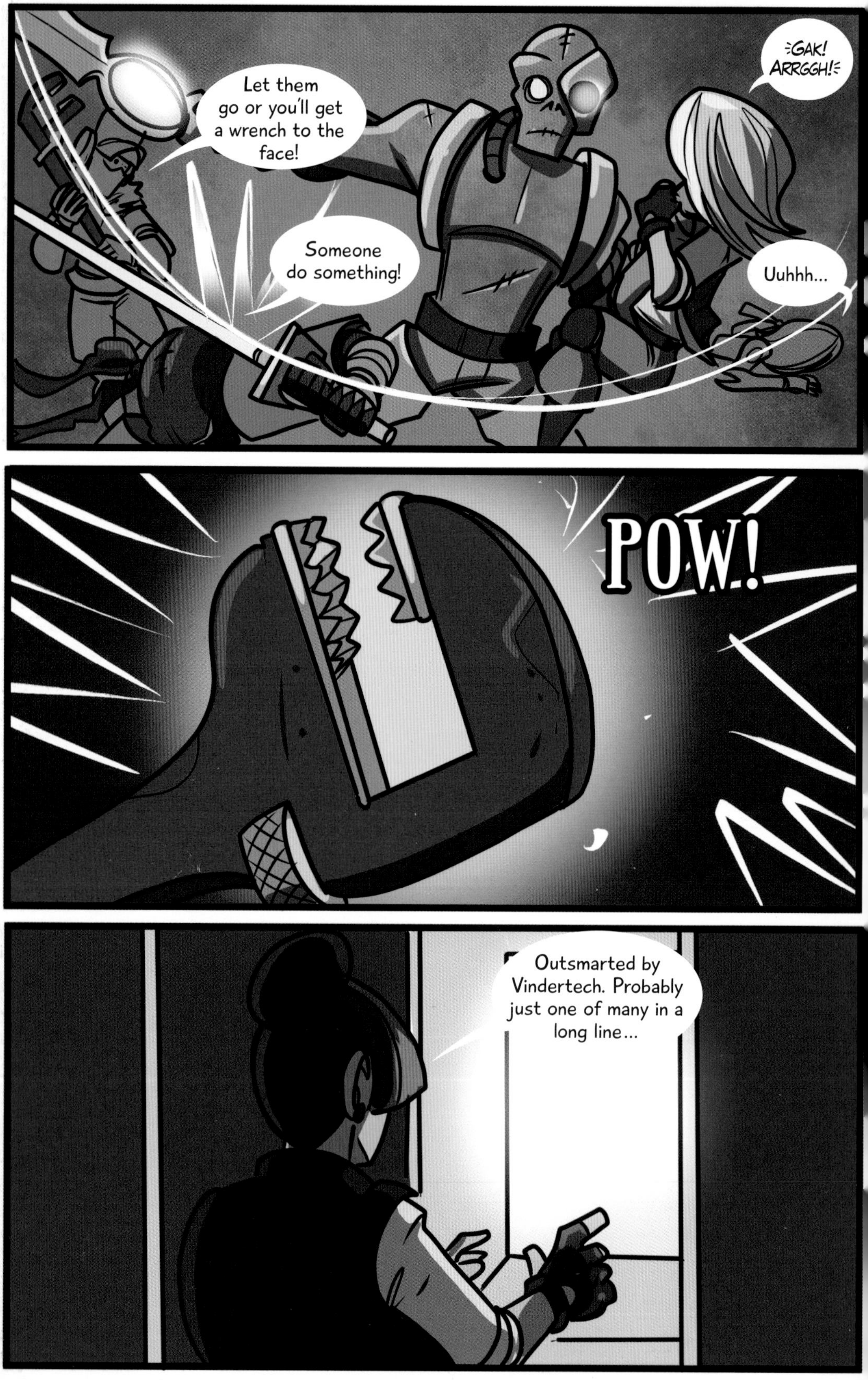
Let them go or you'll get a wrench to the face!
GAK! ARRGGH!
Someone do something!
Uuhhh...
POW!
Outsmarted by Vindertech. Probably just one of many in a long line...

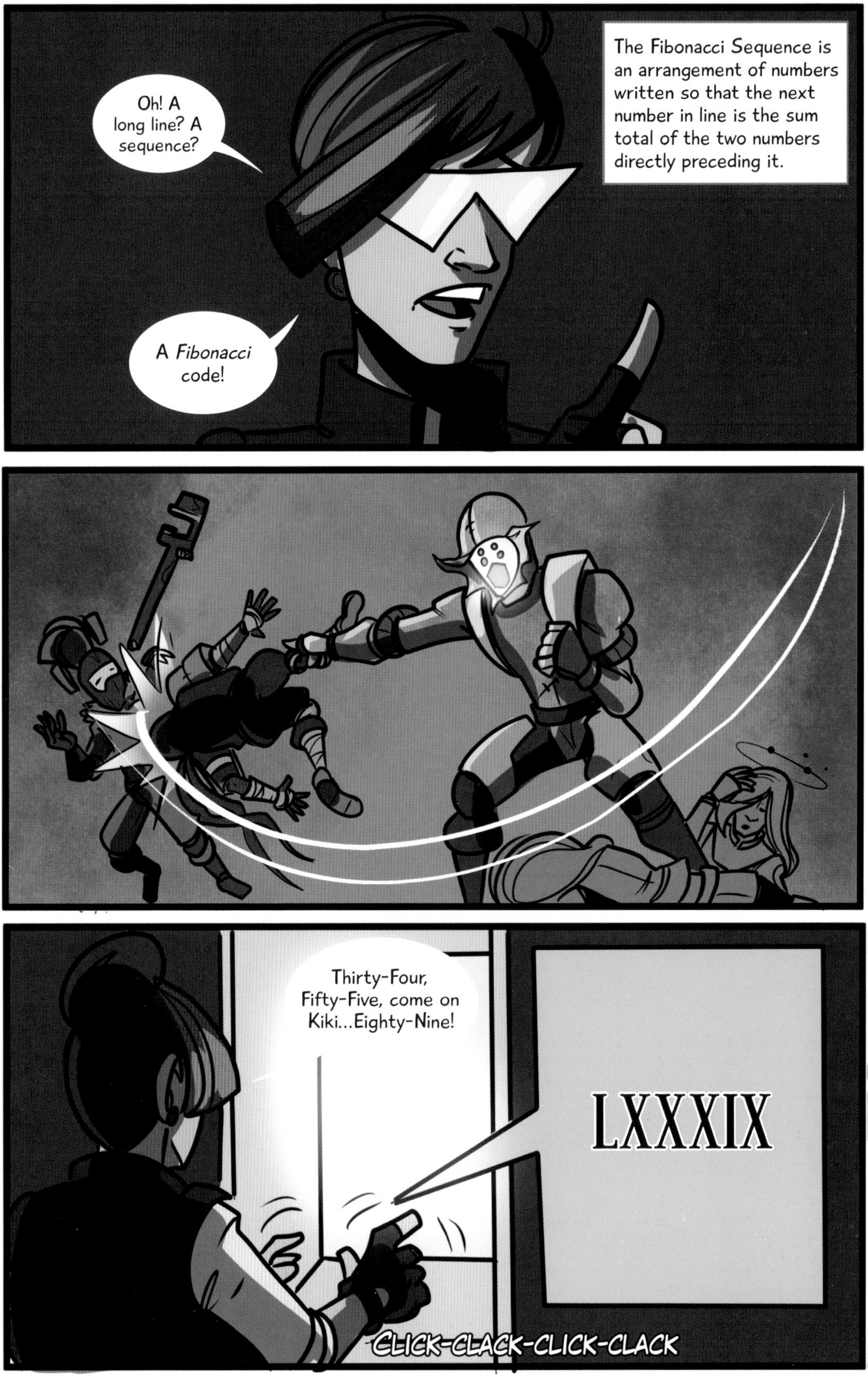
The Fibonacci Sequence is an arrangement of numbers written so that the next number in line is the sum total of the two numbers directly preceding it.
Oh! A long line? A sequence?
A *Fibonacci* code!
Thirty-Four, Fifty-Five, come on Kiki...Eighty-Nine!
LXXXIX
CLICK-CLACK-CLICK-CLACK

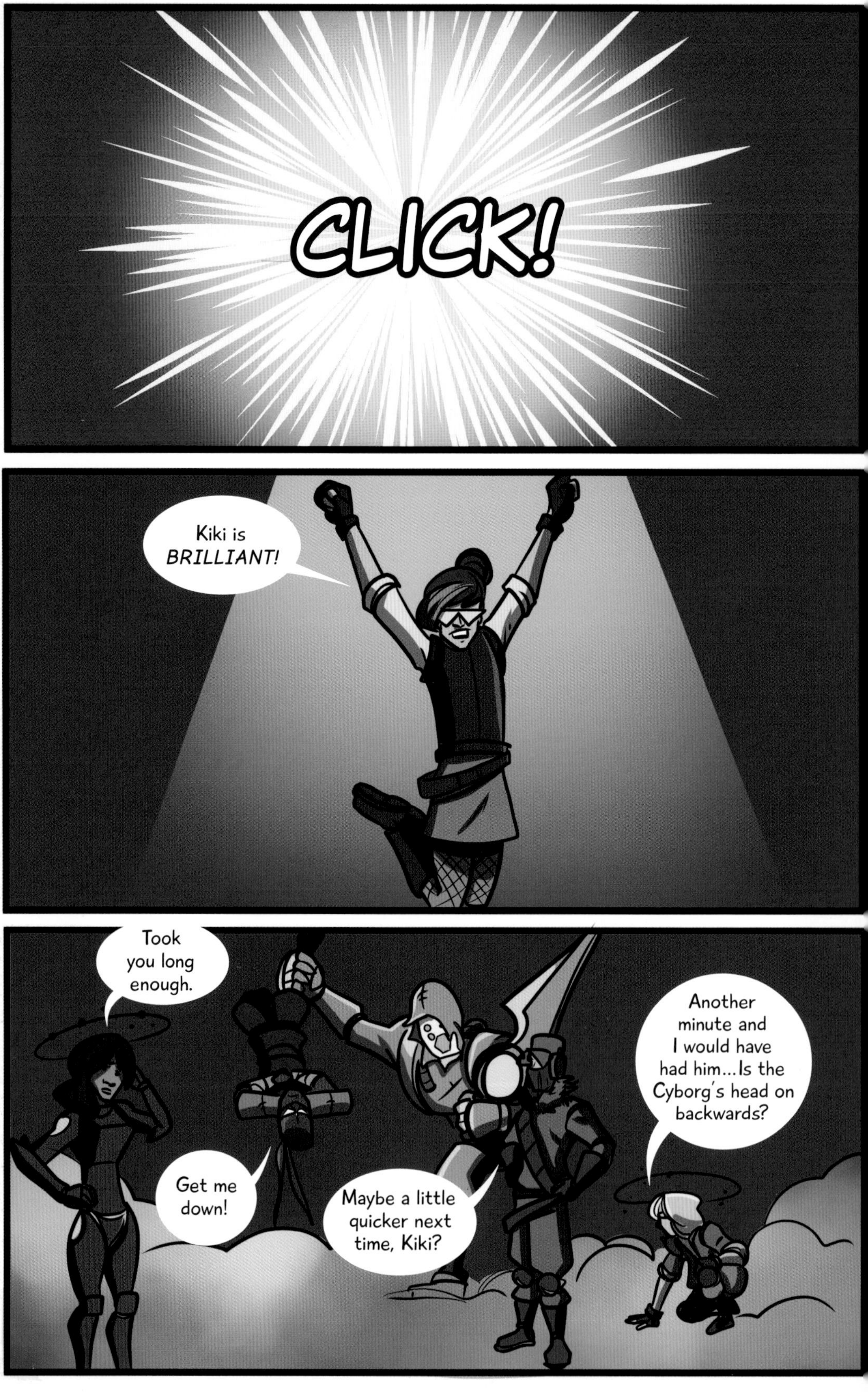

CLICK!
Kiki is *BRILLIANT!*
Took you long enough.
Get me down!
Maybe a little quicker next time, Kiki?
Another minute and I would have had him...Is the Cyborg's head on backwards?

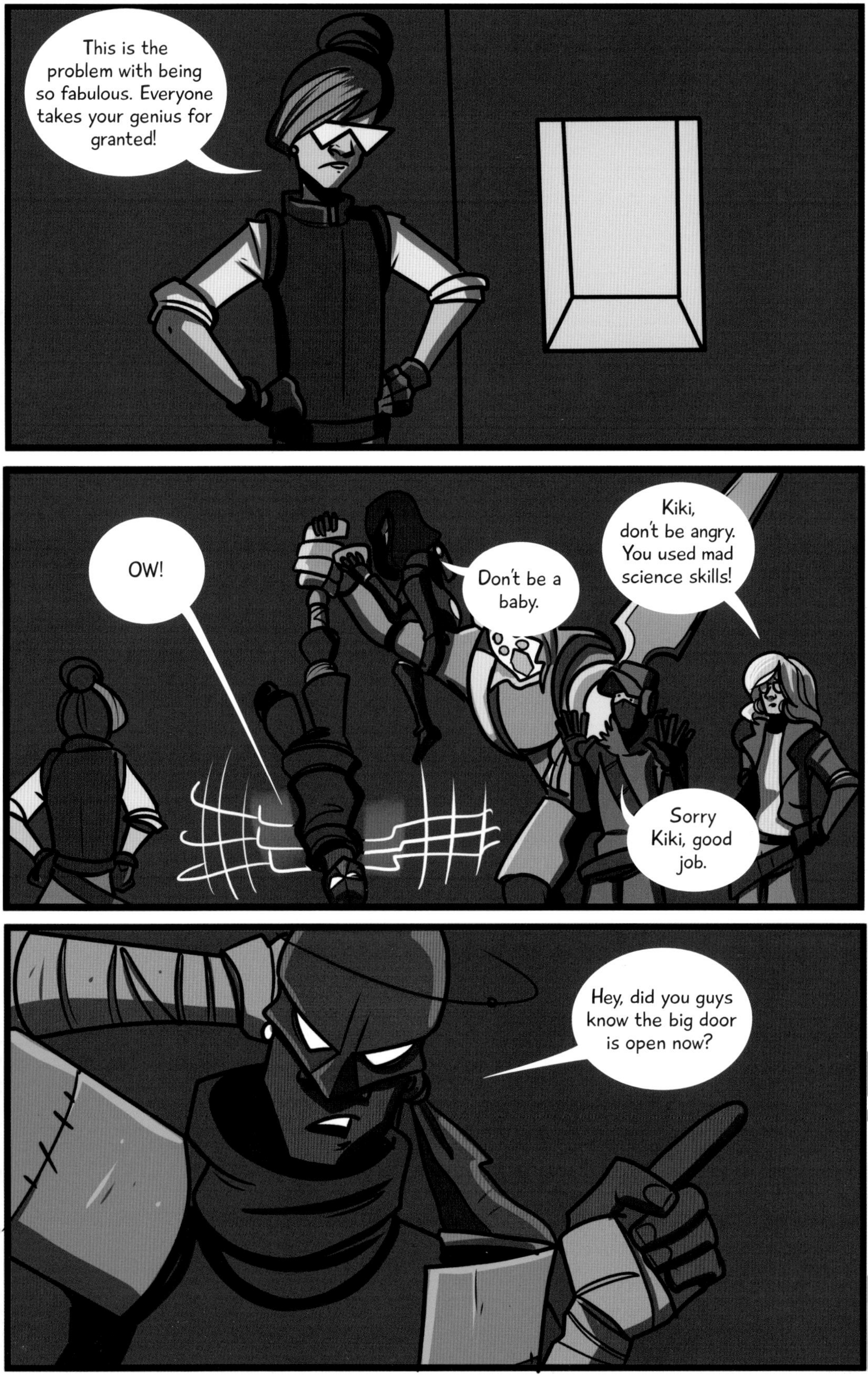
This is the problem with being so fabulous. Everyone takes your genius for granted!
Kiki, don't be angry. You used mad science skills!
OW!
Don't be a baby.
Sorry Kiki, good job.
Hey, did you guys know the big door is open now?

The way is clear.

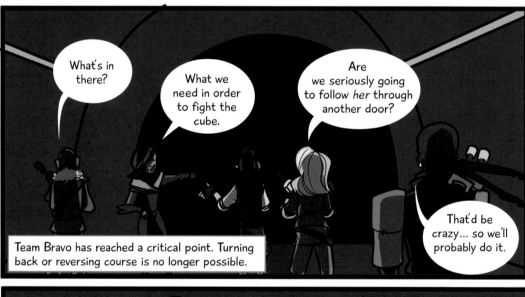

What's in there?

What we need in order to fight the cube.

Are we seriously going to follow *her* through another door?

That'd be crazy... so we'll probably do it.

Team Bravo has reached a critical point. Turning back or reversing course is no longer possible.

You guys fought dinosaurs, fell out of the sky, were shot at, blown up, and went hand-to-hand with a freaky robot monster—

Are you really telling me you're not a little curious about what we're after?

I hate it when she's right.

Let's hope "curiosity killed the cat" doesn't apply to what happens next.

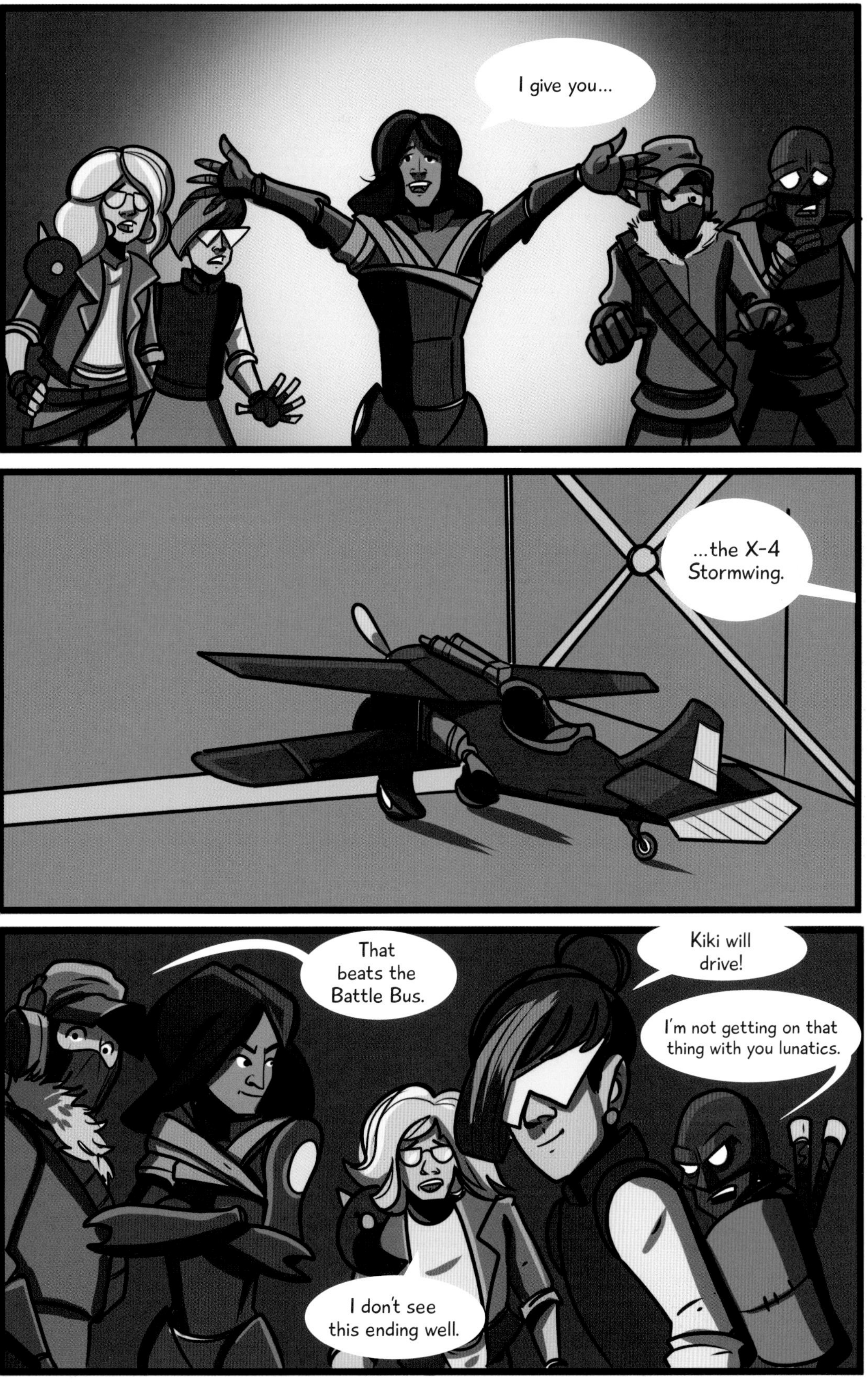
I give you...
...the X-4 Stormwing.
That beats the Battle Bus.
Kiki will drive!
I'm not getting on that thing with you lunatics.
I don't see this ending well.

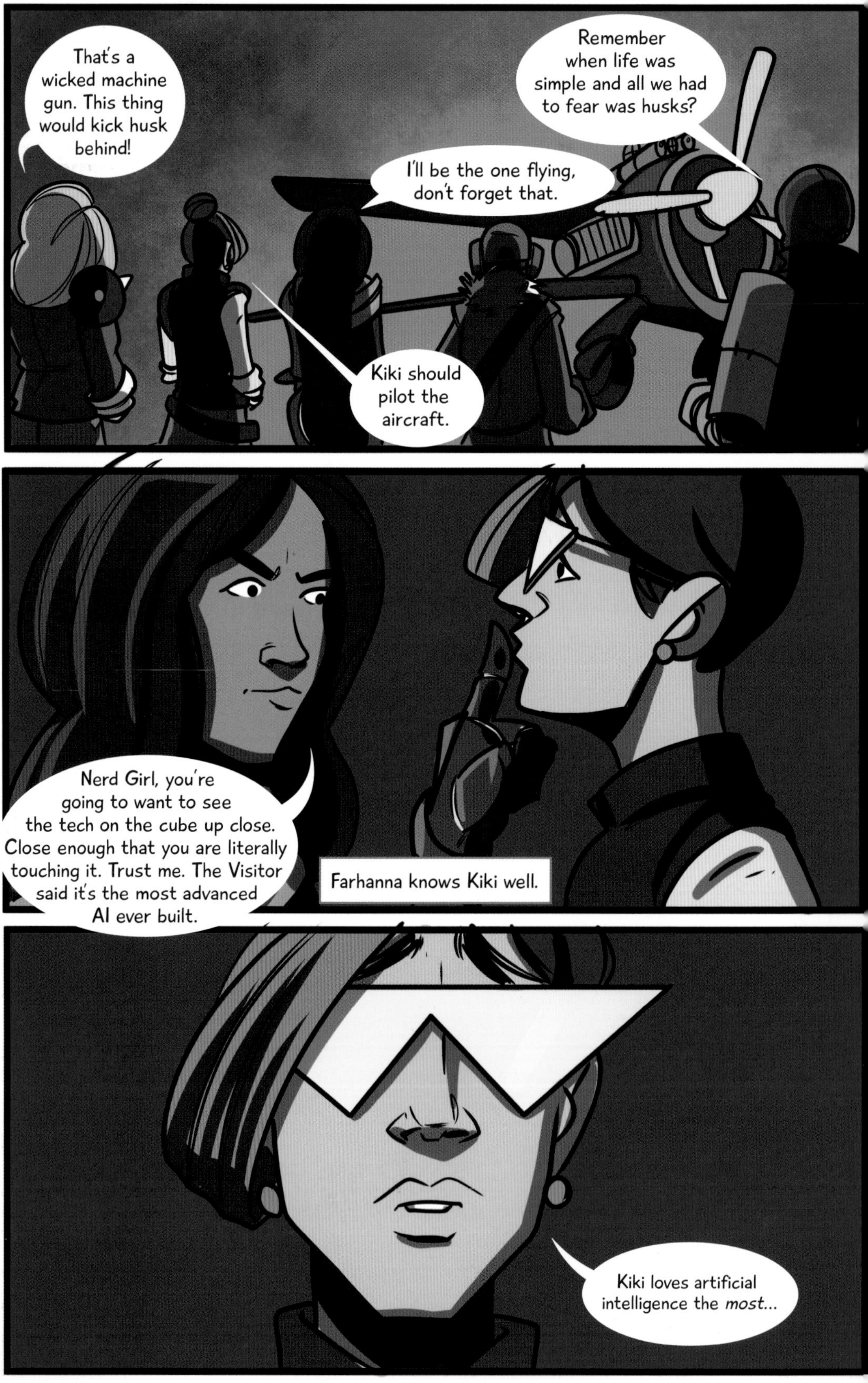
That's a wicked machine gun. This thing would kick husk behind!
Remember when life was simple and all we had to fear was husks?
I'll be the one flying, don't forget that.
Kiki should pilot the aircraft.
Nerd Girl, you're going to want to see the tech on the cube up close. Close enough that you are literally touching it. Trust me. The Visitor said it's the most advanced AI ever built.
Farhanna knows Kiki well.
Kiki loves artificial intelligence the *most*...

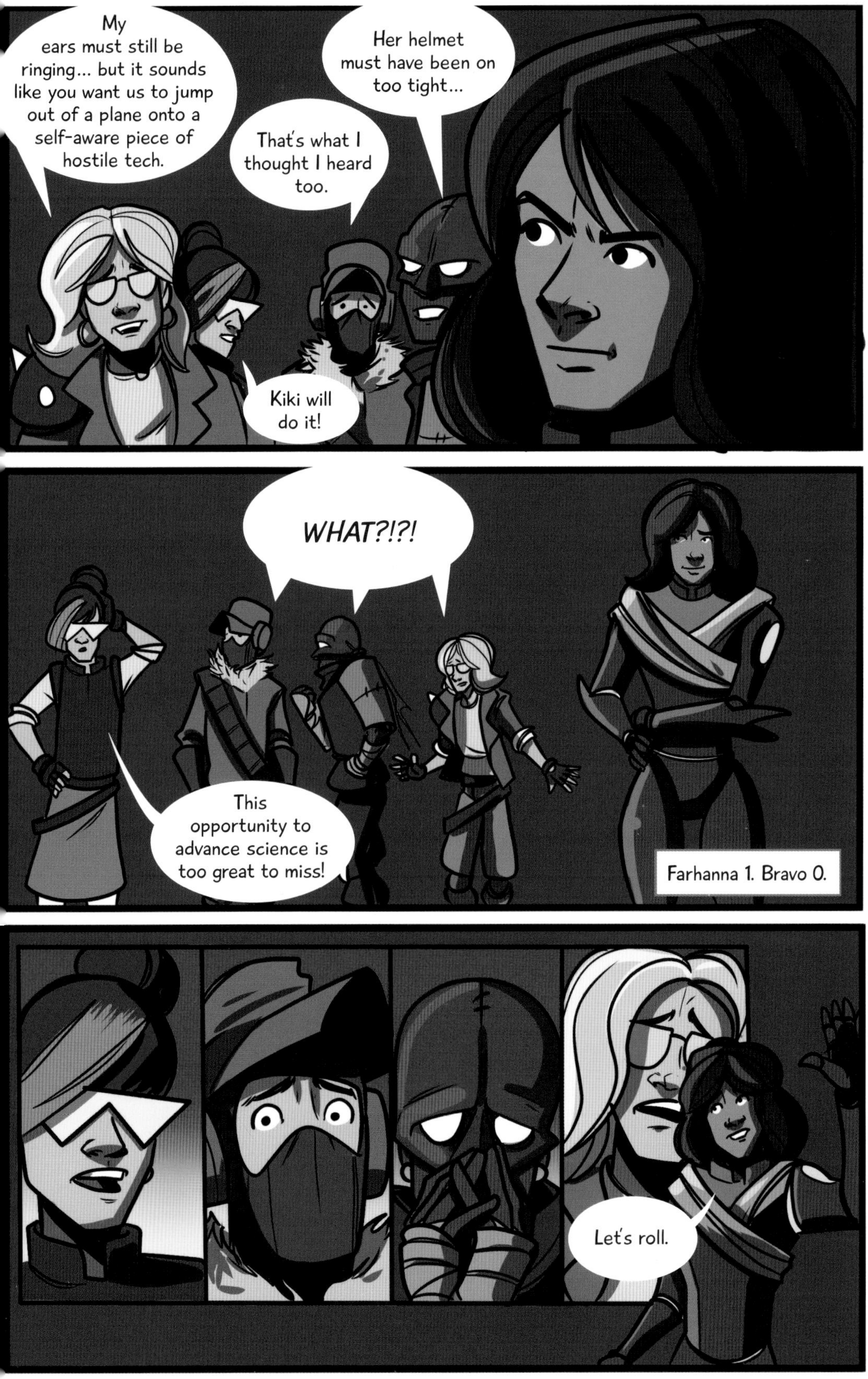
My ears must still be ringing... but it sounds like you want us to jump out of a plane onto a self-aware piece of hostile tech.
That's what I thought I heard too.
Her helmet must have been on too tight...
Kiki will do it!
WHAT?!?!
This opportunity to advance science is too great to miss!
Farhanna 1. Bravo 0.
Let's roll.

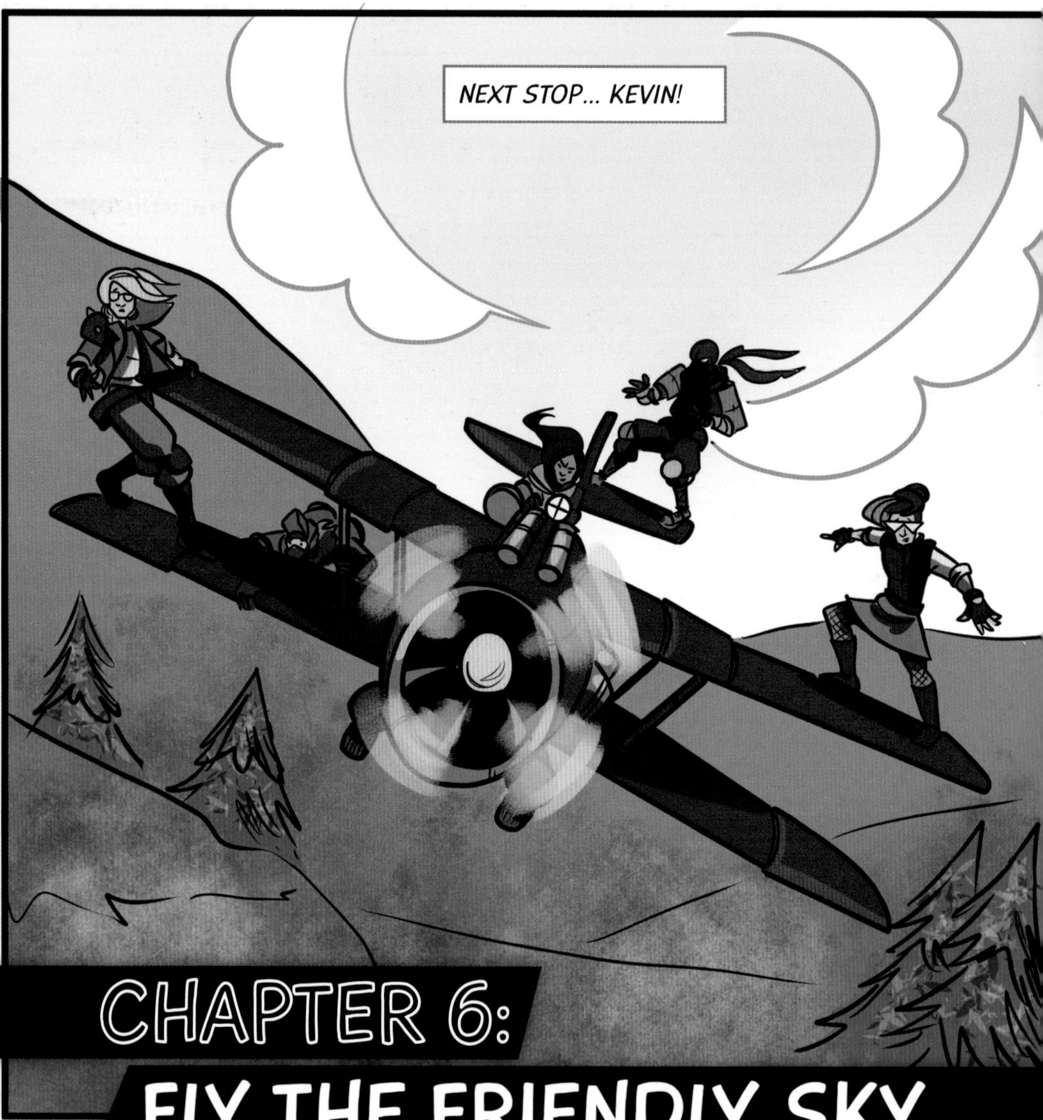
NEXT STOP... KEVIN!

CHAPTER 6: FLY THE FRIENDLY SKY

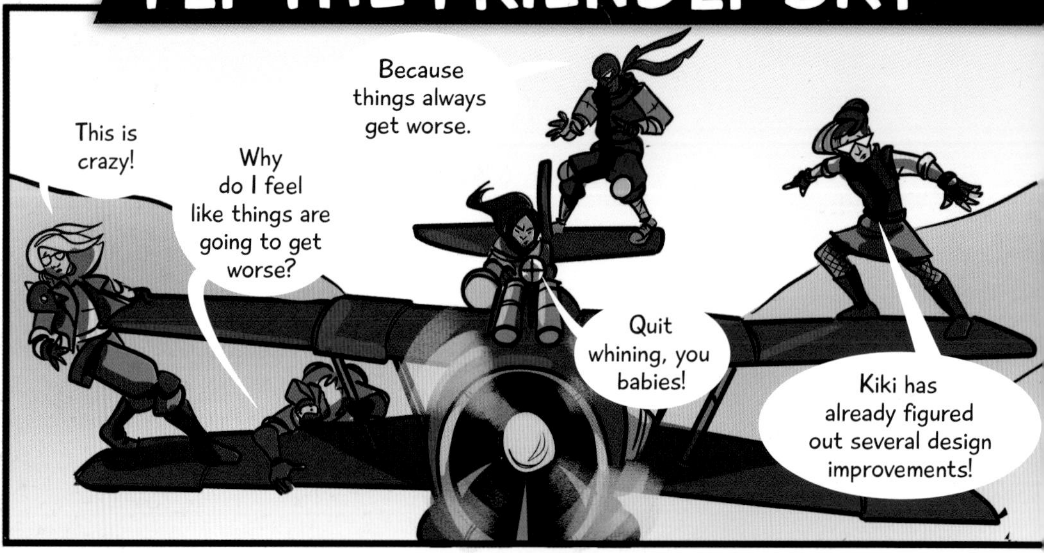
This is crazy!
Why do I feel like things are going to get worse?
Because things always get worse.
Quit whining, you babies!
Kiki has already figured out several design improvements!

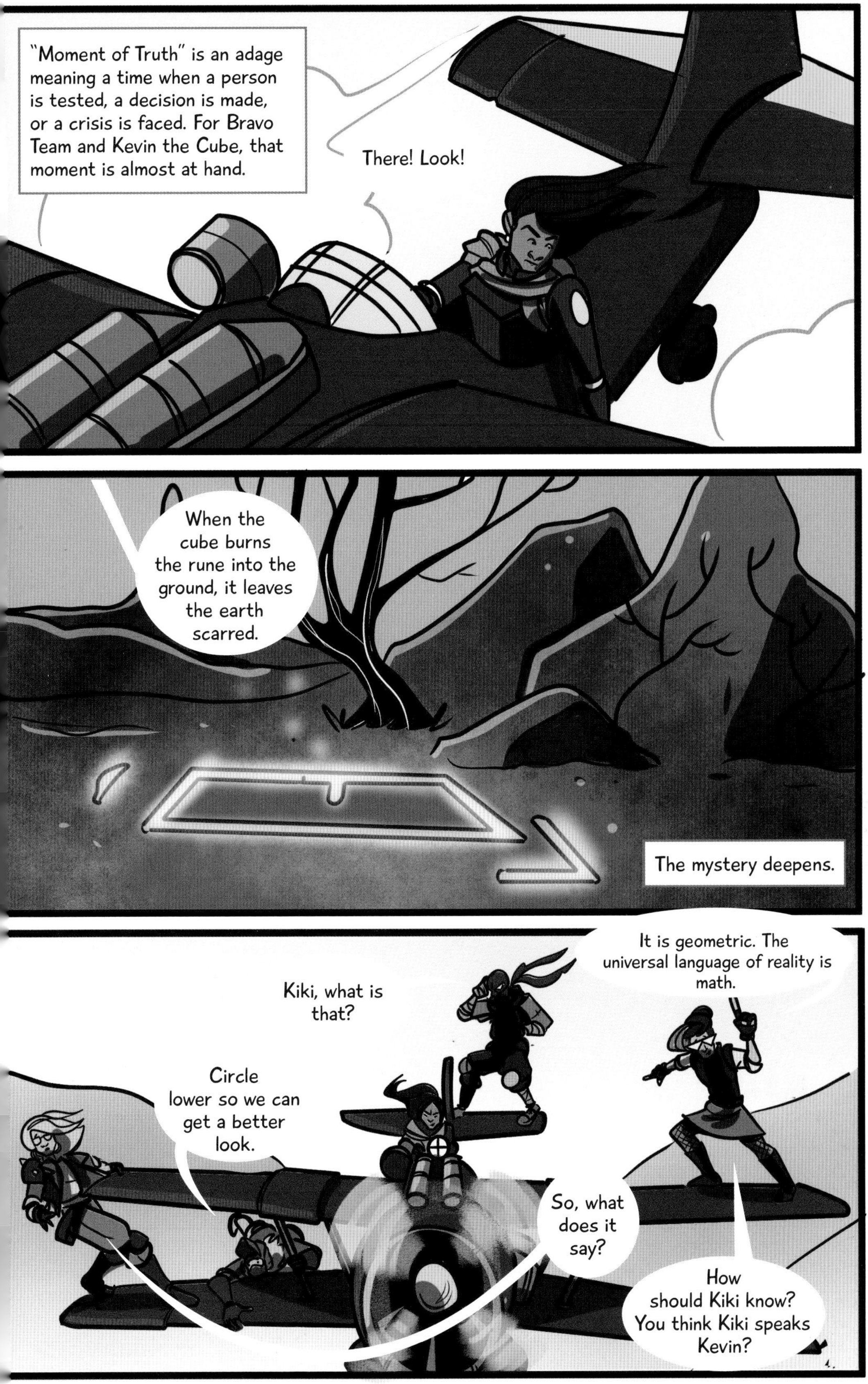
"Moment of Truth" is an adage meaning a time when a person is tested, a decision is made, or a crisis is faced. For Bravo Team and Kevin the Cube, that moment is almost at hand.
There! Look!
When the cube burns the rune into the ground, it leaves the earth scarred.
The mystery deepens.
Kiki, what is that?
It is geometric. The universal language of reality is math.
Circle lower so we can get a better look.
So, what does it say?
How should Kiki know? You think Kiki speaks Kevin?

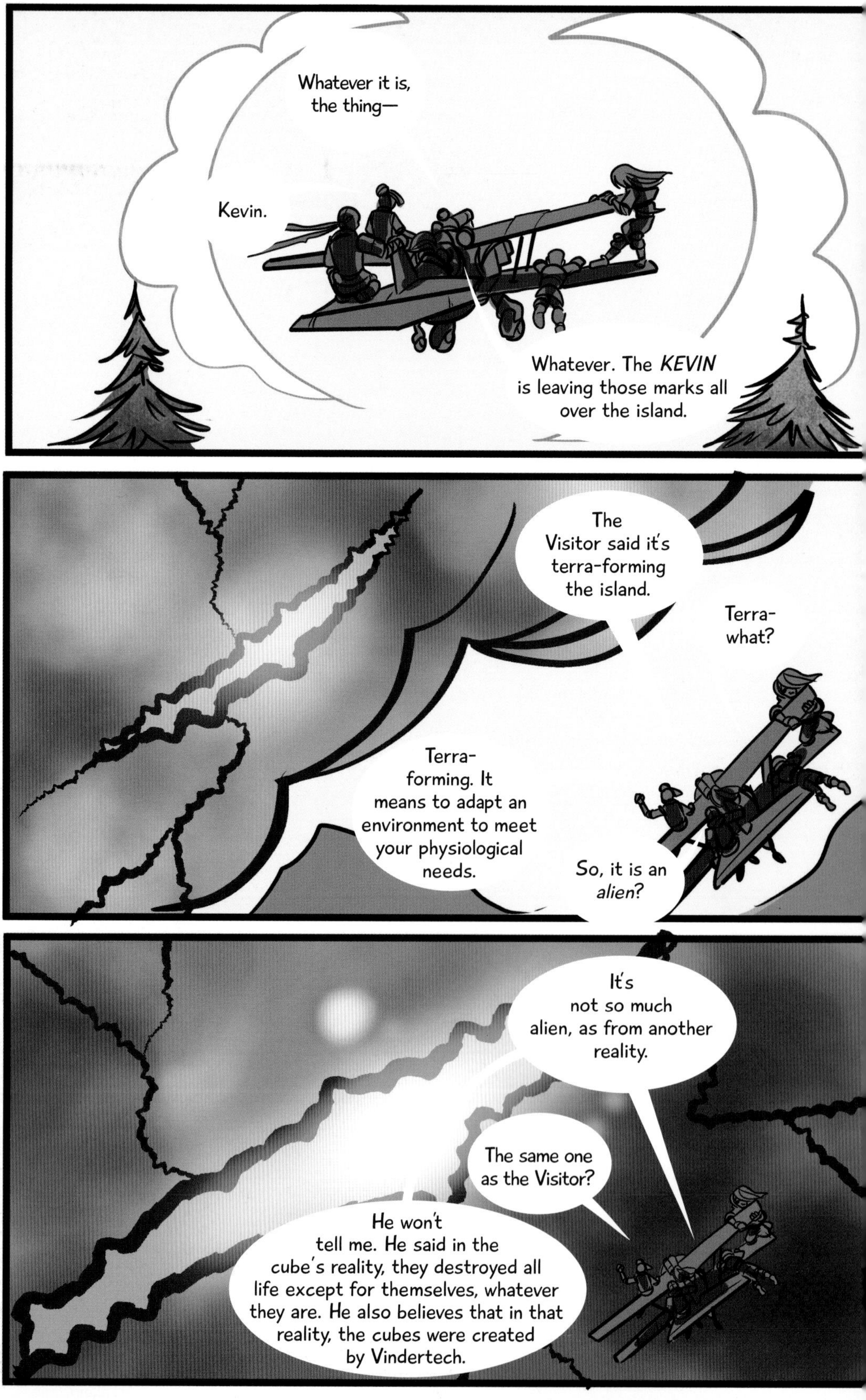
Whatever it is, the thing—
Kevin.
Whatever. The *KEVIN* is leaving those marks all over the island.
The Visitor said it's terra-forming the island.
Terra-what?
Terra-forming. It means to adapt an environment to meet your physiological needs.
So, it is an *alien*?
It's not so much alien, as from another reality.
The same one as the Visitor?
He won't tell me. He said in the cube's reality, they destroyed all life except for themselves, whatever they are. He also believes that in that reality, the cubes were created by Vindertech.

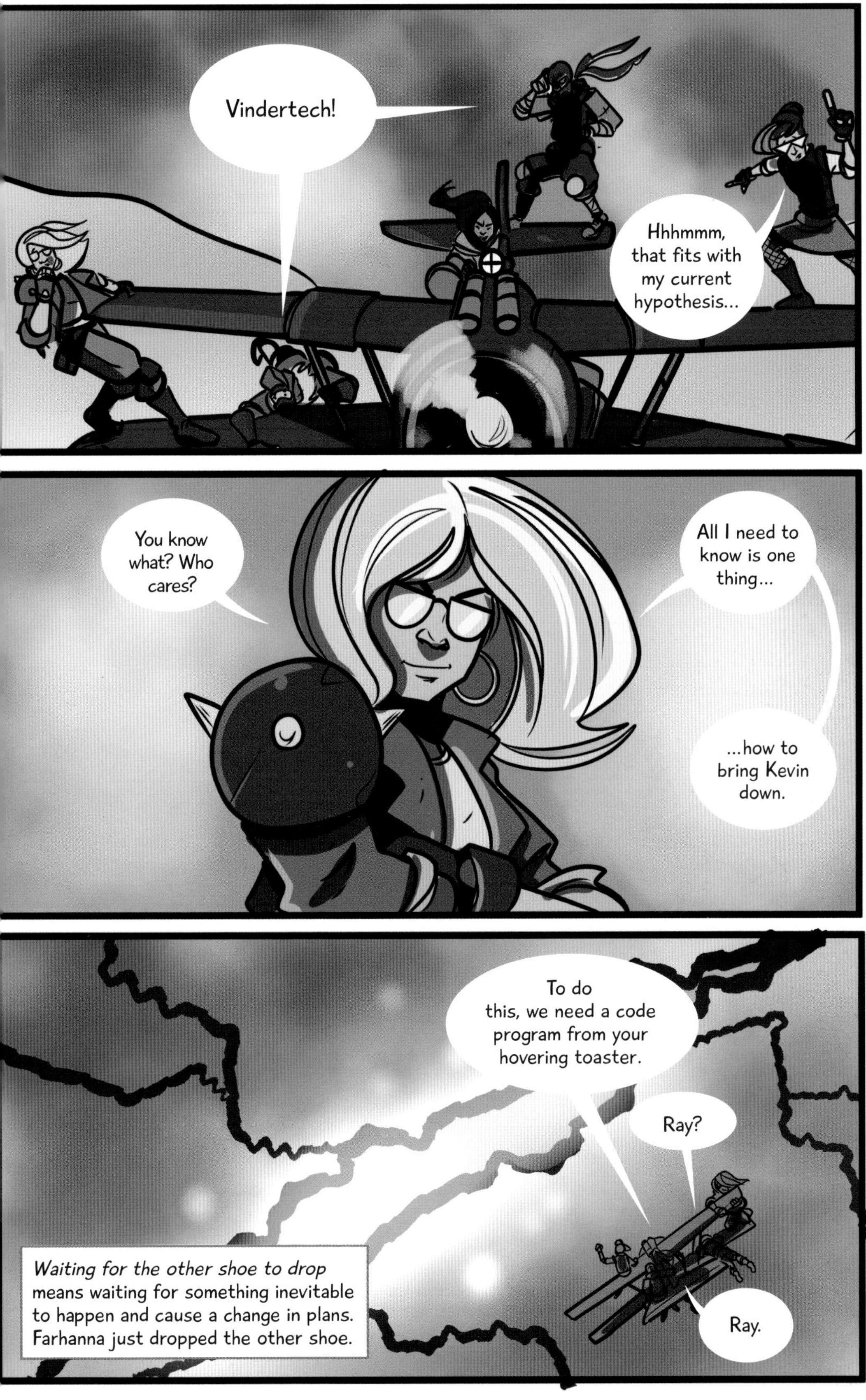
Vindertech!
Hhhmmm, that fits with my current hypothesis...
You know what? Who cares?
All I need to know is one thing...
...how to bring Kevin down.
To do this, we need a code program from your hovering toaster.
Ray?
Ray.
Waiting for the other shoe to drop means waiting for something inevitable to happen and cause a change in plans. Farhanna just dropped the other shoe.

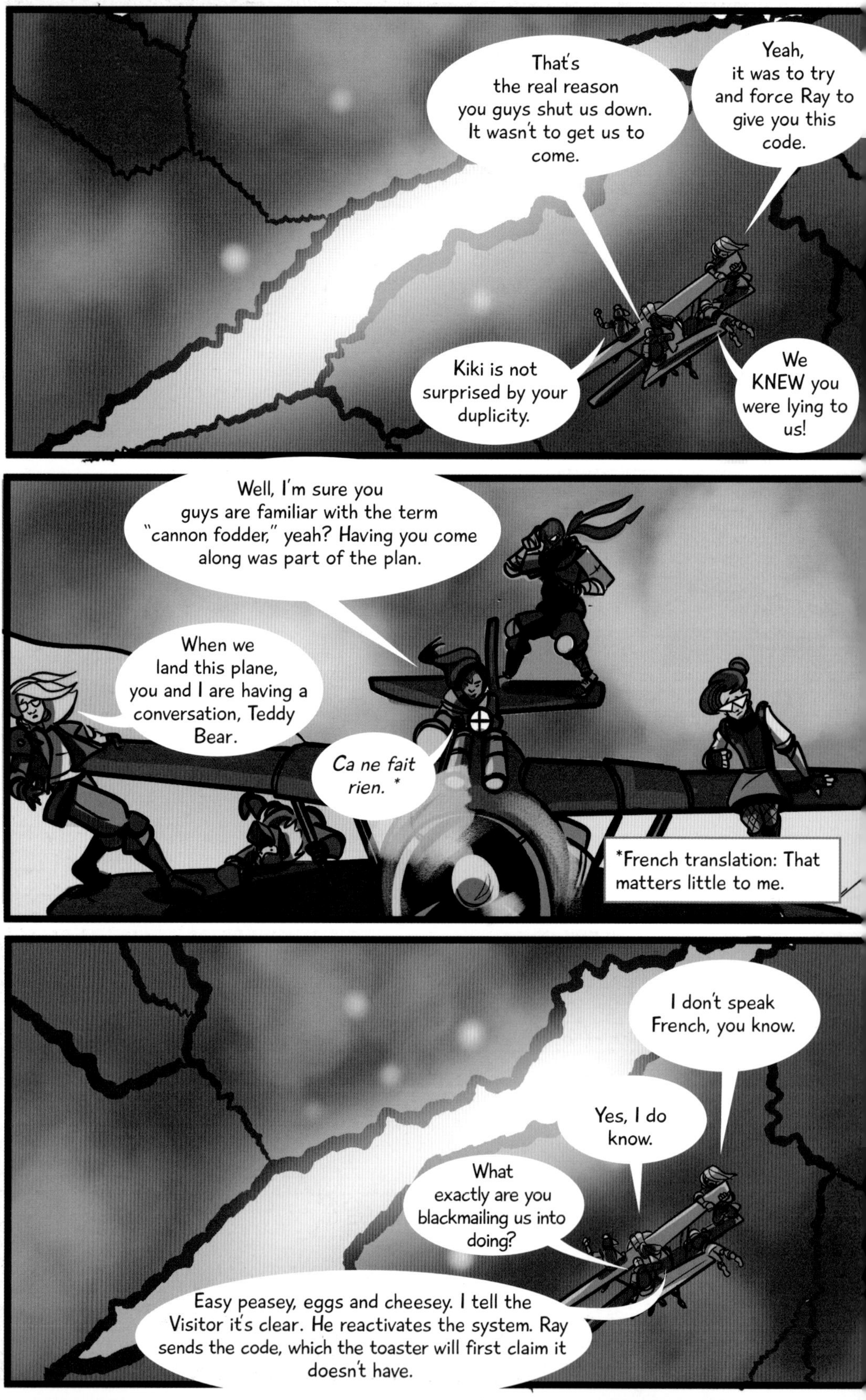
That's the real reason you guys shut us down. It wasn't to get us to come.
Yeah, it was to try and force Ray to give you this code.
Kiki is not surprised by your duplicity.
We KNEW you were lying to us!
Well, I'm sure you guys are familiar with the term "cannon fodder," yeah? Having you come along was part of the plan.
When we land this plane, you and I are having a conversation, Teddy Bear.
Ca ne fait rien. *
*French translation: That matters little to me.
I don't speak French, you know.
Yes, I do know.
What exactly are you blackmailing us into doing?
Easy peasey, eggs and cheesey. I tell the Visitor it's clear. He reactivates the system. Ray sends the code, which the toaster will first claim it doesn't have.

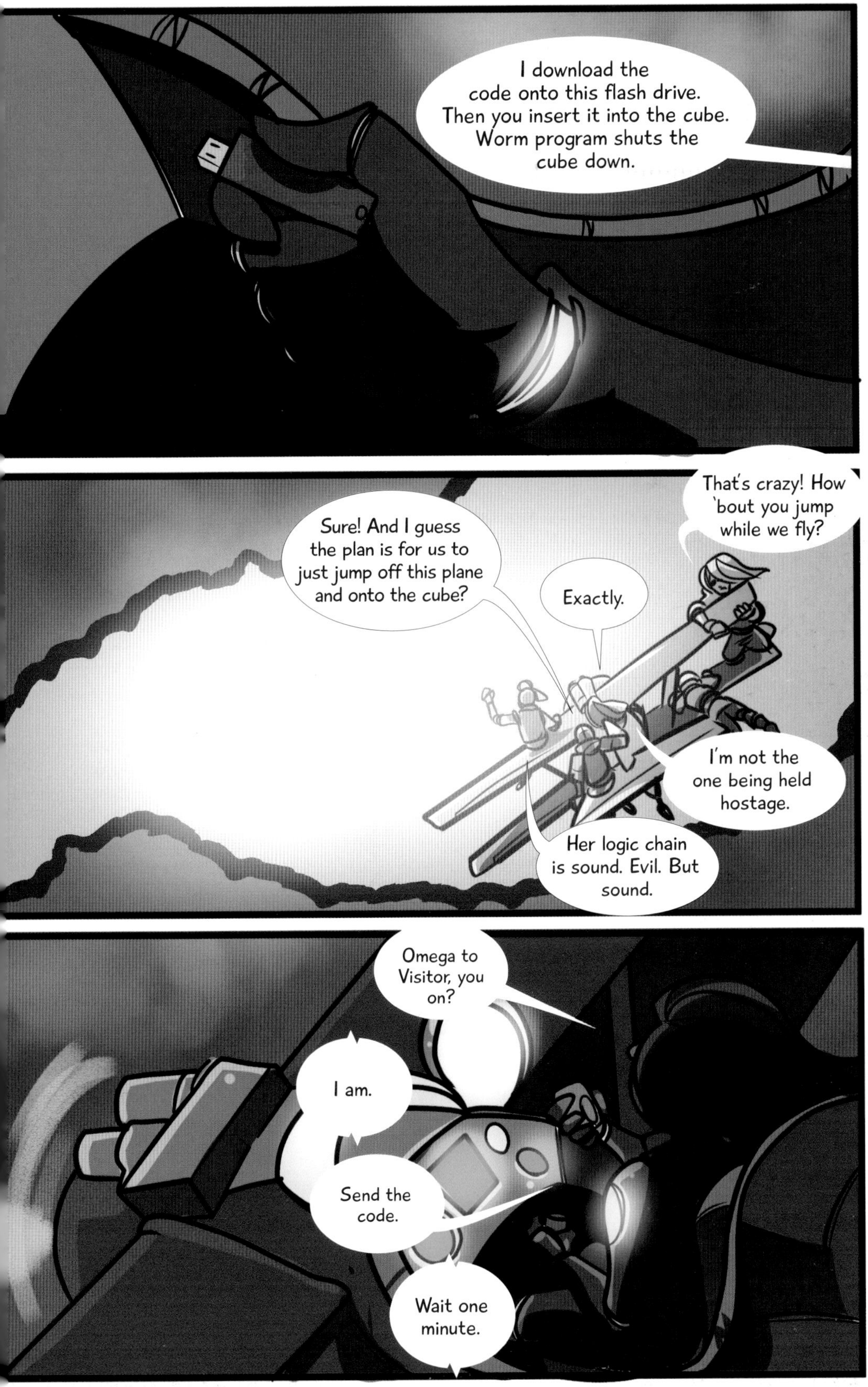
I download the code onto this flash drive. Then you insert it into the cube. Worm program shuts the cube down.
Sure! And I guess the plan is for us to just jump off this plane and onto the cube?
Exactly.
That's crazy! How 'bout you jump while we fly?
I'm not the one being held hostage.
Her logic chain is sound. Evil. But sound.
Omega to Visitor, you on?
I am.
Send the code.
Wait one minute.

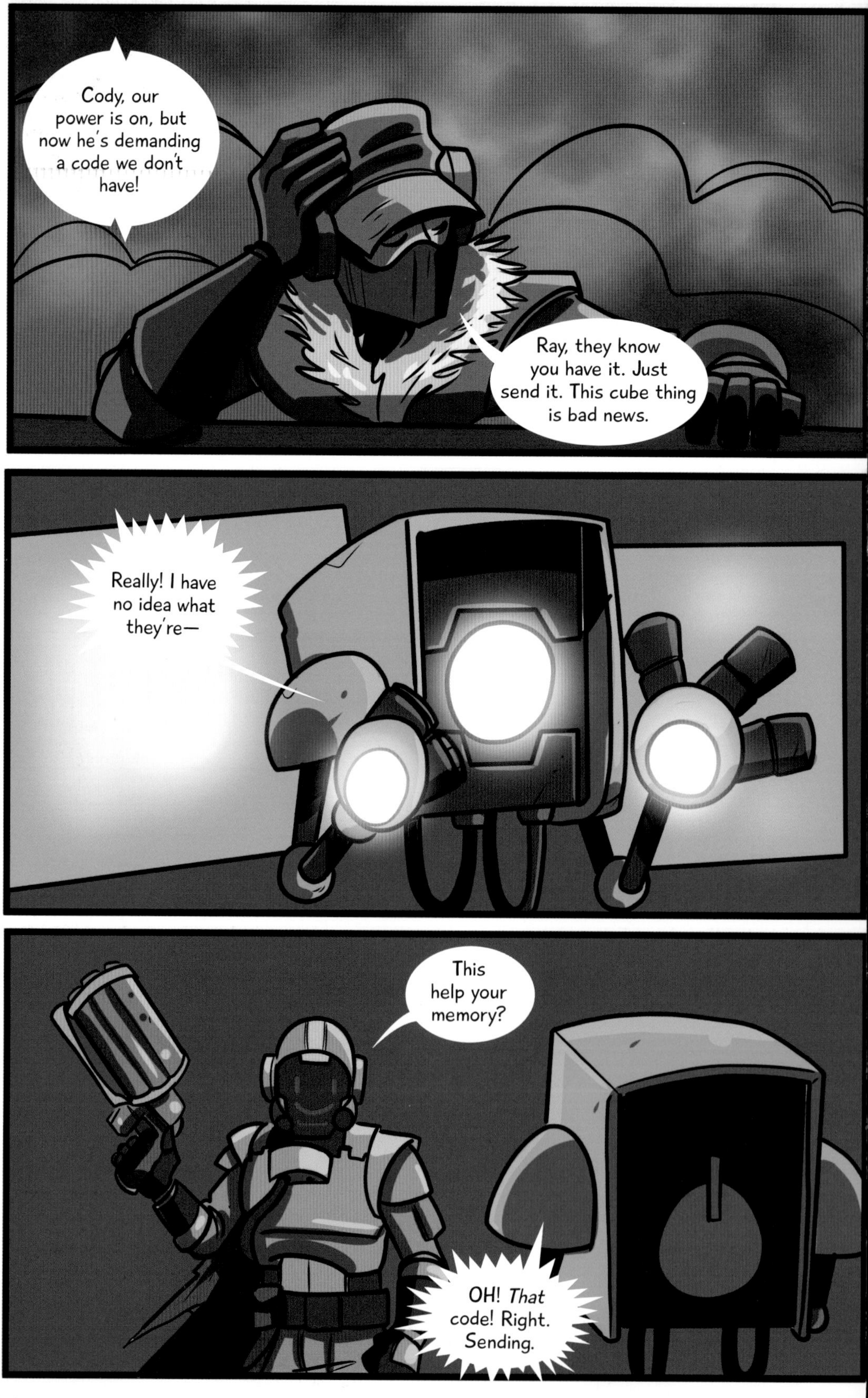
Cody, our power is on, but now he's demanding a code we don't have!
Ray, they know you have it. Just send it. This cube thing is bad news.
Really! I have no idea what they're—
This help your memory?
OH! *That* code! Right. Sending.

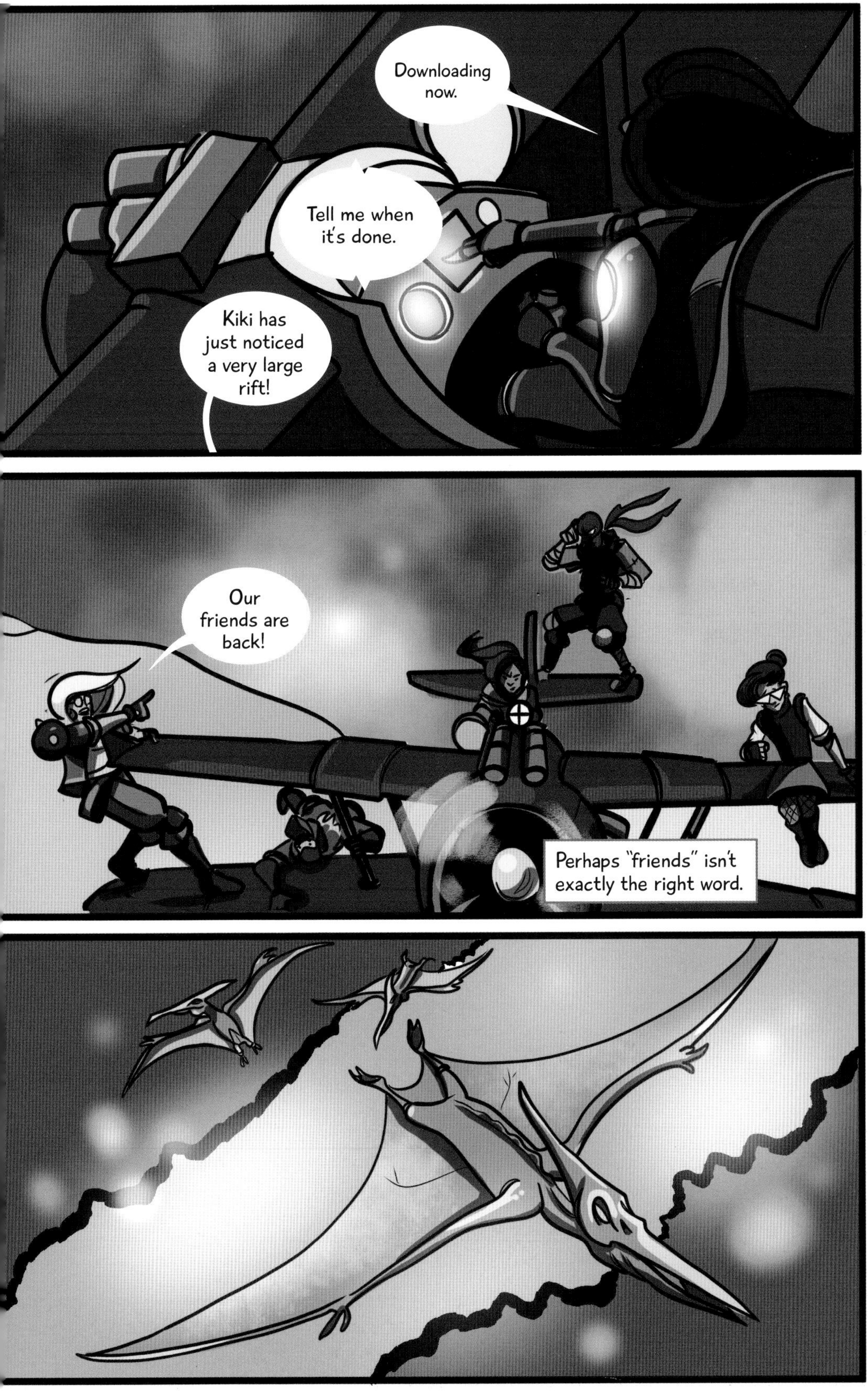
Downloading now.
Tell me when it's done.
Kiki has just noticed a very large rift!
Our friends are back!
Perhaps "friends" isn't exactly the right word.

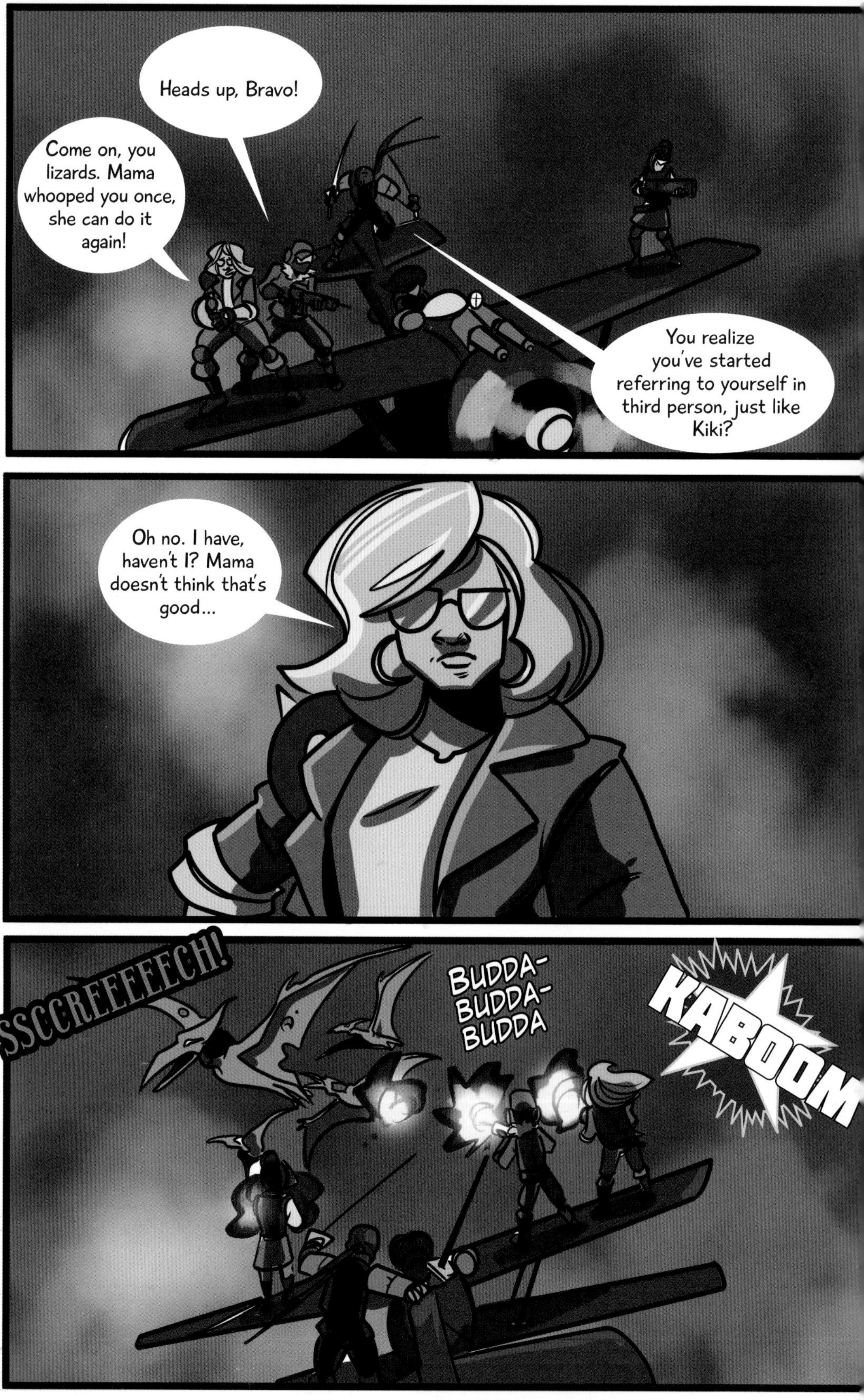
Heads up, Bravo!
Come on, you lizards. Mama whooped you once, she can do it again!
You realize you've started referring to yourself in third person, just like Kiki?
Oh no. I have, haven't I? Mama doesn't think that's good...
SSCCREEEEECH!
BUDDA-BUDDA-BUDDA
KABOOM

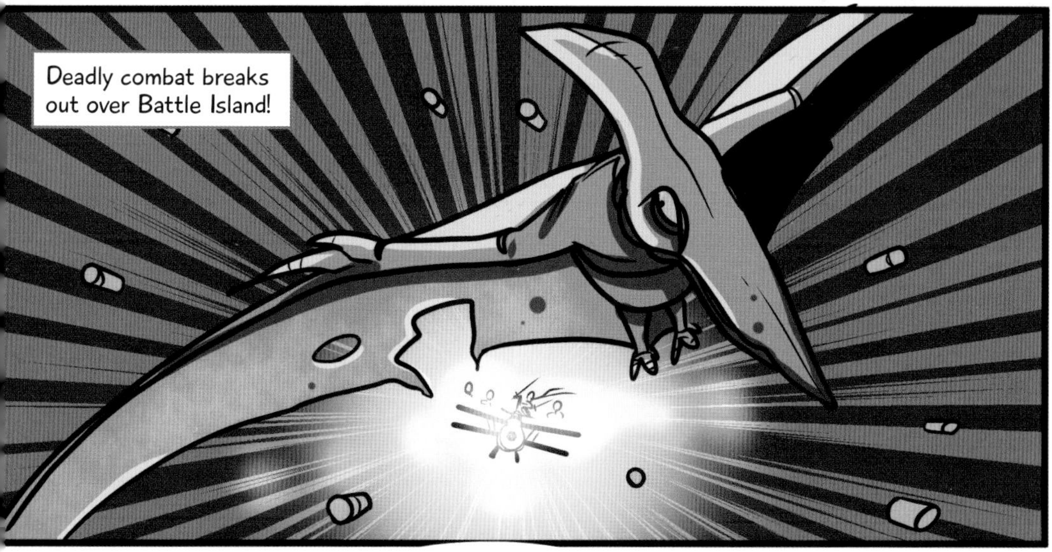
Deadly combat breaks out over Battle Island!

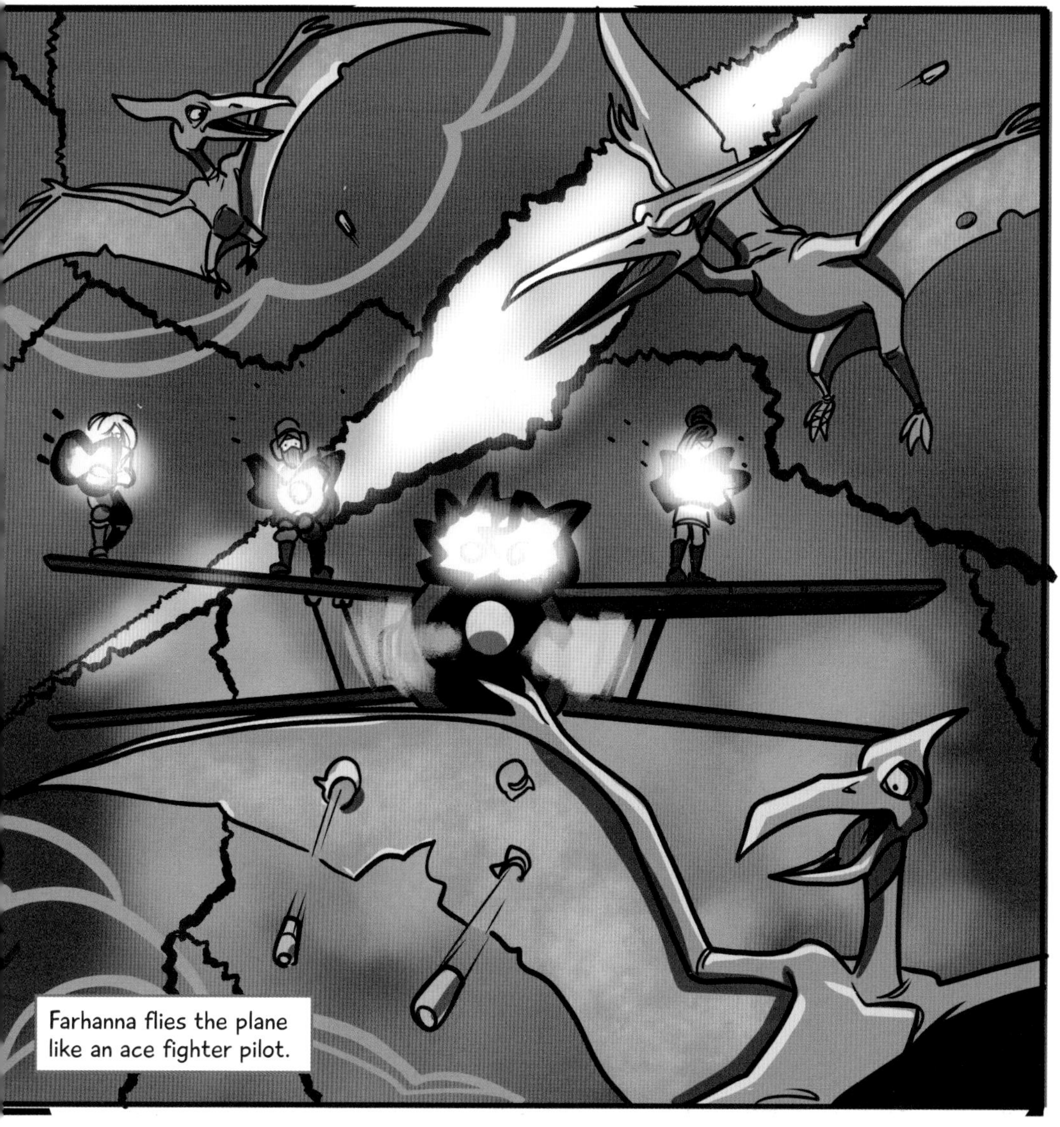
Farhanna flies the plane like an ace fighter pilot.

There is Kevin!

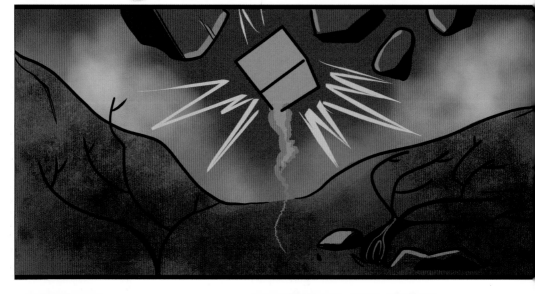

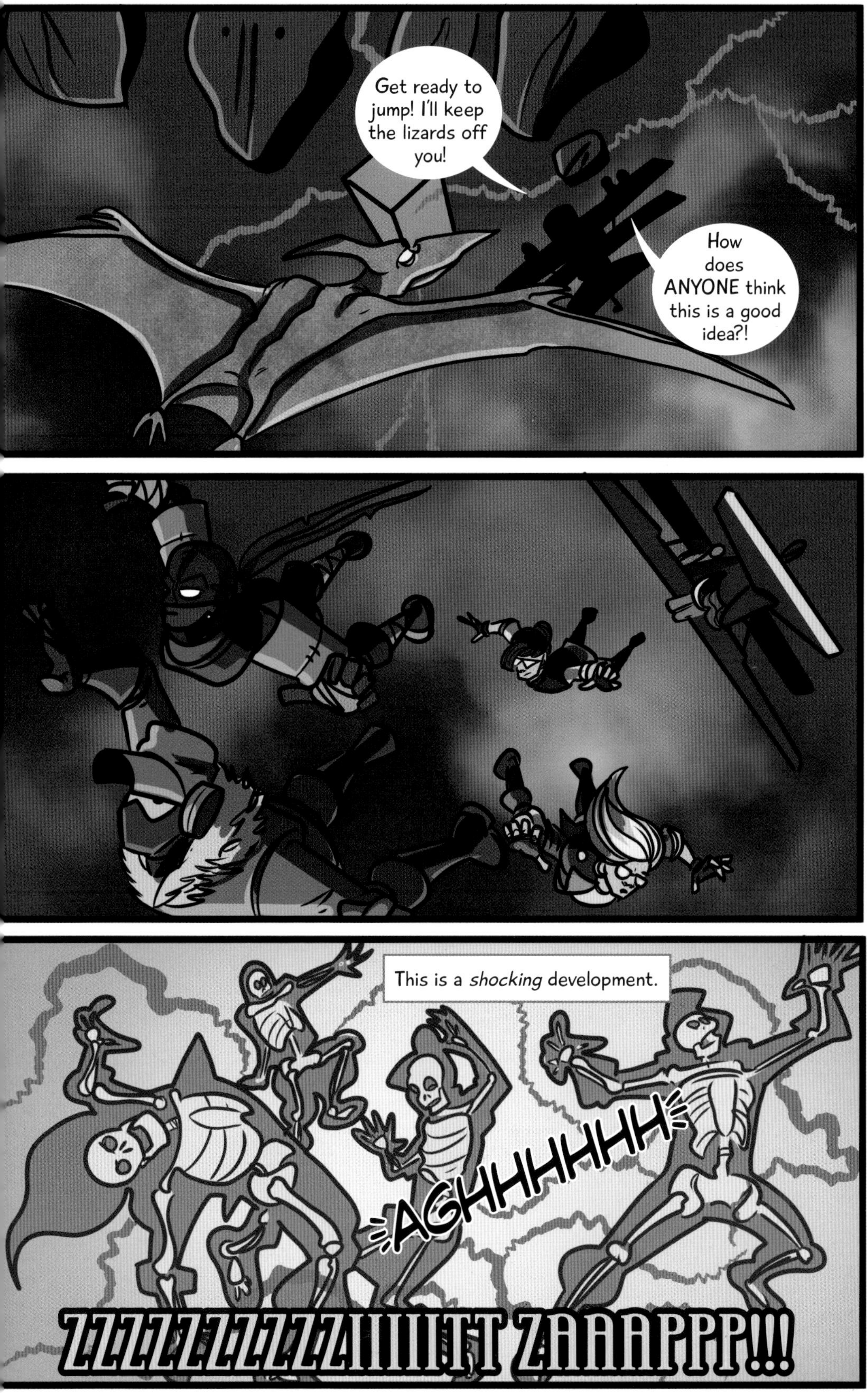
Get ready to jump! I'll keep the lizards off you!
How does ANYONE think this is a good idea?!
This is a *shocking* development.
AGHHHHHH
ZZZZZZZZZZZZIIIIIITT ZAAAPPP!!!

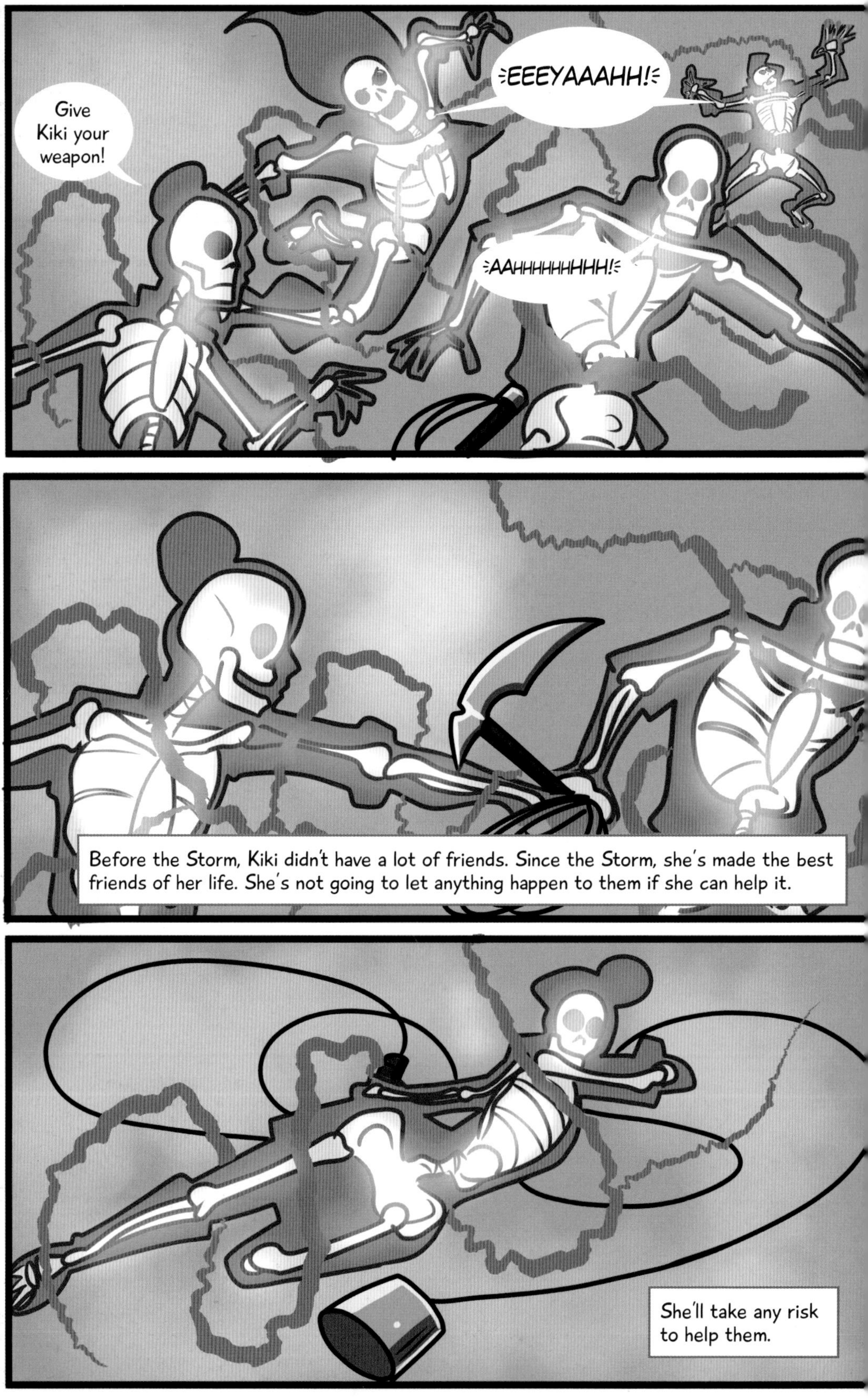
Give Kiki your weapon!
EEEYAAAHH!
AAHHHHHHHHH!
Before the Storm, Kiki didn't have a lot of friends. Since the Storm, she's made the best friends of her life. She's not going to let anything happen to them if she can help it.
She'll take any risk to help them.

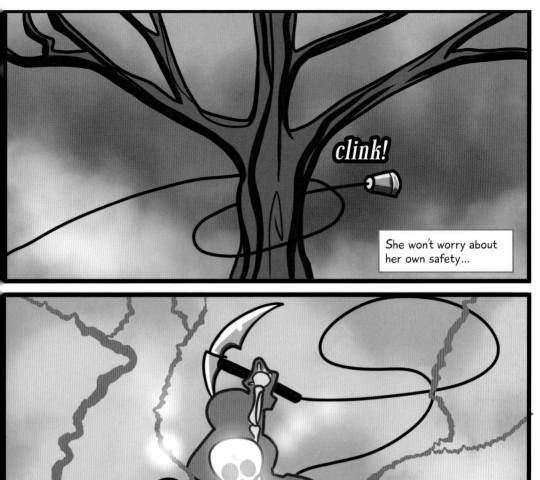

clink!

She won't worry about her own safety...

... no matter how dangerous the situation may be!

ZZZZZZZAAAAAAPPPPPPP!

CRACK!

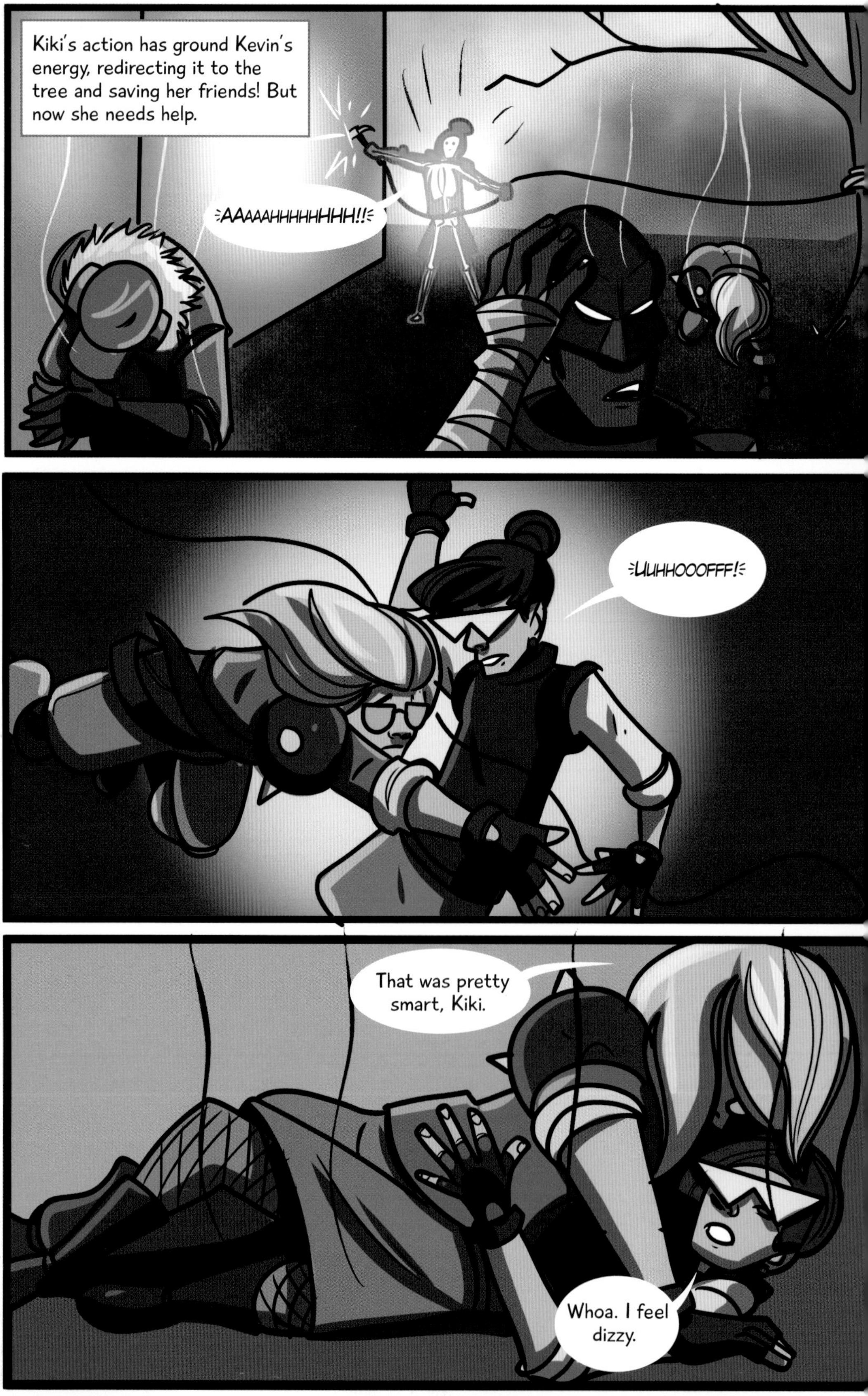
Kiki's action has ground Kevin's energy, redirecting it to the tree and saving her friends! But now she needs help.
AAAAAHHHHHHHH!!
UUHHOOOFFF!
That was pretty smart, Kiki.
Whoa. I feel dizzy.

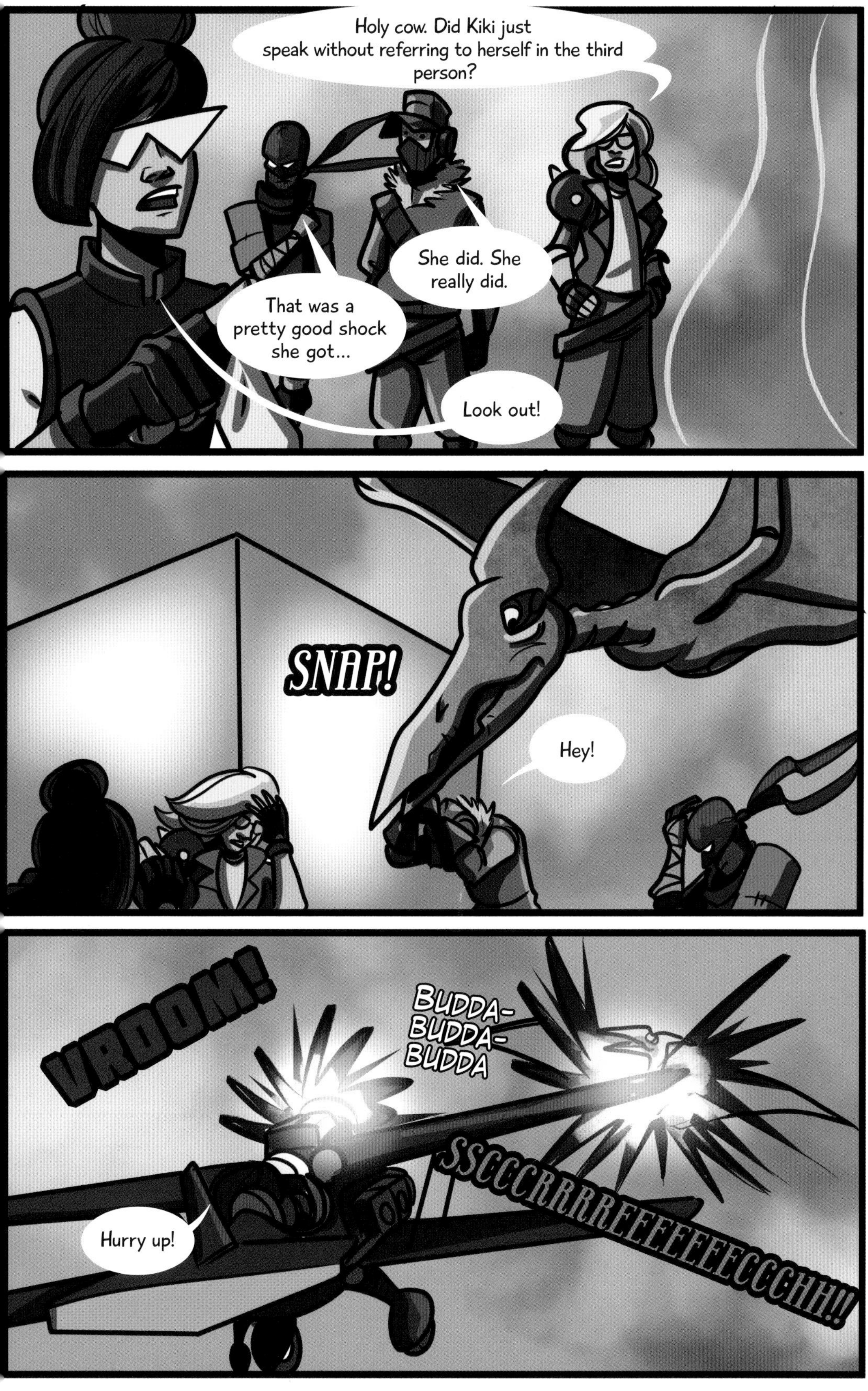
Holy cow. Did Kiki just speak without referring to herself in the third person?
That was a pretty good shock she got...
She did. She really did.
Look out!
SNAP!
Hey!
VROOM!
BUDDA-BUDDA-BUDDA
SSCCCRRRRREEEEEEEECCCHH!!
Hurry up!

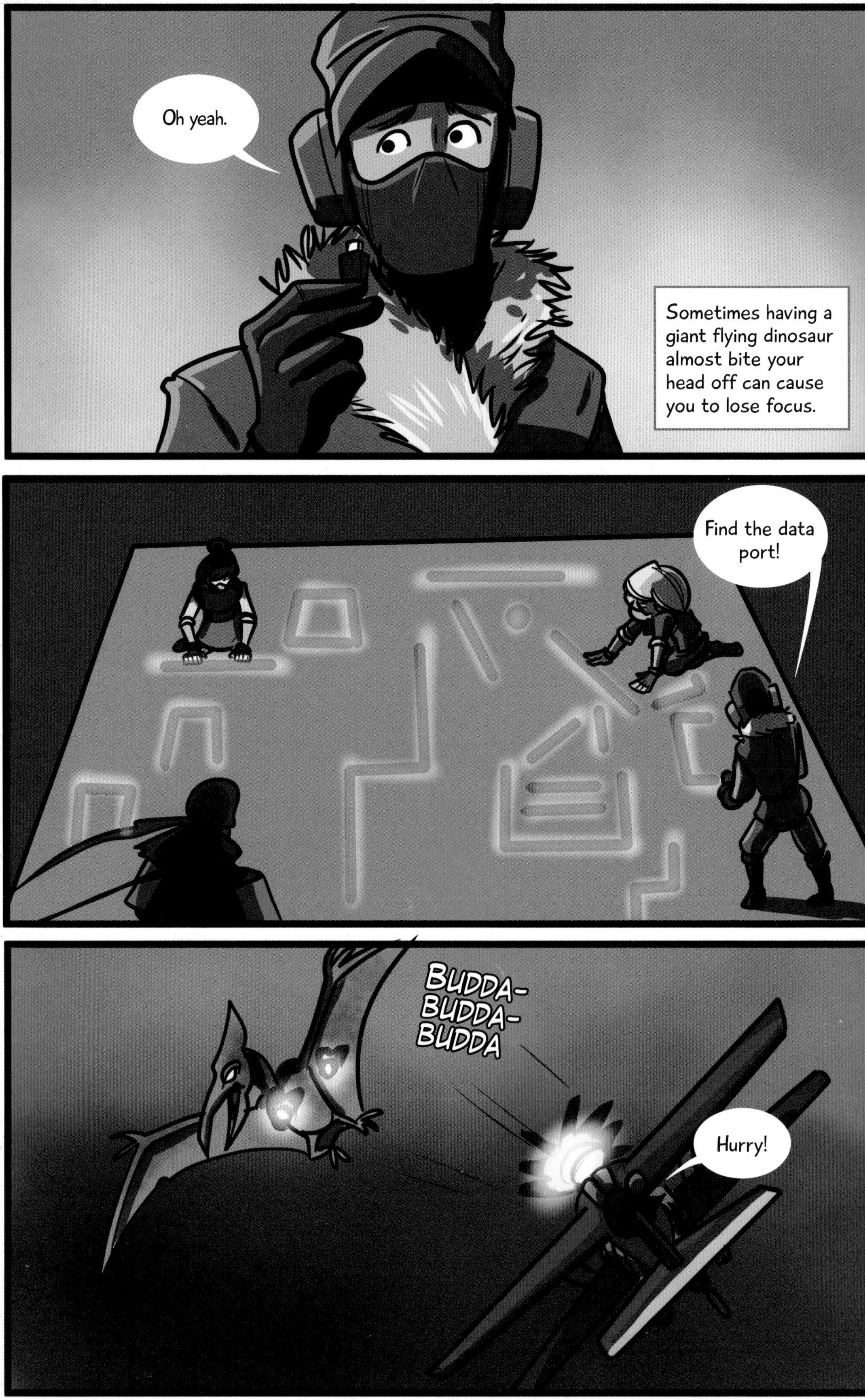
Oh yeah.
Sometimes having a giant flying dinosaur almost bite your head off can cause you to lose focus.
Find the data port!
BUDDA-
BUDDA-
BUDDA
Hurry!

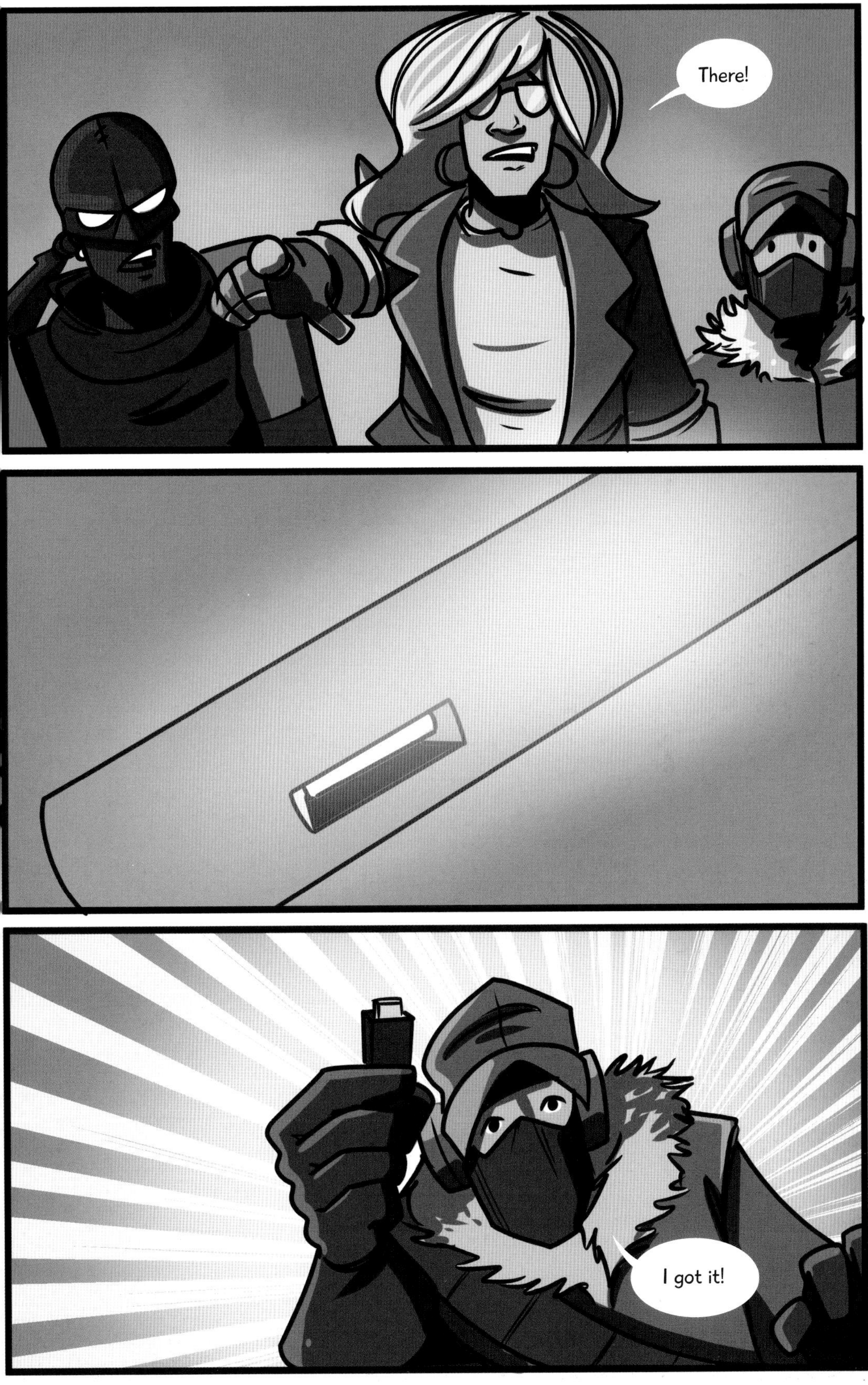
There!
I got it!

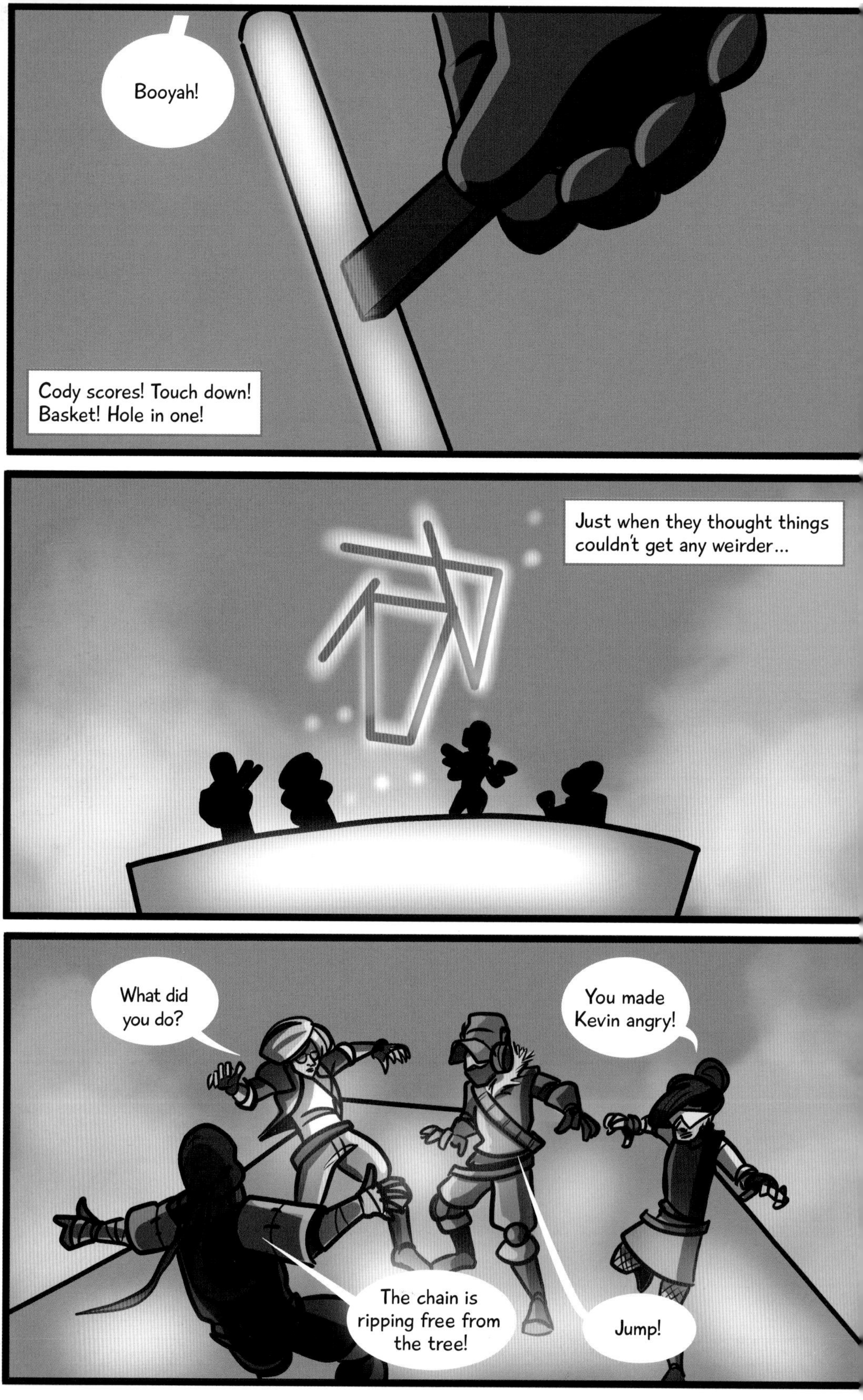
Booyah!
Cody scores! Touch down! Basket! Hole in one!
Just when they thought things couldn't get any weirder...
What did you do?
You made Kevin angry!
The chain is ripping free from the tree!
Jump!

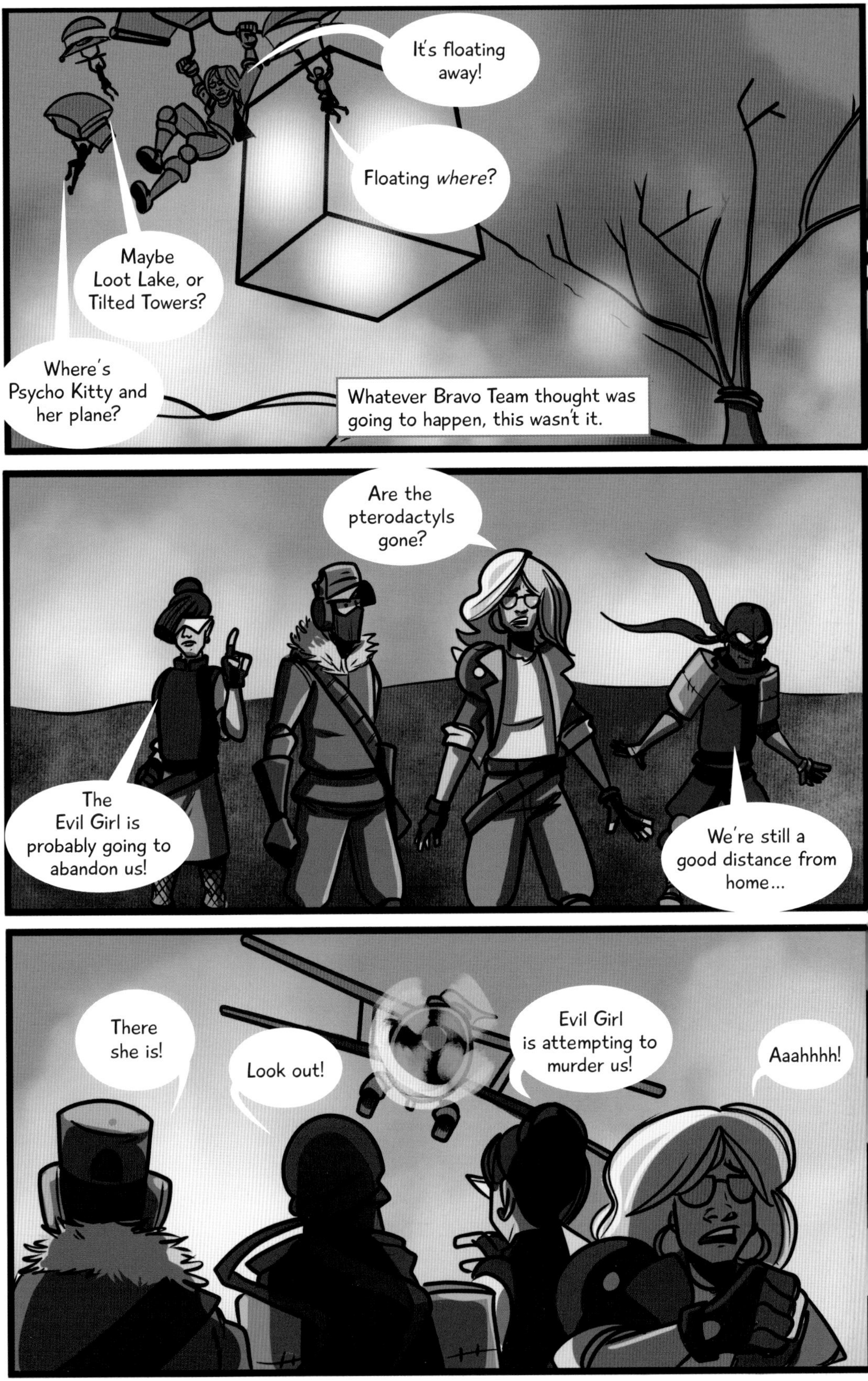
It's floating away!
Floating where?
Maybe Loot Lake, or Tilted Towers?
Where's Psycho Kitty and her plane?
Whatever Bravo Team thought was going to happen, this wasn't it.
Are the pterodactyls gone?
The Evil Girl is probably going to abandon us!
We're still a good distance from home...
There she is!
Look out!
Evil Girl is attempting to murder us!
Aaahhhh!

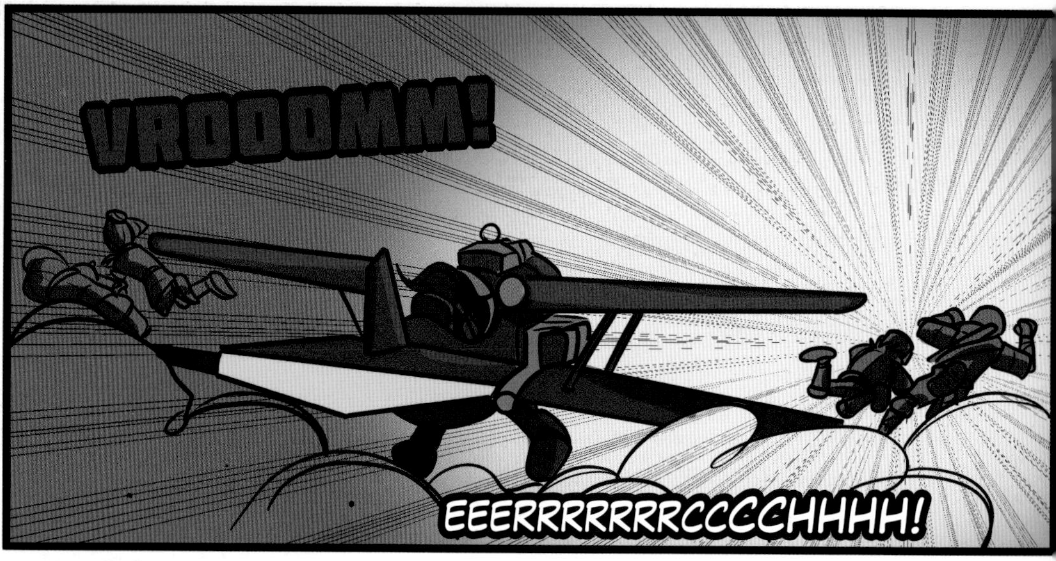
VROOOMM!
EEERRRRRRRCCCCHHHH!

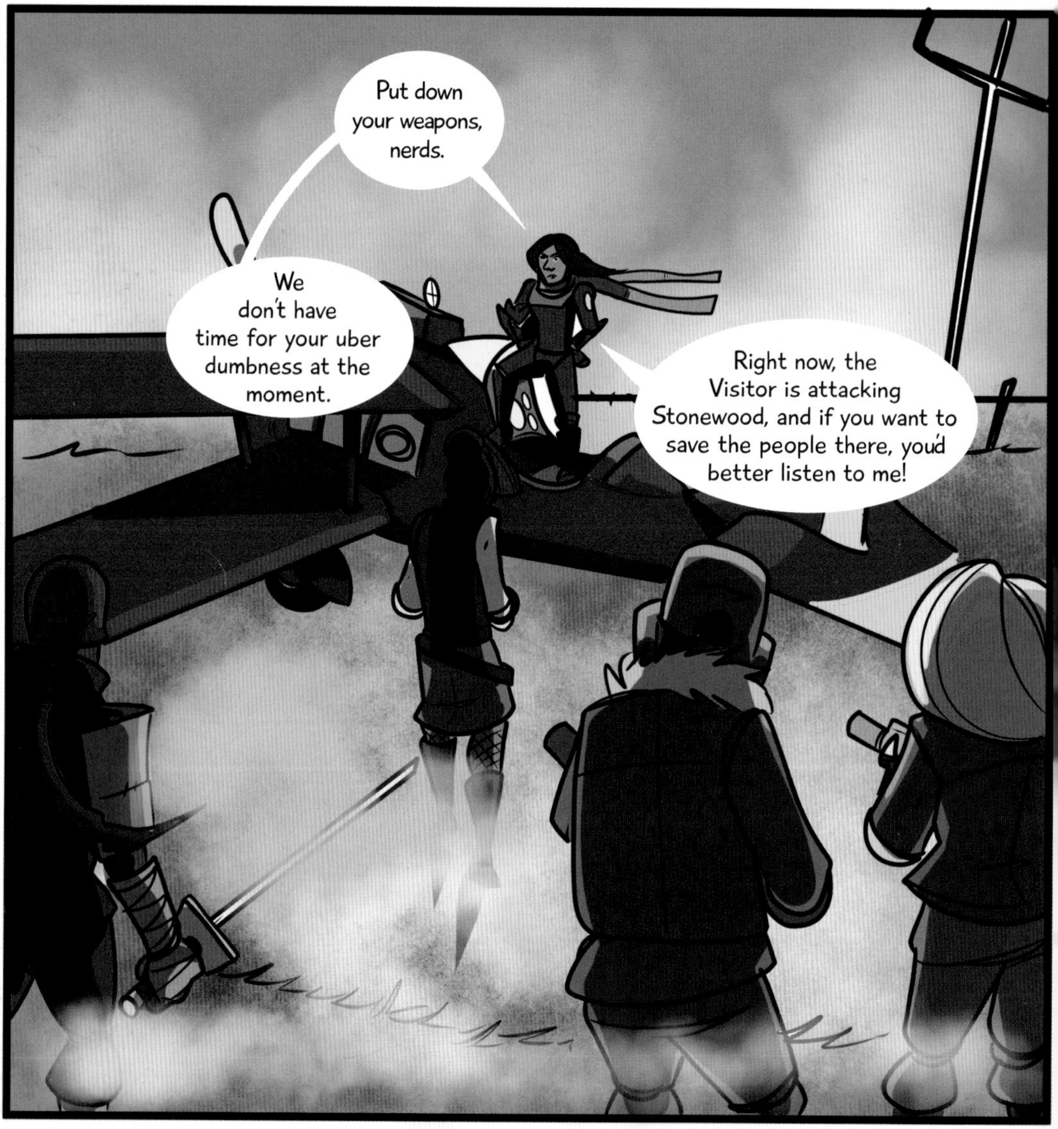
Put down your weapons, nerds.
We don't have time for your uber dumbness at the moment.
Right now, the Visitor is attacking Stonewood, and if you want to save the people there, you'd better listen to me!

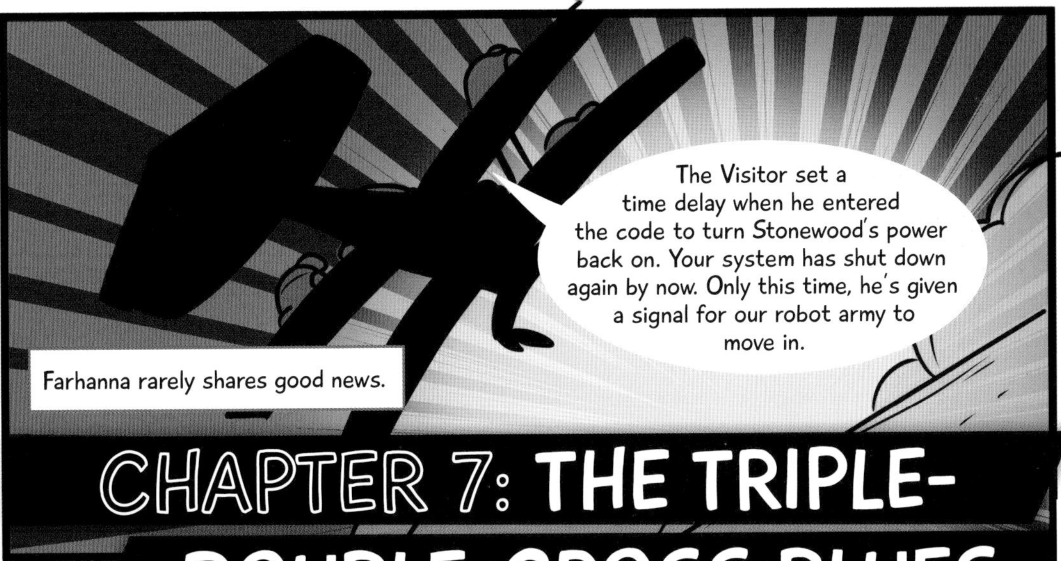
The Visitor set a time delay when he entered the code to turn Stonewood's power back on. Your system has shut down again by now. Only this time, he's given a signal for our robot army to move in.
Farhanna rarely shares good news.

CHAPTER 7: THE TRIPLE-DOUBLE-CROSS BLUES

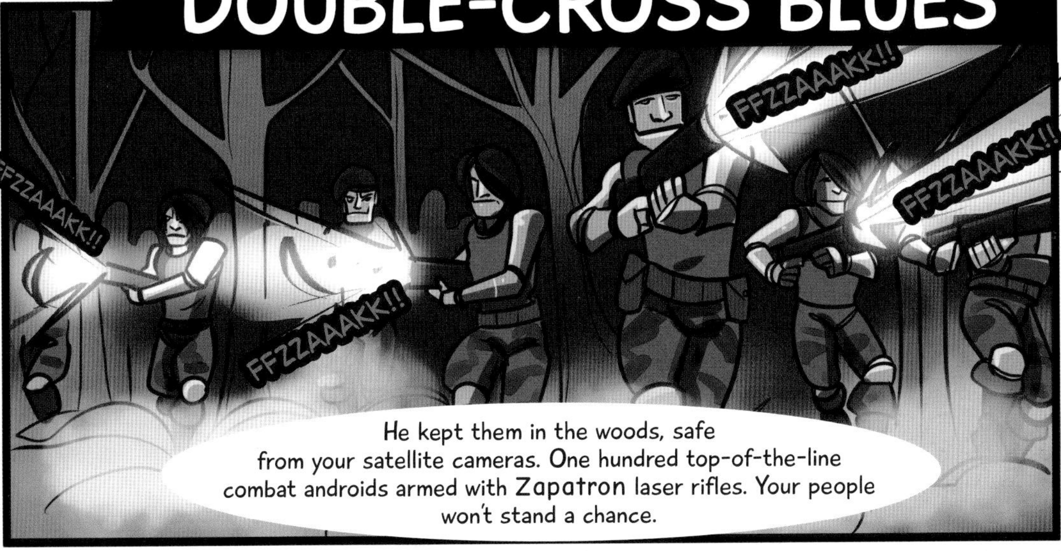
FFZZAAAKK!!
FFZZAAAKK!!
FFZZAAAKK!!
FFZZAAAKK!!
FFZZAAAKK!!
He kept them in the woods, safe from your satellite cameras. One hundred top-of-the-line combat androids armed with Zapatron laser rifles. Your people won't stand a chance.

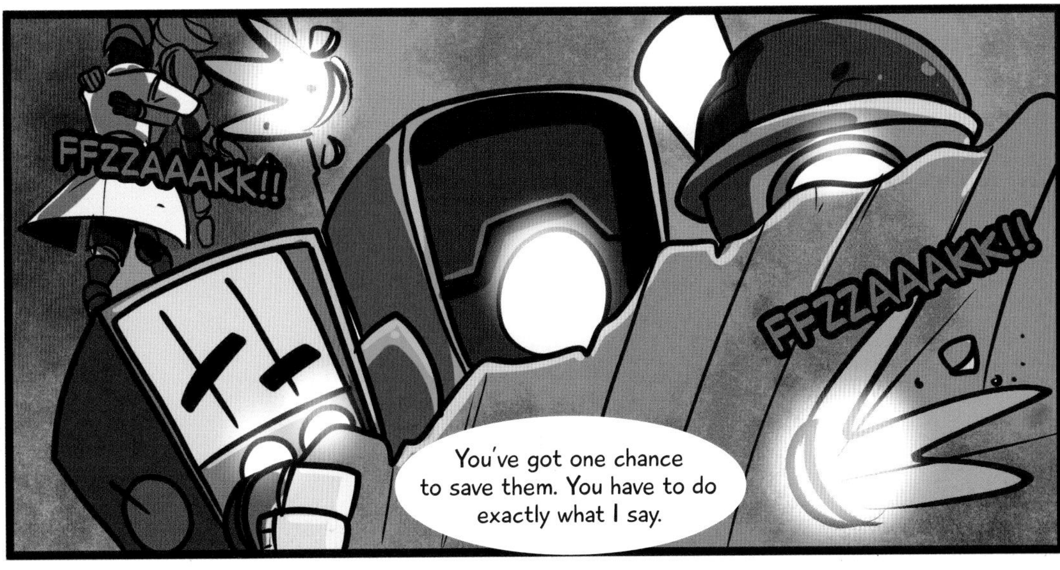
FFZZAAAKK!!
FFZZAAAKK!!
You've got one chance to save them. You have to do exactly what I say.

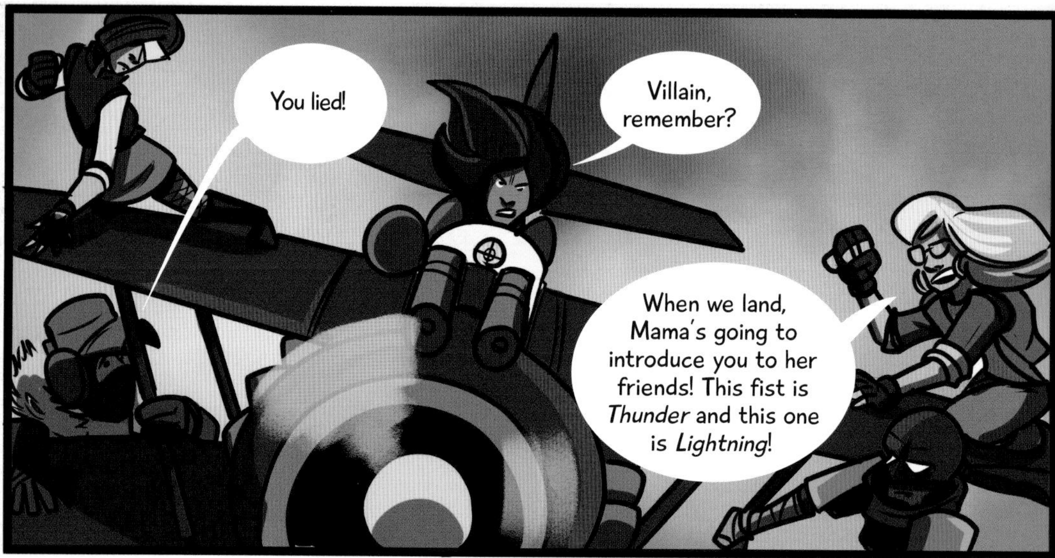
You lied!
Villain, remember?
When we land, Mama's going to introduce you to her friends! This fist is *Thunder* and this one is *Lightning*!

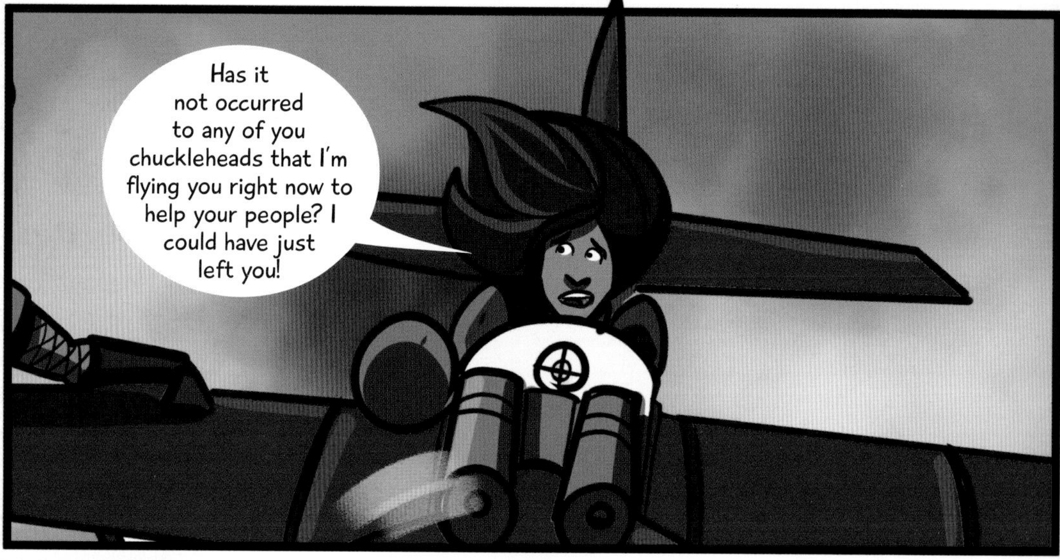
Has it not occurred to any of you chuckleheads that I'm flying you right now to help your people? I could have just left you!

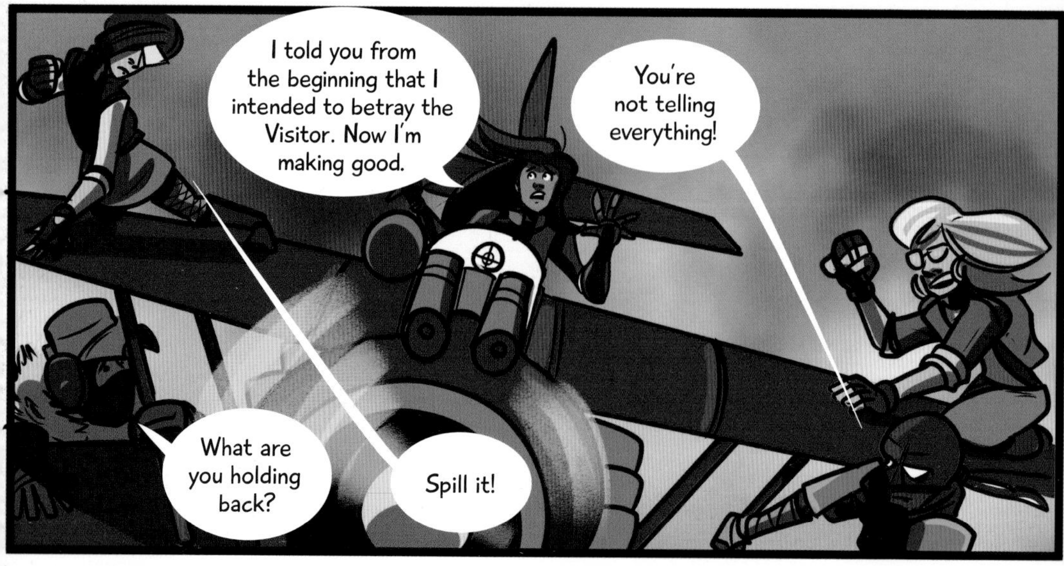
I told you from the beginning that I intended to betray the Visitor. Now I'm making good.
You're not telling everything!
What are you holding back?
Spill it!

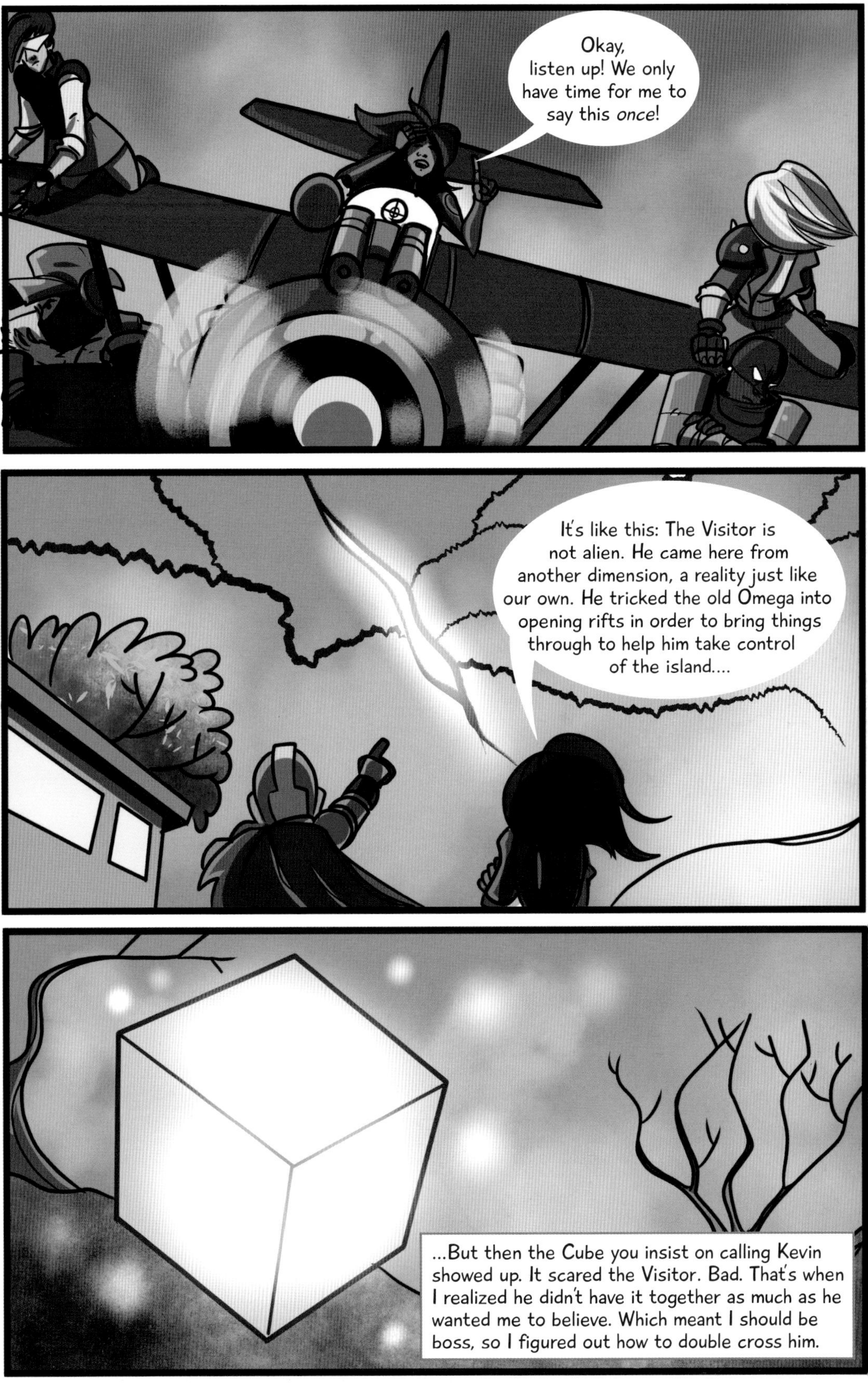
Okay, listen up! We only have time for me to say this *once*!
It's like this: The Visitor is not alien. He came here from another dimension, a reality just like our own. He tricked the old Omega into opening rifts in order to bring things through to help him take control of the island....
...But then the Cube you insist on calling Kevin showed up. It scared the Visitor. Bad. That's when I realized he didn't have it together as much as he wanted me to believe. Which meant I should be boss, so I figured out how to double cross him.

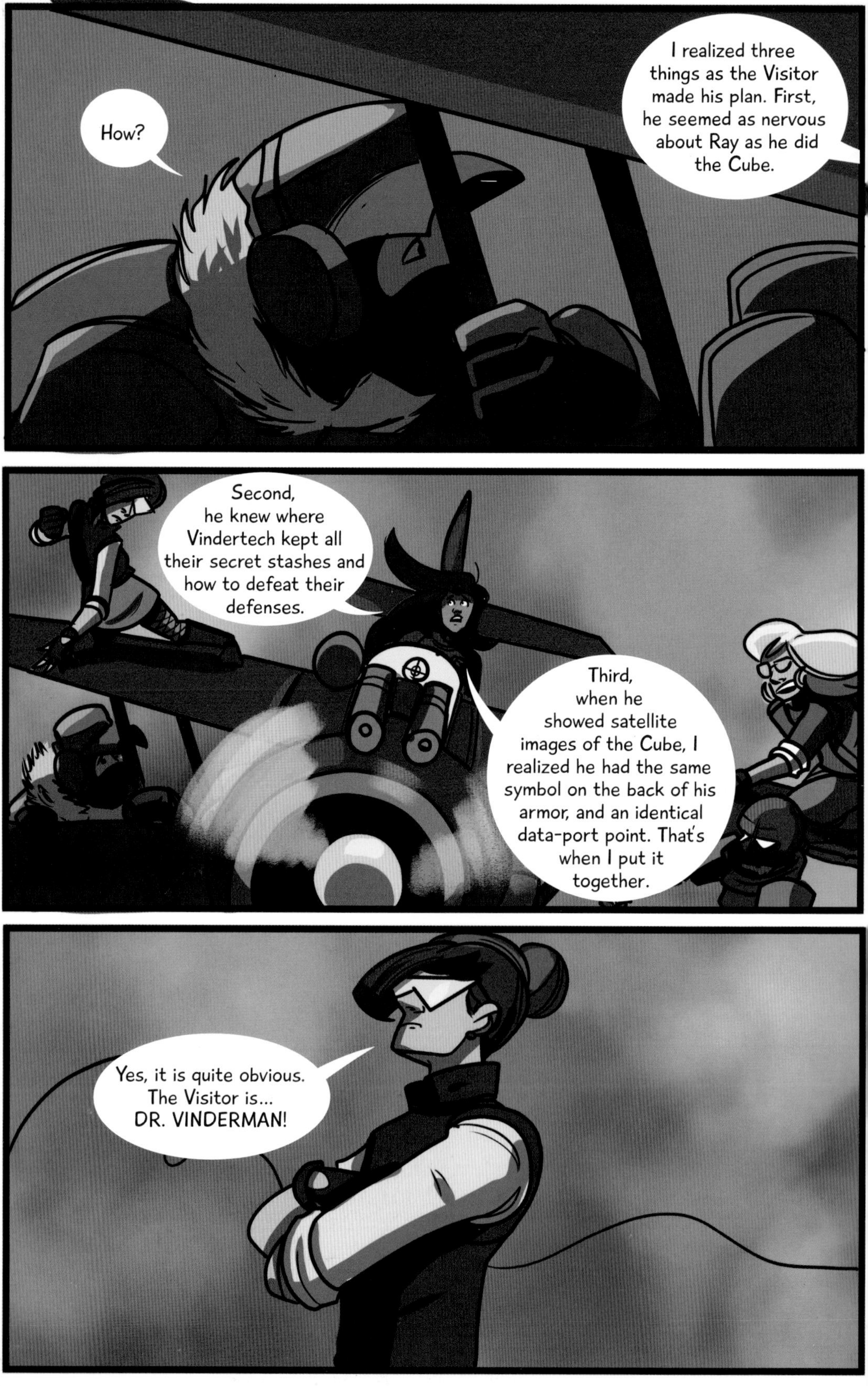
How?
I realized three things as the Visitor made his plan. First, he seemed as nervous about Ray as he did the Cube.
Second, he knew where Vindertech kept all their secret stashes and how to defeat their defenses.
Third, when he showed satellite images of the Cube, I realized he had the same symbol on the back of his armor, and an identical data-port point. That's when I put it together.
Yes, it is quite obvious. The Visitor is... DR. VINDERMAN!

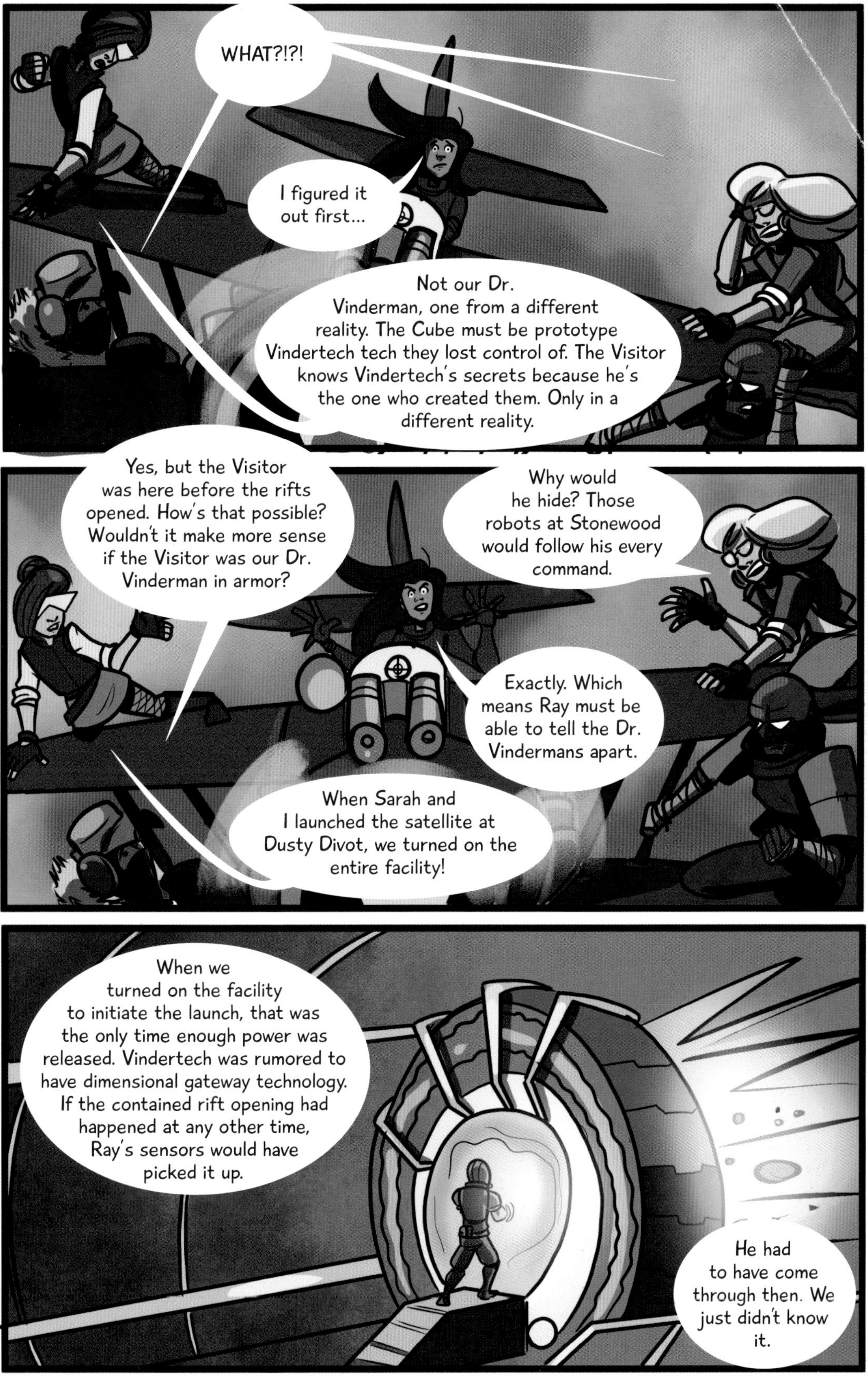
WHAT?!?!
I figured it out first...
Not our Dr. Vinderman, one from a different reality. The Cube must be prototype Vindertech tech they lost control of. The Visitor knows Vindertech's secrets because he's the one who created them. Only in a different reality.
Yes, but the Visitor was here before the rifts opened. How's that possible? Wouldn't it make more sense if the Visitor was our Dr. Vinderman in armor?
Why would he hide? Those robots at Stonewood would follow his every command.
Exactly. Which means Ray must be able to tell the Dr. Vindermans apart.
When Sarah and I launched the satellite at Dusty Divot, we turned on the entire facility!
When we turned on the facility to initiate the launch, that was the only time enough power was released. Vindertech was rumored to have dimensional gateway technology. If the contained rift opening had happened at any other time, Ray's sensors would have picked it up.
He had to have come through then. We just didn't know it.

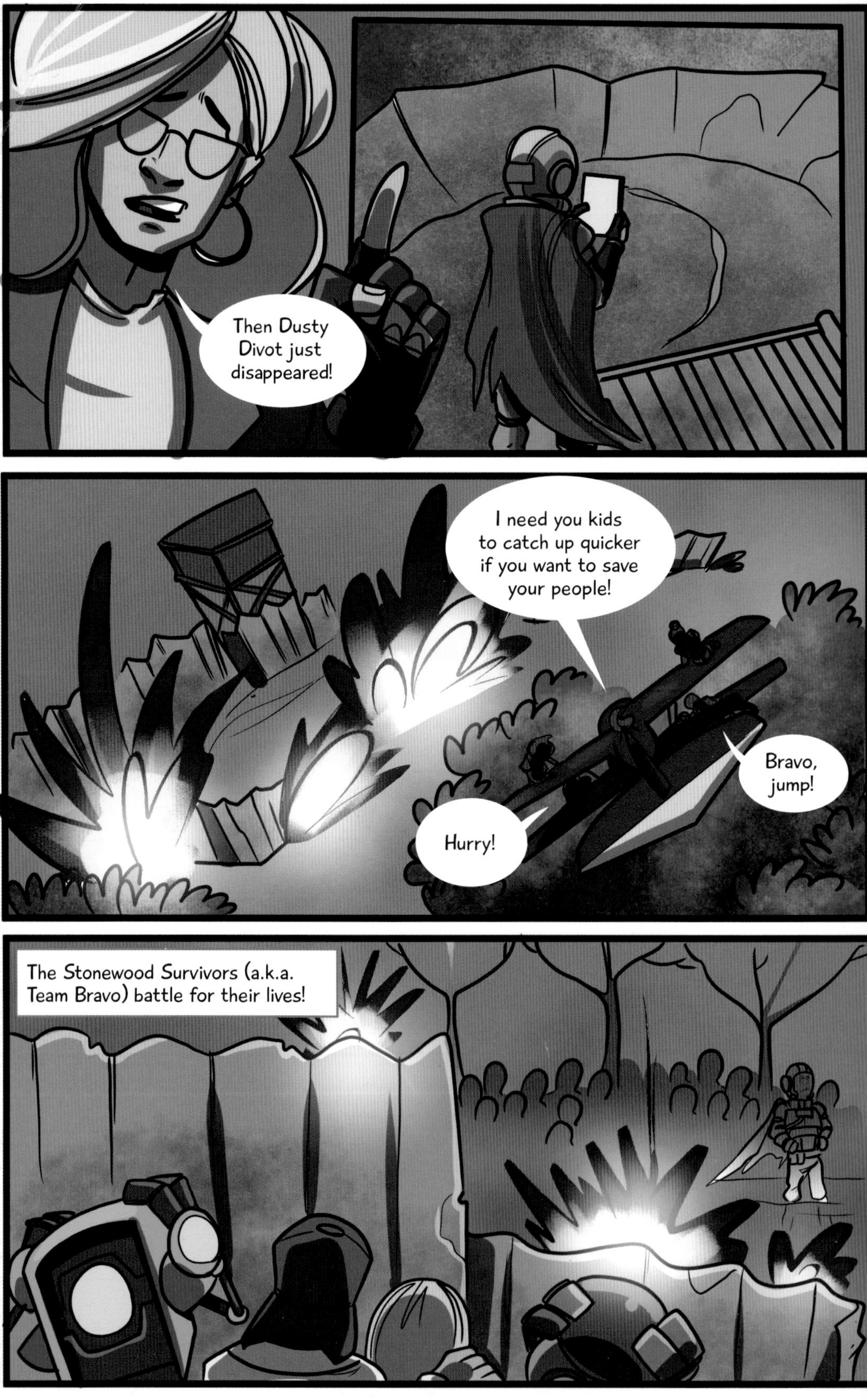
Then Dusty Divot just disappeared!
I need you kids to catch up quicker if you want to save your people!
Bravo, jump!
Hurry!
The Stonewood Survivors (a.k.a. Team Bravo) battle for their lives!

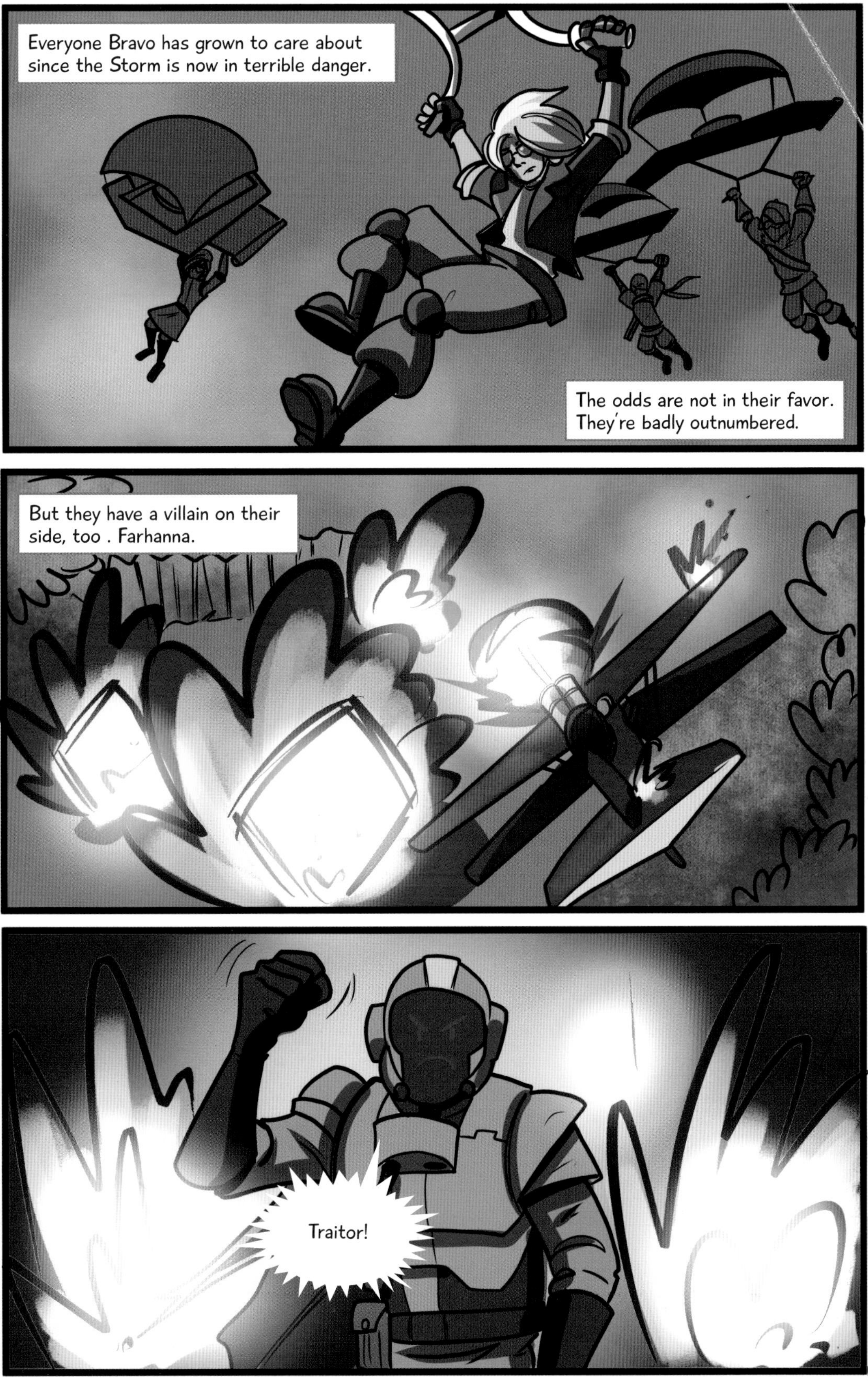
Everyone Bravo has grown to care about since the Storm is now in terrible danger.
The odds are not in their favor. They're badly outnumbered.
But they have a villain on their side, too . Farhanna.
Traitor!

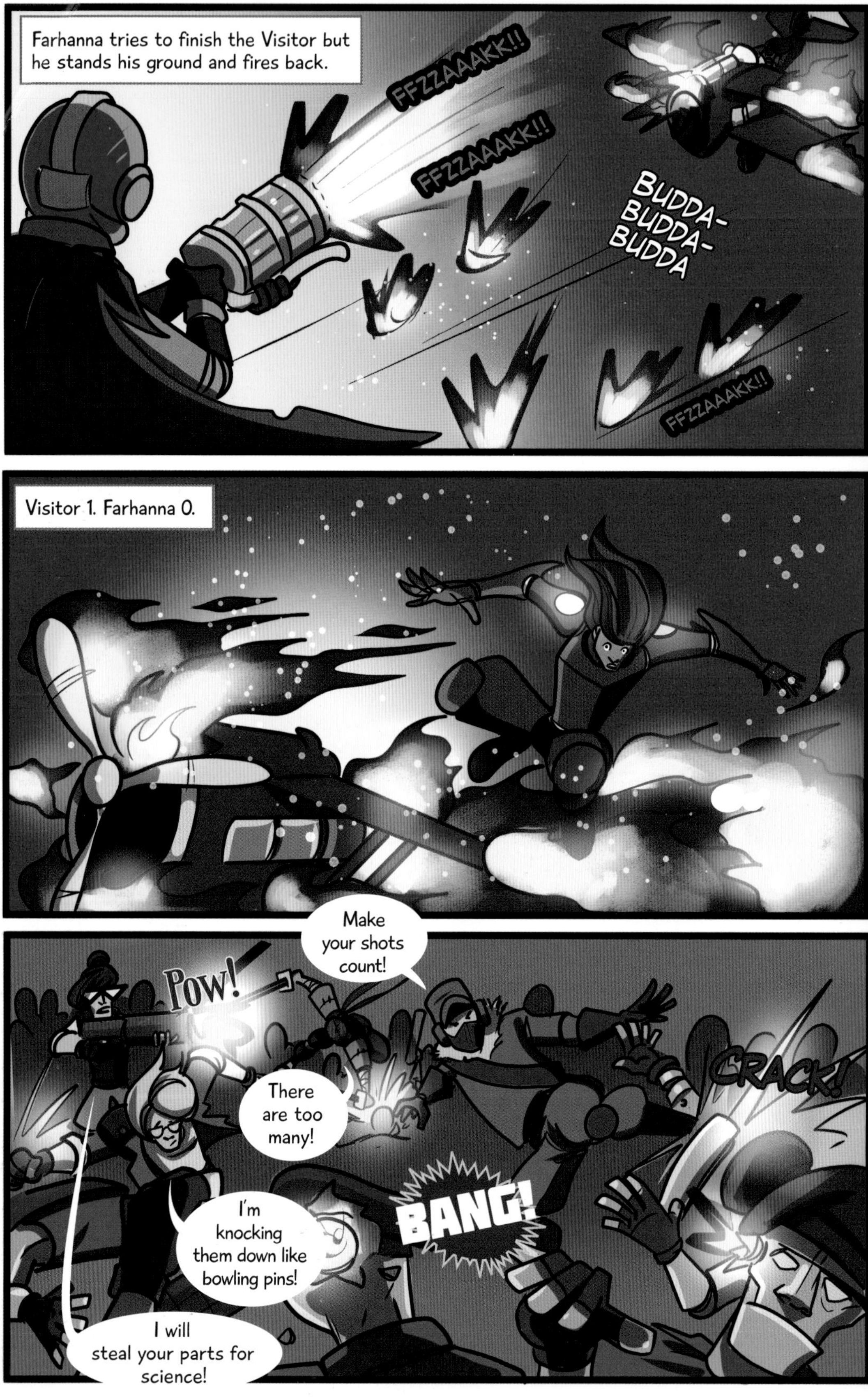
Farhanna tries to finish the Visitor but he stands his ground and fires back.
FFZZAAAKK!!
FFZZAAAKK!!
BUDDA-BUDDA-BUDDA
FFZZAAAKK!!
Visitor 1. Farhanna 0.
POW!
Make your shots count!
There are too many!
CRACK!
BANG!
I'm knocking them down like bowling pins!
I will steal your parts for science!

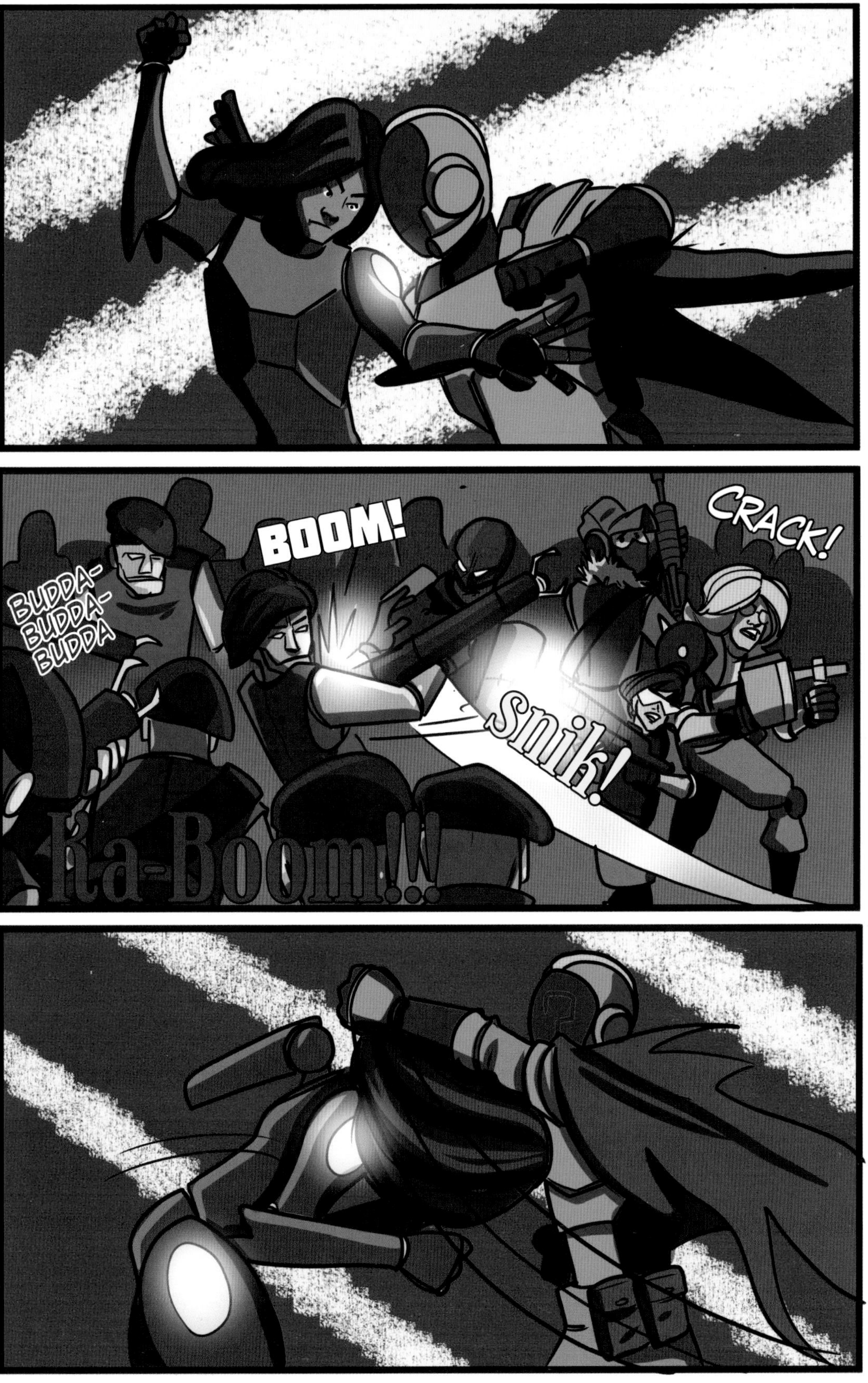
BOOM!
BUDDA-
BUDDA-
BUDDA
CRACK!
Snik!
Ka-Boom!!!

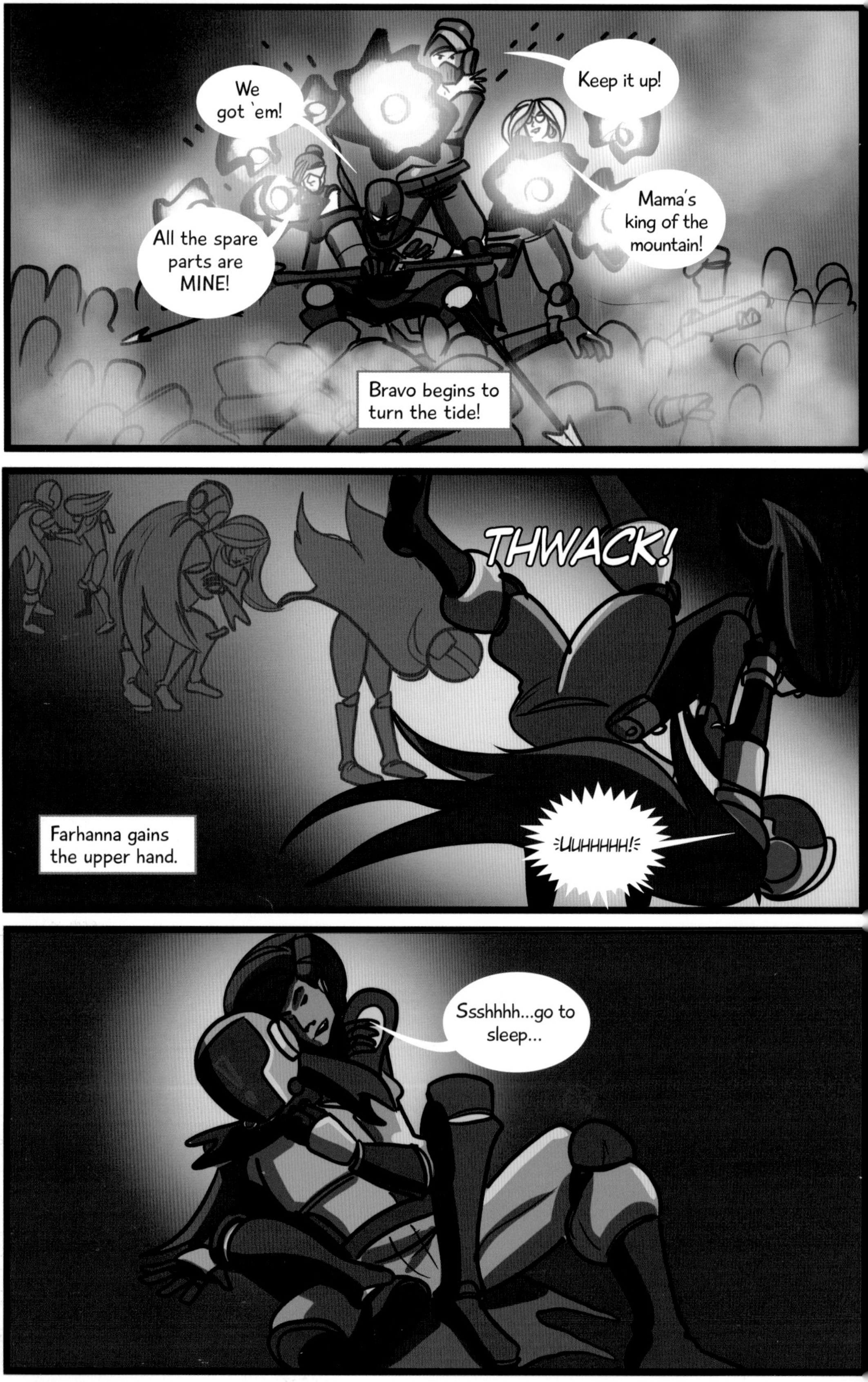
We got 'em!
Keep it up!
All the spare parts are MINE!
Mama's king of the mountain!
Bravo begins to turn the tide!
THWACK!
Farhanna gains the upper hand.
UUHHHHH!
Ssshhhh...go to sleep...

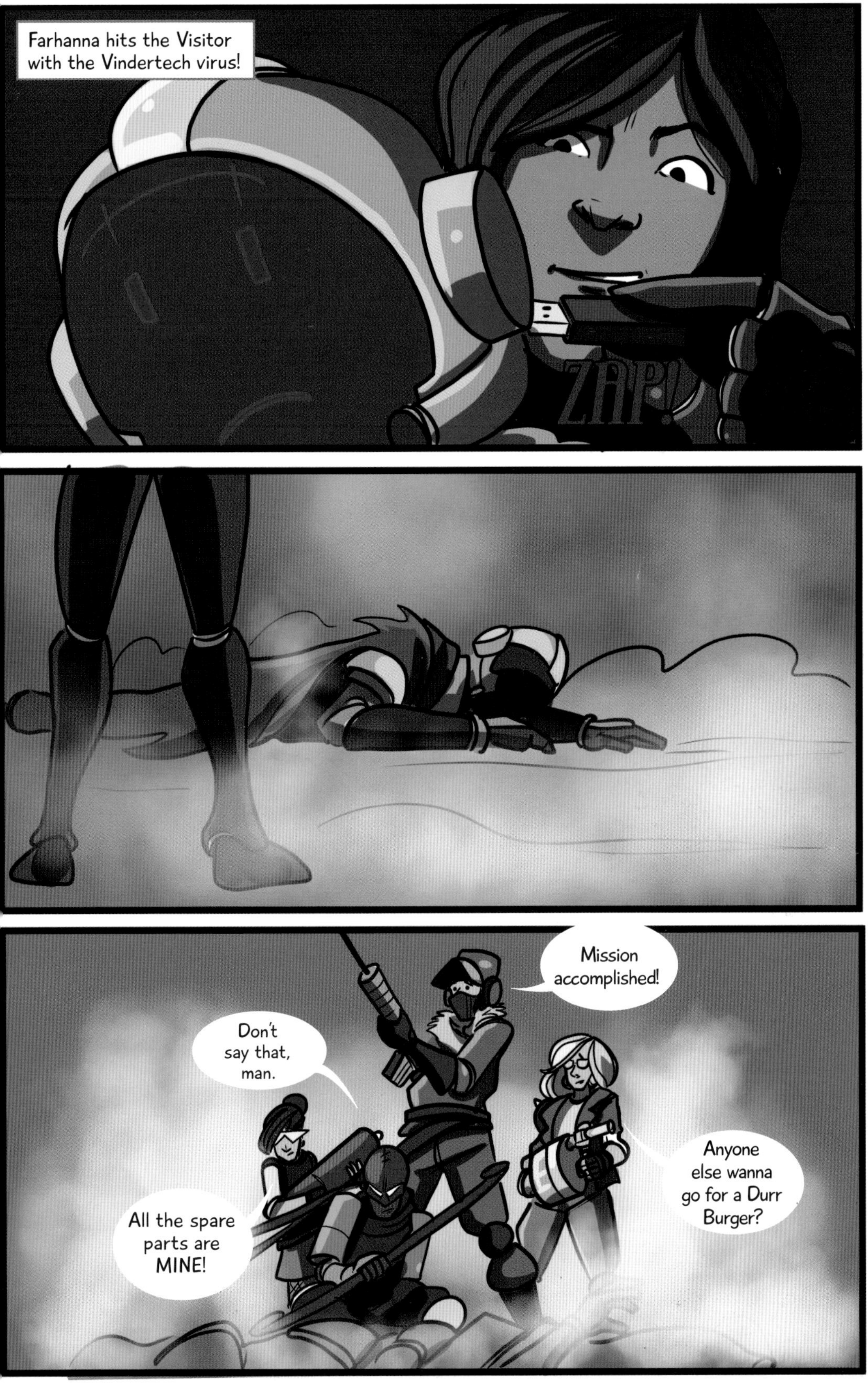

Farhanna hits the Visitor with the Vindertech virus!
ZAP!
Mission accomplished!
Don't say that, man.
Anyone else wanna go for a Durr Burger?
All the spare parts are MINE!

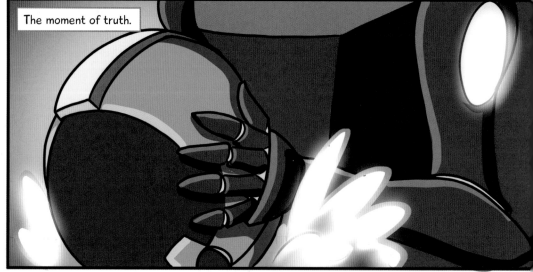

The moment of truth.

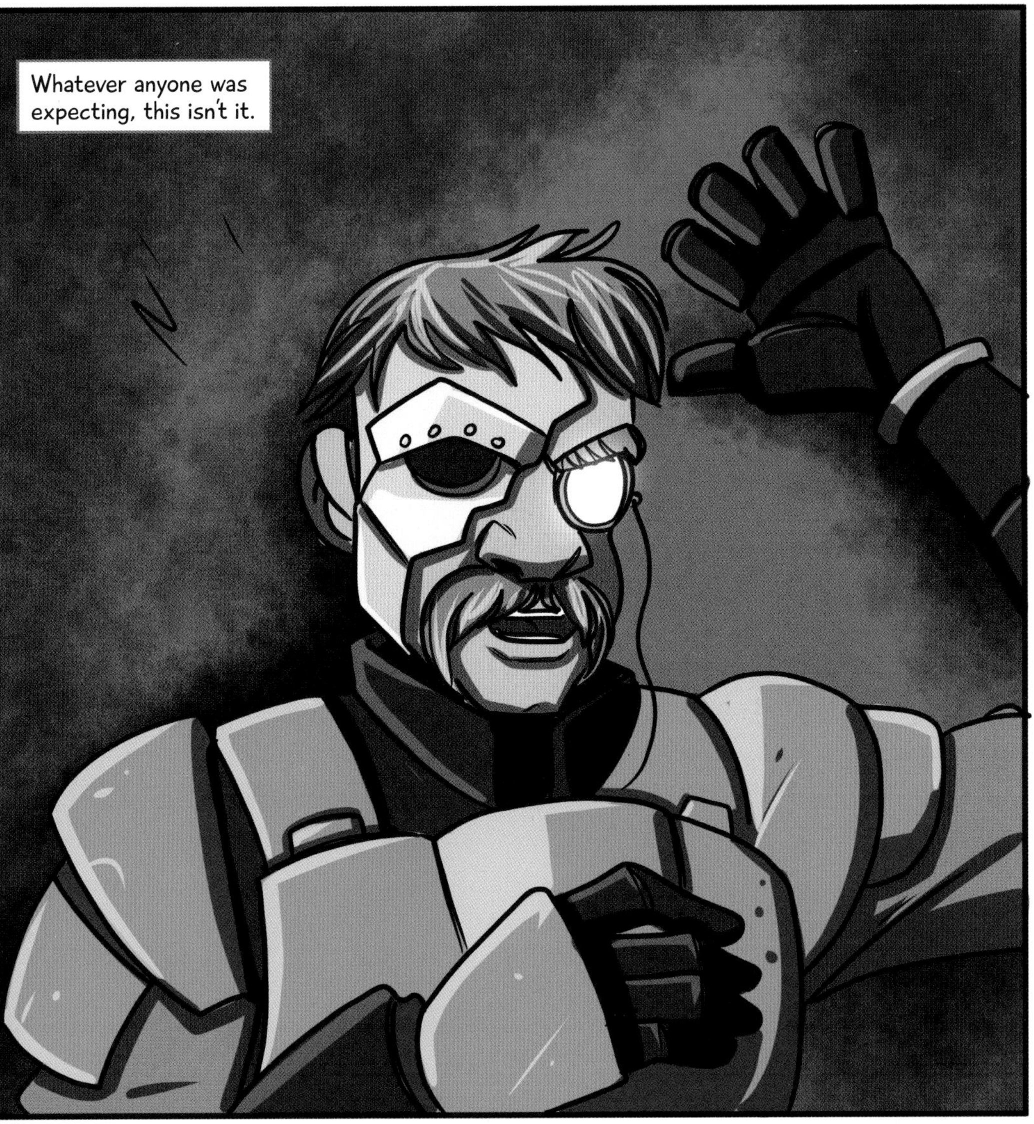
Whatever anyone was expecting, this isn't it.

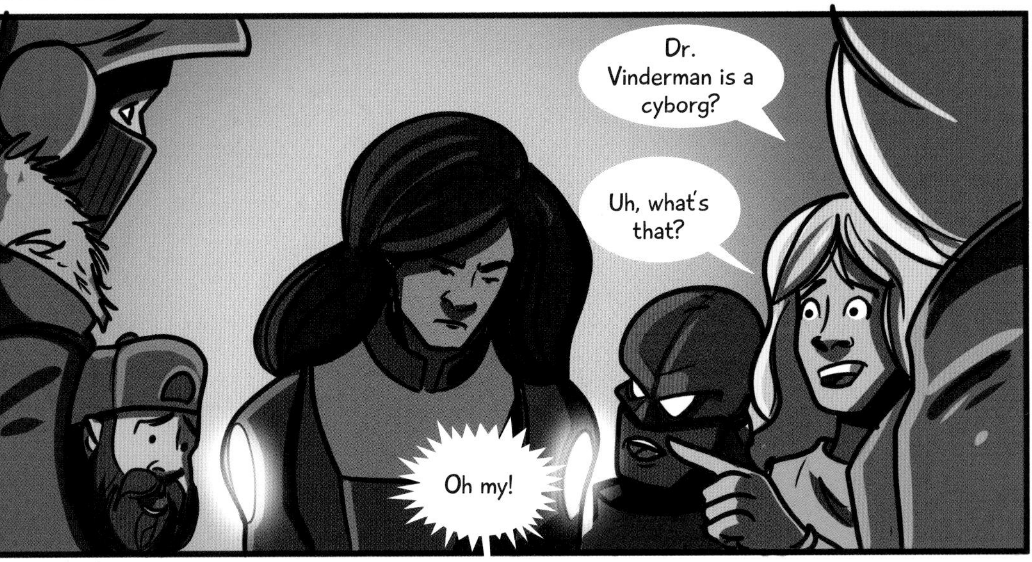
Dr. Vinderman is a cyborg?
Uh, what's that?
Oh my!

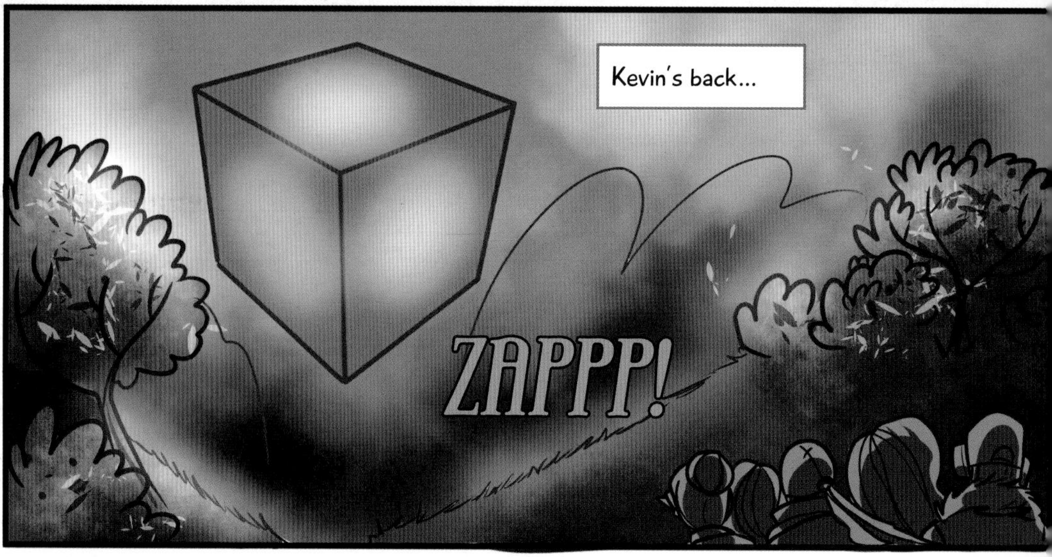
Kevin's back...
ZAPPP!

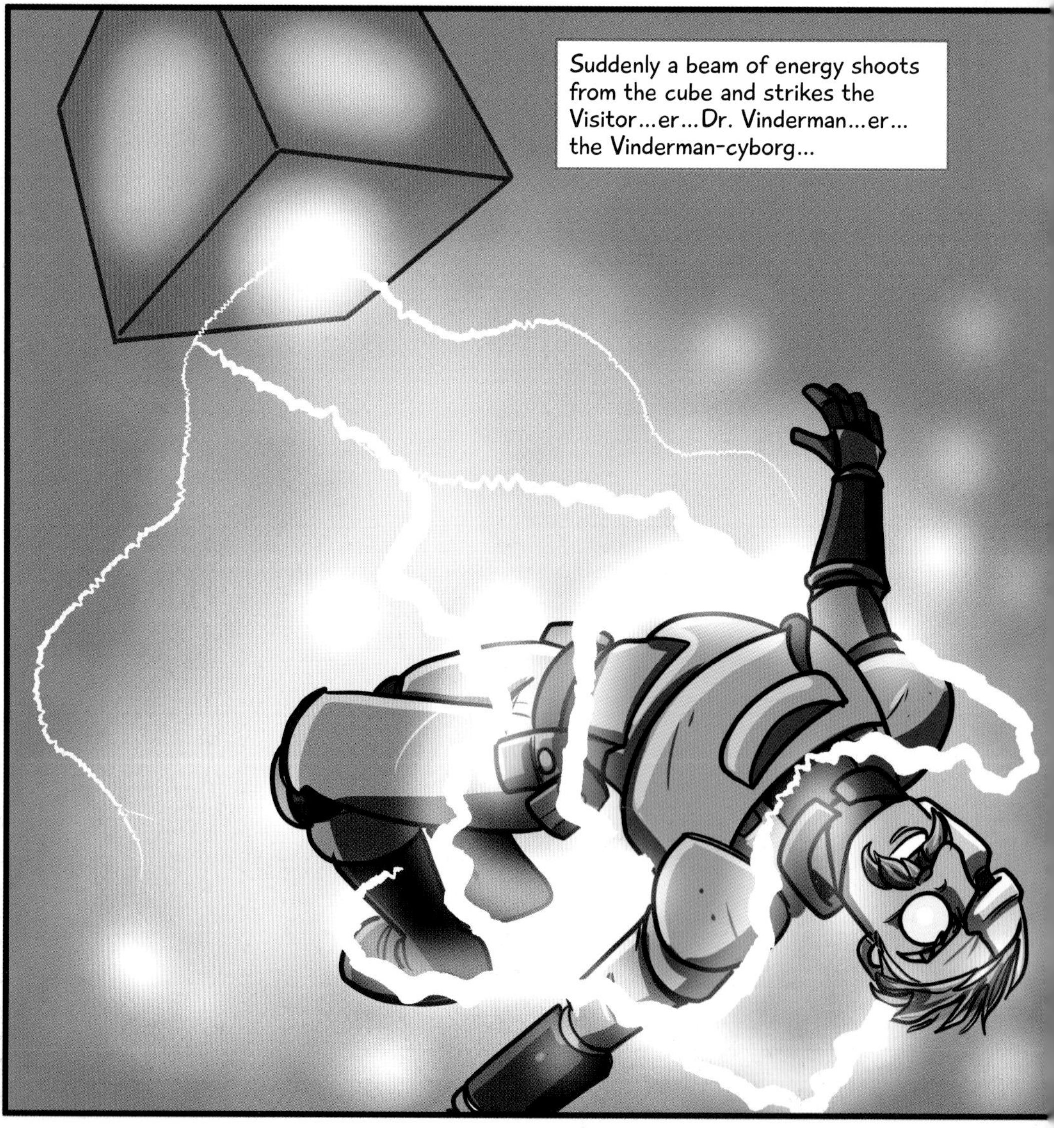
Suddenly a beam of energy shoots from the cube and strikes the Visitor...er...Dr. Vinderman...er... the Vinderman-cyborg...

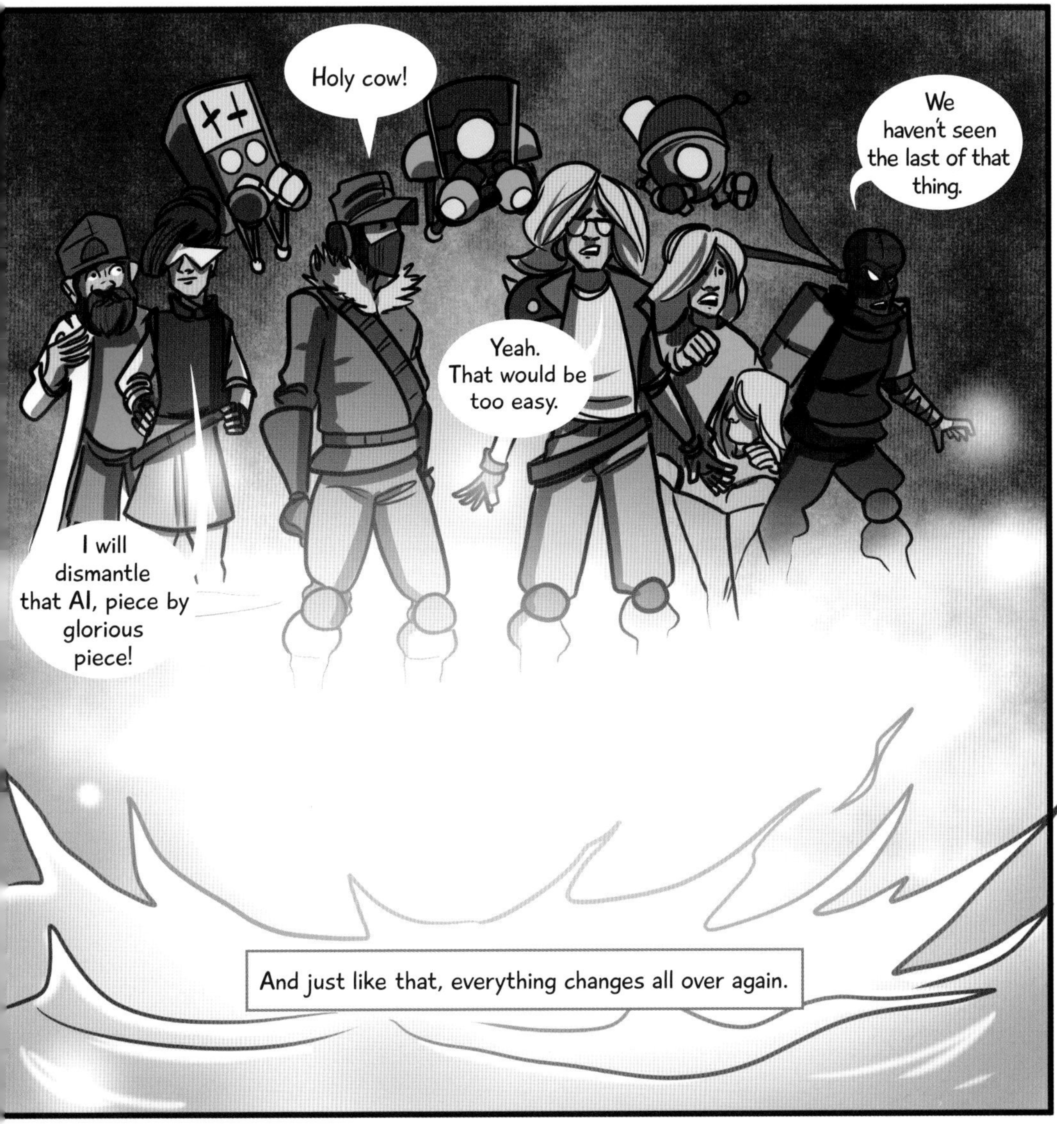
Holy cow!
We haven't seen the last of that thing.
Yeah. That would be too easy.
I will dismantle that AI, piece by glorious piece!
And just like that, everything changes all over again.

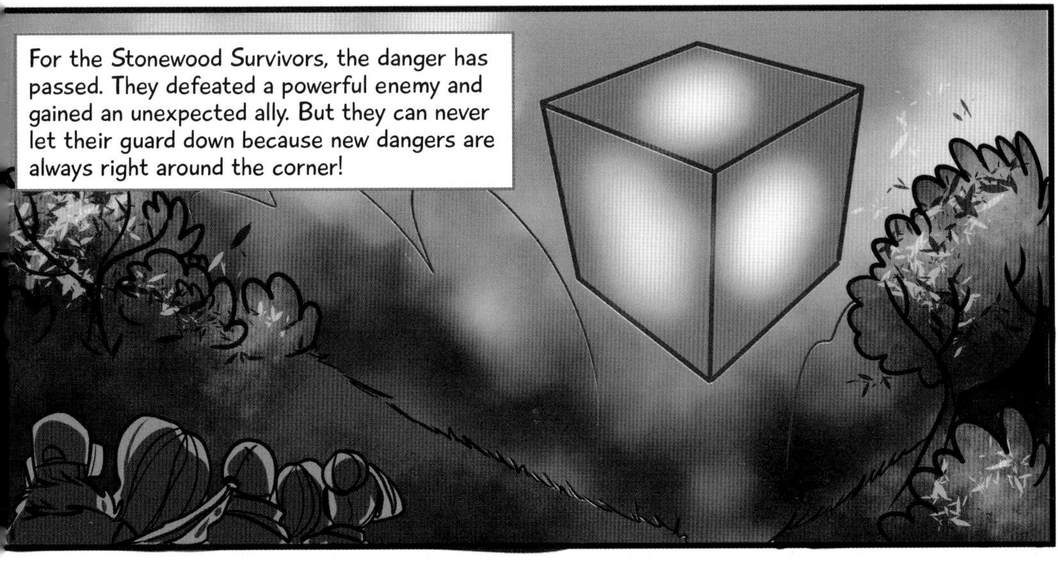
For the Stonewood Survivors, the danger has passed. They defeated a powerful enemy and gained an unexpected ally. But they can never let their guard down because new dangers are always right around the corner!

Also Available from the Storm Shield series!

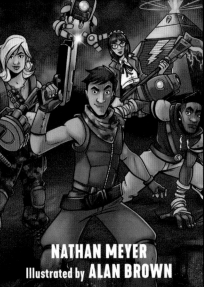

UNOFFICIAL GRAPHIC NOVEL #1 FOR FORTNITERS

LAST HOPE FOR SURVIVAL

NATHAN MEYER
Illustrated by ALAN BROWN

UNOFFICIAL GRAPHIC NOVEL #2 FOR FORTNITERS

TRACKING THE MASTERMIND

NATHAN MEYER
Illustrated by ALAN BROWN